Val Greathead grew up near Halifax in West Yorkshire. She worked as a costume designer for Tyne Tees Television and Central Television before joining the Arts University, Bournemouth, where she became head of the School of Performance. During this period, she contributed to books on costume and fashion illustration and on learning and teaching in higher education. Val lives in Wiltshire with her husband, Tim, and this is her first novel.

For my parents, Brenda and David Reid, who instilled and encouraged my love of books.

Val Greathead

GLASS IN THE SUGAR: ANNA'S STORY

AUSTIN MACAULEY PUBLISHERS™

LONDON • CAMBRIDGE • NEW YORK • SHARJAH

A CIP catalogue record for this title is available from the British Library.

ISBN 9781528932325 (Paperback)
ISBN 9781528967006 (ePub e-book)

www.austinmacauley.com

First Published (2020)
Austin Macauley Publishers Ltd
25 Canada Square
Canary Wharf
London
E14 5LQ

Without the love and support of my husband, Tim, I would never have achieved what I set out to do. Thank you for being there for me.

I would like to thank my family for their love, help and encouragement; my son, James and his wife, Ally; my stepdaughter, Georgina and her husband, Ben; my sister, Heather and my brother, John; my brother-in-law, Richard and sister-in-law, Katie; and my lovely mother-in-law, Mavis, who sadly died without having been able to read *Anna's story*. And of course to my parents, David and Brenda Reid, to whom this book is dedicated.

I would like to thank Doctor Gabrielle Malcolm for her excellent mentorship, coffee and laughter throughout the writing process. It has been the best experience. Also, thanks to Jayne Woodhouse and our group of writers for those wonderful Wednesday mornings. Thank you to Stephen West for helping me visualise all the characters. His drawings inspired me. I would also like to thank the team at Austin Macauley for their help and support.

Thank you to Peter and Fleur Nell for insightful and practical help during my research. I will never forget the South African veldt-style barbeque served in their back garden in Wiltshire. Thanks to Robin Hodges, whose military knowledge is staggering. Thank you to Grace and Lynnie Reed and Annie Jeanes, because until I asked them, I knew very little about horse-behaviour. Thank you Monaya Abel for helping me to better understand one of my characters.
I would finally like to thank my special girlfriends, who have tirelessly listened, contributed their specialist expertise, advised when asked and generally put up with me. So, thank you to Fiona Ffoulkes, Alison Sankey, Charlotte Edwardes, Sharon Ibbotson, Joanna Crawford, Lalla Hitchings, Jenni Sundheim, Fran Lailey, Ellie Nixon and all my gym gang.

Table of Contents

Timeline of the Anglo-South African or Second Boer War 1899–1902

1899

31 May–5 June: Conference at Bloemfontein fails to maintain the peace.

9 October: Boers issue ultimatum.

11 October: Ultimatum expires and war begins with Boer invasion of the Cape and Natal.

13 October: Boers besiege Baden-Powell at Mafeking.

15 October: Boers besiege Kimberley.

30 October: Boers besiege Ladysmith.

10–15 December: Black Week-Battles of Stormberg, Magersfontein, Colenso.

17 December: RMS Dunottar sails for South Africa with Field Marshall Roberts, new Commander in Chief of British Forces on board.

1900

10 January: RMS Dunottar arrives at Cape Town.

23–24 January: Battle of Spion Kop.

15 February: Relief of Kimberley.

28 February: Relief of Ladysmith.

March: British begin erecting blockhouses.

15 March: Roberts offers amnesty to Boers prepared to surrender (so-called 'hands-uppers').

5 April: Action at Boshoff.

17 May: Relief of Mafeking.

24 May: Orange Free State annexed to British dominions as Orange River Colony.

5 June: Roberts occupies Pretoria.

16 June: Roberts issues proclamation on burning of farms.

15 July: Boer General de Wet flees Brandwater Basin with thousands of Boer civilians and commandos.

31 July: Remaining Boers capitulate to the British in Brandwater Basin.

September: Announcement that refugee camps for Boers who surrender will be set up at Pretoria and Bloemfontein.

22 September: Refugee (concentration) camp established at Bloemfontein.

25 October: British annex Transvaal.

29 November: Kitchener replaces Roberts as Commander in Chief.

27 December: Emily Hobhouse arrives in South Africa to visit concentration camps.

1901

28 January: Campaign to round up Boers in the Transvaal.

10 February: Boer General De Wet invades the Cape.

28 February: Abortive peace talks open at Middleburg

July Committee under Millicent Fawcett appointed to inspect concentration camps.

25 December: Action at Tweefontein.

1902

28 February: Extensive British drive culminates with success at Lang Reit.

11 April: Battle of Roodewal.

6 May: Action at Hulkrantz.

31 May: Treaty of Vereeniging signed; Boer forces surrender.

Part One
A Foreign Land

Chapter 1
Cape Town, January 1900

I grip the guard rail to steady myself against the rolling motion of the ship and away from the commotion below. My nerves begin to settle. The salt tastes sharp and the sea air cools my cheeks, hot from re-arranging my uniform and the contents of my luggage. From the promenade deck, I have an uninterrupted view of the giant continent as it rises majestically from the ocean, and as Devil's Peak looms and duty beckons, I savour the final sights and sounds of our long voyage. In the certain knowledge of Britannia's supreme rule, the ship slices through the water and the waves tumble apart, gulls cry out their welcome overhead and small white terns plummet from dizzy heights then flash into the gunmetal sea. And there I see them. A mass of military vessels moving through the water. Balletic, they seem to glide in time, as if to music. Purposeful, co-ordinated, confident.

Table Mountain glowers over this uninvited display of British military might amongst which I recognise the troop ships because they have great painted numbers on their sides. They remind me of toys, and I am transported back to the Round Pond in Kensington Gardens and the outings my brother and I so enjoyed with our grandparents when we were small.

Thousands of miles away from London now, I think of Henry, and how fine he looked in his uniform when we waved him off with his regiment late last summer. Because he has inherited our mother's fine features, porcelain skin and blonde hair, whereas I am tall, dark and olive-skinned like our father, we are the subject of raised eyebrows when people meet us for the first time and discover that we are not merely siblings, but twins. Twenty-one-year-old twins, identical only in height. Most important, in our playful rivalry, *I am the oldest by five minutes*, as I often remind him when he is trying to take charge, which he usually does.

Now, however, Henry's regiment have been in the thick of the action up country and I wonder about his involvement in the bloody battles that have been the subject of much gloomy talk on board.

"Quite something, isn't it?" says a voice, startling my thoughts back to the present. I swing around to face him and find myself looking up into unfamiliar, bright, hazel eyes. I nod. Indicating towards the shoreline, the uniformed stranger returns the smile that I finally manage.

"Hard to believe what's going on there," he says, and for a fraction of a moment, the spark vanishes from his eyes, then is reignited when he asks, "Do you know which hospital you will be at?"

Refusing the cigarette he offers, I shake my head this time, pull my red cape tight around my shoulders and silently reflect on the whirlwind events that saw me board the RMS Dunottar Castle, bound for Cape Town on 17 December 1899, just one week after enrolling into the Princess Christian's Army Nursing Service Reserve, and two months after the outbreak of the South African war.

The stranger holds out his hand towards me.

"Robert Dawlish. Captain. In the Yeomanry. About to join my lot at Maitland Camp, just outside Cape Town."

Like his eyes, his voice is clear and direct and he speaks with no accent, providing no clue as to where he is from.

"Oh…Captain Dawlish, hello. Yes. My name is Anna. Anna Lieberman. I am in the army nursing reserve…but I think you have probably guessed that."

I am suddenly conscious of how I look in my uniform and realise that my corset stays are going to be unbearable in the heat that is already building even though the sun has only just risen.

"Ah, good, she speaks! A pleasure to meet you, Miss Lieberman. An interesting surname. But you don't sound German?"

Something about his voice or perhaps the very direct way he looks at me causes me to blush, but before I can reply, a familiar animated figure, complete with her own red cape comes fluttering towards us through the sea of khaki that now surrounds us. As usual, disobedient strands of blonde hair have escaped from beneath her cap to add to the happy chaos that is my friend, Marjorie Makepeace.

Marjorie immediately finds time to disarm Captain Dawlish with one of her bewitching smiles before she grabs my arm. In a beat, his attention switches to my beautiful companion, and I see from the way his eyes shine that he is delighted with what he sees.

"Quickly, Anna, quickly! Let's go to the other side and we might be able to see him."

Marjorie pulls me away with alarming enthusiasm. As we dart through the crowd, I twist back towards Captain Dawlish, but he is gone, submerged in the sea of uniforms. I manage to keep up with Marjorie as she swoops and flaps in the breeze, laughing as we collide into our other friend, Joy Bradleigh, almost knocking her over and then we all three converge on the starboard deck just as the Dunottar Castle pulls alongside to dock.

I first met Joy on the second day of our voyage from England, when she was almost blown away as she tried, in vain, to save the bonnet of a rather frail fellow passenger during a vicious sou'westerly gale. I smile to myself as I remember her many other good deeds, not all of which were particularly welcome. A passionate needlewoman and convinced that Marjorie and I would find the herringbone stitch as useful and gratifying as she did, Joy repeatedly ushered us into some quiet corner of the ship to teach us her beloved embroidery techniques. It was probably when a completely absorbed Marjorie stitched the sample, she was working on firmly to her own skirt with a stitch unrecognisable as herringbone or any other that Joy had to admit defeat. I again regard Joy's girlish looks and diminutive figure as she laughs at Marjorie's exuberance, and find it impossible to believe that she is a married woman of six years with three children under five.

"I really don't know where he is now." Joy had been unusually subdued on the evening before we reached our destination when we talked about her Ted, her husband, an officer in the British army. "All our troops need railways, bridges, water and he is a Royal Engineer, so he could be attached to any regiment, in any part of the country."

Marjorie and I know relatively little about how the army works and we laugh when Joy tells us that, because the Royal Engineers motto is 'UBIQUE' – which roughly translated means 'Everywhere' – her husband could, in fact, be anywhere. With no medical training and having come to South Africa solely to be with her husband, Joy has faced considerable and vociferous opposition from many on board the Dunottar Castle, including a rambunctious old colonel who we found ourselves at dinner with one evening.

"I suppose you know, ladies, that the Queen is firmly set against the idea of wives at the battlefield?"

We nodded patiently because her Majesty's view is oft quoted when the subject arises, and it is easier to agree than to argue. The colonel took a self-righteous sip of his port and continued, "Queen Victoria is not at all happy that Roberts wishes to bring his wife over here. Not at all the thing for our new Commander in Chief. Really, madam," he addressed Joy, "it is not too late to reconsider your position. After all, a woman's place is in the home, is it not?"

This view is typical. A minority express the opposite, however, but they tend to be quieter, less perfunctory. One such individual, a kindly man with a huge handlebar moustache, made a gentle rebuttal, "Now, now, Colonel, surely it is a good thing for this young gal to be with her husband, huh? Plenty of time for staying at home once children arrive, don't you think, huh!" and a lifetime of laughter lines wrinkled around his eye when he winked at Joy. I awaited my friend's usual response with dread. But Joy did not tell the sweet moustachioed gentleman about the three children she has left behind. She did not explain that they are staying at her husband's parents' sprawling mansion on the Isle of Wight. She did not say that she loves her husband enough to come halfway across the world to be with him. Worn out with the hostility she has received up until now, she decided that, for once, saying nothing was better than the truth.

Marjorie and I come to her defence often, but I suspect that secretly, Marjorie does not entirely support Joy's decision to abandon five-year-old Charles, three-year old Katie, and especially baby John, who at six-months-old, and because he was born prematurely, is a small, somewhat sickly infant. I am not entirely sure why I think that Marjorie harbours this secret disapproval. It's just that she is never one to leap to Joy's defence. And sometimes she hesitates or looks down at the ground when I voice my ardent view that if Joy wants to be with her husband and doesn't make more work for the hard-pressed medical staff, then she will certainly be more help than hindrance.

Throughout the voyage, there has been much talk of the fighting so far in the war against the South African Boers, and my fellow passengers express great dismay that British troops are now besieged at Mafeking, Kimberley, and Ladysmith. The week of 10 December brought three significant defeats for us at Stormberg, Magersfontein and Colenso, and now goes by the name of 'Black Week' amongst the troops. So, despite efforts, ten days ago, to welcome the new century with some kind of jollity, the atmosphere on board our requisitioned former mail ship was decidedly sombre. Now, as we prepare to disembark, our mood is celebratory and at odds with what we have experienced during the journey and I experience a rare feeling of patriotic fervour.

Frantic activity on and off the ship heralds what is to happen next.

"There he goes, look! He is so splendid," gasps Joy, the white muslin frills of her dress squashed against the guard rail and copper curls bobbing under her straw bonnet. "But it's so terribly sad about his son. The poor man."

We ponder on the news of Lieutenant Freddy Roberts' death at the battle of Colenso that reached us on the last day of the old century, and my heart aches for the father who has lost his only son. An Infantry guard of honour marches into position beside the dock and Lord Roberts, inscrutable, in Field Marshal's dress blue uniform and with the white plumes of his headdress flying, heads down the gangplank, followed by his staff, in sober khaki. Roberts, who is the new Commander in Chief of the British forces in South Africa and probably the most esteemed of my fellow passengers, gets into a horse-drawn coach and drives off.

We wave our farewells to Joy as she climbs into a smart carriage with two other ladies that I do not recognise, destined for one of Cape Town's hotels. Feeling a little bereft after Joy's departure, I lean next to Marjorie and we peer at the unfolding scene below, not quite sure what to do next. We must be looking lost because the woman who is to be the sister in charge at the hospital where Marjorie and I have been posted approaches and issues curt orders that we must, 'get yourselves to Number One hospital at once and stop dithering!'

We quickly make our way to the dock-side, which is teeming with horses, people and military paraphernalia, and after what feels like an age, Marjorie and I are crammed with our luggage into an aptly named 'Cape Cart'. This is a curious horse-drawn vehicle with two wheels and a huge hood, which our native driver has pulled up. The cart is devoid of paint or upholstery, covered with years of grime and tied together with pieces of frayed rope. All these vehicles would appear to be similarly decrepit, but unlike many of the others, at least our horse is relatively free of mange. The cart's cracked leather hood has the advantage that it protects us from the scorching sun and the small rocks, which the hot wind picks up from the dusty road and hurls up at us. Despite the protection provided by the hood, the fine dust finds its way into the carriage, and soon a film of grime covers us and gets in our eyes so that we find ourselves coveting the huge eye-goggles worn by our driver.

As we bounce through the streets, Marjorie points out groups of local women whose headwear gives them the appearance of cheerful flowers. The ingenious bonnets – called 'kappies', our driver tells us – are made from linen and come in a variety of colours, but mostly, they are pink or white and have layer upon layer of gathered fabric tied under the chin. The flounces are very deep, to protect the wearer from sun and dust, and the women's faces are almost hidden. One of the tiniest girls sports a boldly patterned costume of vivid green and yellow. She returns our curious stares with the widest, whitest grin and a merry wave. As the vibrant throng of women and children melts into the melee of Cape Town's back streets, I wonder whether the child finds my starched white nurse's cap as intriguing as her frilly bonnet is to me.

The homes and vehicles present a colourful jumble. Some are low, stuccoed native cottages, others are modern cut-stone houses, whilst here and there are magnificent government buildings standing imperiously to attention. All together, they form a colourful backdrop to a myriad of electric trams, donkey carts, hansom carriages, ox-wagons and the cavalry troops that clutter the roadways wherever we go.

We realise the disadvantage of the cart's hood as our journey takes us away from the main thoroughfares of the town and the road becomes increasingly rutted, with rain-made ditches and channels criss-crossing the road. Despite the speed that we travel, and my repeated instructions to the driver to make haste, I am sure that he has not taken the most direct route and my anxiety increases. We are jolted up, down and sideways with each turn of the cart's wheels, our heads collide either with one another or with the unyielding hood every few seconds.

By the time we reach No. 1 General Hospital, Wynberg, just a few miles south of Cape Town, we have been battered into disarray and spend a few moments straightening our caps and gathering our rattled senses. But at last, we have arrived. I breathe in the surprisingly fresh, scented air and realise that a beautiful pine forest surrounds us. The hospital is a huge collection of military style barrack huts against the beautiful backdrop of Table Mountain with Simon's Bay glimmering in front.

We notice a stream of people heading into what must be the refectory building and decide to go straight there once we have found our quarters. At least in our quarters, I can take off or at least release these wretched stays, which are beginning to make me feel light headed, possibly because I almost never wear them at home. The dust and heat have made us thirsty and our breakfast on board the Dunottar Castle, barely touched due to the excitement of our arrival, was six hours ago.

More daunting than the scale of the hospital is the arrival of Sister Jenkins, who glares at us as she spits a remark in our general direction.

"Sister Makepeace, Nurse Lieberman, what are you doing here? You are billeted at Number Two Hospital and you are late."

"Sorry, Sister, but I thought your instruction was that we head to Number One Hospital." Marjorie sounds wounded and upset, but the Sister's instructions given to us on board the ship to meet her at No. 1 Hospital had been clear and definite, so I grip my mouth into a tight straight line to avoid making an unpleasant interchange worse.

"Your insolence is noted." Her small flinty eyes meet Marjorie's. "You will both go directly to Number Two Hospital and begin your shift immediately. You have missed luncheon. And for goodness sake, straighten your caps. We do not encourage slatterns here."

No. 2 Hospital appears to be a makeshift addition to what must once have been the parade ground of the barracks that is now No.1 Hospital, and when I look around, I understand why Sister Jenkins has billeted us here. There are no actual buildings, just row upon row of marquees and tents. The combination of canvas accommodation plus the spiralling temperatures and gruelling wind will make nursing here somewhat testing. As we stand and gape at the prospect, a short, stocky nurse in an unfamiliar uniform approaches us.

"Ninety-nine," she barks in a deep, heavily accented voice. We must look as confused as we feel. "Tents. There are ninety-nine of them. How do you do? I'm Martha. From Australia. There's a group of us from Adelaide, all here for the Imperial cause."

Marjorie and I introduce ourselves and we learn from Martha that every nurse is allocated six tents, each with between five and eight patients to look after.

"Can you believe we are treated as officers? But you don't need to call me lieutenant."

I immediately like this tiny, gruff woman who looks to be in her late thirties.

"Where are our rooms?" asks Marjorie, whose delicate complexion is flushed and who is wilting fast in the sun.

"Right there," Martha points to the edge of the parade ground.

"Tents?" Marjorie's eyes are wide.

"It's not too bad. And you will get a house soon enough," Martha chortles gaily. "We get a box to sit on. And another box for a table. Oh, and there are beds. One each. We have to share the boxes though."

Before long, we are laughing and swapping stories, then Martha escorts us to the central administration office where Marjorie and I are given our billet. At the far end of our tent are three camp cots on each side, facing one another in an orderly manner, blankets tucked in neat and tidy. Nearer to us and just inside the tent are the boxes, as Martha described – one box to act as a table and three to sit on.

"Home at last."

Marjorie launches herself onto one of the beds, and it creaks ominously. I barely have time to loosen my stays before we are swept up by one of the senior Sisters who introduces us to our 'men' and their assorted shrapnel injuries and shell shock. The small, clean puncture of the nickel bullet is one thing, but the gaping wounds from the expanding bullets makes the bile rise in my stomach. The first man that I treat is shell-shocked and thinks that I am his mother. And so, my new life begins.

Chapter 2
Three Weeks In

Just as Martha described, we moved to a small house and five of us share a maid with the nurses next door. We have coal and our wages cover what we pay our servant girl, plus the rent and there's £1 for food, but the price of everything is shockingly high and it's hard to make our money stretch to buy what we need.

"Not again!"

Faced with brick-heavy sour-dough bread and runny tinned butter for breakfast for the fourth day in a row, I cannot help but complain. We could buy yeast bread at the shops but it costs sixpence a pound, and since we eat four pounds per meal, we would soon be broke.

"Honestly, Anna! Not everyone has devilled kidneys and scrambled eggs delivered to them on a silver platter by the servants you know, madam!" A deferential Marjorie lowers her eyes, and I cuff her affectionately when she curtseys as she places the bread and butter on the table.

"So, what do the poor girls of Dame Edith's Convent Boarding School eat for breakfast?" I ask her, half joking but genuinely, I want to know. Marjorie's family is complicated, and I am certain that she would not wish to discuss her status as an illegitimate daughter and the miserable upbringing she suffered because of it with Martha and the others, not yet at least.

"You've read Oliver Twist?" she replies laughing.

I think for a second, "Gruel?" I say, and she returns my playful wallop.

"Seriously, Marjorie. What did you have at school for breakfast?" Martha asks.

That trademark smile vanishes as Marjorie searches her memories; some I know too painful to discuss in our present company.

"Fresh bread. And dripping. It is quite delicious."

"Bread an' drippin'?" Florence is the fourth member of our ragtag family whose Yorkshire accent is so pronounced that rarely does she speak without being asked to repeat herself. "That's nowt. Yur were lucky to get owt t'eat."

Fortunately, on this occasion, when Martha, Marjorie and I share a look of non-comprehension, the final member of our household, Rose, who has just arrived and hails from Burnley, Lancashire, nods and helps with an almost-simultaneous translation. "In other words," she says, "think yourselves lucky, ladies, because having anything at all to eat is better than having nothing."

At the hospital, we heed Florence's wise words, because on many an occasion, we would have welcomed bread and dripping like long-lost friends, so grim is our daily fare. And despite the paucity of what we all regard as decent nourishment, most of our patients make good progress on their diet of tinned beef, bread, jam, tea and sugar. However badly they are hurt, the first request from most Tommies is for a 'wee drop' or 'a bit of tobacco' before they ask for a piece of paper 'to send a line so they won't be scared at home'. Today is no exception, and I have already distributed all but one of my own pencils and the day's paper ration. Out of the corner of my eye, I notice that I am being watched by a young soldier who has two fingers splinted together on his right hand and a shattered left collar-bone. "Can I help you, Private Hoyle?" I say and offer him my very last pencil.

"Thank you, nurse. I'm not so good at this writing lark. Never was much for school. But I've watched you with your pen an' all. You write a lot at night."

"So, I am found out!"

His puzzled face makes me smile.

"I do sometimes write my journal at night," I admit. "When I see or think, I see you are all asleep."

He grins, "Won't tell, promise. If…" he looks around, conspiratorially, "you help me to write home?"

I feel such pleasure at his request that my reply comes out as rather an explosion, "Of course, it would be my pleasure!"

He grins at my keenness, "You read too, don't you, nurse?"

I smile back, "Guilty as charged. Does your shoulder keep you awake at night?" When he nods, I ask if he would like to borrow one of my Dickens novels to pass the hours.

"That would be smashing, nurse. Except I can't read. Never was at school long enough to learn." He swallows his pride and adds, "I don't suppose you could read to me?"

So it is, in the dead of the next night, to the accompaniment of gentle background snoring and occasional moans from the other men, I move my chair next to Private Hoyle's bedside and open the book I have chosen for him.

"Whether I shall turn out to be the hero of my own life, or whether…"

Private Hoyle tugs my arm, his eyes alight, "Is it about a soldier, miss?"

"No, it's a story about a young boy, who has a bit of a difficult time at school. His name is David too. David Copperfield."

The next day is glorious and I am at one with the world after a restorative Sunday morning Matins service, even though my indecisive faith means I do not join in with all of the ritual. Somehow, my silent prayers for David Hoyle and the other young chaps under my care have steadied my nerves and I feel prepared for what will be a difficult day ahead. And who knows, perhaps there will be peace on earth if we pray often enough?

The walking-wounded like Private Hoyle are quite usual, but many arrivals are stretcher cases, shot through thigh, foot or spine and I know today will be more gruelling than most because many of my current patients are critically wounded and there are two with inoperable spinal injuries who will not survive the weekend.

I attend my ward, ready to commence duties when I stop short. The familiar sight of my brother Henry's shock of blonde hair greets me. I run to where his stretcher lies abandoned on the ground. I can tell from the way his wound is dressed that he has been shot in the back and the lead weight of care consumes me as the Lord's peace drops from me. I want to kill whoever has done this to my twin. But then a sweet, unfamiliar face looks up me, and I silently thank God and sink to the boy's side in relief and agony.

"Hello," I say and squeeze his hand, "my name is Anna, I am a nurse. I thought for one minute that you were my brother, Henry."

"Hello, nurse Anna; I'm Albert, but my mum and dad call me Bertie. Lucky you, having a brother – there's just me at home." He smiles, raises his head slightly, stares in turn at his legs and at me. He cannot understand that his legs will not move. I steel myself as to how I might tell him that because of where the bullet smashed his spine, they never will.

"Tell me about Henry. What is it like, to have a brother? Do you have a sister too?"

"Well," I reply, "there's just Henry and me. We are twins and we were twenty-one last year, although..." I look around to make sure that Sister Jenkins is not engaged in her customary eavesdropping, "I had to pretend I was twenty-three to be accepted onto the army nursing course in London."

Bertie laughs and echoes my covert whisper, "Aha! Me too, Nurse Anna. They thought I was eighteen when I joined up."

He waits for the orderly to pass.

"But I was sixteen. Seventeen now though, and I've a girl at home. She makes up for not having brothers or sisters." He produces a tobacco tin from thin air and I must look aghast because he roars with laughter. "Don't worry nurse, I'm not going to light up. Here." Gingerly, he opens the lid with his good hand and passes me a pristine photograph of a very beautiful girl with pale skin, thick curly hair and freckles. She folds one hand over another so that the tiny diamond she wears on her left hand is proudly visible.

"Niamh. Her family is from Ireland. My da' calls her his 'pudding'."

I cannot help laughing at this incongruous nickname. Bertie laughs too.

"I know, funny, ain't it? You can't tell from this, but it's because her hair is the colour of treacle sponge. She says when we get married, we are going to have at least six puddings of our own!"

"You are a very lucky man." I hand back Niamh's photograph which he studies for a moment, then presses it gently into its place of safekeeping. He looks at my ringless hands.

"Aren't you engaged then, Nurse Anna?"

"Not yet," I say, wondering ruefully if I ever will be.

He glances at the pile of books under my arm. "Too much reading and not enough fun, nurse. You need more parties! I will be sure to tell Sister Jenkins." He pulls a face and I laugh with him, until I realise that he winces not at the thought of Sister Jenkin's response, but because he is in considerable pain. I pull back the covers to check his wounds and see the type of angry red rash that only means one thing. I go to find the doctor at once.

This bright and hopeful seventeen-year-old with the beautiful fiancée whose hair is the colour of treacle sponge did live long enough for me to write to his parents in Liverpool on his behalf. He never did understand why his legs, which were still there after all, would not work, however hard he stared at them.

Such is the cruel nature of their injuries that often I am glad when death releases my patients, but not this time. This time I am angry and in trouble again with Sister Jenkins. Reprimanded for un-professional behaviour, I have been assigned to clearing the slops and disposing of old dressings for one week and it is in the windowless furnace room that Marjorie finds me.

25

"Why, Marjorie? Why Bertie?" I ask.

"You did the right thing, Anna," she confides.

"Sister Jenkins did not think so. And Bertie died anyway."

"Disagreeing with a doctor's diagnosis is completely against what she believes, Anna. And we have never exactly been her favourite nurses."

"Even though I was right."

"Even though you were smart enough to spot the secondary infection."

"If the doctor had amputated, Bertie might have lived."

"I know, Anna. I know."

Despite being forbidden to do so by Sister Jenkins, Marjorie and I attend Bertie's funeral, making sure that he is buried with the photograph of his golden girl, Niamh, in his breast pocket. I do write to his parents. The most difficult letter I have ever written. I describe for them the church service for their son's burial. I try to tell them things that I think probably won't appear in the standard letter of commiseration they will receive from their son's commanding officer. I tell them how his eyes lit up at the memory of family Christmases together and especially his mother's plum pudding with rum sauce, how he loved to listen to my storytelling which became popular with his comrades on the ward – until Sister Jenkins put a stop to it. And how he looked forward to kicking a football against the wall at the back of the house again. He had never understood that the bullet through his spine meant he would not walk again and no one ever had the heart to dissuade him from his dream of playing for his beloved Everton.

Bertie is the fourth burial in as many days, but thankfully the funerals become less frequent as the weeks pass by and the 'lucky ones' return home. Sadly, most of them must head back into the fray. And in the last week of January, just when everyone thinks the worst is over, Spion Kop happens.

I watch the wounded emerge like silent stone ghosts from the ambulance train. Their uniformed bodies and sun-burnt faces are caked in baked on mud, so they have an all-over pale dust colour through which the blood of their wounds seeps. They are layered with battle, weather and fatigue. Marjorie is right there, at once serene yet purposeful, attending to the wounded, but at first, I can only watch. I think back to the glittering, whispering seascapes, the magnificent drama of Cape Town's mountains and the sweet scent of the forest that greeted my arrival here, until these guilty thoughts are repressed by the metallic stench of blood, the sight of flat, dusty parades of stretchers and the groans of agony and despair. I pull myself together and walk in amongst the pain.

"Here, let me help," I move to face these pitiful, broken men, then call one of the orderlies who stands smoking nearby to help me move a man with a shattered collar bone and broken leg to the operating theatre, where queues are already forming.

"Nurse Lieberman?" It is the first time I have encountered the doctor since my spell out of the ward after Bertie died and I steel myself for another dressing down.

"Doctor Edwardes?" I buy time.

"Nurse Lieberman, I wanted to make sure that you had received my message," he responds to my blank look quickly, "Ah. I see. Sister Jenkins has not spoken to you? Quickly, man, quickly!" He gestures another orderly towards the line of stretchers on the ground. "Well, let's not beat about the bush, Nurse Lieberman. You did well to spot the infection that took hold of that young soldier. If he had come to me earlier, I should have amputated at once. Not easy to do, to identify what was wrong with him. Well done, nurse." He is gone before he can see my pain and pleasure. Pain that Bertie need not have died, pleasure in knowing that I made the correct diagnosis. Anger ignites inside me towards Sister Jenkins and I wonder what drives her.

Some days later in the aftermath of Spion Kop, we receive an invitation from Joy. She wants us to join her and her new friend Lady Maud Roddeston for lunch at their hotel in the centre of Cape Town. At the news of this social event, Marjorie's smile, which has been uncharacteristically absent for days, returns and she twirls me around the tent, much to the amusement of the patients. Marjorie and I have been tending the injured, from 'Black Week' to Spion Kop with no respite for three weeks. The thought of a trip to the Mount Nelson Hotel, plus the fact that Sister Jenkins is nowhere in sight, makes me brave enough to return Marjorie's embrace and join her and the soldiers in a less than tuneful rendition of The Blue Danube waltz as we cavort giddily around the beds.

So, it is that two days later, we decide against the Cape Cart mode of transport, and treat ourselves to the luxury of a hansom cab. The drive this time is so smooth we can take in some of the scenery without having to hold onto one another or our caps. We arrive outside the hotel at the appointed hour and Marjorie's smile grows even wider as she takes in the setting.

"Something beautiful to put in your diary for a change, Anna!" she says and I nod, relieved that I will indeed have something other than the horrors of war to reflect upon later when I write my journal.

The Mount Nelson Hotel is nestled right up to Table Mountain and surrounded by a riot of colour and lush greenery. Acknowledging a shared purpose perhaps, two young, spruce and clean-looking khaki-clad men give us a bit of a salute as we pass one another beneath the fir trees. Their purposeful stride and confident look gives me the impression that they must be newly arrived and I feel a sort of protective apprehension for them, and yet proud at the same time. They make me wonder, what on earth we are all doing here in this hot, windy foreign land, fighting Boer farmers who have just as much right to be here as we do? I wonder why I have come here at all, wish I had not listened to my brother, Henry, and think that maybe my father was right.

"I could certainly get used to this place!" Marjorie breaks my reverie, and she bends to examine one of the colourful exotic plants whilst managing not to flirt with the officers for a change. I breathe in the scent of the bougainvillea, cannas and roses and think how magnificent the mountain looks up close.

Joy greets us as we enter the hotel lobby, wearing a softy draped day dress in a shade of lilac that perfectly suits her complexion and auburn hair.

"Anna! Marjorie! It is so good to see you both," she says. "How are you? I want to hear all about your work at the hospital. Oh, I have so much to tell you! Come, this way."

Above me, the vaulted ceiling is held in place by statuesque ribbed columns to form a decorative canopy. The breath-taking grandeur reminds me of the Walsingham House Hotel on Piccadilly where my parents took Henry and I for dinner just before he joined his regiment and I feel a pang of home-sickness. I glimpse rows of palm trees and cascades of vivid pink oleander through the tall French windows that line each side of the passageway, and I am reminded that this is not London. Not London at all. But as I take in all the splendour, I do wish that I could wear the beautiful lapis and bronze paper taffeta gown I wore that day instead of my dull uniform.

Joy ushers us into a huge airy room, buzzing with muted, lowkey chatter and the chink of glass and cutlery. Polished floor to ceiling mirrors alternate with lavishly draped windows through which yet more luxuriant plants are visible. I cannot even begin to name them. Beyond rise the mountains, majestic and proud.

Back in the dining room, Marjorie stifles a giggle and nudges me. She nods towards the centrepiece of the buffet table. Three naked, voluptuous china figurines hold bowls that overflow with fresh fruits of every colour imaginable. Not a sight a young woman from Dame Edith's Convent School will be familiar with, I suspect. It is a sculpture worthy of Michelangelo and bears a feast fit for the Queen. Smiling at Marjorie's wonderment, Joy squeezes each of us by the hand and I ponder out loud whether anyone would mind if I were to take some of the grapes and oranges back to the hospital for the patients. Joy shakes her head in despair at my lack of decorum. She pulls us away, "Come and meet Maud. We have some champagne on ice."

Surrounded in the elegant dining room with high ceilings and stately columns, and the smart clientele sipping chilled champagne, it is hard to believe that we are in a foreign country. It is even harder to imagine that we are at war. The reason why we are here, though, becomes clear on inspection of the other diners. British officers in khaki, or the occasional smart blue dress uniform fill most of the tables. Some men sport bandages, others display fresh looking red scars and a few sets of crutches line the walls, waiting like anxious dance partners.

Dotted here and there are other English ladies like us, most dressed in last year's frocks, with eyes full of thinly disguised anxiety, borne with an outward cheerfulness that doesn't fool me. By contrast, several women stand out with a carefree attitude and voluptuous décolleté. Glittering with confidence, they are bedecked in extravagant gowns and breath-taking jewels. This is a sight I have certainly never seen in the London, or even in the Berlin hotels where I dined once upon a time with my father. Joy whispers that these ladies are South African millionairesses, their showy attire and brash manners are the mark of their connection with the diamond mining upcountry.

We halt at a table with the best view of the garden and our hostess stands to greet us. What strikes me first about this woman, who looks to be perhaps ten or fifteen years older than me, is the way in which her ample bosom is thrust forward, giving her the odd but very fashionable 'S-bend' shape. When she shakes my hand, I notice her broad frame and firm grip, and when her eyes meet mine, I see that she is at least the same height as me, if not an inch or so taller. Joy introduces her as 'Maud Roddeston', and even though Joy is a mere Mrs and not a Lady, I soon begin to understand why they have become friends.

"Anna, please do have some champagne," Lady Maud has lifted the bottle herself even though the wine waiter is hovering nearby. I must look as petrified as he does, which I am rather, because it takes me a second or two to smile and pick up my glass, and then everyone laughs when Lady Maud says, "I promise I won't bite. Although, I do know that I have a bit of a bark! My husband tells me off about it all the time. Apparently, I terrify some of his men. Can you believe it?"

28

We all politely agree this to be an 'impossibility', even though it is perfectly clear that Lady Maud could intimidate whomsoever she chooses. It is only when Marjorie asks if there are children in the Roddeston household that I see the briefest flicker of fragility cross Maud's face. There is a resoluteness, however, in the way she holds her head and although clouded by sadness, her grey eyes are full of strength and humour. As we sip our consommé, Lady Maud entertains us with stories about her north-country family estate before she launches into hair-raising tales of hunting for tigers with Maharajahs in India that almost distract us from the exquisitely cooked roast rack of lamb. By the time dessert comes, I have quite warmed to this extraordinary woman. Like Joy, Lady Roddeston has come to South Africa to be with her husband and so is entirely sympathetic. Perhaps it is because of the way she describes her husband's bravery in previous campaigns, the fact that his name is Sir Lancelot and he rides an enormous grey stallion that Marjorie and I rather fall in love with the idea of this modern-day Knight of the Realm and his own Guinevere.

"Miss Lieberman!" I hear a voice that is familiar and yet I cannot place it. Two tall, handsome officers in khaki approach our table, and Marjorie raises her eyebrows and regards me with a look of respectful appreciation.

"My Anna, you are a dark horse," she murmurs for my ears only. I ignore her remark and manage what I hope is a friendly greeting for the officer I met so briefly on the Dunottar Castle.

"Captain Dawlish, it is a pleasure to see you again. How are you finding Maitland camp?"

At this, Lady Roddeston says, "Maitland? Then you might have come across my husband, Colonel Lance Roddeston?" And before we know it, Captain Dawlish and his dark-haired comrade-at-arms who we discover is a Lieutenant, also from the Yeomanry, have joined our table and are regaling us with tales of their time at the camp. Soon, the conversation turns to the different reasons that bring us all to South Africa and I see Joy close her eyes for a second, take a deep breath and prepare that answer she will give these strangers. I speak quickly, before anyone else can.

"I never planned to become a nurse," I begin. "In fact, both my parents were quite set against the idea. Particularly my father."

Thoughts of the heated arguments over my decision to become a nurse assault me and I close my eyes in an effort to dispatch the unpleasant memories.

"What did he think you should be doing?" asks Captain Dawlish. "Getting married?"

"Well, no, actually," I smile at the thought of my academic, German-Jewish father, the lawyer, and his absolute love of learning.

"He rather expected me to continue with my studies, maybe Somerville."

"Oxford. Not the usual place for girls."

I am not sure that his tone is entirely friendly, and thoughts of my relinquished scholarship nudge me accusingly. "You see, I was educated first at the North London Collegiate School for girls and..."

"Ah, the indomitable Misses Buss and Beale!" interrupts Lady Roddeston.

"Why, yes, Lady Roddeston, indeed. Their reputation as champions for the education of young ladies is well known. If not universally approved of." Captain Dawlish fixes his gaze on me even though he addresses Lady Maud.

I feel the heat of embarrassment spread from my neck to my face and decide to ignore his tease when I continue, "Our head teacher, Miss Buss, was tremendously supportive of my love of languages. She seemed to think that I showed potential in that field. My father is from Berlin, you see, and I was already a fluent German speaker when I joined the school."

"Ah," Captain Dawlish speaks again. "Why, Miss Lieberman, thank you for answering the question I posed all those weeks ago, when your friend, Miss…?"

"Sister Makepeace," grins Marjorie and flicks me a quick sideways glance from beneath her blonde eyelashes.

"When Sister Makepeace carried you away from me in such a hurry just as we were becoming acquainted on the ship. And so, Miss Lieberman, you are indeed German," he says.

"Half German, half English," I retort, trying not to feel defensive.

"As indeed are several of our Queen's grandchildren," Joy chirps, relaxed and letting out her breath now that she is not in the line of fire for once. "I have come across some of them at Osborne House."

This remark causes a flurry of interest from all of us, and we encourage her to explain.

"My husband's parents live in East Cowes and my father and mother-in-law work for the Queen. We love the Isle of Wight and go there often."

"And how is Sir John? I have not seen the Lanchesters since Ascot," Lady Maud enquires.

Joy is prettier than ever when she blushes, "I'm sorry, Anna, Marjorie." Her eyes are full of fun and childlike sheepishness. As the realisation hits, I cannot be cross with my friend, but Marjorie finds it impossible to contain her outrage.

"*Sir* John?" Marjorie sounds as peeved as I feel deep down. "The *Earl* and *Countess* of Lanchester?"

"The very same," Joy admits. "Ted is their oldest son."

"Which makes you a future Countess of Lanchester," I volunteer.

"Well…yes. Quite likely," Joy says before Lady Maud joins the fun,

"And should Ted wish, he could use his courtesy title…"

Joy interrupts, "…of Lord Bradleigh. Which he chooses not to. Therefore, I am Mrs Joy Bradleigh, not Lady Bradleigh." Joy is adamant now. Marjorie's face is a picture of astonished disbelief and Captain Dawlish leans forward, elbows on the table. His chastisement apparently forgotten, he interrogates the precise nature of the working relationship between Ted's family and the Queen. Simpering a little and not revealing any more surprises, Joy adroitly offers up information that her enchanted audience finds equally compelling. Except for Captain Dawlish, that is. His questions ignored, he pushes his chair back abruptly, makes his excuses and heads off to find a cigar. Keen to endorse my own German heritage, Joy reminds us that Queen Victoria's youngest daughter, Beatrice, married her own German prince, Henry of Battenberg at Whippingham Church on the Isle of Wight. Apparently, Princess Beatrice and her family spend a great deal of time at Osborne House, the Queen's residence on the island.

"Ena," she continues with warmth, "Princess Beatrice's youngest daughter, dotes on my eldest son, Charles. She mothers him rather. And my little Charles is devoted to Beatrice's youngest boy, Maurice. Maurice is four years older than Charles, and they both love playing at soldiers. Maurice is the youngest of the Queen's grandchildren and I think he enjoys having a little admirer who he can order about!"

At this, I feel a shudder run through me. Where will this war lead our next generation of young men? I need to step into the garden for some air. At my movement, Marjorie brushes a stray lock of hair from her face then gives me a little wink and a nod in the direction of the exit. I guess my hair must need attention, so I grin back and head towards the powder room.

Champagne-flushed cheeks, not rumpled tresses are what greet me when I look in the mirror and I despair at Marjorie's assumption that I will be carrying face-powder just as she does. I splash cold water onto my face and exit the ladies' room, still grinning and shaking my head, wishing that I was as sophisticated as my friend.

"You have a very pretty smile, Miss Lieberman. You should deploy it more often."

Although I recognise the smooth, accent-less voice, I trip down the step in surprise and find myself in the arms of Captain Dawlish. The scents of tobacco smoke and laundry soap mingle in my nostrils and the heat of his body warms my own through the thin cotton of my uniform. I try and pull away, but it is only when one of the waiters needs to pass that Captain Dawlish releases me. He smiles and makes a gracious bow.

"You were lucky that I was here, Miss Lieberman."

I brush myself down and realise that my hands are shaking.

"Yes, thank you, Captain Dawlish. I am indebted to you."

"Perhaps then you will grant me one small favour?" He does not wait for a reply before he ushers me gently through the French doors into the garden.

"A little air, for the shock. You might have had a nasty fall. Here, rest awhile." His firm hand finds the small of my back and he guides me to a small bower shaded with vines where there is a wooden swing upon which we sit. Finally, I pluck up the courage to look him in the eye. He is undeniably handsome. I feel ridiculously nervous but smile at him nevertheless.

"Miss Lieberman, please permit me... Your lips are quite as beautiful as your smile." He cups my face in his free hand and draws me to him. Beads of sweat stand expectantly on his brow and above his mouth where his neatly cropped moustache quivers in anticipation. The heat is stifling.

"No. No, please, Captain. Not here, Captain." I push him away harder than I intended.

"No, Captain. Not here, Captain. Please, Captain!" His unkind mimicry completely captures my naiveté but does not convey whatever it is that makes my stomach churn. His smile is gone and his mouth twists oddly, to reveal a gold tooth next to his top right incisor. His hand lingers low down on my back as he stands.

"I do look forward to your change of heart, Miss Lieberman. It is my experience that young women usually say 'no' when what they really mean is 'yes'. Yes, please, is what they want to say."

My heart is thumping when I return to the table and slip into my seat, thankful that no one even looks up, so engrossed are they in Joy's anecdotes about life on the Isle of Wight. Captain Dawlish resumes his place soon after and clicks his fingers for some brandy which is quickly provided and downed before he grins at me then addresses Joy to enquire as to her husband's whereabouts.

Now she has realised that none of our present company is going to denounce her for being in South Africa, Joy decides to reveal that she has at last received a long-delayed letter from her husband's commanding officer, Colonel Speakes. She pulls a much-handled envelope from her reticule.

"You see, look at the date! It was posted ages ago. Now, where is it?"

She scans the letter and begins to read, "…so although your husband was injured at Spion Kop, he has been successfully treated at the field hospital here in Frere, and the surgeon thinks there will be no lasting damage."

This is indeed good news as I have nursed many of the casualties from Spion Kop and from the Modder River Battle which happened weeks before we arrived. I witnessed several amputations due to limbs being horribly mutilated by shrapnel then left for too long before treatment. Colonel Speakes' account of the situation of his field hospital is not entirely encouraging.

Joy reads on, "…Frere is a raggedy straggle of tin shacks that is no more than a dot on the parched landscape. In fact, it is not a town at all but just a station on the railway line that bisects Natal and there are many challenges here. However, there is a certain 'bonhomie' about our hospital because all the chaps who are able enough but who are not blessed with the necessary skills are very keen to adopt the role of nurse. I am sure that you can imagine the banter!"

The letter is infused with caustic humour and the Colonel appears optimistic that Ted will soon be fit enough to join the relief forces headed for the besieged towns of Ladysmith and Mafeking. The slight tremor in Joy's voice grows as she reaches the letter's conclusion, but after a sip of champagne to calm herself, she reads the final paragraph.

"So, my dear, be reassured that your husband is in extremely good hands and will not be permitted, however ardently he insists, to return to front-line action until he is fit to do so. It is my belief that the bullet wound to his arm which appeared initially to be a glancing hit, went a little deeper than we first thought, but of one fact I am certain. With complete rest and the attention of our best surgeon, Mr Treves, he will soon be restored to full health.

I remain yours sincerely,

Colonel Alexander Speakes."

Whilst Joy reads about the trials of her husband and the bravery and resourcefulness of the men in camp, I manage to calm my rampaging heartbeat and soon everything is as it should be. Captain Dawlish appears relaxed when he smiles at me kindly now and again, and I begin to think that perhaps I have over reacted.

As we discuss the injury to Ted's arm and his apparent keenness to return to the front line, Joy expresses her frustration that she has not been granted a pass to visit her husband.

"I really cannot understand why I am not allowed to go there. There is such a shortage of staff, one would think they would welcome more help."

Lady Roddeston looks kindly at Joy, "Ted is in a field hospital, right by the action. It is dangerous. There is that, plus the condition of the railway, which the Boers keep blowing up. Maybe supplies are scarce. You would be another mouth to feed…" Lady Roddeston starts another sentence, thinks better of it and signals to the waiter for more coffee.

And you are not a trained nurse, Joy. And maybe Ted's condition has worsened, I think to myself.

Joy, however, does not seem to notice her friend's hesitation and instead is somewhat pacified by Lady Roddeston's explanation. As we drink coffee and discuss the war, Lady Roddeston's dedication to her own husband, our troops and the British cause becomes infectious and I get that patriotic feeling again. News that my brother, Henry is neither wounded nor besieged, but forging ahead with his regiment in the north, plus the jovial and positive tone of his letter has filled me with renewed ardour for the work of the Imperial Army. Despite the incident in the garden, I find myself at one with my decision to be here and put to the back of my mind the plan forming in my head to return to London. We hear from Captain Dawlish and his companion Lieutenant Parker that many of the recently arrived troops left England in a hurry and have not had time to have their uniforms properly fitted and so Joy, delighted to find someone at last who might truly appreciate her skills as a needlewoman, promises to bring her sewing kit to the camp where Colonel Roddeston's Yeomanry are based.

Captain Dawlish studies Joy, one eyebrow raised, looks at Marjorie and then expresses his appreciation, saying that he knows how much his men will appreciate Joy's offer. He then picks up on Lady Roddeston's observations about what is happening at the front.

"There's talk at the camp about typhoid up the line. It is not fighting that's the problem there now, but the contaminated river water, apparently."

Although we have only seen a few cases so far in No. 2 Hospital, since the afflicted are mainly dealt with at nearby Rondebosch, we have heard rumours that the hospital at Bloemfontein will soon be requiring more nurses to cope with the large numbers of typhoid sufferers.

I see Marjorie pursing her lips when Joy agrees to consider travelling north to one of the towns where hospitals are fast filling up with men suffering from this terrible illness. Despite her sunny disposition, bravado and courage, I know from what happened during the long ocean voyage that Joy is not very strong after the difficult birth of her younger son, John, the previous year and I hope she doesn't take on too much. Lady Roddeston has a few words of caution, but the two men are fully supportive of Joy's intention.

Meanwhile, Marjorie excuses herself from our table and is talking animatedly with another attractive uniformed man who returns her twinkle with the eager face of a man recently arrived but who has not yet experienced battle. She and I exchange the briefest of glances and I try to hint at my disapproval in a smile-come-grimace because we both know that flirting with officers and doctors in public has been absolutely forbidden by Sister Jenkins. When she and the young officer disappear into the garden with their coffee, I feel a sudden pang of jealousy because I am not at all brave when it comes to breaking the rules and I feel particularly shy when it comes to initiating conversations with young men. Not for the first time, I wish I was more daring and I wonder again if I have misjudged Captain Dawlish. My olive skin, now further darkened by the hot Cape sun, full mouth, aquiline nose and brown eyes with their pronounced arched brows reflect back at me from one of the dining room's tall mirrors and I wish I was more femininely pretty and not so tall. I am suddenly aware of another reflection in the mirror. Captain Dawlish returns my stare and I look quickly away.

Chapter 3
We Move to Bloemfontein Hospital

Back at No. 2 Hospital, Marjorie can't wait to tell me about the young man she met at the Mount Nelson Hotel.

"What do you mean you did not notice?"

She is quite exasperated at my feigned disinterest and I give in.

"Yes, Marjorie, I agree. He is a terribly good-looking chap."

She looks up at me, expectant and waits for me to continue. I sigh and grin. "Alright, tell me more! What is his name, where does he come from, does he have brothers?"

She pulls me onto the bench beside her. "Sadly for you, Anna, both his brothers are younger than him. Both still at school. Happily for me, he is a twenty-five-year-old bachelor."

I raise my eyebrows.

"Oh, yes, sorry," she says. "His name is Captain Rosevere. Captain Jack Rosevere of the South Lancashires."

"And?" I ask.

"And we are going to write. And meet, if we can. He may be able to take leave in Cape Town."

"My, and all this happened in the ten minutes you two spent together in the hotel garden?"

"I know. It does seem impossibly sudden, but there you have it. What, with the war and everything, why not? Now, Anna dear, is there anything you want to tell me about your beau. You were gone quite a while. In fact, Lady Maud commented on your absence."

"Surely, she did not think...? Marjorie, surely you do not imagine...?"

"Well, what should we think? It was obvious to everyone that Captain Robert Dawlish is captivated by you!"

Marjorie is very quiet after I explain what happened outside the ladies' room and in the garden.

"Have you ever kissed a man?" she asks me and gives me a look worthy of my mother so that I look down at my knees.

"I have never kissed a man, Marjorie. I did not kiss Captain Dawlish because I did not know how to."

My friend seems to think that this is very funny because she laughs for at least a minute.

"What is so amusing?" I chastise her.

"Anna, you did not kiss Captain Dawlish because you did not want to!" She gives me a huge hug and shakes her head. "Honestly, what am I going to do with you? If I ever see that man again, he will get a piece of my mind!" Her agitation is reflected in the way she slips into a thicker London accent than normal, and soon we are reminiscing and laughing about some of the particularly ardent patients Marjorie nursed at the Royal London Hospital, which is where we first became friends. Marjorie had witnessed a particularly sharp dressing-down given to me by a rancorous sister and then decided to take me under her wing, which selfless act caused her as much trouble as it saved me from. The older nurse was equally as vindictive as Sister Jenkins but had the additional venom of a viper and all we young trainee nurses were at the mercy of her poisonous tongue.

Managing to stay mostly out of trouble with Sister Jenkins, we have been back at No. 2 Hospital for nearly a week after our lunch with Lady Maud and due to the smaller than usual number of patients, we have had ample opportunities to discuss Marjorie's oft-doomed love-encounters. She entertains the whole ward quite unintentionally with an exuberant story about an actor who fell off the stage during a performance of *All's Well That Ends Well* and actually broke his leg. He used to quote Shakespeare's love sonnets at her in the most inopportune medical situations and she is in full flow with the story of *'Shall I Compare Thee to a Summer's Day?'* whilst lancing a boil when the screech of an ambulance train interrupts her.

Jacketless, mute and blistered with sunburn. How different are the wounded boys from the spick and span, khaki-clad men who left Waterloo not so very long ago, amid a storm of cheers and flag-waving. An occasional call for assistance disrupts the grim entrance of this troupe of players, now returned in bloodied glory. I detect a north country accent in the dying gasp of one young trooper who has only a single limb left and wish there was something I could do to hasten the inevitable. When I kneel to hold his trembling hand, the fellow next to him seizes me and pulls me close so tight that I find my face pressed to his chest. "Mother, oh mother," he sobs, and I give in to his embrace. As more injured men arrive and call to us for attention, it becomes apparent that all these casualties hale from Manchester, Oldham and other towns West of the Pennines.

"Thank you. Now, take this man to the theatre tent."

Marjorie slips swiftly from raconteur to life saver. She accepts our new patients, directs the orderlies and turns to me, "Anna, please dress this man's wounds. What is your name, soldier?" She lowers her face to hear his name and repeats his whisper. "Raymond. This is Nurse Anna. Anna, please look after…"

Marjorie raises her eyes and her face turns ashen.

My eyes skim to where her gaze is frozen upon the remaining half face of the twinkling officer she flirted with at our lunch in mirrored dining room of the Mount Nelson Hotel. The face belongs to Captain Rosevere. Captain Jack Rosevere of the South Lancashires. He holds one arm aloft as though asking for something, so I go to help him. The Captain's eye is fixed upon my friend, however, and when she goes to him, Marjorie's would-be suitor presses a battered, almost full packet of cigarettes into her hand. The handsome mouth is all but gone, but I see what would have been a smile in the way he squeezes my friend's tiny wrist and nods towards one of the other injured men. Marjorie smiles back and with a steady hand, passes on the gift, which is gratefully accepted by its recipient. Then she strokes what is left of Captain Rosevere's forehead.

I summon two orderlies. "Please take this man to the Portland Hospital. Immediately," I add when I see the mutinous look they give one another, trying to muster a confident tone because it is Marjorie who would normally give the orders and she is unable to speak. It is quite a journey, but the surgeon at the Portland is an expert in facial reconstruction and I sense agreement in my friend's tacit nod. We both know that sending Captain Rosevere there is his best chance. Possibly his only chance.

After the initial onslaught of wounded men has been dealt with and as the weeks pass, we get to know some of our patients a little better. Marjorie slips away to the Portland Hospital from time to time and we all cover for her. We are always delighted to hear of Jack's progress, which we agree is as much to do with Marjorie's illicit visits as the surgeon's expertise. When Jack first wears the mask made for him as part of the facial reconstruction process, Marjorie comes back from her visit very subdued. Then, when she does not return in time for her shift for the fourth consecutive day, I begin to imagine the worst.

"Shall I do it?" Florence offers. She and I are on duty together and it is becoming increasingly difficult to invent a plausible excuse.

"No, it's my turn," I say and make my way to the ward where Marjorie is meant to be on duty.

Sister Jenkins folds her arms across her chest and her eyes narrow as she watches me approach.

"Good afternoon, Sister, I am afraid that Sister Makepeace is unwell and won't be able to work her shift today."

The senior nurse purses her lips and I am just about to offer my services when a dishevelled Marjorie flies through the door. Cap-less and red-faced, her eyes are inflamed and her voice has none of its usual sparkle.

"I am sorry to be so late, Sister," she manages dully.

Sister Jenkins turns to me, "Your friend appears to have made a miraculous recovery, Nurse Lieberman. That will be all." Her tone leaves me with the impression that Marjorie is not going to have an easy afternoon, and I leave with a heavy heart.

Shortly after two the next morning, our dormitory door creaks open. I watch Marjorie move noiselessly around the room before she slips ghostlike into her bed. She does not need me to ask the question.

"It's Jack. He doesn't want to see me again."

"But why, Marjorie?"

"He says that he cannot love me."

"Do you believe him?"

"No," she says and does not reply when I ask if she wants him to love her. Neither does she answer when I want to know if she loves him.

Impregnable, Marjorie guards the inner keep of her feelings and we do not speak of Captain Jack Rosevere after that night. At first, my friend distances herself from the new patients, but as more wounded men arrive from all over the British Empire, her warmth and tenderness return and the armour of self-protection gradually slips away. Marjorie cannot help herself and she has a directness that the men find as irresistible as her pretty face. When she meets an injured soldier for the first time, her voice is always full of compassion but never pity. I listen to the way she manages not to patronise when she gives an order. I see that she goes to hold a blind man's hand before she speaks, and how this gains his trust and encourages him to talk. But even those who are still blessed with sight sometimes find it impossible to look

36

Marjorie in the eye, for fear what they have seen might somehow communicate its horrors. Many are unable to speak, but for some it is an utter relief to be able to chatter about this and that or nothing in particular. Others are keen to impart their views and report on what they have seen.

"It helps get it out of their minds," Marjorie retaliates when I quiz her after she has been talking with one shell-shocked sergeant for almost twenty minutes, only for us to receive a dressing-down from Sister Jenkins because we haven't completed our rounds. "Maybe the poor man will get one decent night's sleep before he meets his maker!" She is angry at my intervention even though she knows she can ill-afford the wrath of Sister Jenkins, plus we have already worked fourteen hours without a break and there are many more medical matters to be dealt with before the luxury of sleep.

Transport and communication problems mean we are faced with the constant challenge of dealing with week or fortnight old injuries. There seems to be no hope for prevention of gangrenous limbs and gaping septic wounds. However, yesterday, a new sight greeted us on the arrival of a fresh cargo of wounded down from the Modder River. We had already heard that the dirty water there was being further contaminated by dead horses and human carcasses before being consumed – un-boiled – by thirsty, desperate troops and we were preparing ourselves and our facility for the worst.

"What are those things they are holding?" Marjorie looked aghast as we peered over a group of men who each clutched a piece of some sort of vegetation over their bloodied wounds. One of the Tommies lifted the huge leaf to reveal a deep laceration. Burnt deep sienna brown by the sun, and hat-less, his once-blue army shirt was in shreds and stained black with dried blood.

"Special field dressing, Sister!" he laughed and waved the leaf about, causing much mirth amongst his comrades-at-arms. Despite the horrific nature of the shrapnel injury, his one-week old wound was, miraculously, uninfected. "Not sure it'll protect me from the Modder-typhoid though."

I knew by the sores around his mouth that he was right.

It was not the antiseptic properties of the leaves, whose name I never knew, that most aided the soldiers' recovery. "You look like bloomin' Vesta Tilley, waving them leaves about like you were on't' bloody Music Hall stage! Ya big girl!" was the comment that started it. By the end of the week, several of the more mobile chaps had combed nearby river banks for more of the leaves and those that didn't become much-needed dressings, formed props for a kind of musical review. It was a wonderful tonic.

Once the rumours of a typhoid epidemic at Bloemfontein are finally confirmed, Sister Jenkins summons us one morning in early March. She addresses about twenty nurses who she splits into two groups. The first is made up of the girls billeted in my tent, plus the adjacent tent with whom we share our maid. The second group are ten girls who have been at No. 2 Hospital since November last year. Most of them have been nursing for some years and Sister Jenkins dismisses them with a curt, "You are my most experienced nurses and will leave for Bloemfontein tomorrow. Go immediately and pack your things."

I am relieved to hear that our group is to remain at Wynberg for the time being and may not even be called to Bloemfontein because the epidemic will soon be under control. I cannot wait to share these welcome tidings with Marjorie who hasn't been able to attend the meeting as she is assisting Doctor Matthews with the removal of a stubbornly embedded bullet from a trooper's shoulder.

Marjorie's skills in the operating theatre have been noted and the best surgeon asks for her all the time. Sister Jenkins stands erect before us and her steely eyes meet mine when she scans our group. It seems that I am the only nurse not looking at the ground.

"Where is Sister Makepeace?" she demands, fixing me with her stare, and I hesitate for a second too long. "So, she is assisting Doctor Matthews again, is she?" The spiteful tone and deep inhalation make my blood run cold. "Thank you, Nurse Lieberman. Dismissed."

When Marjorie sinks into her bunk next to mine very late that night, white-faced with tiredness but smiling, I guess she must have already heard the good news that we are not to go to Bloemfontein, not yet at least. I grin at her and offer her a piece of congratulatory chocolate that has come my way from one of the newly arrived Tommies.

"What are you doing?" I ask as she pulls her travelling valise from under her bed.

Marjorie plumps the bag on to the mattress.

"Sister Jenkins feels that since I didn't have the courtesy to attend her meeting, I should go to Bloemfontein tomorrow, with the other group."

I stand in such haste that I knock my inkwell over and dark liquid pools over the half-written letter to my uncle and aunt in Germany.

"Shhh…" comes a sleepy rebuke from the curled-up body in the corner bunk and I speak in a whisper.

"She cannot do that! It is not fair. She knew that you were helping Doctor Matthews."

Marjorie looks at me, her smile one of defeat. Or is it acquiescence? "I did explain that, but she chose not to accept it as a good enough reason and she…" I wait for my friend to finish her sentence.

"Well?"

Marjorie crams rolled-up stockings and handkerchiefs into the already bursting valise before answering. Her voice is thick and low.

"She made it quite clear that she thinks we are trouble makers. A bad influence on one another and the other nurses. She says she expects it of a person such as me. Meaning my bastard status, I suppose. But that you should know better."

Fury boils inside me and I make towards the door, ready to take on the woman who is sending my best friend into the hell of Bloemfontein. A hint of a smile wavers on Marjorie's lips when she catches my arm. "Leave it, Anna, please. It will only be worse for me if you go to her."

As usual, she is right, but I vow to get even somehow.

Florence, Martha, Rose and I are not called to Bloemfontein for three more weeks. When the agreed day in April arrives, Sister Jenkins makes sure that we travel on the very last train and the night is pitch-black when we leave Cape Town station so we will see nothing of the scenery for the first part of our journey. Martha remains undaunted throughout and has somehow procured a feast of pickled eggs, cheese, and fresh bread. With a flourish of her cape and a triumphant 'Ta-daah!', she also produces a bottle of champagne to cheer our spirits. Although this in itself is a valiant attempt to outwit Sister Jenkins, who has forbidden alcohol on our journey, what happened next would have most outraged our former superior. I recorded the events of that evening in some detail.

My diary:
4 April 1900, one o'clock
I wish Marjorie had been there to share the fun. Imagine our surprise when Martha disappeared at the first station stop on our journey, only to return with <u>three</u> more bottles of champagne and two corporals from the South Australian Mounted Rifles! We toasted 'good-riddance' to Sister Jenkins and then played cards with Owen and Pete, the Australian soldiers, all evening. I'm afraid I got very giddy after the first three glasses of champagne. Worse still, when we gambled, I lost all my matches – which we used instead of coins – before anyone else and then had to do a forfeit. Not only am I a terrible poker player, but neither can I dance, as everyone discovered when I pirouetted straight onto Owen's lap. He didn't seem to mind though, and even gave me a beautiful pin brooch in the shape of a funny little Australian bear called a Koala. It had belonged to his favourite aunt and had been his mascot so far in the war. I really love it, and it was terribly sweet of him to give me such a precious thing (I think he likes me quite a lot), but I have decided to give it to Marjorie when we get to Bloemfontein because I think she could do with a bit of luck and I think that might be a better thing to do than all the terrible acts of revenge we planned for Sister Jenkins.

Martha grumbles from her bunk that the sound of my nib scratching away is keeping her awake and the increasing volume of her distress threatens to wake the others. Reluctantly, I put away my pen, pin the Koala bear brooch to my uniform and smile at the memory of our evening which ended too soon when Owen and Pete went back to their carriage well after midnight, taking all the empty bottles with them. I thread the tiny brass key that locks away my secrets back onto the chain around my neck and sleep the champagne-induced slumber of no responsibility.

The strangely fresh, cool sharpness of the morning air hits us when we awake the next morning. Exhilarated, we scramble like silly, giant puppies to get ourselves dressed quickly so we can investigate where the night's journey has brought us. When the blinds are pulled open, we discover that our train is twisting up through the snow-capped Hex Mountains, the sun is shining and the sky is a deep, dazzling blue. So clear is the air, that everything stands out as if magnified. A truly magnificent sight. As we wait in a siding after breakfast, an ambulance train passes by and a group of Tommies cry out, "You're going the wrong way! We're headed to Cape Town!" Then, laughing, we are on our way again and I feel alive in the company of such scenery, fresh mountain air and the companionship of my three friends. Gradually, the mountains reduce to hills, or kopjes as they are called here, and we are on the great Karoo.

This arid plateau where there is nothing but huge kopjes covered with boulders and where dry, sandy desert stretches in every direction is like nothing I have ever seen. The vast skies and boundless earth broken only by the merest cloud and the occasional stunted sage bush. My attempts to sketch the scene are not particularly successful, but even so, I am quite hurt when everyone laughs at my drawings of the local livestock.

"But their legs, Anna!" Martha barks when she can stop laughing.

"Theis no sheep lark theis int Dayles," remarks Florence. We nod, no longer needing Rose's assistance to understand our Yorkshire friend.

"They certainly have unfathomably long legs," I add. "In fact, they could easily be mistaken for goats with their funny long tails and gangly limbs." I grin at Martha, who glances back at my drawing and says,

"Well, I suppose you have captured their stumpy ears," and then everyone laughs.

"What on earth do they eat though?" Rose wonders out loud and we discuss how many sage leaves they will need to consume each day to maintain their weight and health, a discussion led by Martha who is the only one among us to have any experience of the desert. She is ably assisted by Florence whose knowledge of the various breeds of sheep that inhabit the Pennine hills and Yorkshire Dales is impressive.

Creaking and shuddering to a final standstill at Bloemfontein station, we descend onto a platform alive with activity.

"Here, here!" Martha cries out to a Chinese man wearing an enormous straw hat that almost covers his wrinkled face. Pushing a steaming barrow, he winds his adept way between disembarking passengers, piles of trunks, heaps of precariously balanced boxes, other hawkers, tradespeople and hundreds of soldiers – some on horseback. We all wave and smile our best smiles at the tea-seller. But then he is gone, hat and all, swept away in the crowd, leaving our thirst unquenched and our spirits quashed.

A familiar, welcome figure emerges from the throng, tendrils of blonde hair flying loose. She throws her arms around me and then hugs each of the girls in turn.

"Welcome to Bloemfontein, City of Refuge! As the soldiers say."

Marjorie! She is wrapped in a wool cape that I have never seen before and I shiver. Sensible Rose and Florence are wearing the warm outer clothing we have been told we would need. I ignored the direction and now I sorely regret it. Martha, bizarrely, does not feel the cold and strides ahead, coatless. As Marjorie and I embrace and the chilly air fills my lungs, the misnomer of what the town is affectionately called by exhausted soldiers who arrive here straight from the front, strikes me at once. 'Refuge' is the one word that I would not have chosen to describe this place.

"All these people!" I cry as I am nearly pushed over in the scramble to leave the station.

"Before the war, only seven thousand people lived here," Marjorie ducks, narrowly avoiding a soldier's knapsack that has been tossed from one man to another. "There's nearer forty thousand now."

Looking around the chaotic muddle of smoke, men, horses and piles and piles of bags, boxes, trunks and saddles, I can believe it.

"But where do they all live?" I ask my friend who seems to be knowledgeable on the subject.

"Everywhere and anywhere. Anywhere there is room for a bed. And even where there is not," Marjorie laughs. "You will see. Here, you are freezing." She hands me a shawl and I gratefully pull it around me, not before she admires my gold koala bear brooch and cries when I give it to her. Once I have persuaded her and the others that I am nor betrothed to Owen or planning to go to Australia at the end of the war, we head west across the town, admiring the impressive Parliament Hall, Grey College and Post-Office buildings en route to our destination. Despite my initial doubts, the overall impression of this pretty town situated high above sea level on the veldt is positive, and I am very happy indeed to see my friend again.

At No. 8 Hospital, in the middle of the veldt, the scale of the place and the chaos takes me by surprise. I learn from Marjorie that Joy is here and has been at Bloemfontein for some weeks, helping the over-burdened medical staff. Because of her husband Ted's apparent proximity to the fighting and the impossibility of obtaining a civilian travel pass, Joy has put all her energy into the task of caring for the hundreds of men suffering with typhoid. I find her in one of the spaces allocated for nursing staff accommodation and I force myself to conceal my shock at her appearance. Joy's beautiful fine-boned face is gaunt, her curly auburn hair needs a wash and the stench of fever seems to linger on and around her. Her once white clothes are grey. I try to ignore the smell and the way she looks as I put my arms around her and insist, she takes a break.

Chapter 4
Joy

We step through the lines of soldiers lying on the ground and make our way out of the building for some air. As we share meagre rations of tinned corned beef and black tea, Joy says that it was only after our army had occupied Bloemfontein in March that the scale of the unfolding medical catastrophe became apparent.

"We had twenty funerals yesterday. And twenty the day before. And twenty the day before that. All from enteric fever." Her voice is flat with exhaustion, she stares into her cup of tea. "There are not enough beds, Anna. There is hardly any food and there is no milk. We have no water for washing."

I hear from Joy that every available building in the town has been converted into a typhoid hospital. She has not heard from her husband, Ted since learning of the injuries he sustained during 'Black Week' and of his determination to return to the fighting. However, she has nursed a young corporal who fought with Ted at Colenso who was able to pass on first-hand news of what he believed to be Ted's improving condition and that he might already have joined the Mafeking relief column.

"What can be done, Joy?" I ask. "What can I do?"

She shakes her head as I pull her close and make a mental note to contact Lady Maud Roddeston and see what strings might be pulled to find out Ted's whereabouts.

Our meal and conversation are short-lived respite from the battle within. We are called back inside the hospital to deal with casualties from the latest ambulance train delivering its wretched cargo from Boshoff. What follows is a forty-eight-hour black nightmare. During these two April days and nights, I do not see my bed. My work is interrupted only by visits to the canteen to snatch a hurried, scanty meal of yet more corned beef and black tea. The time, in between meal breaks extends from five to eight hours and I lose count of the injured and dying men we lift from the ground. At first, I ignore the griping pain in my stomach, protesting, when Marjorie asks, that I am probably hungry but will be fine once I have eaten a meal. Finally, compelled to throw myself on my bed, I stay there for three hours, with a raging attack of fever and a temperature of 103.

In vain, I cover my ears to stop the background cacophony of clanging, crying desperation that insists I stay awake. A glass of whisky brought by a sympathetic nurse whom I do not recognise induces an hour's heavy sleep, but when I awake, I am again gripped with fever. I shiver in my ice-cold sweat and the walls heave when I try to sit up. My voice becomes trapped in my belly when I cry for Marjorie and all I can hear is the thud of blood in my ears. The pounding sound moves to my eyes and forehead, and I am forced to drop to my knees. I drag my unwilling body out of bed, and as I crawl to the door my legs twist and then collapse beneath me and everything turns black.

I do not know how long it is before I hear fragmented voices: "Hush, she is awake…" And then: "Not typhoid, thank God," then another, unfamiliar male voice: "Anna, can you hear me?"

I feel the cool metal of a stethoscope on my hot skin. Then, at last, a voice I know: "Anna, drink this." The liquid wets my parched lips and loosens my tongue which has become stuck to the roof of my mouth. Then blackness.

I hear the humming at the same time I feel a brush pass through my hair. "Again," I hear myself say, "please," and I open my eyes when the humming stops, to see what I think is a look of happy shock on Joy's face.

"Oh, Anna, you are back. We were so worried. Now, you must promise to take better care of yourself!" And she hugs me before scurrying away to find the doctor and Marjorie.

I never did discover what was wrong with me. No one ever knew. Soon, I am fully recovered and we all work long days for the next few weeks, often from seven-thirty in the morning until ten at night. Although there are many casualties who need surgical intervention, these are heavily outnumbered by typhoid sufferers.

The irascible Sister Jenkins herself, who arrived at Bloemfontein just days after we did, proved not to be invulnerable after all. She is just one of the nurses who has succumbed to the disease. She recovered enough to be sent back to the Cape, and so thankfully, life for Marjorie and I has improved in one respect at least. Our new nurse superintendent, Sister Francis, is kind and gracious. It transpires that it was she who brought me the life-saving glass of whisky on that darkest of nights.

"We thought we had lost you, Anna," she confides during one of our shifts.

"Yes," I recall the sound of my friends' voices fading in and out, feeling myself slipping away even though I did not want to. "I do feel lucky to be here. But why did I live when so many do not?"

Sister Francis thinks for a moment, then brushes the red dust that has rubbed onto my skirt from sitting too often on the ground, "It was just meant to be, Anna."

We are forced to treat many patients on the floor because there are not enough beds, and due to the lack of water for washing, even the officers are covered in lice. It is worse than the receiving room in the east end, where I spent months after I had finished my initial nurse's training. Hurled around by strong winds, the dust is a huge problem in this country as it intrudes through every crack and crevice and forms a powdery red surface on everything. Along with this comes a disease most particular to this campaign, the veldt sore.

We usually see these small, suppurating blisters on the soldiers' hands and necks, but sometimes they invade the whole trunk, more particularly the lower body and legs. The sores remind me of those I have seen on the hands of plasterers back in East London and if not treated, will leave permanent, crater-like pockmarks. I am certain the veldt dust is responsible for them here. Simple to treat in small areas, the soldiers' sores are often compounded by sunburned skin, left too long to fester and accumulate in great number on one poor body. There is no excuse here. There is no poverty. Just the damned war. In Shoreditch, a plasterer would present with a single ailment – the very same sores, except for those with tuberculosis of course.

I remember Mr O'Malley with his family of eleven all stick-thin and flea-infested. They somehow found their way onto the ward where I treated their father's terrible sores. How these motherless waifs survived in their one roomed hovel was a mystery to me, but survive they did. Possibly because they made a little money from the safety pins, needles and other 'useful' bits and pieces that disappeared during their hospital vigils. I do hope so.

In South Africa, multitudinous medical conditions compound the severity of the soldiers' terrible injuries and make me long to be back in the slums of London. Here, we are also terribly short of some necessary articles for our work, but I have discovered a marvellous tool for applying poultices. At first, I was using the tiny silver letter-opener given to me by my mother, but one of the Tommies gave me his bayonet to try and now I can spread the embrocation onto a patient's skin in half the time. We have had to buy more linen from the haberdashers in Bloemfontein to make new aprons and Joy stitches late into the night when she isn't tending to the sick. It is hardly surprising that she suffers from terrible headaches because she will not stop working, however often Marjorie and I insist.

We hear of the relief of Mafeking in the middle of May, but when Marjorie and I look for Joy to share the good news and to find out if she knows whether Ted has been involved in the fighting, she is nowhere to be found. The room she shares with three other women bears no trace of her personal possessions and a stranger is seated on Joy's bunk.

"Has Joy moved quarters?" I ask, failing to inject my voice with a friendly tone.

"Sure," a Canadian accent explains the unusual nurse's uniform, "I think someone said she's at the little hospital with the stoep." Returning my own inhospitable manner, the young nurse does not look up and her features remain hard and unsmiling as she continues to read her book. The upset I feel at this dour woman taking over my friend's place is inexplicable, but my face burns hot as I stride out of there, followed by a subdued Marjorie.

Our search for Joy ends at nearby Bishop's Lodge, a pretty, red-brick house not far from No. 8 Hospital. The late Bishop apparently had no relations, so all his belongings are just as he left them and the place is crammed full of lovely paintings and ancient books. We agree that working in such an interesting environment must be some compensation to Joy for the difficult conditions within.

Marjorie and I approach the building and step onto a veranda that in summer will be garlanded with passion flower vines. Pausing in the shadows, we breathe in the cool dampness and exchange a look. Only too familiar with the scenes of human misery that are sure to lie beyond the building's picturesque façade because this is where the more serious cases are sent and nursing the patients here is only for those of the strongest disposition. Joy, I fear, should not have been asked to work in this place as she has no nursing qualification and little experience, but I suppose it is for her kind disposition that she will be appreciated.

Bishop's Lodge is the latest building to be designated as a typhoid hospital and on entering, we discover that fifteen of its sixteen beds are occupied by sick women. The sixteenth bed is where we find Joy. We rush over, but I see by her face that we are only just in time to say goodbye.

"She wasn't admitted until yesterday," the sister in charge tells us when we ask why we haven't been informed. "But she was already very weak. I don't know how she carried on as she did for so long. Please, stay with her."

Joy's eyes open and a little colour flushes across her pale cheeks when she hears my voice. She tries to move and what might have become a smile turns to agony when she tries to part her cracked lips. Upon her whispered breath is his name, "For Ted. For my husband."

I stroke the papery skin of her hand, "We will find him, Joy. We will bring him to you. I promise."

Her shallow, choked breathing turns to agitated rasps, as in desperation, she clings onto life. Frightened hands grip the bedclothes repeatedly, grasping, searching. By now, Marjorie is weeping openly and I am struck dumb with fear. When Joy begins to flail her arms as though she were trying to fly, the commotion brings Sister, who takes our friend's arms and holds them still. From the bedside-table, she takes a small parcel and gently folds Joy's hands around it.

"Here, my dear, is this what you were looking for?"

A long, slow exhalation follows and we wait as Joy's eyes close and her face becomes still once more.

"It is time. I will fetch the Padre," the Sister tenderly brushes a damp tendril of Joy's beautiful chestnut curls away from her eyes. With a final dogged, shuddering effort, our dying friend turns to me, pulls my hands close, whispers jumbled words that doesn't really make sense, something she wants him to forget. Then I hear, "Please give these to him, Anna. Tell him…tell him…"

And she is gone. Melted to a memory.

I agree to write to Joy's parents for whom the Sister has an address, but as I clutch the sheaf of letters that Joy pressed into my hands with her last action on this earth, I know that I have a much more onerous task to perform.

Chapter 5
Major Oliver
Anna's Diary

May 29th 1900

I have been at Kroonstad hospital for over a week now, and at last have time to put pen to paper. Although it is less than six months since I arrived in South Africa, it feels longer somehow and I am beginning to feel at ease in this country. The early morning frosts here remind me of England – Kroonstad is further north up the railway line from Bloemfontein – and I am glad of the cooler temperatures. One of the other pleasures that I have found in this straggling town with its enormous white Dutch church that looks to be made from porcelain, is to spend time with Lady Maud Roddeston. Maud has become like an older sister to me and she knows of the guilt I feel about surviving my fever when Joy didn't escape the typhoid and of my dilemma over her letters. Should I send them to her parents? To her husband's commanding officer? Or should I keep them safe until somehow, I can find out where Ted is – if he is still alive of course. Unlike Marjorie, who believes that I should take care of the letters because Joy entrusted me with them, Maud thinks that they would stand more chance of reaching him if I were to forward them via Ted's regiment. Perhaps that is what I will do. It is three weeks since Joy passed away, but I still think of her every day and hope that her family have received my letter by now. Some of her last words did not make sense at all and they puzzle me still, but perhaps one day, I will work out what she meant. It was before she gave me the letters. Something she had forgotten. Or something she wanted Ted to forget. What was it? I wonder.

I have met a very interesting patient. His name is Heiman. The Boers usually make it clear that they would rather be treated by their own, but Heiman is different. He comes from a town in the Orange Free State that I have never heard of. His family are originally from Germany and he loves to converse with me in either his or my language about politics, history and art. He reminds me of my father. Perhaps, one of the reasons that I feel more at home these days. Heiman gave one of his soldiers a dressing-down the other day because the young lad spat at Marjorie, who in truth was being even more direct than usual. This is exactly the sort of thing my father would have done and I told Heiman so. Since then, after we discovered that both our families have relatives in Bavaria, we have become friends. Heiman has been helping me to get to know this country. We draw maps of the different states of South Africa, with all their towns, rivers and mountains and he tells me something of their turbulent history. Maud joined us this morning when she dropped off a new consignment of gifts for the patients, and we had an especially testy discussion the absolute sovereignty of God in salvation (my father would have made a far more informed contribution than I was able to, but Heiman and Maud were at it hammer and tongs for ages), before a tot of the finest malt whiskey made everyone friends again.

In Kroonstad, just as in Cape Town, Maud seems to know a great many people and she uses her contacts and not insubstantial funds to help whoever, whenever and wherever she can. Although she says there is 'nothing left to buy in this wretched town', Maud continues to relieve the shops in Bloemfontein of a surprising quantity warm clothing, champagne, brandy and other delightful delicacies. These she distributes to nurses and patients alike and when they run out, she sends funds to her friend, Lady Foley in Bloemfontein who replenishes supplies and sends them to us. I forgot to mention that when she brought in the brandy and tobacco this morning, Maud gave me a set of the most exquisite linen napkins and silver napkin rings. Hardly a priority in my current circumstances, I know, but at least mother would approve.

Next to my journal entry, I begin to make a sketch of the beautiful napkin holders in the shape of swans and smile at the memory of the yesterday's conversation with Maud.

"I am so pleased to be in the Kroonstad Hotel, Anna," Maud confided. "Had Nan and I availed ourselves of the lodgings that were suggested by Mr Solomon, we would have been out on the streets during the day."

"On the streets, Maud?"

She laughed at my misapprehension, "Yes. Because the only vacant sleeping accommodation that we were able to find was occupied during the day by sleeping nurses who work night shifts. But sadly, I am still having to drink from those ghastly thick glass tumblers. It is impossible to find fine crystal here. And there is no oil for heating to be found anywhere. But there seem to be plenty of napkins. Here, Anna, these are for you and the girls."

When Maud went on to complain of having to make do with only three tablecloths, I thought of my mother, with her similar high standards, who is also terribly well-connected and to who I owe a letter. I sigh, put away my sketching pencils and take out my best writing paper. It is late and I have an early shift tomorrow.

Duty the next day begins in one of the tents, which houses some of the more seriously injured and disturbed men. My eyes take a while to become accustomed to the dim, brown Holland-coloured twilight. A large marquee of double folded canvas keeps out the sun; a few shafts of light twinkle through here and there, occasionally lighting the faces of the men. Some are lying, some are standing, some sitting, and range of injuries are not dissimilar to those I have treated at the Cape and in Bloemfontein. I look up from reading the notes left by the night sister to consider how best to approach the complex needs of these patients.

Two young men, both lieutenants, appear to be suffering from bad cases of shell shock and one man, a Major Oliver, is in danger of losing a leg after his shrapnel injury became infected at the field hospital where he was first treated. Aided by our new X-Ray machine which can locate embedded bullets, six of the men have had surgical treatment so their dressings will need attention and the night-sister is concerned that an older man, Major McRoberts from the Highland Regiment, is showing signs of enteric fever. If so, he will have to be moved.

Something about the man in the corner bunk with his bandaged arm and a badly damaged leg captures my attention. The man must have sensed my stare because he looks up from his book and catches my eye as I study his face for clues. Caught out, I wave a fresh wad of bandages at him and he gives me a look of pretend-horror before he turns promptly back to his book. The Scarlet Letter is a surprising choice, if my mother's opinion is anything to go by, and I make a mental note to ask what he thinks about the book's controversial subject matter.

Through three openings in the canvas where air finds its way in from time to time, I catch glimpses, crossed by a web of guy ropes, of other surrounding tents. Each one is neatly enclosed by a border of whitened stones to prevent people from tripping over the ropes at night. Orderlies run from tent to tent minding their patients. I see another nurse with familiar strands of stray blonde hair flying lose as she breezes across the open space between the straight lines of marquees. I wave, then watch as Marjorie stops for a moment's chat and a little bit of a flirt with one of the doctors, who I do not recognise immediately, but I smile and shake my head because, as usual, Marjorie can't resist chatting up a handsome man. She grins, pixie-like, waves back and tucks some disobedient hair behind her ear.

I can see groups of patients in clean, dark-blue clothes. They walk about, or sit, taking the air; some hobble on crutches, some have arms in slings, heads bandaged, or patched and mended in some way or other. I'm confused at how I feel when I realise that many of these men will soon be well enough to go back to the fighting. And then what? Back here for us to mend them again? Or worse. After one week, I am already sickened by the sight of fatigue parties, each one bearing aloft their stretcher, with its silent burden covered by the Union Jack.

As I shudder in the cool air at the thought of the ever-increasing number of little burial mounds on the veldt, the new patient with the intriguing taste in literature beckons, so I make my way across the dry mud floor through the neatly organised, linen-covered tables, bowls, jugs and magazines to his bedside. Spotting his name scribbled across the notes beside him, and taking in his shattered leg, I ask, "Can I help you, Major Oliver?"

Major Edwin Oliver's reply is drowned out by clattering metal and shrieks of confusion as a bounding mongrel, wearing army puttees that have been specially fashioned for him, careers enthusiastically through patients and paraphernalia, only coming to a halt when his collar is grabbed by one of the orderlies. Sheepish at first, Durban, the camp's mascot, enjoys the chaos he has caused and barks around for a reward before he is hustled away by his owner, a young, red-faced corporal.

"I am so sorry, Major Oliver, but I didn't catch your reply. I am Nurse Lieberman. Anna Lieberman. We have not met before. Is there something you need?"

He closes his book and our eyes lock. I take in the thatch of dark hair, grown a little longer than is typical for an officer, and which frames his face. His straight nose, dark eyes and serious countenance remind me of the portrait of a very young Prince Rupert of the Rhine that is one of my favourite paintings. This soldier, however, is older and even more handsome than Prince Rupert. I feel heat rising up my neck and curse inwardly because there is nothing I can do to prevent my face from adopting its customary bright red giveaway badge of girlish inexperience.

"Do you have a dog, Nurse Lieberman?" asks Major Oliver, who ignores my silly embarrassment and gives me a smile that leaves me momentarily speechless

"Not out here, Major," I laugh at the very thought. "I think Durban is enough dog for this hospital. Do you know he even has his own waterproof cape with little panniers marked with the red cross, so he can carry surgical dressings for us? The patients love him. But I am sure that wasn't what you wanted to ask."

"No, it wasn't, but Durban reminded me of the dog we have at home, Billy. My wife chose him and spoils him. But he doesn't have his own clothes, I am happy to say." The Major smiles and fixes his gaze on me again. "I need some help with something, Nurse Lieberman. Or may I call you Anna? It is just that what I have to ask is…something rather personal."

I nod my head, willing him to ask me anything, anything at all. I just want us to continue talking.

"Thank you. Thank you, Anna. What I wanted to ask… I really wanted to see if you can help me find my wife."

"Your wife, Major? Is she here in South Africa?"

"Edwin. Do please call me Edwin. I really don't know where she is. I have heard nothing from her in weeks and weeks. I do know that she was intent on coming out, but then there was the battle at Colenso, then the relief of the siege, and now this." He indicates towards the web of wires and wood around his injured right leg and manages to knock the book he was reading to the ground. I reach down quickly to retrieve it.

"Collected works of Christina Rossetti. I love her poems," I say, rather too informally, given we have only just met and he is married, but he doesn't seem to mind and I hold out the ragged anthology to him. "It appears to be much travelled."

He nods and takes the book with both hands.

"A parting gift?" I ask, and he nods again. I wonder if he has his own favourite.

"Do you have a favourite?" he says at the very second that I ask him the identical question and we laugh together like idiots when at the exact same moment, we pronounce 'Goblin Market' to be the very best poem Miss Rossetti ever penned. He appears not to notice that I blush again and thank goodness he doesn't ask why I like that poem particularly.

"But my wife…who gave this to me…prefers…now where is it?" He flicks the pages until they fall open and then begins to read.

"Remember me when I am gone away,
Gone far away into the silent land;
When you can no more hold me by the hand,
Nor I half turn to go yet turning stay.
Remember me when no more day by day
You tell me of our future that you planned:
Only remember me; you understand
It will be late to counsel then or pray.
Yet if you should forget me for a while
And afterwards, remember, do not grieve:
For if the darkness and corruption leave
A vestige of the thoughts I once had,
Better by far that you should forget and smile
Than you should remember and be sad."

Major Oliver raises his eyes to mine and when he smiles, a thousand tiny lines light up his face. "She thought it might help, if I didn't make it back. But here I am, still!"

Only when I know that I can speak without letting my emotions give me away, I say, "How can something so very sad be so unutterably beautiful and heart-warming?"

The touch of his hand sets off a tremor that ripples up my arms, gathers pace and leaves me confounded by the aftershocks that rock me from my scalp to my toe-nails. I realise that Edwin is speaking and he repeats himself when he sees that I have regained my composure.

He smiles that smile again, "I see that you are a great romantic, Anna. My wife has a sweet, kind nature too. Some would say that she is too sentimental. Perhaps she is. But she would do anything to help others. It is one of the many reasons that I fell in love with her. She gave me this collection of poems on the day she waved me off."

"But it was not this book that you were reading earlier?" I breathe deep to calm my pounding heart.

His eyebrows raise in unison with the corners of his mouth. "How observant you are." He pulls a less-thumbed volume from beneath his pillow and hands it to me. "I got a bit of stick from the padre for reading it. A Canadian doctor gave it to me. Said he thought it might broaden my view of the world. Do you know it?"

I flick through the pages and nod, thankful that my heart is now beating a thudding but more normal rhythm, "I know of it, but I have not read it. My mother is quite religious and forbade it in the house. She is Roman Catholic. My father is Jewish and said he didn't care if I read it or not." I wait for Major Oliver to ask the question that most people do when they discover that my parents have different faiths. He says nothing, and so I study the cover and hand back the book. "I was not aware of its full title: *The Scarlet Letter – A Romance.* Would you say that it is, given that she is an adulteress?" Am I testing him or myself by using a word I have never before spoken out loud?

He passes *The Scarlet Letter* back to me and says, "I will let you be the judge, Anna. I shall be most interested to find out what you think." This is not where I had expected our conversation to lead, but I thank him and pocket the book. I begin the question I wanted to ask about his wife, but the day's sister in charge swoops into the tent and orders me to go and assist with another amputation. It is the sixth such operation this week.

Next day, I wait until the other nurse finishes the busy morning shift and I am left alone with my patients in the quiet of the early afternoon. It is particularly calm now that the doctor has finished his rounds and the men can relax. And for once, there is no sound of the big guns, whose sporadic thunder is not good for anyone's nerves. Because Doctor Matthews is concerned about the possibility of an infection returning to Major Oliver's leg, I go over to him armed with a thermometer. I do not have much time, because I am due to help with the expected new arrivals from up the line. At the thought of my task, the Major manages to grin and grimace at the same time, "Let's get on with it shall we, Nurse Anna?"

As I wait for the thermometer to do its work, I decide to break the silence of anticipation.

"You said yesterday that your wife wished to come to South Africa, Major?"

"Yes. I was torn about it, rather. We both were. The children, you see. But she felt that her skills would be of use."

I shake the thermometer, which reads what it should. Not just married, but children too. I cannot believe that I am even thinking these thoughts. I show him the reading. Normal. "Her skills? Is your wife a nurse, Major?"

"Edwin, please. No, she isn't a nurse…but she is so terribly kind and good…and we just wanted to be together…she wanted to come…but the children had to be cared for. She arrived here on the Dunottar Castle in January. It wasn't safe for her to join me, and so we wrote when we could. But I haven't heard from her in weeks. I know she was helping at Bloemfontein. Her name is Joy." My heart flips, then I remember that his name is Oliver, not Brandleigh.

"Joy? Joy Oliver?"

"Yes, and no," his smile lights the tent. "Yes. My wife's name is Joy. But she uses Brandleigh. It is a courtesy title from my father. It is my title. But my surname is Oliver. I rarely use the prefix. Either of them."

The prefix. Both sir and lord. Sir Edwin Oliver, Lord Brandleigh, son of the Earl and Countess of Lanchester. His name is Edwin. And Ted. Ted – Joy's pet name for him.

I reach down to retrieve one of the metal dishes scattered yesterday by Durban and brush a speck of dust from the rim, then place it gently back on the table.

"Nurse Lieberman? Anna?"

"I met your wife, Major Oliver. Edwin." I deliberately avoid any honorific address, "I met Joy. We travelled together from England on the Dunottar Castle. We became friends. Good friends." My head spins.

"Why, that's wonderful! Did you see her again after you arrived in South Africa?"

His face is alight.

"I did. I did see her. Often."

The light behind his eyes fades as he searches my face. At that moment, a clearly annoyed Marjorie flies into the tent, gathers herself and ushers me hastily away. She has come from the latest ambulance train with its many wounded and dozens of new cases of the typhoid fever that continues to lay waste to the British troops and I should have been with her at the receiving station ten minutes ago. I turn and through the swiftest of glances, I try and communicate that I will return soon.

Marjorie and I work swiftly and silently for many joyless hours among the afflicted. All the time, I cannot help but wonder why unkind fate has drawn me so cruelly close to my dear, dead friend's husband.

"Anna?" Marjorie sounds troubled and I realise that I have been standing over the same corpse for several minutes.

I try to pull myself together. "I am sorry, Marjorie. I…" I feel myself begin to shake.

"Stop, right now!" she commands and recruits two additional orderlies to take over. "Here, come." And she leads me away from the stinking agony of death, disease and despair. "Tea." She grabs steaming cup from an astonished orderly and thrusts it into my hands. "What happened just then? It's not that you haven't seen dead boys before." Her tone softens and she passes me a handkerchief, "Do dry your eyes." She laughs as she usually does at the very unladylike way I blow my nose, and then I tell her.

51

"Edwin is Ted," I say. "Joy's Ted."

"Joy's Ted? But Joy is…was…Brandleigh," she speaks our dead friend's name in her quietest voice, "And Edwin's name is Oliver. Edwin Oliver."

"Sir Edwin Oliver, Lord Brandleigh. Son of the Earl and Countess of Lanchester." I slot the final pieces into the puzzle.

"Oh, Anna," she locks those blue eyes onto mine. They are not smiling. "What a mess."

For the next few hours, we separate the living from the dead, summon the Padre for others, and as the urgency fades, my conflicted thoughts return to Joy's husband and I know what I must do.

The sun is long set by the time I can see him again. Before I make my way back to Edwin's bedside, I take refuge in my own tent and emit a long breath, relieved to find myself alone. The five girls that I share this canvas home with must be either eating or still working. I take one of the keys from around my neck, retrieve my writing box from beneath my bunk and unlock it. Hidden underneath my diary, I feel for the soft velvet ribbon, and as I lift the bundle towards the glow of the lantern, an almost imperceptible rustle breaks the silence. The name inked in hand-written script on the top envelope flickers briefly as I face the task given to me by my friend.

Soothed a little by the becalmed night air, I am guided through the rows of tents by the white-painted stones that mark the guy ropes; the precious parcel awaits delivery in the folds of my apron. Its recipient is the only man awake when I reach his tent and lift the flap. Edwin watches me until I sit and rest my lantern beside him.

"Tell me," he says blankly.

Reluctant envoy, I pass the letters to him. "Your wife…Joy…entrusted these to me before she died." I curse the tears that run hot on my cheeks. "I am so sorry."

Gently, he takes the bundle. Helpless, I watch his shaking hands as he struggles with the ribbon. When he begins to read his beloved wife's farewell, I stand to leave.

"Please stay, Anna."

I need to remind myself to breathe when his eyes meet mine and I have no idea whether I want to run away or to stay. He senses my mood because he raises himself despite the pain in his shattered limbs and takes my hand. "Anna, please don't go." His voice is rusty with emotion. "Please," he appeals. And I know then that I want to stay with him. I want to stay with him more than anything.

"My darling, Ted,

If you are with Anna, she has found you somehow. She is so kind and I am giving her all the letters I managed to write since I lost touch with your whereabouts. Did she tell you yet that we met on the ship that brought me to South Africa? That we worked together in Bloemfontein? Maybe you are in hospital, not too badly hurt please, God, and I pray not with the enteric fever. I hope you are not alone when you read what I must write now. There is so much I dearly want to say to you and my time is running away. I only wish we could have found one another."

The words blur into a golden pool, but he reads on. And then he reads it all once more. In Edwin's trembling whisper, I hear again the tender voice of my friend in her final words to the man she loved.

"Say goodbye to the children from me and give Billy a pat. I know he is naughty sometimes, but he is a good dog really. It seems silly to say thank you, my darling,

but thank you. Thank you for our wonderful boys and beautiful daughter. Thank you for your love. I am holding you now in my heart. Goodbye, my darling one. I am so sad to leave you. I love you so very, very much."

Drifting through the darkness on the night breeze, I see that Joy's final words are as precious to him as their wedding vows.

"She asked me to tell you something." Joy's whispered dying words that I did not understand at the time now make sense. My tears are a river. "'Forget. Forget and smile', she said. Like the poem."

"Oh, Joy," he whispers, and as I relish his touch and hate myself for being so selfish, I share his grief and we both remember why she suited her name so well.

That night, I lie awake in my bed, turning this way and that, and when I do drift into sleep, I am immediately awoken by Joy. Joy humming as she brushed my hair when I was ill, Joy trying to teach me the herringbone stitch, Joy reading letters from her oldest son back in England, Joy's soft laugh as she regales tales of her dog, Billy's antics to the sick and wounded soldiers, Joy's despair at the lack of food and clean water at Bloemfontein. Her voice haunts me through the night, and when morning comes, and it is time to get back to my work in the wards, I resolve to question her husband. What possessed him to agree that Joy should come to South Africa? Why did he not write to her when he was injured? What will he say to their children? I throw back my bed covers, fling on my uniform, bundle the tatty mess that is my hair beneath yesterday's crumpled cap, slap some water from the jug onto my face and stride through the torrential rain in the direction of Edwin's ward to the disgruntled groans of my fellow nurses whom I have woken with my hasty toilette.

"What made you think that it was alright for her to come here?" I glare at my dead friend's husband who is already awake despite the early hour. "To this God-forsaken, disease-ridden country. You knew how weak she was after John was born."

Since yesterday, his eyes have dimmed and there is only red where there should be white. I will not give him time to think. I just want him to answer me. "Well? What have you got to say for yourself, Major Oliver? Sir Edwin? Nothing? There is nothing you can say, is there?"

My voice has risen from a hissed whisper to something uncontrolled, loud, broken. "Why didn't you write to her? Send a telegram? Anything!" My shouts have turned to sobs.

The rain drums down and the distant artillery thuds its relentless reminder of what Joy died for.

"Anna." Marjorie has appeared at my side and her firm hands manoeuvre me from where I tower, dripping wet, over Edwin's bed to the chair beside it. Marjorie narrows her eyes and studies my face, and his, in turn before she directs a question to him, "Major Oliver?"

His eyes refuse to meet mine however hard I fix my stare, but he nods at Marjorie who then releases her hands from my shoulders.

"Ten minutes and no more," she says quietly and leaves us as smoothly as she arrived. It is as though she was never there.

I am as a sunken ship, my cargo of anger dissipated across the seabed. Waves crash way above me, but I am at the bottom of the ocean in the gloomy, murky depths of sadness and despair. Edwin joins me in the wreck's stillness and hands me a small

53

metal tin with a raised, slightly rusty embossed lid. "The letters I wrote but was not able send," he says. "Open them."

How can I possibly read this man's letters to his wife? I refuse the casket with its lost treasure, but he presses it onto my lap.

"Read them, Anna. Please read them. I asked her not to come. But she was her own person. She wanted to be here. Conflicted, yes, but it was her wish to come to South Africa."

"But you could have stopped her." This untruth reverberates inside my head. I knew Joy. I know I am wrong. I hear my forlorn tone echo back at me. I know it is not his fault.

"I loved her, Anna. So much. I wanted her with me. I am sorry for it, but I wanted her with me."

I feel myself floating in the flotsam and jetsam of our lives, all upturned by the war and hand back the metal box.

"I know. I am so terribly sorry. I loved her too."

The morning light is beginning to ripple through the canvas so I can just make out the script on the letter he hands to me.

"This might explain a little of what happened," he says. When I unfold the paper, I see that it is addressed to Mrs Joy Oliver and dated 24 December 1899. It is no wonder that the letters did not reach Joy. Joy Brandleigh. I look up and he encourages me to read on.

Dear Mrs Oliver,

I am writing to you because your husband, Ted cannot write due to his injuries, but being the persuasive man that I'm sure you know him to be, he has convinced me to be his scribe.

He wants you to know that he is certain that he will recover from the shrapnel wounds to his arms and right hand, they are bandaged thoroughly which is why he cannot hold a pen, and that it is not possible for you to be here because no wives are allowed so close to the front lines. He says it is simply too dangerous. And my dear Mrs Oliver, he is quite right.

Your husband has urged me to impress upon you that his condition is in no way life-threatening and that it is his intention to re-join the Ladysmith Relief Column as soon as his hand and arm are recovered. Knowing his courage and determination as I do, there is no doubt in my own mind that this will be the case. Now, Mrs Oliver, I am going to switch and write the words your husband dictates to me.

My kindest wishes,
Frederick Treves

Consulting Surgeon with H.M. Troops in South Africa

The envelope of this letter and the next have been marked Return to Sender. I open the second.

Dearest Joy,
I wish…

I stop myself reading his words. It's too much. It hurts too much. I know how they lived for one another. I close my eyes and sense Edwin's intense scrutiny as he tries to read my thoughts.

"Tell me about the Field Hospital," I say and look at him, "Tell me about Frederick Treves." And for the next thirty minutes, interrupted only by Marjorie who comes to make sure her enforced peace has been maintained, I listen.

"Treves always said that the day I arrived at No. 4 Field Hospital was the most horrific day he had ever experienced as a medical surgeon. It was also the day that the new commander in chief, Lord Roberts' son, Freddy was mortally wounded trying to rescue one of the abandoned guns. I was there. He was a brave man."

I tell Edwin that Joy, Marjorie and I had heard the news during our voyage on the RMS Dunottar and then he wants to know about our friendship, our journey and every detail of the time I spent with his wife. He has easily slipped into the habit of calling me by my first name, and unless there are doctors present, I always call him Edwin now, which I prefer to the abbreviated version that Joy liked. I am anxious to find out why the letter I have just seen and the others did not reach Joy, but his eyes plead with such depth and hope to hear about his wife that it now becomes his turn to listen and mine to speak. It is as if I have scarcely begun when Marjorie returns for the second time, impish now that she has to remind me that other patients are waiting.

Over the days, Edwin and I exchange stories, and each morning when I wake, I find myself anticipating the moment when we can resume yesterday's unfinished anecdote or when I might ask him something about Joy or the children that came to me in the night. His face, particularly the warmth and softness in his deep brown eyes, is often my final thought of the day. Occasionally, if I can sneak him in, I bring Durban into Edwin's tent even though it's completely against the rules.

Right now, as I rest before the start of my night shift, what he has told me returns in vivid images. Thankfully, alone in my tent, I reach for my special box and retrieve another letter to Joy that he began to read to me but did not finish. He has trusted me enough to let me take it away. This particularly tattered envelope has been addressed and re-addressed several times. Its original date is 18 January 1900 and comes from the Field Hospital, Spearman's Farm. The handwriting is elegant, sinuous and a little shaky.

Dearest Joy,

At last, this is me, writing, which feels like a miracle. When the bandages came off, my hand refused to obey instructions for a few days, but as you can see, I soon got it back into shape. So much so that the medics think I will be able to get back to Buller and the Ladysmith relief column as soon as next week.

The hospital has moved its location again and we arrived here at Spearman's Farm on 16th January. It's a homestead, typical of these parts, I am told, but to me it has a remarkable Englishness about it. Although small, single storey and surrounded by a great stone wall, and now completely wrecked by the Boers who came before us of course, it has a certain charm. It's my guess that the garden was once beautiful and I think there was a duck pond.

The road is barely passable because of all the heavy artillery that was here and the farm equipment destroyed by the Boers litters the place. Vehicles do get through though. They've tried to put me on an ambulance cart twice now, but there have been many chaps in greater need so I've had to stay with No. 4 Hospital. I don't mind really. Seeing the views this morning, I must say that it is quite preferable to the situations of either Frere or Chieveley. But when we were at Springfield, some of the fellows bathed in the river, which was quite an event especially in this heat and I long to bathe now that I am well enough. I took a stroll around the back of the hospital this morning and only wish I could enclose a photograph. The Tugela River glistened like molten silver, and over the plain and in and out among the kopjes and round the dongas, I could see the road that leads to Ladysmith. Soon, I hope to be there, to release those poor souls who have been besieged all these months.

Well, my dear, I digress. Let me return to the incredible and beautiful scenery. The panorama from this spot is boundless. You can even see the ridge of Spion Kop (news of the battle there may have reached you) and the far hills behind Ladysmith are the shade of deep purple that I know you love so much. Here I am, writing so much about the country, about Ladysmith and Spion Kop and Buller! When you receive this letter, it may all be censored, but know that it is simply not possible to censor the love I have for you, my darling, and for our children. I look at the photographs every day even though they are somewhat dog-eared after all this time in the heat and rain and hail and dust that this land throws at us. Anywhere and everywhere, it seems.

I have just heard that a dispatch rider is set to go out soon and I may be able to persuade him to take this letter, which I am sending to the Mount Nelson Hotel. I can only hope and pray that it reaches you.

My fondest love,
Ted

I gently re-fold the letter that, with its many addresses written and crossed out, must have travelled hundreds of miles in search of its intended, much-loved recipient. How I wish it had reached her. How I wish I could have helped her to find him. Why did I not ask Lady Maud to help when I thought of it?

When I next have a whole day off duty, I spend the morning with Lady Maud so that we can distribute the armfuls of new warm clothing from the most recent supplies sent by Lady Foley from Bloemfontein. The new owner of a fine wool sweater, which she has kept back especially for him, I watch Edwin succumb to Maud's charm as did I when first introduced to her at the Mount Nelson Hotel in Cape Town.

"Can you believe that I too am staying in a hospital?" she says as she tells him of the Kroonstad Hotel where she has a room but where most of the accommodation has been turned over to the wounded and sick. As at Bloemfontein, many buildings including churches are now home for typhoid sufferers, but with the colder weather, there has come a reduction in new cases. It is true that places to sleep are more rare and precious than stones from Kimberley's diamond mines, and I relate the tale of Florence and Rose who are forced to share a very small bed – one sleeping in it during the day and the other at night.

"And what of Colonel Roddeston?" enquires Edwin at the end of our afternoon together, during which time, we have managed to hoist him in and out of a makeshift wheelchair fashioned by one of his sappers to provide him with a guided tour of the hospital environs. For once Lady, Roddeston does not have a quick or witty retort and she studies her reticule, pulling the drawstring and gently touching its embroidered surface.

"Maud?"

My fears are only partially confirmed when she answers, her voice calm but clipped, "I have had news. News that Lance is injured and is at Lindley."

"But when did you discover this? Can you not go to him?"

"I am waiting to hear from the commissioner if I might be granted a pass to proceed up the line. Of course, I do have Nan and provisions."

I remember Nan from Cape Town. She is Lady Maud's companion and is a qualified nurse.

"But I have been told that it may not be possible to obtain a pass. So, I have decided to seek other ways of getting myself and Nan up to Lindley so that I can be with Lance."

"Other ways, Lady Roddeston?" Edwin's tone is tight and creases have formed across his forehead.

"I know, Major Oliver. I realise that Lord Kitchener is very much against us ladies being at the front. But I thought that perhaps I might go with one of the convoys. I spoke with General Cox who thought that if I found myself a cart, I might be able to go with his."

She looks suddenly and uncharacteristically as though she might cry, and when pressed, tells us that as she tried to finalise the arrangements, she had been severely reprimanded by one of the junior officers and had subsequently received a message from General Cox, who said that he was obliged to retract his permission. And to further compound her troubles, Nan had been taken sick this morning.

"So, as you can see, I am rather back where I started. No Nan and cart-less."

"And that is the best place, Lady Roddeston. Your husband would not appreciate your becoming caught up in the fighting and there is much of it. I am sure Sir Lancelot is in good hands."

Lady Maud nods but continues to fiddle with her purse and I am left with the impression that we have not heard the last of her valiant attempts to go to her husband. She asks if Edwin is well enough to undertake an outing from the hospital into Kroonstad, which of course he is not, and so she and I make a tentative arrangement for me alone to accompany her when I next have a free day, on what she tells us is a delightful river walk.

It is not until I accompany her across the camp to deliver the last of her gifts for the men that she lets down her guard.

"He is all I have left, Anna. I cannot imagine life without Lance."

We walk shoulder to shoulder, but I stop when she does.

"I had a daughter, once. You remind me of her a little. She was tall and dark-haired like you."

Now I understand. I hear her sorrow, feel her pain. "Oh, Maud, I am so very sorry," is all I can offer and I take my friend's hand.

"We named her Alice. She would have been fifteen next month," Maud continues and searches the horizon for faraway memories. "I had other babies, but none of them lived for more than a few weeks."

"Oh, Maud. How terribly sad. Tell me about Alice. What was she like?"

I listen as Alice comes alive again in her mother's mind… "Brave, rather shy, very beautiful and great dark eyes with black lashes, just like yours, Anna. And she loved books too." Maud talks for such a long time that I know I will be in trouble again, but I really do not care and vow that I will do everything in my power to help reunite Maud with her husband.

As the typhoid loosens its grip and we appear to be receiving less and less battle-injured troops, I find myself with a little spare time. The quietest parts of my day are around dawn and late in the evening, and it is at one such midnight hour that I discover that a letter from Edwin's young son in England has somehow found its way to our hospital. Perhaps I should be embarrassed that the orderly has given me the letter to pass on. But I am not. That other patients and one of the doctors have commented upon my frequent bedside visits to Edwin has made me cautious, I must admit, and even Marjorie has stopped her slightly barbed jokes about how much time I spend with him. I curse to myself tonight however, when my friend spots me as I cross the camp, wrapped in a dark cape and head bowed in an effort to be invisible. Her demeanour is quite rigid, and so despite the darkness, I sense her disapproval. Damn the moonlight. Eyes fixed ahead, she passes by. I let out a breath of relief, lengthen my stride and quicken my pace, but Marjorie is right beside me.

"What are you doing, Anna?" she hisses at me in a whisper even though there is no one near.

"I think you know," I respond, tightly.

"How can you? How can you flirt with our dead friend's husband?"

"How can I flirt?" I hiss back, "You have a nerve, Marjorie! There is not one day goes by that some man or other, or more than one…three or four even, are the subject of your avid attention! What right do you have to disapprove?" I stop dead in my tracks because Marjorie halts abruptly. I have hurt her.

"What about Joy? Our friend. She is barely in her grave."

"He likes to talk to me about Joy. He loves to talk to me. We have a great deal to say. It helps him. He has told me so. He tells me often." It is my voice. They are my words. Cracked, small, disconnected somehow, but mine nevertheless. My nostrils flare as I breathe deep; mouth tight shut.

"Of course, he does. He is grieving, Anna. You are taking advantage of her death and his grief! You should be ashamed."

"I am not ashamed, Marjorie," I say. Calm, in control.

"How can you not be ashamed?" she demands, her eyes on fire.

"Because I love him," I say.

And I continue on my way, to where the man I love is waiting for me, leaving Marjorie firmly rooted to the spot.

I feel a calm certainty when I reach his tent and watch him now, tracing in my mind every line that is etched on his handsome face. As Edwin reads the letter written in the rounded, deliberate and neat hand of his five-year-old son, Charles, I am filled with the desire to wipe the tear from his dark lashes. I lean a little closer. I move my face towards him, breathe in his scent and then I kiss his pain away. I taste the bittersweet saltiness only for a second because he lifts his arm as if to push me away.

His actions are slow, deliberate and firm when he cups my face with his hands. I hear my own soft gasp when he pulls me towards him, his mouth soft, warm and moist. He tastes of sun and dust and heat. As the touch of our lips becomes harder and deeper, the pounding sensation that reverberates around us is for once not caused by the nearby guns.

Back in my tent, only minutes since I crept from his bedside, I already long to see him again, feel his touch once more. And tomorrow, I am to meet Lady Maud in Kroonstad for our river walk, which means that it will be nearly twenty-four hours before I can go to him. Alone on my bed, in shafts of pale light, I imagine his caresses dancing along the moonbeam to me. I reach for the invisible kisses, catch them and sink into the dream of his embrace.

Chapter 6
Lady Maud's Plan

Maud is right. Kroonstad is an untidy, unprepossessing place with no fine buildings, few shops with barely any provisions and plenty of obstacles even for our walk along the riverbank. Because I have not been able to invent any justifiable reason to stay behind with Edwin, I have taken a cape cart into the town as planned. When I arrive at our appointed meeting place, Maud is already seated at one of the elegant restaurant tables next to a grinning, khaki-clad officer. I hold out my hand, delighted to meet Sir Lancelot, and happy that he appears not to be injured in the slightest way.

"Anna, this is my brother, Archibald. Archibald Young. Archie, allow me to introduce my very good friend, Anna Lieberman."

"Very pleased to meet you, Miss Lieberman. Maud tells me that you are an excellent nurse, as well as a great friend. Please call me Archie. Colonel Young or Archibald are so terribly formal, don't you think?"

"It is a pleasure to meet you, Colonel...Archie."

I turn to Maud but she anticipates my question before I can speak.

"No more news of Lance, I am afraid, but I may have found a way to reach Lindley."

Before she can divulge more, the waiter appears in the smartest, cleanest uniform I have seen in months. With a flamboyant flourish of his cloth, he takes our drinks order and soon, as we sip our champagne, the talk turns to progress of the war, upon which subject, Maud's brother, Archie is most well informed. The rich timbre of his voice and the unhurried way he speaks is quite a contrast from the furious pace of the hospital wards and I find my thoughts drifting. Edwin. Edwin. I say his name over and over in my head and imagine his face, his touch, his kiss. It is only when Archie coughs and I realise I have neither heard nor answered his question that I am forced to snap out of my daydreams. Emboldened by more champagne, we toast the latest British victory at Diamond Hill and I ask Archie what he thinks about Lord Roberts' latest proclamation, which Edwin and I have already discussed. Archie's reply is clear.

"If the Boers decide to blow up railway lines and stations, and use farms as bases for their commando activity, they cannot expect us not to strike just because women and children are living there."

"But is burning them to the ground the right thing to do?" I ask, knowing that Edwin thinks it is not.

"What would you suggest as an alternative, Miss Lieberman?"

It feels wrong to tell him that we should not be at war at all, so we change the subject and three courses, much merriment and several cups of coffee later, we set off towards the river.

From a distance, the banks seem to be well-wooded, but as we approach the drift, or ford as we call it in England, what looks initially like a forest reveals itself to be mostly mimosa bushes and reeds. We amble along the riverbank past a large dam that creates a deep pool, admiring the wispy willows as they trail picturesquely over and into the water. I visualise myself strolling here, arm-in-arm with Edwin when he can walk again, and search for the future in the black water. To my horror, however, it is an image of Joy's face that ripples up from the pool. I do so very much want him for myself. I cannot help it. But I know that Edwin and Joy belonged together. They were meant to be together. They would be together now if I had done something, anything to help them find each other.

I force myself to join my companions as they appreciate the tall bulrushes and where our stroll is interrupted by the first of many barbed wire fences. Archie and Maud think that the fences have been made to mark the gardens that run from some of the better class houses on the hill down to the river. Then Maud catches the fine lace of her gown on a particularly high fence, causing Archie and I to laugh hysterically as we become entangled with both Maud's dress and the spikes of the wire. We are almost free when a loud Afrikaans voice commands our attention.

"What do you think you are doing?"

Archie extricates himself and puts on his most sensible voice when he answers the elderly Boer gentleman.

"Sir, we are merely trying to get through."

The Boer spits something in Afrikaans that, judging from the way Archie's eyes become indignant, must be quite rude. Before Archie has time to speak, the Boer speaks quickly in the same insolent tone, "No. There is no way through, you must go back." He views Archie with disdain, whilst Maud and I barely merit a glance. "I have just put this fence up to prevent soldiers going along here."

With quiet authority, Archie says, "You have no right to do so."

"But I do," is the Boer's reply. "The soldiers do a great deal of mischief and destroy everything."

Still quiet but firmer now, Archie says, "You should not go to war if you do not want soldiers here."

There are more grumbling curses from the Boer and there is a brief, curt exchange in Afrikaans until suddenly, he throws up his hands and stalks off through the woods. His parting comment suggests that the war is not over yet and his people might still get the better of it. At this, Archie just laughs and we continue our promenade a little further. Ladies' clothes are not really at all suitable for the thick undergrowth and our spirits sink as Maud and I both find ourselves caught up in some thorny bushes.

From within the undergrowth, we hear a deep voice that bids us to go, "This way, sir, ladies," and we find ourselves following the invisible man, heading up a hill where, as we reach a weathered wooden gate, our guide reveals himself to be a tall, native South African dressed as if he were about to work in the fields. "This path leads to a small clearing where you pick up the road back into town." He doffs his cap and disappears as quickly as he arrived. It happens with such rapidity that we do not even think to thank him until he is out of sight. Archie shouts our appreciation after him and shakes his head before turning to us.

"So typical of these chaps. Bet he works for that Boer farmer who, no doubt, treats him like the slave that he probably is. We are recruiting many such native men into the British army. They make excellent scouts."

We continue our walk with a discussion about what it might be like to be a scout in this huge land of kopjes, dongas and mountain ranges, which, Archie explains, might feature strongly in the next phase of the war. We take the path that leads us to the road and then, somewhat sobered, head back to the hotel.

With a steady hand, Maud pours from an enormous teapot and the question of how she intends to reach Lance finds its way into our conversation.

"Are you going to tell us about your plan, Maud?" asks her brother.

"Well, I have found a Boer farmer who is prepared to take me up to Lindley in his ox cart. I just have to pay him a fee and pretend that I am his niece."

"A Boer farmer! How do you know you can trust him?" I ask.

"He already works for us, for the British. Has done since he took the oath. Perfectly trustworthy. I have it on good authority. His name is Klaus. Klaus Meyer. He has a wife and children on a farm at Senekal near Bethlehem and took the oath to protect them. Doesn't believe in the war at all."

"But, Maud, have you ever travelled in an ox cart? It's quite a way and across dangerous country," I look at Archie for back up.

"Maud, this is nonsense. You cannot just go off with some man you do not know, to find Lance in heaven knows what state. Even if you were to get there, the likelihood is that your wagon will be intercepted and all your provisions captured either by a Boer commando or by the British – if as you say you would be travelling as a Boer woman. Goodness, Maud, you could be imprisoned as a spy!"

The slight quiver of Maud's mouth suggests her resolve has weakened and she looks at me. After a pause, she drops a startling question, "Would you come with me, Anna? It would be too much for Nan, she is simply not well enough for such a journey, but you are different."

Archie leans forward and his teacup clatters into its saucer. Before he can speak, I say, "No, Maud, absolutely not. I will not accompany you."

"Thank goodness one of you has a modicum of sense," Archie's face relaxes and he sits back in his chair, lifts a piece of shortbread and takes a long drink of his tea before I finish what I started to say.

"I will not accompany you, Maud, but I will go alone with your farmer. I will disguise myself as his niece. We will find Lance and when we do, I promise I will nurse him until he is well enough to travel."

Archie chokes on his biscuit. Maud stares at me wide-eyed. It is hard to say which of the three of us is the most shocked.

Part Two
In the Veldt

Chapter 7
Anna's Plan

Later that night, I rehearse in my head the words that will best explain my plan to Edwin. But at his tent are a doctor, the night nurse and two orderlies, alongside an agitated soldier of about twenty. A new patient repeatedly tears at the fresh blood-steeped bandages around his forehead and shouts that he must get back to his post. He has to be held down by the orderlies so that the doctor can examine his injuries.

"Can I help you, Nurse Lieberman?" the Sister asks curtly.

Her face is red and I think that she could probably do with my help, but since I am not on duty, I invent a reason for my late visit.

"I have come to collect a book I lent to Major Oliver. In exchange for these." I hold up my copy of *Great Expectations* and *Wuthering Heights*, which books I will not be taking on my journey to Lindley. "Two of my favourites," I add, rather lamely. A third book remains hidden among the folds of my apron.

"Be sharp about it then, nurse," orders the Sister and I scurry past her.

"Poor chap thinks he is dead," says Edwin softly, as the younger patient continues his fight with an invisible enemy. "Will not eat, cannot lie still. He stood too close to one of the Boers' Long Tom cannons and its explosion knocked him unconscious." Edwin's look of concern changes to one of interest when I hand him my Dickens and Brontë novels, but it is impossible to read his expression when I slip The Scarlet Letter between his sheets. "Ah, thank you, Nurse Lieberman, I shall very much enjoy these," and then a much quieter, "and what did you think of Hester Prynne's crime and punishment?"

I turn to rearrange his pillow, "I think that Hester was very much a victim of circumstance and of her time. She committed a crime in the eyes of the church but who could blame her for it? She thought that her husband was dead. I felt more upset about the child and the way Hester was shamed."

He nods and says, "A scarlet letter, stitched to her clothing. 'A' for adulteress. A sign for all to see what she had done." His eyes search for my reaction.

"That particular badge of dishonour was quite unnecessary," I say.

"These things are not always straightforward, are they, Anna?" he speaks quietly, fixing me with his gaze.

When Sister looks over to see what is taking so long, Edwin offers me another book to play out our ruse, and my heart beats a little faster when I whisper that I will see him the following day. What he does not know yet is that tomorrow will be my last in Kroonstad, for the time being at least.

"Crime and Punishment. I did not imagine you to be a fan of Dostoyevsky," comments Doctor Matthews on my way out. He grins knowingly, and I pray that no one asks me what I think of the book, which of course, I have never read.

Next morning, Edwin's tent is again teeming with activity. The young man has realised that he is alive after all, but his elation is so loud and animated that one of the nurses is now dedicated solely to keeping him calm. This type of reaction to being under prolonged artillery bombardment, so familiar to me now, requires great patience, perseverance and much individual nursing care.

"Poor devil," says Edwin, who is pale through lack of sleep.

I have decided that although it does not really need doing, changing the dressing on his thigh wound will give me the opportunity to be close enough to him that our whispered conversation will not be overheard.

"Lie still, Major," I enact my role as nurse, roll down the blanket so that his leg is free, cut away the bandage and begin to attend the wound.

"How was your walk with Maud yesterday?" he asks.

"I met her brother, Archie. He's a colonel with the artillery and treated us to lunch and champagne. Then we walked along the riverbank. Now, move your leg a little to the right, please, Major." I raise my voice a little for the benefit of the others in the tent, "I am just going to bathe around the wound."

He grins up at me and plays the game, "Thank you, nurse."

His hand gently brushes mine when I reach across him, and I take a deep breath.

"I am going to help Maud find her husband," I say, and then respond quickly and quietly to his puzzled frown, "It will only be for a few days, a week or two at most. But I cannot tell you any more of the plan. I hope you understand. The less people know, the safer it will be. I am to leave tomorrow evening, so I will see you before I go."

Edwin's eyes are now wide and a fiery expression crosses his countenance. Twisting it firmly, with as much authority as I can muster, I secure the end of the new bandage as Marjorie approaches. Her look is quizzical because she and I both know that the dressing was only changed yesterday.

"I appreciate what you are doing, thank you, Nurse Lieberman," Edwin's voice is guarded but warm, and I think he does understand why I have decided to help Maud. I wish I could explain to Marjorie because I know that she will understand, but it is important that, for now, my mission remains secret. Maybe Maud will tell her once I am gone.

I decide to drop a brief note to Sister that will explain my absence as a sudden and unexpected family emergency. I do not mention my brother, but she knows that Henry has been involved in the action in the Northern Transvaal and my hope is that she will assume I have gone to him. She isn't at her station, so thankfully I do not have to speak my lies aloud. I make my way through the dark camp and almost trip over the white stones just by my quarter, even though they are perfectly visible.

"Whoa there, Nurse Lieberman!" The familiar voice of the orderly from Edwin's ward interrupts my anxious distraction and I feel myself steadied in capable arms.

"Cecil!" I steady myself, "Lucky for me that you were here. Is there something I can help you with?"

He grins, "No, nurse. I have something for you. From the Major." He winks and passes me a thick, cream envelope. "I'll be off then, but see you tomorrow, as agreed," and with another, more exaggerated flick of his right eyelid, he is gone. Despite his irritating and oft repeated comedic antics, Edwin and I trust Cecil implicitly and that is why I have asked him to escort me to meet Maud and her 'Boer uncle' tomorrow. I begin to lift the flap of Edwin's letter but decide to save this precious moment until I have packed.

Barely are my journal, pens and drawing pencils assembled, when Cecil reappears in the doorway. For once, he neither smiles nor winks. "You have to come now. We have to leave now."

"But we can't!" I think of Edwin and how he will feel if I do not say goodbye.

"I am sorry, Anna, but I've had this from Lady Maud."

A very few words are scrawled across the ripped paper he holds up. I buckle the straps on my carpet bag once I have torn a page from my journal.

He seizes my luggage, "This way," he orders in a voice I have never heard him use. I scribble half a dozen words and thrust the folded note towards my co-conspirator. Cecil nods as he pockets my unsealed vow of forever-love that I pray he will remember to give to Edwin tomorrow.

Poised and erect, Maud awaits my arrival part-way between the hospital and the Dutch church in Kroonstad. She alights quickly from her carriage, greets me with a rib-crushing hug and passes a small valise to me. The first thing I pull from the bag is a linen cap with a voluminous frill just like the ones Marjorie and I noticed the locals wearing when we first arrived in Cape Town.

"This is what Boer women prefer. It will protect you from the sun, although at this time of year in Lindley, you are more likely to need these." She extracts wool gloves, a thick flannel petticoat, and a knitted shawl and hands them to me. "Make haste, Anna. You can change here in the carriage. And, Anna..." her gloved hand clutches an envelope so tightly packed that I wonder it has not burst already. "It would have been my daughter's birthday yesterday. Please give this to Lance. Photographs. I have written it all down. Everything. In case...just in case. And, Anna...make sure he knows how much I miss him and how I long to see him. Sometimes, we forget to say these things."

I hold her hand tight longer than we have time for and then we are abruptly away, the horses' hooves thudding dully on the dry road.

By the time I have assumed the disguise and parcelled up my uniform, Maud's carriage has halted behind the enormous church. Maud tethers the horse and as we step down a tall figure emerges into view. Even in the half-light of dawn, the man's red hair and beard are striking and his height and girth make me think that I will be in safe hands. He nods at Maud, who hands him a fat envelope. His fee, I remember. Feeling rather like a young woman about to embark on her first dance of the season, I look down at my feet and only raise my eyes when Mr Meyer addresses me.

"Guten Abend, Fraulein Lieberman." The German is a surprise and I do not reply immediately to his greeting. Then I remember my manners.

"Guten Abend, Herr Meyer."

"Please, Miss Lieberman, you say Oom Klaus to me. Afrikaans for uncle. Please I say Anna to you?" His discomfort is only momentary and Maud tells me that it is because he is embarrassed about his poor English.

"Please do not worry, Oom Klaus," I say. "My father is German and I am a fluent German speaker. Perhaps, if I teach you some English, you might help me learn Afrikaans?"

The introductions over, I turn to Maud. We face one another, her eyes fixed intensely on mine.

"God speed, Anna. And thank you," she says. She hands me another package carefully wrapped. "This contains an old Bible and a hymnal plus a little money. You Boer ladies are renowned for your piety and hymn singing."

At this remark, Klaus smiles. Maud and I embrace and then I am climbing into the Voortrekker wagon that will take us the fifty or so miles to Lindley.

I look down at her, suddenly feeling a lump in my throat at the thought of how much she is counting on me.

"I will find him, Maud," are my parting words and I treasure the talisman of gratitude in my friend's eyes when she leaps aboard to give me one final tight hug.

Then she watches, wordless, as Klaus ushers me onto the seat in front of the covered part of the wagon, a big tent-like structure with a wooden cart base. Much paraphernalia hangs in and outside the vehicle and I am curious about the purpose of everything, but the sky is brightening and we need to get moving. There are four pairs of oxen, and although the cart is not huge, I imagine that we will not be able to travel at great speed. At the crack of the whip, Klaus calls it a *sjambok* in Afrikaans, the muscled beasts pull slowly away and I shuffle next to my new uncle who sits on the chest that forms the driver's seat. I pull a blanket tight around my shoulders to contain my anxiety and excitement.

Klaus thinks that we can comfortably achieve between twenty and thirty miles the first day, providing there is somewhere for the oxen to graze. We will aim, he says, to travel alternately for six hours and rest for six perhaps today, due to our early start. He knows the area well as he has lived in the North Eastern Free State all his life and our conversation, mostly in German interspersed with English and the occasional Afrikaans word, flows smoothly and for several hours. However, when I speculate that by my reckoning, we should reach Lindley in two days, his mood becomes noticeably more edgy. Our progress so far has kept us within sight of the Vals River and it is close to the deserted banks that he halts the wagon and rests the sjambok.

"There is one thing that I did not tell Lady Roddeston," he says, looking straight ahead. Panic rises into my chest. "I have told you about my farm. At Senekal."

I nod. I have learnt that the Meyer family farm, some way west of the town of Bethlehem, has herds of sheep and cattle and produces maize, fruit and many different vegetables.

"It sounds idyllic, Oom Klaus."

"The reason I took the oath of allegiance to the British was to protect my family. And my home. We are the fourth generation to farm the land there."

"I understand this, Oom Klaus. But what does it have to do with our mission?"

"I have not seen my family, my wife, Magrieta and my children for months. We have a new baby, Jacobus, who I have never met."

With a jolt, I realise what he is about to reveal. We will not be heading straight for Lindley but will make a circuitous detour to include a visit to Klaus' family near Senekal some thirty-five miles South West of Lindley. At best, this extra leg will add two days to our journey.

It is many silent, tense hours later that we outspan. I see that Klaus has chosen this sheltered place to camp for the night because now they are unhitched, the oxen can forage on nearby thorn bushes. Other trees and accompanying thick vegetation provide a screen for us against the wind and the gentle rush of nearby water soothes my ill temper as we sit by a small fire, chewing a kind of savoury biscuit.

"The river is close by," offers Klaus with a cup of hot coffee. It seems like a peace offering, so I take the cup of steaming liquid. "You can bathe there in the morning."

I have been trying to find words with which to banish the strained mood of our little camp and the idea of what my parents would think of my bathing naked in a river in this wild country whilst travelling in disguise to goodness knows where with a strange man makes me laugh.

"You have never swum in a river?" his beard quivers with mirth. When I tell him that the River Thames in London is just not suitable either for bathing or swimming and that my father has tried, but failed to teach me to swim during our summer holidays at my uncle's lakeside house in Germany, Klaus promises that he will teach me not only to swim but to hunt and fish too.

"Klaus, we have to reach Maud's husband in Lindley as soon as possible. There is no time for swimming or hunting."

"Anna, we must hunt to eat. And we will have time when the oxen are resting. I have taught all my children these things. My eldest daughter is about your age and she is an excellent swimmer. You are eighteen years old, I think?" He scratches his red beard thoughtfully, "You can ride a horse, yes?"

"No, Klaus. Oom Klaus. I am a nurse. And I am twenty-three years old. A twenty-three-year-old nurse who lives in London and who cannot swim or ride a horse." Embarrassed, I remember that I need not lie to my new uncle about my age, but he is already concocting a plan. Klaus slaps his thigh and grins at me. I think he's feigning shock but it's hard to tell.

"That is settled then. I would like to teach you now, but since we don't have a horse here, this lesson might have to wait for another time."

A short time and two more drinks later, we are still laughing about our very different lives. When, despite the coffee, I cannot quite stifle the yawn that has been threatening, Klaus springs up and pulls a bed roll from the covered part of the wagon.

"I will sleep underneath and you will sleep inside," he says and I notice that as well as his bedding he holds a rifle.

"Is that necessary?" I ask him.

"Just a precaution, Anna. I am a good shot."

"And I suppose you will teach me to shoot too?"

With our laughter, Klaus hands me the lantern and the day ends on an affable note. Alone under the canvas of the wagon, at last I can open Edwin's letter. The paper is thick and creamy white and the envelope so well sealed that I have to improvise my hair comb as a letter-opener.

My dear sweet Anna,

What a shock you gave me when you spoke of your intention to go to Lindley! But since we have come to know one another, I do understand you well enough, I think, to appreciate why you must go. And when you return, within the month, I expect, I will be much improved and will be physically able to stop you running off again! Please do not worry about Sister Makepeace. Once you are safely away, I will explain everything to her. I have seen the closeness of the friendship that exists between you and know that she too will understand, as she understands the relationship that has developed between you and I, my darling Anna. Not everyone will look favourably upon us, as I am sure you must realise. Because, as we know, these things are never straightforward. Just know, my dearest, what others may think worries me not. What I know, see and love is your beauty, your wonderfully fierce spirit and your desire and determination to help Maud – amongst others. I know from Sister Makepeace (after she and I spoke yesterday, I think she now realises that my intentions are honourable and that I am not a dastardly bounder) how much you cared for Joy. So, my dearest Anna, as I sign off this too-brief note, be assured of my love for you and know that when we meet again, I will offer you something more than a mere letter to bind our future hopes.

Yours with deep affection,
Edwin

How can I put into words how his promise makes me feel? It is so definite. So certain. So perfect. I imagine the joy of our reunion in a few weeks and am soothed into a deep sleep by my beloved's words to the accompaniment of the soft burble of the river and the rustle of the trees in the night breeze.

It is the crackle of the fire that wakes me, and as I move my stiff limbs out into the cool morning air, Klaus is busy putting the yokes back on the oxen.

"Guten morgen, Anna." As usual, he sounds as if he might break into song at any moment, so mellifluous is his voice and I smile at him.

"Good morning, Uncle Klaus, I trust you slept well?"

He replies first in German, but I ask him to speak in Afrikaans. "I did sleep well, thank you. I have lit the fire, but because I let you sleep, there is no time for you to make bread today. So, we will eat some mealie porridge that I will make."

I dare not tell him that I have never made bread in my life because our cook at home would never have let me near her kitchen. And if he knows of yet another lack in my education, for certain he will insist on teaching me to bake. So, I summon some courage and nod in the sagest manner I can muster. Neither have I eaten mealie porridge, but I know that it is made from maize flour, and I grimace at the thought of the gritty texture. I think longingly of the poached eggs on toast, kippers and breakfast tea served at my parents' house in Hampstead before I remember the pressing matter of the morning's toilette and make haste through the copse towards the river, clutching my soap and wash cloth.

Refreshed and tinglingly clean, I stroll back, ready for mealie porridge and the next six-hour trek. Klaus is out of view behind the bushes that surround our camp, and I can clearly hear him talking to someone called Sampson. His tone is that of a father to a son. Cajoling. Soft. Imploring. Then his voice rises and he appears to be losing patience. "You lazy good for nothing!" he shouts, and when I hear the crack of the whip, I run quickly to the boy's aid. Only there is no boy, only one ox who stands stubbornly away from the rest.

"For goodness sake, Oom Klaus!"

"Ah, Anna, good, we can eat breakfast."

"I presume this is Sampson?" I say.

"Yes. Sampson. He is new. Not used to pulling the cart," Klaus pats the huge beast with great gusto as though he were patting a giant dog. "And these are Chaka,

Rooinek, Donder, Drakkie and Goliath. My farm boy usually drives, but I could not ask him on this errand. He knows them better than I do."

"And these last two?" I ask.

Klaus shifts his weight from one leg to the other and his blue eyes twinkle at me, "This is Tafelberg. Table Mountain in English. Look, his head is flat on top just like the real thing." Klaus imitates the flat-headed beast and I tell him that he would be good at charades, of which game he knows nothing, so I spend a few minutes trying to explain.

"And him?" I look at the last member of our team.

"Engelsman. Englishman. You see, he is a bit skinny and more reddish colour than these others," Klaus grins at me as he wallops Englishman good and hard.

Once Sampson, Tafelberg and Englishman are persuaded back into harness and we have eaten the mealie porridge, which I enjoy, despite its odd softly grainy texture, Klaus damps down the fire and we board our wagon.

The conversation that began over breakfast continues as the wagon rumbles on its way. Although my Afrikaans is coming along nicely, we speak in German because it is a little easier for me.

"So, Oom Klaus, how did your grandparents meet if he was German and she French?"

"Both their families were part of the Great Trek from Grahamstown about sixty years ago. Many people moving north from the Eastern Cape in their *kakebeenwoens*."

"Where were they going in their wagons? Why were they trekking?"

Klaus regards me with curiosity, "These people, my people did not want to be part of your British Empire. They seek their own land. To be free people."

"Were they not free under British rule?" I ask and Klaus peers at me.

"There were rules that my ancestors did not like. They want to keep their slaves. They want to be masters in their own land."

"But where did they go, Oom Klaus? The land must have been wild, untamed. Dangerous."

"Yes, Anna. There were wild beasts then and warrior tribes. My grandmother and grandfather were lucky. They settled in what is now the Orange Free State. They have fourteen children who live. My father is oldest of four boys and ten girls, and I am oldest of six boys and five girls." He runs his fingers through his long red mane. "All children in Meyer family have same hair as my grandpa. And same spirit."

It is early afternoon when we next outspan and the sun beats hot and fierce. My hair and face are so thick with red dust that I could easily be mistaken for a true member of the Meyer family. We are in the shade of a group of trees, but there is no sound of the rushing water that I crave to cool myself with. To take my mind off the heat, I investigate all the drawers on the outside of our cart to discover a treasure trove of candles, bottled fruits, flour, salt, animal pelts and dried herbs. Water bags are hooked beneath the carriage and all my medicines and nursing supplies have been stowed between the double floor of the vehicle.

"Well, Uncle, what a shame there is no river here. It is the perfect weather for a swimming lesson!" Thank goodness I can joke and that there is no possibility of going in the water. Klaus flattens his mouth into a crestfallen expression and urges me to follow him. He picks up two of leather bags and a second gun that I have not seen before, stouter and heavier than the rifle. The level, wooded ground of our camp descends steeply through thick bushes and suddenly, gleaming before us is a flat calm lake.

"It is dam, made by one of the farmers," Klaus announces, his previously crestfallen face now lit up by a huge grin. "We can replace our water and you can swim."

I feel the sweat trickle down my back and the water tempts me.

"But Oom Klaus, I have no bathing costume."

He replies while he fills the two leather bags.

"What need for a special costume, Anna? You have the underwear, yes?"

What is there to do but nod?

"Well then, it is good. Yes?" He has switched back to English in a further effort to persuade me into the water. He hoists the refilled water bags over his shoulders and gives me five minutes to get myself appropriately attired and into the dam before his return.

The silky cool wetness envelopes my body and by the time I am semi-submerged, I do not care that I'm dressed only in my underwear. I splash water over my face then plunge my head beneath the water and feel slippery mud ooze between my toes. At the sound of a blunt splash, I turn around and Klaus emerges from his dive just downstream. He surfaces from the deep water, dives again, resurfaces, smooth as a porpoise, sleek as a snake. He is transformed.

"Watch me, Anna. Then swim to me. Come. It is not so deep."

Smiling, he stands up to his chest in the river dam and the water laps gently against his body. His look of determination confirms that if I do not swim to him now, we might be here for a long time, so I make frog-like circles with my arms like my father taught me and push myself towards him. I'm sure he moves away from me, but I press on, kicking my legs, flapping my feet.

"Well done, Anna!"

He grabs hold of my arms as I try to find the riverbed with my feet, but discover that although Klaus is still standing, I am now out of my depth.

"Good. Good. Now I turn you round and you swim until you can stand in the water."

I am thankful he is speaking German now, not Afrikaans, so I understand what he wants me to do and manage to swallow only a mouthful of water when he pushes me off towards the riverbank.

My body is tingling with effort and achievement when we emerge, dripping and laughing from the lesson, about an hour later. I have been so absorbed that we might well have been in the water for longer, but at the conclusion of whatever time was spent, I am quite able to swim, not stylishly but unaided from one side of the dam to the other.

"I leave you here to dress. Dry yourself a little in the sun first. You will be hungry so I go now to prepare food."

I spread myself across a warm rock, close my eyes and let the late afternoon sun dry my body and clothes. I am dozing when the distant sound of a gunshot breaks my reverie and I quickly pull on my skirt, blouse and boots, fastening the ties of my kappie as I scramble up the path towards the wagon, slipping and sliding in my haste. Hands bloodied, Klaus peers up from beneath the wide, floppy brim of his felt hat. Triumphant, knife gleaming in the setting sun, he holds up a plump skinned rabbit. Supper.

Not content that he has taught me to swim, it is now time for me to learn how to shoot.

"Before we eat."

When Klaus throws down the gauntlet for this challenge, my spirits sink because I know that it will be many hours before we might sate our hunger. As instructed, I press the thick end of the gun into my shoulder, take aim at the tin can that is atop a pile of stones, close my eyes and pull the trigger. A hollow clang, followed by the thin clatter of tumbling rock and metal announces that I have hit the target with my first ever gunshot.

"Better to shoot with your eyes open, Anna," says Klaus, a little chagrined at my success. His grin is broad, which makes me think he is also a little proud.

The day has been uncharacteristically warm for the time of year, Klaus tells me as we roast chunks of the rabbit on long sticks over a fire that takes the chill off what is becoming a cold night. I have already dropped two pieces of my supper into the smouldering embers as I endeavour to master this unfamiliar culinary practice. As ever, my new uncle is patient and shows me again exactly how to securely skewer the meat. The only thing I have ever cooked on an open fire before today is chestnuts, and Klaus seems delighted to hear about this and other of my family's Yuletide customs. Of all things, he loves the idea of charades and wants me to play this game with his family when we arrive at the farm and I sing some of my favourite carols to him even though Christmas is six months away.

By the end of our second evening together, we both know several new words in languages with which we are unfamiliar. I can count to ten in Afrikaans, Klaus knows the first verse of *Away in a Manger* in English (it is the only carol I can think of that mentions oxen) and wrapped in thoughts of comfortable companionship plus four blankets against the cold, I fall into a deep and dreamless sleep.

The next day dawns crisp and clear and I awake to Klaus berating Tafelberg, who refuses to leave the thorn bush he is chewing.

"His flat head does not hold very much brain," Klaus says and cracks the sjambok hard on the animal's hindquarter. With a sulky expression, the beast moves toward the yoke and the team of oxen are ready, which is more than can be said for me. I stretch out the night's long slumber from my limbs and Klaus thrusts a steaming can of coffee into one hand and a kind of dried meat into the other.

"Biltong. Volstruis." This is new Afrikaans, and Klaus sees my puzzlement so offers the German.

"Strauss."

This word is not in my vocabulary either, so Klaus decides to show me through the game of charades. In the pink dawn light, red beard bobbing, he struts around holding his arms to his side, flapping his hands and craning his neck from side to side until tears of mirth run from my eyes because I realise that I am eating breakfast of dried ostrich. Such a dish has certainly not yet reached North London.

Progress is good on our third day, and when we stop to rest the oxen, Klaus anticipates that we are less than six hours from the Meyer family farm and will probably arrive there by midday tomorrow if we make an early start. And soon after that, we will be on our way to Lindley and to Colonel Roddeston. My second shooting lesson does not go so well as the first because this time, I am firing at live, moving targets and I find it even more difficult to keep my eyes open when I am aiming at wild versions of an animal I used to keep as a pet when I was a child. The idea that Horatio, a lop-eared rabbit that lived in his own little wooden house, was taken for walks on a lead by my mother and won a smart rosette for being 'best in show', leaves Klaus, for once, completely lost for words.

Our encampment has brought us to an arid spot away from any water where huge mounds of red earth rise up, some taller even than Klaus. Once the animals are grazing on their usual thorn bushes, my Boer uncle unhooks a shovel and a pick from beneath the wagon and heads towards one of the smaller mounds. I keep my distance after an initial foray confirms that these small precipitous earth mountains are anthills and I am not at all keen to make the acquaintance of the enormous insects who live here and who rush up Klaus's long arms stinging him as he works. His broad shoulders gleam with sweat as he hacks relentlessly into the hillock, then he stops, swats a few of the insects who persist in their retaliation, waves the shovel in the air and beckons.

"Your bread oven, Anna. We have time here for you to make bread."

I stare at the cavern that Klaus has carved out, and notice for the first time that the top of the anthill has also been hollowed out and forms a kind of chimney. I rub my hands together and await more information or instruction.

"I will make the fire, Anna. You prepare the flour and the bread kettle."

He sees my blank face and again his shock is real.

He shakes his head. "You English girls have a most peculiar education," he ponders for a minute. "But you have trained to be a nurse. This is useful and your charades are funny. Now, I show you how to bake bread in a miershoop oond."

I help him to gather stones to line the bottom of the oven and kill a few last ants and light the fire. Klaus gathers the ingredients for the dough from the side drawers of the wagon and we quickly mix flour, salt, sugar and a little fat. Soon enough, we are warming ourselves by the anthill-oven, and as the bread bakes, I explain about the cook and housemaids employed by my parents, that we have no need of a gardener because my mother tends to our very small outside space and my father does not keep a horse because he drives an automobile. I learn that Klaus's wife, Magrieta and his daughters Isabel and Hentie, aged eighteen and fourteen, are expert at bottling fruit and making preserves, whilst ten-year-old, Lizzie loves to look after the younger siblings, Dietlof and Eva. As well as the new baby, Jacobus, there are two older boys, Christo and Frederick, who Klaus has left in charge of the farm and who are apparently excellent horsemen and hunters. I'm looking forward to meeting them all and to tasting Magrieta's famous peach chutney, which will accompany the lamb we will eat. It is only now, because it is days since I thought of it, does my guilt at not yet having reached Maud's husband in Lindley, boldly present itself. So, thus motivated, I fetch my diary and wrapped in blankets, I begin to write.

Dear Edwin,

You will not believe what I ate for breakfast today! Nor, I suspect will you believe me when I tell you that I have baked bread in an anthill. An activity, I suspect, even in your idyllic childhood on the Isle of White, you have not encountered. Very soon, we will be on our way to Lindley to find Colonel Roddeston, but for now we have made a small detour to the south (near Senekal) so that Klaus might see his family and meet his new baby son, Jacobus, who he has not yet seen, since he has been working for us in Kroonstad. I can see why he is held in such great esteem by our chaps. His knowledge of this country is immense and he is brave and funny. I think he must be a wonderful papa to his children and he is a gifted teacher. He tells me that he will teach me to ride a horse, of which creature, I am terrified. But thankfully, with not even a donkey available, I am saved! Because of him, I am now able to bake bread, swim and can handle a gun. Now, please do not worry. The most dangerous creatures we have encountered on our journey thus far are some of this country's strange lanky-limbed, long-tailed sheep and a few scared rabbits that usually end up in the pot. I have not managed to shoot one yet because (so Klaus tells me) I always close my eyes when I pull the trigger. In fact, as each day comes and goes, we make steady and very easeful progress with only a little drama. We have come across a few abandoned farms but we have not seen a soul so far.

Although, it will not be possible to send the letters that I have written to Edwin and Marjorie every day so far, and for safety, I keep the key to my diary's secrets around my neck on a chain, I hope that when I get back to the hospital at Kroonstad in a week or two that we will all be able to laugh together about my adventures. For the umpteenth time, I re-read the note that Cecil brought to me. As usual, I hear Edwin's clear, soothing voice and a shiver runs through me to my fingertips as I trace the words I hold so dear.

...So, my dearest Anna, as I sign off this too-brief note, be assured of my love for you and know that when we meet again, I will offer you something more than a mere letter to bind our future hopes.

Yours with deep affection,
Edwin

Although he has asked me to call him Ted, I have told him that I prefer Edwin, because it sounds more distinguished. I have not found a way to explain yet that, as Ted was Joy's name for him, I cannot bear to think of my dead friend every time I say his name. I write until the candle gutters and disconnects me from my recollections. It is Edwin's face, his gentle brown eyes, soft mouth and firm touch that are my final day dreams before sleep whisks me away into the South African night.

Chapter 8
The Meyer Family

We travel for over five hours and then we see them. The blood-ripped carcasses litter the landscape before us like hurled stones. Bloated and stiff-legged, it is only the dust-white fleeces that render them recognisable as sheep. Silent and grey-faced, Klaus halts the wagon and dismounts. All the merriment and anticipation of the moments before we rounded the bend in this rugged track are gone as we survey the murdered beasts. An unexpected sound reaches us. It is a sound so strange to this landscape that at first, I cannot place it. Thin, reedy voices accompany the faint, muffled sound of a piano before the hymn's tentative verse reaches its chorus crescendo.

Back on the wagon in an instant, Klaus gathers his guns, pulling me with him as he dismounts, secures the wagon and drags me towards the music. Through charred remains of what look like pumpkins, I struggle to keep up, and when I trip over a rock, find myself pulled roughly along before I can get back on my feet. He stops when I cry out but does not let go of my wrist when he helps me up. He says nothing and I feel fear clog my veins as we run towards a blackened, roofless house. The barn next to the farmhouse is only partially burnt out with half its roof still intact. When we finally come to rest outside the firmly shuttered wooden doors, I realise it is from in here that the singing continues to reverberate. My lungs are fit to explode and Klaus's face has turned from grey to a deep, angry red. He thumps the door.

"Magrieta!"

Sudden silence punctuated by a baby's cry. Klaus grips my arm so tightly that I think it might snap.

"Open the door, Magrieta! Open the door!"

"Pappa?"

"Open the door, Christo!"

After a scuffle of excited chatter and movement from within, the sound of wood against wood, and then a heavy crash followed by some Afrikaans words of consternation, one of the double doors begins to creak open. Unable to wait a moment longer, Klaus flings the door completely back on its hinges to reveal a quivering pile of humanity that launches itself upon us. This time when I find myself on the ground again, Klaus lets go of me. I use my hands to push myself backwards and find the wall against which to rest my back.

So many sooty, dishevelled children all talk at once that it is hard to tell one child from another. I manage to spot seventeen-year-old Christo though, because he's an elongated version of his father with no beard and it is Christo who spots me watching, listening.

"Hallo, Christo. My naam is Anna. Anna Lieberman."

This simple Afrikaans greeting does not fool him though.

"What is this English woman doing here, Pappa?" He switches his glare from me to his father, and I feel the expectant but hostile gaze of the rest of the Meyer family upon me.

"Anna has been my traveling companion. She is a nurse and we were going to the aid of her friend's husband. I have been paid handsomely to do this."

"But she's the worst kind of uitlander, Papa," one of the other boys adds.

"A foreigner she may be, son, but she is not a bad person."

"My friend Maud's husband is wounded at Lindley. Your Papa is taking me there so that I might tend to his wounds and return him safely to his wife."

I badly want them to like me.

"What will you do with her now, father?"

I face the owner of this voice who must be Klaus's oldest daughter, Isabel. Her long red hair hangs down her back in a dishevelled plait and like the others her face is streaked with soot. I try to smile but somehow, my face is frozen and all I manage is a rigid stare.

"I do not know, Isabel."

There is little warmth in the look Klaus gives me, and the fear in my heart turns to ice.

It is Mrs Meyer who comes to my rescue.

"Does she have medical supplies?" Magrieta asks her husband.

"In the wagon. Is there something you need?" Klaus takes his wife's hands in his.

"Frederick, show your father," she urges her second son forward and I see a long, inflamed cut on his burnt right arm that needs immediate treatment.

"I went back into the house, Papa. With Christo. To get Mamma's piano. But something hot fell on my arm."

I remember the tinkling sounds of a piano as we had approached the scene of devastation and look across at the barn. The mission to retrieve his mother's instrument had obviously been successful.

"I can help Frederick if you will allow me," I offer, not daring to move until I am instructed. Magrieta nods at Klaus who bids Christo accompany me to the wagon.

"Put that down, son. You won't be needing it," and Christo takes the butt of his gun from the small of my back and tosses it to the ground. As their eldest son pushes me roughly from the barn, Klaus and his wife talk in rapid, low tones. It is when she raises her voice in anger that Magrieta confirms my fears.

"It was the English soldiers, Klaus. You said if you took the oath, they would leave us alone."

I decide it is best to say nothing, and so we walk in silence to the wagon.

Christo untethers the oxen and jumps aboard.

"Get up," he says as he picks up the sjambok, whips the beasts into movement and we are underway before I have properly climbed up, so that I fall awkwardly, flung into the back of the cart like a bag of provisions. In a mere thirty minutes, my status has changed from rescuer to prisoner, my mood from delighted optimism to overwhelming anxiety, and when Christo commands the wagon train to a halt outside the barn, I look around the rugged expanse of farm land encircled with ragged topped mountains and wonder how I can feel so trapped in such beauty.

I accompany the Meyer brood to the river, closely escorted by Christo and Frederick, whose injured arm needs to be bathed before I can tend to the burns and cut. Curiously nestled within the tall reeds of the riverbank are several iron bedsteads.

"This is mine, Papa!" calls ten-year-old Lizzie as she leaps onto a semi-concealed, partly submerged bed frame.

"And mine too!" Little Eva, who is five, bounces on top of her older sister. Soon, all the family except Christo and Frederick occupy one mattress or another. The two older brothers stand guard over me and we survey the scene from the bank. I do not know why the boys do not just get onto their bed, since there is no possible escape route for me.

"This is where we hid from the British soldiers when they kept coming for us. And after they burnt the house and killed the animals," volunteers Isabel, casting me a sharp look to make sure I've heard the emphasis she places on the nationality of the soldiers.

"We had to be very quiet," says Eva. "We were not even allowed to sing. But Jacobus kept crying. He would not stop." Eva admonishes her little brother with all the authority of her five years.

"Yes, Eva. Because he is a baby and because he was hungry," Magrieta speaks at last. I imagine the cold dampness of their ordeal and cannot stay silent any longer.

"But why, Magrieta? Klaus has taken the Oath of Allegiance to the British. Why did they burn your house and your fields? Why did they kill the sheep?"

Christo is quick to respond, "You should ask your Commander Roberts. It was his orders the men told us they were following. If we hadn't been able to hide here in the reeds, they would have come back for us and taken us to one of the camps."

At Magrieta's sad smile, Klaus puts his arms around her and she looks at me as she speaks, "Our commandos had blown up the railway just to the north. The farm burning is retribution by your army. Terrible for our farm and two of our neighbours. But it is worse for the families nearer the railway, I hear. The women and children are gone. Some are roaming the mountains in their wagons and others have been sent to the camps."

"What camps?" I ask Magrieta.

"For the people who have nowhere to go. So many with no homes now. Men away fighting. No servants."

Klaus looks puzzled, "Where are our boys? Where are Khama and Andreis?"

"They said they could not work for us anymore," Magrieta's short-lived smile has gone. "They said they didn't want to be captured and taken away. They said they were going to Pretoria."

"To work for the British, no doubt," Christo faces his father accusingly. "Look where that got us!"

Magrieta is wading back through the river towards us now. She has handed baby Jacobus to Hentie, another tall, fierce-looking girl with tumbling red hair who seems not to speak. "Christo. Apologise to your father."

"No, Magrieta. The boy is right. I did what I did for you and the children. I sacrificed many friendships and gained many enemies within our own people. And now, despite my turning against my own country to keep us safe, we have lost everything that my family built up over one hundred and fifty years."

"What will you do, Papa?" asks Isabel.

"What I should perhaps have done at the outset, Isabel, my dear. Fight for our people. Fight for my country. But not before I have found a safe place for you all."

"But Papa, we can stay here, on the veldt. Use the wagon, cook outside. Hunt and fish. Like the Rohn family," Frederick has become suddenly animated.

"It is too dangerous, son. President Steyn's, de Wet's and other commandos are in the area and there are many, many British. There will be fighting for sure."

"If you are going to join a commando, Papa, then so am I. Frederick and Isabel can look after mother and the others," Christo stands, feet solidly apart as he faces down his father.

"I did not say that I was going to join a commando. There is other work to be done here to support the Boer cause and that is what I plan to do. With Nurse Lieberman's help. You, son, will take your mother and the others to my sister's house in Bethlehem."

Christo and I shout in unison and our cries of protest drown out one another's words. Then I see the same look embed itself on Klaus's face as the day he taught me to swim and I know there is no point in arguing.

Several noisy hours later, Frederick's arm treated and bandaged, we sit around the fire's glowing embers sipping the last of the black coffee and chewing biltong. When Klaus and Christo rise purposefully, I assume this is the sign for us all to retire, and I am pleased because at last, I will find out what the sleeping arrangements are to be. But the two men pick up their hats, jackets and rifles and hoist ammunition belts across themselves.

Sensing a shift in purpose, Magrieta turns the poisonous looks she has been flashing at me into a softer gaze as she turns towards her husband. After bending low to kiss her, Klaus guides his wife to one side, his huge arm encircling her tiny frame. They return after a brief hushed exchange and Klaus is swamped by a riot of his red-headed offspring, at least two of whom are a head taller than him. "We will be back by dawn. Isabel will sort out your bedding, Anna. You will all be safe in the barn tonight."

Rigid, I awake to the sound of galloping hooves. British soldiers! Rosy grey morning mist hangs over the barn's half-roof and I await the sight of my rescuers, willing them to be here soon and hoping they will believe my story. I remember my diary and touch the key that hangs around my neck. Surely there is enough in what I have written to prove that I am a nurse in the British Army Reserve. How I wish that I had brought my uniform. Curious to see why they are laughing and seeming so excited I follow the others who rush to open the barn door. My excitement slumps to the pit of my stomach when I see that it is Klaus and Christo, not British soldiers, who dismount from two fine large horses, one chestnut the other grey. Behind these are two smaller, stockier animals.

"Basuto ponies!" Frederick cries. "Which is mine?"

"Christo will have the grey mare and yes, you, Frederick will take this small pony. You will ride beside your mother who will drive the wagon with Isabel."

"Thank you, Papa, thank you!" Frederick is bursting with joy. "But where did you get them, Papa?"

Klaus does not answer his son and instead hands me the reins of the other Basuto pony, "This one is yours, Anna."

The animal gives a nonchalant snort and I drop the reins in fright. I gasp when he shows his huge teeth and the children laugh.

"He needs watering and a good rub down. The boys will show you."

After we have sorted out the horses and eaten a breakfast of fresh bread cooked perfectly by Isabel on the stove in the farm's ruined kitchen, I find myself alone with Klaus whilst the others go about the business of packing the wagon ready for their departure.

"Klaus, I do not know how to ride a pony. How can we go to Lindley when I cannot ride? How will we carry all my medical supplies without a cart?"

"I thought you understood this, Anna. We are not going to Lindley."

"But the horses. I thought the horses were so that we could continue with our mission. Maud has given you money. A lot of money. We promised her!"

"Your British have destroyed my livelihood, Anna. It is lucky that I still have my family. As for the money, it will be most beneficial for the Boer cause."

"But what about me, Oom Klaus? I do not belong here. How can I get back to Kroonstad?"

"I will not pretend, Anna. You are not going back. You are my security. Because you are British. Because you are a nurse. Your Britishness and your skills will be useful."

"I will not help the Boer commandos, Klaus. I cannot."

"But you can, my dear Anna, and you will."

Chapter 9
Hostage

We are all awake early the next morning in anticipation of the portentous day ahead. I trail behind the others as we make our way from the barn where we have slept on the hard floor again to the kitchen of the burnt-out farmhouse. I rub my arms against the cool brisk air and look around into the tangled void of purple gorges and black ravines for clues as to how I might get away. Klaus did say that there are many British soldiers in the area, so all I have to do is find some.

When, after breakfast and somewhat begrudgingly, Frederick hands me everything I need to saddle my Basuto pony, now dubbed Willem, my sense of dread is quickly superseded by the realisation that if I can learn to ride, escape is possible. I practically snatch the saddlebags and other riding accoutrements from him, leaving Frederick to exchange a puzzled look with his father. Klaus pursues me to where the horses are tethered and gently takes the saddle, blanket and bridle.

"Watch me," he says and I make sure that I observe his every move. Willem bites me when I try and repeat the action Klaus uses to make the pony open his mouth so the bridle can be inserted. Other than that, I learn quickly, so once I have repeated the harnessing manoeuvre three times with no further attack from the pony, I know that I won't forget. Mounting the beast is another matter entirely however, and by the day's end, I am aching all over and covered in bruises. I must bide my time, however, until Magrieta and the children have left the farm, escorted by Christo and Frederick in a little convoy, and begin their journey towards Bethlehem. So I make good use of the time to practice, in the face of bumps of bruises, to gain my seat on Willem and plan my escape.

Firstly, I fasten the girth strap too loosely, and as soon as I put my foot in the stirrup, I find myself tangled up beneath Willem's belly. Then my too-long skirt catches in the stirrup and I hear a loud rip before I land painfully on the ground. I do manage to straddle the horse at my third try, but the stirrups are set too low, making my feet dangle alarmingly and I slide forward in the saddle. Several attempts and minor injuries later, I am seated comfortably astride, feet secure and reins in hand. However, Willem is so disgruntled with my ineptitude that he stubbornly refuses to budge. No matter how hard I dig into his ribs with my knees or click my tongue or jiggle the reins, he stands impassive.

"He is sulking," says Klaus, unhelpfully, so I dismount, but catch the ripped hem of my skirt as I go, and once again, I land on my back with a thud.

"Enough for one day, Anna. We will put him to graze now."

Klaus relieves me at last. I dust myself down and think how I might fix my torn skirt using one of the needles from my nursing supplies. I have no time for myself.

Klaus has constant plans for me and I have to follow him down to the family's bedstead hideaway in the river.

"Take off your skirt and come here," he orders as he wades to the nearest bed. With Klaus waist deep in the reeds and occupied with the bedstead, I seize my chance. Slowly, I back away and then I turn and run.

Why I do this I do not really know, because of course he is faster and stronger than me. He is out of the water and on my tail and in less than a minute, I hit the dusty ground with a thud. His solid body knocks the air out of me and I am smothered by him – dripping and panting. Klaus pushes me roughly and I think he might grind me into the dust of this hateful land. His eyes shine with hurt and anger.

"Your British are responsible for these beds being here and you will help me get them out," he says and pushes himself off me.

"It will be easier for you if you are not hampered by these," he gestures roughly at my skirt and petticoat. "But it is up to you."

Crushed and resenting him, I work for three laborious hours, minus my thick flannel underwear and woollen skirt. Finally, we have dragged all the mattresses to the sunniest spot outside the barn where they lie rippling in the wind and soaking up what little remains of the afternoon's warmth. At least there will be something comfortable to sleep on, I think to myself, still inwardly furious and disappointed about my failure to flee.

By nightfall, even though we have moved them into the barn, the mattresses are still damp, my clothes are not yet dry and the temperature has dropped. Several sheepskins have appeared, which will add some warmth and comfort to the night and a pile of blankets will keep off the chill. After a wordless supper of rusks left for us by Magrieta, washed down with coffee, Klaus picks up his blanket and guns, leaving the flickering candle with me in the barn.

"I shall sleep in the farm kitchen. Will you be warm enough, Anna?"

I nod and thank him, seeing how he leaves all the fleeces for me. After the candle is snuffed out, I gaze up at the moonless night through the broken roof tiles and try to make sense of what has happened, but after the day's exertions, my eyelids soon begin to droop. Just as I feel myself drifting into sleep, I hear the unmistakable sound of a heavy plank sliding into place. It is no surprise to me that Klaus has secured the barn door from the outside.

The days and nights begin to assume a routine. Klaus locks the barn once he thinks I am asleep and makes sure it is unbarred before I awake in the morning. On some nights, I hear him ride off and return hours later, always alone. He has rounded up some of the chickens that escaped the British soldiers and we have fresh eggs each morning for breakfast with the bread that I have become adept at making, glad of the heat of the oven now that July's weather has turned colder. We tend to ride and hunt after breakfast and Willem has become used to me now that I have progressed from a slow trot to a cautious canter. He is a sturdy animal and seems to enjoy our forays into the beautiful Brandwater Basin as much as I do. His ears wriggle to-and-fro with pleasure when I cajole him in either English or Afrikaans, and I am convinced that he grins at me when I him saddle him up.

In the deliciously cold, frosty mornings, the mountains that surround us assume a soft heathery colour that remind me of an autumnal Scotland.

"A natural fortress," Klaus tells me when we ride through Slabbertsnek. "Impregnable to British columns apart from a mere half a dozen routes that are passable for ox wagons and large guns."

It is one morning in mid-July that a lone figure on horseback gallops into sight breaking our tranquil daily pattern in a swirl of dust and thundering hooves. I recognise Christo's grey mare but not before Klaus is on his feet and striding towards his son.

"The British, Papa," Christo breathes hard and fast. "They have taken Bethlehem."

"Where are your mamma and the children?"

"I told them to head into the Brandwater Basin. By the Retiefsnek Pass. Many wagons and horses are going there, Papa. General de Wet and President Steyn are meeting at Viljoen's Farm tomorrow."

"Yes, I know, son. I am going there tonight."

Klaus and his son speak in Afrikaans, but I have been well taught and understand almost every word. Klaus calls over to me in English.

"Anna, we must leave. Please pack up your things and make ready."

So, we are heading for Viljoen's Farm somewhere between Retiefsnek and Slabbertsnek, I muse to myself as I walk over to the barn. Klaus mooted the possibility of English scouts in the area and that lifts my spirits a little. I cannot hear the animated discussion that ensues but guess they are deciding what to do with me because Christo keeps looking over in my direction. The initial angry dialogue turns to a quiet exchange and the glare of animosity disappears from Christo's face. I have no idea what will lie in wait for me where we are going, so I try to put anxious thoughts to one side and gather a sharp crescent-shaped cutting tool that I add to my few other possessions. If I do manage to think of a way out of this predicament, it could be useful.

Once Willem is saddled and loaded up with my nursing supplies, biscuits, mealie flour, coffee and water, I watch as father and son embrace before Christo rides off.

"Where we are going, it is dangerous," says Klaus. "You are my niece, daughter of my wife's German brother-in-law. We will speak only Afrikaans or German in front of my family and other people. Never English. Unless I say. Is that understood?"

"But your family. They know I am British."

"Christo will tell the others what to do. They will treat you as their cousin."

Armed worryingly with my new identity, I manage to keep pace with Klaus as we head North West. We pass cattle kraals and gardens surrounded by low stone walls or mud-brick fences, and I recognise the hedges of prickly pear – the ordinary cactus of these parts. We ride in silence for many hours until just as darkness gathers, the track opens out slightly to reveal several dwellings in the near distance silhouetted by the setting sun. The long shadows have violet and opal tints but they disappear and quickly turn to that murky dark hue that is not yet black. We halt a hundred yards or so short of the buildings by a small thicket next to a stream and I am instructed to tether my pony once I have watered him. I begin to shiver in the cold evening air so the fire that Klaus lights is welcome.

"Heat up some water for coffee. I will return shortly."

He canters away and I can just make out the rider who greets him as he approaches the farmhouse.

As night falls, the temperature drops, so I feed the fire, drink hot coffee and wrap Maud's shawl tight around me against the cold until I hear the gentle pounding of hooves that announces Klaus' return. He nods as I hand him some coffee.

"Damp the fire and gather your things."

I think he senses my apprehension. "You will sleep in one of the outbuildings. It will be warmer."

"What have you told them about me?"

"That you are my niece and a trained nurse. That you will accompany me."

"Where to, Klaus?"

"Oom Klaus. I am your uncle, remember? You must call me Oom Klaus."

"Where will we go, Oom Klaus?"

I think the sound of my thundering heart can probably be heard for miles. Klaus turns away to face the mountains. He is quiet for a moment.

"There will be much fighting, Anna. Many Boer commandos are making their way here to the Brandwater Basin. It is the only part of the Orange Free State that the British haven't taken. There will be many women and children too. But first President Steyn, General de Wet and others of our leaders will meet to decide how best to manage the situation."

"But what can you do? You are not part of a commando."

"That is right, Anna. But I know these passes through the mountains. I can find my way even in the dark. I will be a scout."

"A scout?" I feign lack of knowledge even though I remember fine well from my conversation with Lady Maud's brother, Archie, how valuable and important scouts are for both sides in this war and how the British have recruited many native Africans to their ranks.

"Someone who finds where the British are and what are their plans."

"And then?"

"We report back."

Sickened, I register that he does not speak in the first person.

"We?"

"Sometimes I take you with me. Sometimes I go alone. There will be much for you to do. Now, make haste, we go to the farm."

He checks the dying embers of our camp and guided by the glow of the fire at the farmhouse, we lead the horses to our night's resting place.

A hush descends on the party of twelve or so men who are gathered around the blaze, their laughter turned to curious dancing stares as they watch Klaus escort me to the smallest of the farm's outbuildings. By the firelight, I can see that the interior is full of straw and several blankets are piled in one corner. Klaus pulls some out.

"You will be comfortable in here. Warm enough, I think."

When the door closes behind me, I hear a bolt slide into place and I curl up in the straw like an animal.

It is still dark when I'm dragged roughly from my haunted sleep. I don't recognise the rasping voice which urges me to accompany him and I don't like the way his grasp lingers a little too long on my shoulder. In Afrikaans, I ask him where I might find Klaus, but he only laughs and pulls me to my feet.

"He is busy. You will come with me. To the kitchen. There is work for you there."

Outside the dawn has frosted the landscape in a silver coat and even the cobwebs glitter. Passing the glowing remnants of last night's fire, I am guided onto the wooden stoep of the farmhouse whose balustrade is littered with saddles, harnesses, leather bags and all kinds of what seems to be ammunition, through to the kitchen, where the clock reads seven o'clock.

"You will make coffee and bread for the breakfast. We are fourteen. The latrines are behind the large barn," the rasping man orders me.

As they gather in the dining room, the faint hum of the men's voices becomes less sleepy. I busy myself with the preparation of the meal. A slatted wooden door with round air holes reveals laden pantry shelves where rows of glass jars full of preserves and chutneys are neatly stacked. I add three types of jam to the wooden tray I have packed with plates and cutlery before making my way across the corridor. As I enter the dining room, the now raucous chatter stops at once and I face the daylight stares of the men from last night's bonfire. Klaus steps forward and relieves me of the heavy tray.

"This is my niece. Miss Anna Lieberman. She is a trained nurse and makes excellent bread."

There are a few quick nods, one or two smiles and some disinterested turns of heads away from me as the conversations begin again. I feel the probing stare of a man of relatively small stature but whose broad chest and confident manner seems to draw the attention of the others. He waits for a moment and begins to speak when I make to leave.

"The Basin is an ideal place for us to regroup and to procure food for our commandos. Then we move as planned, and fight."

As I retreat to retrieve the bread and coffee, I hear general murmur of agreement. There is one dissenting voice that advocates remaining in the Basin indefinitely due to its potential as a fortress and because of the plentiful food stocks, particularly wheat. The owner of this voice whose beard is notable by its length and sparseness has the power to silence the background muttering that cradles the discussion whenever he speaks.

Head down, I busy myself with unnecessary trips in and out of the room, delivering more bread and pouring coffee into half full cups. By the time I have served and cleared away the breakfast, I have begun to understand the importance of the Brandwater Basin to the Boer cause. I have gathered that the short, stocky speaker is General Christiaan de Wet. He commands reverential silence as the assembled company listens to details of his plan. They will briefly remain in the area before regrouping to the north west to mount the attack on the British rail and other lines of communication.

"Our chief strength is our mobility. Ideal for the open plains and low hills but not here. If the British cut off all the exits, as we know is their intention," and he looks directly at Klaus, "we will be cramped in this Basin and what good will that be?"

The last man I hear speak has a familiar mellow tone. It is Klaus.

"The British have stayed in Bethlehem for too long, President Steyn." I see that he addresses the man with the long, thin beard. "They will leave the day after tomorrow on the Senekal road, and although there are many, I believe that it will be possible for us to leave the Basin by Slabbertsnek, if we move with haste."

There begins discussion about guns and wagons and other Boer leaders called Prinsloo, De Villiers and Crowther, but I have no pretext to remain so I make my way to the kitchen with the final tray of crockery.

What I have not been prepared for during my eavesdropping on the men's conversation is what happens once the washing up is complete.

"Be quick about that." I look up from my work. "You are needed outside. Come."

Bringing the damp drying-up cloths to hang out, I follow the stranger's bidding. I recognise Tafelberg's flat head first, then see Sampson, Englesman and the others. Next to the wagon, mounted and fully armed, Christo and Klaus are poised, ready.

"Get in, niece. Your things are in the back," Magrieta snaps in German. Whip in hand and looking as though she might easily use it on me, she sits straight-backed next to her stone-faced daughter, Lizzie, who holds baby Jacobus. Behind our wagon, there is another, and another and many, many more beyond. The wagon train winds across the valley floor, eventually disappearing around the distant curve of the river. I lose count at sixty. In front, the familiar shape of my pony, Willem moves impatiently from side to side and I see that it is Isabel astride him, beside yet another wagon driven by an elderly native man that carries the rest of the Meyer family. With typical insolence, Willem shakes his head when he sees me and moves in my direction, but Isabel berates him firmly and steers him away, casting a look of derision my way before turning her back. Laden with ammunition belts, Frederick gallops up and urges his mother to move our wagon.

As we lumber into action, the heaps of medical supplies, blankets and other miscellaneous items lurch towards my crouched body. From this teetering pile, I rescue a rogue sheath of papers that contains an assortment of maps and other sealed documents. Determined to find out where we are or where we might be headed, I try to unfold the largest of the maps, but its flapping causes Magrieta to turn around and when I see the look she gives me, I immediately re-pack the map.

Into all this muddle has been flung my valise, in which should be my diary, the maps of the area I drew with Heiman, the Boer patient, and Edwin's letter. Heart fluttering, I unfasten the catch and breathe again. Someone has packed these precious possessions along with my washbag, the few items of clothing I own, and a thick fleece. Frederick calls to Khama, the driver of the other Meyer wagon and I realise that I am still gripping the damp cloths from breakfast.

Chapter 10
Escape

For several days, the land unfolds. Our long wagon-train trundles through sloping wooded gorges from which time-striated red and gold rock thrusts towards the sun. As a group, we move and camp as a clockwork army whose winding mechanism allows only one speed. There is no fuss and little noise except for the daily hymn singing, which I avoid. Instead, I make my way to where the horses are tethered. No one questions me on this daily pilgrimage to fuss over my Basuto pony, Willem, whose company I feign to miss. Today, he pretends not to know me and turns his head coyly to one side, despite the apple I try to give him and which cost me dear. Through gritted teeth, I whisper that if that is how he wants to behave, I will eat the fruit myself or exchange it back for the precious pencil I swapped with one of the scouts. At this threat, Willem nuzzles my ear and I give in because I crave affection. Any affection. Time on my own does allow me to study the hand-drawn maps of the area that I created with Heiman's help back in Kroonstad Hospital. It is frustratingly difficult though, to work out exactly where we are. Other than these activities, we make coffee, eat biltong and sleep.

On the morning of the third day of our trek, I watch the passing countryside through the flap at the back of the cart. I am the only passenger on the Meyer's wagon as usual. Magrieta and Lizzie keep their backs toward me and do not include me in their conversation during the five-hour trek. A cursory 'we break here', in Afrikaans is accompanied with a sliver of biltong and a surprising soft peach, which is almost fresh. We halt in the lee of a steep hillside to our left and there is a great stretch of farmland to our right, given over to crops. Just a few yards ahead, stands an imposing farmhouse with a veranda that is at least eighty feet long and twelve feet wide, bordered by a white-painted lattice-work fence.

I have had my fill of these people and there are more than enough of them to sort out the oxen and make a fire, so I slip away towards the house. Despite its initial grand appearance and untouched wooden stoep, it becomes clear that this once-beautiful building has been sacked along with so many others. Fragments of mirror jut up through a thick carpet of feathers, mattress-hair, clothes and broken china. Through the gaping kitchen window, whose frame has been smashed for firewood, the stench of rotting flesh reaches me before I see the dead sheep piled in the back yard.

In another room, probably once a study, I find a packet containing unopened English newspapers and fall upon them like a starved person. I tear at the wrappers and devour the news from home. Some of the stories are familiar, such as Lord Roberts taking Pretoria on 5 June, and I make new and surprising discoveries. China is at war. Foreign diplomats had been given twenty-four hours to get out of Beijing and the German ambassador there has been murdered; the Irish Home Rule Party has a new leader in John Redmond; in Vienna, Archduke Franz Ferdinand has renounced the rights of his heirs to the throne of Austro-Hungary so that he can marry Countess Sophie Chotek von Chotkova. Then I spot an account of a Boer commando that has embarked on raids down in the Cape Colony, and I pour over the article, its accompanying map, and ponder the inconceivable notion of the war moving so far south.

"Dit is goeie nuus, isnt dit?" The man's voice is not loud but its closeness and the hot, sour breath that delivers his question shocks me into momentary silence.

"Yes indeed, it is very encouraging news."

I recover myself only to realise that I have spoken this lie to General Christian de Wet in English. His broad frame blocks any movement on my part and I await the consequence of having been found out. But he smiles and in Afrikaans, says that he has heard from Klaus of my fluency in English and he is happy that I will be able to use this skill to assist the Boer cause. When he congratulates my brave decision to undertake such a perilous mission, I have no idea what he is talking about and I realise that Klaus has kept me in the dark in more ways than one.

I find Klaus tending to the horses on my way back to the kitchen. He is alone and there is no one else within earshot.

"So, uncle dear, were you planning on consulting me before we embark on this 'mission'?" Hands on hips, I spit out my sarcasm, infuriated by his grin of mock shame.

"I did mean to tell you, Anna, but..." and he doffs his hat at an older woman who gives me a suspicious look as she passes, "...but, it is hard to get to see you alone." His pretence of guilt is replaced by that bold assuredness which I know cannot be countered. "We will accompany General de Wet's laager when we move out through Slabberts Nek pass, by 15 July. Then I am to be part of a small field commando and you will accompany me. Until we return here to the Brandwater Basin. We must observe the activity of the British and deliver messages to those Boer generals who remain in the area and..."

"That is ridiculous!" I interrupt. "You are asking me to spy on my own countrymen! I will not do it!"

"No, no, Anna, that is not what I am asking you," he smiles in that sheepish way again and I feel some relief. But his face darkens. "I am telling you that this is what will happen." He moves so close that his thigh presses against my hip, "You will do exactly what I say. Because you are my pawn in their game of chess."

Since we have attracted the attention of another group of women carrying water and food over to the cooking fires, Klaus hands me a bridle and we continue our conversation under the pretence that I am helping him tether the horses. He tells me that once the main laager has made its escape through the pass, our base will be this farm, where the few chickens who are the only remaining residents will be joined by a small number of live sheep, a promised gift from one of the fleeing burgher families. Our hideout will also act as a base for the treatment of injured commandos, scouting activities, commando regrouping and food. So, as well as nursing, cooking and animal husbandry, I am now to spy upon my own compatriots. But as my fury mounts, it occurs to me that being close to British troops will provide the opportunity I have been waiting for. I am walking slowly over to the cooking area and have just begun to plan my escape when the woman who gave me a black look earlier, approaches. She does not look happy and I remember that I should have been preparing food for my group hours ago. Realising that I am in the wrong, I take a deep breath but do not expect the furious beating she meters out.

Despite its size, de Wet's laager runs with meticulous efficiency. We travel in complete silence and I am amazed at how little noise four hundred wagons and carts make. There are even four big guns and a Maxim that seem to glide as on a lake. Each time we outspan, every cart and wagon sashays into the same position as the previous day, guided by a single Boer on horseback. The smooth choreography reminds me of a Covent Garden ballet and I retreat into my memories, only to be called back to action by shouted instruction to unharness the oxen. My body aches due to the punishment I received from the woman for failing to undertake my cooking duty and hunger pains wrack my empty stomach because I was not allowed food last night. Fearful of further retribution, I move quickly to obey Frederick's command. No one stands still. Every man, woman and child have a job to do and seems to know instinctively their place in the proceedings. Within minutes, the oxen are un-yoked, horses watered and tethered, tents erected, fires lit, wagons arranged and sentries posted.

It is just after lunchtime and my allocated task of treating several minor medical cases is complete. I have brought my diary, writing paper and a cushion beneath the shade of a small group of bushes where I will not be disturbed.

Dear Marjorie,

I wish I could tell you of my exact whereabouts, but sadly I cannot. I believe we are somewhere in the Brandwater Basin. And goodness only knows when I will be able to send these letters. Having thought that I would be able to find a post-office in Lindley, that time is now weeks past. Due to very recent events, however, I am hopeful that soon the situation will change in my favour.

Although I know that the Brandwater Basin is not too far from the towns of Bethlehem and Senekal, I have not yet been able to study any detailed maps of this area to determine the exact location and route of the convoy of which I am but a small part. It is my plan to leave these people as soon as I can, but am unsure when that opportunity will present itself.

What I can tell you though, Marjorie, is of the beautiful and rugged scenery hereabouts which is quite breath-taking, especially in the early morning frosts. The mountains remind me a little of Scotland or the English Lake District, although the weather is not at all typical of home. Despite the freezing night-time and early morning temperatures, by the afternoon, we are frying like eggs in the blistering sun. Nevertheless, because of the countryside, I do sometimes imagine that old Mrs Cruikshank might appear from one of the glens, invite me in for afternoon tea and I shall discover that I have awoken from a nightmarish dream. Did I ever mention Mr and Mrs Cruikshank? They run a guesthouse near Perth in the central highlands. My mother particularly loves Scotland and...

I pause, and images of my parents and brother by the deep, glassy water of Pitlochry overtake my mind. How I miss them. How I miss Marjorie. How I wish I could talk to her. But what I wish most of all is to be with Edwin. To hear his stories and questions. To run my fingers through his hair. To feel his touch. As my thoughts waver into the far distance through the heat haze, a party of men from the laager approaches and I instinctively fold the half-completed letter, smudging the ink in tear-blurred haste. The men seem not to notice me and continue across the unshaded ground ahead and towards one of the anthills.

Two of the men who are both well over six feet tall and burly in the extreme, march a third man towards the anthill. This man's head is cowed but every so often, his blood-shot eyes dart manically to the right or left. A fourth man of short, stocky build has gone ahead, and with one deft strike of a shovel removes, the pinnacle of the ants' dwelling. At this action, the cowed man halts, utters a thin but terrible moan and is pressed on by his guards. I curb my instinct to run to the poor, tired-looking wretch who appears to be close to tears and whose body shakes as in terror.

"Get up!" The command rings clear. "Now. Here, take this rifle and hold it. Not like that. Rest the butt between your toes."

Thus instructed, the man grips his weapon and stands rigid on the top of the anthill. The two bigger commandos move about twenty-five yards away in each direction from their comrade, load their Mausers, lay on the ground and take aim. My shriek of horror causes a short-lived commotion and as I rise from my shady place the fourth Boer runs across and takes firm hold of my shoulders. All this while the victim remains stock-still, eyes fixed on the weapons directed at him.

"This is not of your concern." The man loosens his grip.

"But look what they are doing! The ants…the sun!"

"This is General de Wet's way. It is our way. This sentry fell asleep on duty. He must be punished."

"What will happen to him if he moves?" I ask, not wanting to hear the answer.

"If he moves a leg, they will shoot that limb. The same if he moves an arm."

"And if he jumps off?"

The man looks at me as though I am stupid.

"He will not jump off," comes the mocking reply. He looks at me as though he knows all my secrets and I am in no doubt that he could shoot me just for having spoken.

I shake his hand off me and sit down, cursing the pain I feel when I do.

"As you wish," the man gives me a curt nod and returns briefly to one of the prostrate gunmen where a short exchange results in an expressionless glance in my direction and then he is gone. He joins a group of burghers now gathered in a semi-circle just in front the audience.

The savage sun beats down upon the quivering man, who is unable to move his hat to provide the shade for his face that would prevent his already chaffed lips from swelling until I think they will burst. Then the blistering begins. Lips, neck, forearms. I suppress the disgust and anger before the terror rises in my chest. I dare not move for fear that I will be found out, that somehow, they will know that I am not who they think I am. I will receive more than the beating that was my punishment yesterday if the truth is discovered. Do not speak. Do not flinch. Do not react. I make myself rigid, in case I shock the prisoner into sudden movement, but I cannot help watching. His hands tense around his gun. It must be like holding a roasting hot iron. His fingers will be branded. The ruthless sun burns the man's skin through his clothes.

Unable to stand the anguish, he makes an almost imperceptible movement of his shoulder. I flinch and swallow a desperate desire to cry out. One of his guards puts down his pipe and lifts his Mauser to his shoulder. Takes aim. Holds fire. Lays down his firearm. Picks up his pipe. Smokes. I breathe again.

The punished one holds still as a bronze on a plinth. Eyes bulging. About to explode. And still, the sun climbs. Higher, hotter. The scorching heat penetrates the unprotected cells of the ant heap. Then they come. Angry, outraged creatures swarm from their ravaged dwelling. Full of fight, they urge for battle and a desire to take vengeance on whatever has invaded their nest. They crawl into his boots and I imagine them, enraged by his stillness in their attack. The first legion disappears back into their headquarters and re-emerges with new recruits. Soon, the open top of the heap and the victim are covered in a crawling, multi-layered mass of stinging, wriggling agony. He must have moved his leg because the other guard twists his bandolier and glances along the barrel that rests in his left hand.

My decision to interject happens at the same moment as does the commandant of the circle of burghers. We move forward together.

"You will remember this." His stern words are not harshly spoken and he looks directly at me before he turns to the punished man. "You will not sleep again when it is your turn to watch."

"Never, so help me God!" gasps the prisoner.

"Stand down then; you are free."

Writhing like a snake, the liberated man tears off all his clothes so quickly that I barely have time to look away. Tearless sobs engulf his body as he flings his weapon after the ant-riddled garments. Every inch of his poor body has been attacked and is a ragged patchwork of angry, red blotches. When he sinks to the ground, a sympathetic veteran, who I guess might once have endured the same ordeal, rushes to offer a tin brimming with water which the prisoner does not drink but pours over his neck and chest. I hear my name and caring not to find out who has spoken, move quickly back to the laager to fetch my medicine bag.

Within the three days that we remain at the farm with the beautiful veranda, the man's all-over rash is almost entirely gone, and by then I have already witnessed another puzzling punitive spectacle. One of the young men of our group is more anxious than most to get on with the journey out of the Basin and consistently aggravates the seemingly more staid, senior men with his constant demands. His nuisance-making has already resulted in a dressing-down from the commandant who mixes a long piece of scripture with some general words of wisdom, meted out before a large gathering of folk. Klaus says that it would be unlikely for the young man to re-offend, given the humiliation he suffered.

His assumption proves wrong as I witness a group of young men hijack the culprit, bring him to the ground, remove his shirt and put a bridle on his head. Everyone quickly gathers to watch the next piece of the action whereby the bit is crammed into his mouth and firmly buckled there. Amid the badinage of his fellow countrymen and to my astonishment, one of the others takes up the reigns, whips the trouble-maker with a sjambok and forces him to pirouette like a circus pony. First, he canters, then trots and finally gallops around the laager where men pelt him with crusts of rusks and girls giggle and shout 'Are you lonely without your cart?' or 'What lovely ears you have!' before they offer him a handful of grass upon the end of a stick. The women are fervently patriotic and merciless in their contempt for a man who will not do his share of fighting, marching and watching. A good Boer must do all this cheerfully and without complaint.

I spend a good part of each day that I am with de Wet's laager alone in the shade of a small copse at the outer perimeter of the camp. Because my stock of parchment is very low, the script I use now is so small that I find myself squinting as I write. If I am unable to find more paper soon, it will be necessary to stop altogether. Usually, I am uninterrupted when I write to Edwin, Marjorie, Maud, my brother and my parents, but today brings unexpected company in the form of Klaus's eldest daughter, Isabel and my pony, Willem. She speaks to me in English.

"He is yours. Take him."

I resist the urge to hug her and put my arms around the animal's neck instead. His soft nose snuggles under my kappie and he nibbles my ear.

"But why, Isabel?" I ask when she puts the reins into my hands.

"You will need a horse for what you and my father are about to embark upon."

I frown and wonder what she knows of the mission.

"Tomorrow is the 15th. It is the day we will leave by Stabberts Nek. I see by the way you treat the men that you are a good nurse. A good person. You are a brave woman. It cannot be helped that you are English. I wish you well, Anna Lieberman. Auf Wiedersehen."

"Danke, Isabel. Thank you."

Across the gulf of nothing else to say, we exchange a silent understanding before we part. Willem nuzzles the pocket of my dress where he does not find the usual small morsel that I keep for him there. His expression is one of abject annoyance and I swear he looks to Isabel as she makes her way across the dusty ground, wondering no doubt if she is the one with a tasty treat to offer him.

A current of anticipation runs through the camp. Our departure is planned for ten o'clock and since I now have my steed, it is certain that I will no longer be travelling in the wagon. The chance for escape emerges.

"Anna, you will ride at the back of the column with the burghers. And Frederick."

I turn to face Klaus, whose absence has been noticeable in recent days. He answers my un-asked question.

"The advance guard is made up of some burghers and scouts. I will be with this group. We will likely come very close to the English. They will be camped on the Senekal road."

His certainty about the whereabouts of the British army helps me begin to understand the nature of the work that has taken Klaus away from the laager and his family each day.

"So, Uncle, you still believe that this great entourage can be moved through Slabberts Nek Pass, if it is open, that is?" His infuriating grin is as wide as ever.

"It *will* still be open. This I know for a fact, Anna. I understand it is difficult for you. To travel so close to your countrymen."

I see clearly now why Frederick has been nominated as my escort and as the laager prepares for its great getaway, my mind invents a hundred implausible ways that I might escape.

Gun slung loosely across his back, Frederick is by my side as soon as we saddle the horses. There are two more women on horseback but we are not introduced. One woman is much older than me and although stout and rigid as a barrel, gallops at a terrifying pace up and down the line. At the very back of the column, the scale of the operation is apparent. Headed by the advance guard of Klaus and his scout party, we are mass of military and human precision that sandwiches the President's party plus Generals de Wet and Botha between the advance party and the artillery. Mounted burghers flank each side of the ox wagons and cape carts that come next, to form the greatest bulk of the line, which must be at least two miles long. I am with the rear guard, made up mostly of armed burghers but with other miscellaneous persons, all on horseback. I am the only person without arms and ammunition.

We travel for about five hours when a message is relayed that we must move in complete silence from now on, and a blanket of noiseless, invisible invincibility falls on the entire group. Our procession ambles through the red sundown, becoming semi-visible even to one another in the dimming blue-black landscape. Just ahead the pass beckons to the left, having swallowed most of our troop into its shadows. Close by my side, our horses almost touching, Frederick reaches over and gently indicates the orange glow of camp fires about a mile away to our right.

"The British," he mouths as his hand lays firm upon the reins of my mount and his mocking smile emphasises my powerlessness.

As I too become enveloped between the steep, dark sides of Stabberts Nek Pass, I take one more look behind to see the hopeful flicker of the British camp fires disappear from my view. I decide to do it now. I kick Willem as hard as I can and he gallops like a champion back towards the British encampment but the reigns slip from my sweating grip and Willem stumbles on a rocky patch of ground. I grab his mane but we are both tumbling, and I am falling, and crash to the ground.

Chapter 11
Imprisoned

From my makeshift sleeping quarter beneath a roughly arranged length of canvas, I watch his stealthy preparations for an early departure. The light of the un-risen sun is too weak to cast shadows but illuminates the scene well enough and there is no sign of my pony. Accompanied by half a dozen other young men, Frederick speaks a few quiet words before they ride off, and then approaches me. I close my eyes and hope that he will think I am still asleep, but he unsheathes a knife and slices the rope he used last night to bind my ankles together.

"Do not try that again," his voice is steely. "You are lucky that the others think your pony bolted." He cuts the last stubborn tie. "My father wishes it to stay that way, but if it were me…I do not think you are worth the risk."

He cannot resist giving me a kick in my already bruised ribs.

When he is gone, I rub the abrasions on my ankles and watch the camp gradually uncurl from its slumber. A steaming cup of coffee is thrust into my hands by the lively, stout woman who has been riding with my group, and I notice that she wears an oddly fashioned coat made from animal skins, patched neatly together, seams straining to accommodate her girth.

"You look still tired. Drink this. It will wake you," she says.

Fully clothed and wrapped in everything I own, as part of my doomed bid to escape, I nurse the hot tin can. Soon, the heat takes effect and I feel the blood return to my fingertips.

"What is your reason for travelling with this laager?" I ask in Afrikaans.

"Not the same as yours, Miss Lieberman," she replies, taking a sip from her can, "I am, or rather was, a neighbour of Mr and Mrs Meyer. What remains of my family has been living…if you can call it that, on the veldt since my husband joined his commando." She laughs bitterly. "It is not safe to return to our farm, so my family and I ride with General de Wet. Klaus asked me to watch over you. On yesterday's journey. I was sorry that your pony bolted." From her ironic tone, it is clear she knows the truth. "But do not fret, Miss Lieberman, you will have a new, more obedient, horse later today."

Something about the sadness in her face makes me want to like her.

"Thank you for the tea," I say, then, "do you know where your husband is now?" Her eyes crease when she gives the slightest of smiles.

"I did not know for many months. But we were together in the Brandwater Basin for several weeks. He is still there, with another of the Generals. General Prinsloo."

I nod. This is one of the men whose name has arisen in the private conversations I have overheard between Klaus, General de Wet and President Steyn.

"But you have chosen to bring the rest of your family out of the Basin?"

Her assurance turns to thoughtfulness and it is a few moments before she replies.

"We will fight to the bitter end. And this is the right way. For us. For him to fight and for me to keep moving. I want to avoid the camps that are being set up by the British for refugees of the war. I do not know your story, Anna – may I call you Anna? But I do know that neither Klaus nor Magrieta ever mentioned their German niece in all the years I have known them. Until now, that is."

I feel the prickle of nerves across the back of my hands but she continues before I can respond.

"And neither do I want to know your secrets, Anna. That you are a friend to Klaus and Magrieta is good enough for me." With that, she takes my empty cup, wishes me well and vanishes. I did not even think to ask her name.

The command to in-span happens soon after the sun is properly risen and within ten minutes, the random but familiar pattern of scattered sleeping wagons is transformed into neatly organised, close-packed lines, ready to march on. After he brings me a new pony, I breakfast with Klaus who is unusually retrospective and quiet until the others who are assembled around the fire leave to prepare for the journey. He grabs my wrist and pulls me gently back down when I rise. "You have had one beating, yet still you tried to escape. If you try to leave again, the punishment will be worse. Do you understand, Anna?" Although what he says makes perfect sense, what I cannot comprehend is the soft touch that accompanies his harsh words.

"Why is it so important that I stay with you, Klaus?" I badly want him to let go of my arm.

"At first, I was angry. After what happened to my farm. I wanted to keep you here as some kind of revenge for what the British troops did. I am not proud of these thoughts."

"And then?"

"And then I see you are a fine nurse and a caring woman. I realise that you would be truly useful." He pauses and a look crosses his face that I have only ever seen pass between him and Magrieta. For a second time, I want to run away from him.

"And I like you, Anna. I like your spirit. You make me laugh."

"Klaus, stop this. Please stop."

"And you are very beautiful, Anna." He does not move any closer to me, but he is still holding my wrist and the breath of his words lingers longer than it should. My skin prickles.

"Klaus?"

I whip around to see Magrieta's face. She glares directly at me but her voice softens when she turns to Klaus.

"The wagons are ready, husband. We must leave."

"I will come. Get the horses ready, Anna."

I watch until the track ahead swallows them into its steep curve, taking with it the soft burr of their conversation. When Klaus returns, I have saddled both horses, our interrupted conversation remains un-resumed and we wait in silence until the deep reverberations of de Wet's convoy are a distant growl.

Of the small band of seven who remain, Klaus is the only person I know, but I am intensely glad of the others' presence. Their company plus the rhythm of the gentle canter relaxes me enough that I can begin to think clearly. I see that the two extra ponies are loaded with ammunition, my medical supplies, blankets and food, but no spare rifles. The idea that I might find and steal a gun is so absurd, I almost laugh out loud. Even if I were to secure a weapon, I cannot even shoot a rabbit without closing my eyes and holding my breath. Firing at another human being is quite the most ridiculous notion so I shake it off, dig my heels into my new pony's sides and gallop ahead to where Stabberts Nek opens out into the familiar rolling green and gold fields of the Brandwater Basin.

Not knowing whether to head north or south, I slow to a canter until the other riders have caught up.

"This is where we must part ways." An older man with a thick black beard whose face is mostly hidden by the brim of his felt hat addresses Klaus. The two shake hands before the bearded man and three others head north, taking the larger of the pack ponies with them. I glean from the conversation that they will meet us at the farm after a reconnaissance of British troop movement somewhere near Bethlehem.

Wisps of grey smoke and an acrid stench float across burnt stubble to greet us. No longer white, the fence of the long veranda is intact but charred to a chalky grey. The embers are too hot for us to venture inside, so we stand and stare at the piles of debris, in a sea of ash, where there used to be broken furniture, crockery and glass. Not one part of the roof remains. Klaus hoists a large box from the pack pony and drops it with a thud and a clink to the ground. He prises open the box, which reveals a case of the finest Scotch whiskey. It is a brand to which my father is particularly partial and I gasp at its familiarity and at the price that Klaus must have paid for such a prize. Even before the war, just one bottle was considered a luxury at home. Klaus breaks open the seal and hands the bottle first to me. When I decline, he passes the liquor to our comrade who swallows a great gulp, then disappears, saying he will check the barns for damage.

"Fine whiskey," my comment is deliberately sarcastic.

"We have your friend Maud to thank," Klaus is stony faced. I glare back.

"Your fee for taking me to Lindley."

"Correct." He proffers the half empty bottle, but I turn my fury from him and walk away. I do not want him to see how I long to drain the bottle, to drink my memories and fear into oblivion.

Our next days are spent clearing the farmhouse kitchen. It is where I will cook and bake because the range is still functional. Although both barns are un-scathed, the one with slatted wooden sides is coated in ash, thus rendered useless as a hospital ward. By default, therefore, the second of the outbuildings will be used for my patients. Klaus leads me to the third, where I am to sleep.

"But this is a grain store, Klaus. There is no window."

"What need do you have for light at night?"

What need indeed? What point in writing my diary and letters now?

This time, Klaus does not hide the fact that I am to be locked in at night and each evening, either he or the other man, Matthys – also a scout – performs this duty unless there are new wounded men for me to see to and despite the futility, I write to Edwin. I tell him that I love him. I do not say that I might never see him again. I write about the kitchen knife I keep by my bedside because it makes me feel safe, but do not admit how close I came to using it on the night that Klaus locked himself in the barn with me. I do not tell Edwin that I go along with things I don't want to do, things that ignore my wants and needs, and then hate my compliance. Matthys assumed that I really was a relative of the Meyer family, until one day they came to my barn after a drinking spree and I knew something had changed. It was the way both men looked at me. The indifference was replaced with disdain somehow. I know that Matthys still regards me Klaus's property, but occasionally when Klaus is absent, Matthys orders me to undertake tasks that usually he does. Gathering wood, digging over the latrines, heavy work that he seems to enjoy watching me sweat over. I loathe being bullied, yet the way Klaus and his compatriot treat me has become familiar and comfortable, so that before I know it, I am complying, eager to please men who can't be pleased. Especially because I cannot offer what they want me to willingly give. Every day, I look down the barrel of the future, but the bullet never comes. I do not write to Edwin the unbearable truth that my life is devoid of simple pleasures such as amiable conversation, an early morning walk, reading. My books are long since burnt for warmth. Or perhaps as a punishment for something I did or didn't do. Like a dog, I want to shake off my anger, regret and hatred, but my resentment just drips to the ground as I meekly stitch their clothes, mend their broken bodies and fill their growling stomachs.

I write to Edwin that nights are cold, days are hot. I cast off layers as the heat rises and by mid-afternoon, I am usually down to just my linen chemise and thin cotton petticoat. I imagine Edwin's touch and feel Klaus's eyes upon me. By nightfall, I am wearing everything I own, which is not much. What there is of all our clothes needs constant mending because we wear the same items each day, washing them only occasionally. Shoes are a real problem. The soles of my own boots are paper-thin and let in the rain. From cow-hide, I have fashioned new shoes for several commandos whose original footwear has all but disintegrated. These boys remind me of my brother and so I look after them with him in my thoughts. The photograph I have of us with my parents is all but perished, so often has it been taken from its place between the pages of my journal. In that photograph, my mother's blonde curls are piled up beneath the broad-rimmed, ribbon-trimmed hat that we bought together in Liberty of London last summer. How she loves that hat. In the picture, braided up and twisted in the fashion of the season, my hair shines thick and lustrous. Now it is grown so long that I can almost sit upon it. But I care little about my appearance and there are no mirrors in any case. I live in the hope that I do not smell as bad as Klaus because there always remains the other vain hope that I will get away from here somehow.

About once a week, I renew my determination to wash daily and to brush my hair, but I bargain against myself, in the knowledge that Klaus will not think me beautiful in the slightest if I pay little heed to the way I look. And from time to time, I see that look which he usually douses with a glass of whiskey. The knife that I had begun to carry everywhere was confiscated after a second night-time episode in the barn.

I can hardly bear to think about that evening. I have certainly not written about it in my journal. It had been so hot that day that I brought two pails of water to my barn to cool myself down. The men had gone who-knows-where, hunting for God-knows-what (they rarely speak to me) and I was alone. I poured tumbler after tumbler of cold water over my head and rubbed every part of my body until my skin felt like polished crystal. My taut and aching muscles cried out in joy at receiving such attention. I spread my clean, naked body on the soft wool fleeces and began to plait my newly washed hair when a glint from the setting sun caught my eye. I saw the gleaming barrel of his gun before I realised it was Klaus, and by the set of his mouth and the way his tongue poked between his teeth, I think he had been watching for some time. He edged slowly towards the pail where my scattered clothes lay, his gaze fixed on me with an odd expression, not making eye contact. I held myself statue-still. "Anna." His voice slow, low. Without looking down, he hooked my skirt from the ground with the metal end of his rifle and lifted it towards me, indicating wordlessly to approach him. When I did not move, he took a step forward and the crash of the bucket when he knocked it over brought me quickly to my feet. I keep my eyes focussed on the trickle of spilled water that seeps into the earth and do as he bids. I am less than a yard from him when he drops the gun. My skirt falls with it and before I can gather my wits, he kneels at my feet. He is shaking and whispers, "Anna. Anna, you are truly beautiful," and offers up my clothing with a beseeching "Please, take it." I look down at the pulsing veins of his forehead and upcast blue eyes. "Thank you," I say and turn from him to step into my skirt, scooping up my underwear from the ground as I walk quickly away. I smell his closeness just before the shock of his caress brings out the terror that has been lodged inside me. I scream and dive to where I hide my knife, but he is on me and has seized the weapon before I reach it. He is all over me. I close my eyes. "What is…?" And there is Matthys in the doorway. I cover my naked shame with one of the blankets and Klaus jumps up. He brandishes the knife by way of explanation, but does not bother to fasten his shirt. Matthys nods, spits in my direction, goes to where Klaus's rifle dropped to the ground and hands the weapon to his comrade. With much mutual back-slapping, they leave together arm in arm. Not a backward glance for me.

By the end of September, my small hospital ward is empty and Matthys has decided that his future lay not with us, but with de Wet's commando, which by that time had broken cover from its lair near Reitzburg and had crossed the Vaal river.

"Are there any eggs today?" Klaus demands on my return from the daily disappointment of tending to the hens, which are now just three in number. He is too close to me, his voice has the beginnings of that hateful beseeching tone and his shirt hangs loosely around his slumped, bony shoulders. I cannot bear the sight of him.

"Nothing. That's the third day. How much longer must we stay here, Klaus?"

"Until I receive my orders to move. You will do as I say."

"But who will bring those orders to you Klaus? There is no one left. I am sick of hiding. Of waiting. For what? I am not going back to those caves. You cannot make go back there!"

Because he does not respond, I shout louder. I am screaming at him now. I follow Klaus, who has turned his back on me to grab the gun he uses for hunting and is making for the door. Then I see them over his shoulder. Two men in familiar khaki uniforms. At last. We have been found.

Chapter 12
The Rescue

The soldiers – British soldiers – approach me and I feel my shoulders collapse with relief. I switch from the Afrikaans that I was yelling to Klaus into English. "Thank goodness you've arrived," I smile at the two men. I wish there was some tea or at least coffee left that I could offer them. I remember my scant attire and wish too that I had not become so used to the comfort of being only semi-dressed. Klaus, meanwhile, utters a profanity and flees as soon as he registers the British uniforms. The young fair-haired trooper grins and glances at his compatriot, who jerks his head towards the open doorway. In response to the wordless command of his older comrade, the young fair-haired man turns on his heels, bids us farewell in a wonderfully welcome accent that could only have been acquired in the East End of London and sets off in pursuit of Klaus.

I imagine that the young soldier will soon catch up with Klaus, given that we have barely eaten for days and as well as being weak, Klaus is much older than his pursuer. A single gunshot reverberates in the distance. Despite all that has happened, I find myself hoping that Klaus' knowledge of the veldt will mean that he can get away. Grabbing a shawl from its peg and wrapping it around my shoulders, I hold out my hand to my rescuer in welcome.

"Anna, Anna Lieberman. I'm a nurse. A British nurse."

The handsome black soldier extends his hand and grips mine.

"And you speak excellent Afrikaans, ma'am."

I find myself seizing both his hands in return, and think that my face might split in two, so wide is my grin and I do not even begin to explain about Klaus and my reasons for being here. The poor man, who must be one of the many native South Africans who has joined the British, has a look of thirst or hunger, or probably both, and I wish again for something, anything that I could give him to drink or eat. Then I remember the whiskey, bought with Maud's money, that Klaus keeps in the broken cupboard by the range and I turn away to reach for the bottle, explaining to my guest that I cannot provide tea or coffee, but that I do have something a little stronger and would he mind even though it is the middle of the day. I hear him chuckle. The sound of his deep, rich laugh fills me with comfort and I swing around with the half-full bottle and the one remaining glass.

A cough in the doorway announces the return of the fair-haired trooper. "So, you were going to start without me?" he quips and flings down the shotgun. "I am sorry but there's only one glass," I apologise, but he laughs a slow, forced guffaw without smiling and our eyes lock for less than a second. It is time enough for me recognise a look that I have seen before. Despite the overpowering heat, I pull the shawl tight around my body. He takes the bottle and shrugs off his jacket, creating a wave of stale tobacco and rancid sweat. I move towards his companion, who has taken a polite step back and I hand him the glass, which the fair-haired trooper then fills to the brim.

"Nice kappie," the African says, pulling the loose ties of my bonnet playfully with his free hand, but I'm confused because the edge of his voice is harsh with irony. Then he drains the glass, holds it out to be filled again and offers it to me. The sun beats hot through the charred open rafters and the door-less doorway beckons. As I shake my head, he undoes the top button of his shirt to counter the heat, raises the chipped glass in salutation, then slowly and deliberately unfastens another shirt button. And another. When he reaches for the sjambok, I know that I should have run with Klaus.

Part Three
The Refugee Camp

Chapter 13
Arrival at the Camp

At last, the jolting stops. My body lies completely still in the dark. I think that we must have reached our destination, but when I open my eyes, I see just hazy shapes outlined against the light, so I have no idea where we are. My hands reach out and I find that I am lying on my front on hard wooden boards, which are partially covered by a pile of foul-smelling empty sacks. My neck is stiff where my head has been turned to one side. Although we have stopped, the world is heaving and rolling around me. I think I may vomit.

I hoist myself up and grasp at the sacks, but they slip away and I topple sideways onto my back. When a stillness settles and the burning pain across the back of my legs recedes to a throb, I gingerly touch where my skirt should be, to find only bandages wrapping me from waist to ankle, like long johns. Running my fingers up my body, I discover something rough with sleeves that are much too long and a high collar that is cutting into my neck because it has been fastened all the way up. It seems to be some kind of thigh-length coat. Slipping my hand beneath the hem of this scratchy, heavy garment, I feel my bare skin and I wonder why I didn't put on my chemise this morning. Thank goodness, though, I am wearing a kappie to protect my head and face from the sun. But it too feels unfamiliar, maybe because I haven't fastened the ties and the linen cloth smells of wood smoke. Other scents begin to register. There must be some rotten meat in the cart somewhere and my clothes need a wash. As do I. And I really need to relieve myself.

Slowly, slowly, I extend my gaze, trying to take everything in, and as I squint, more of my surroundings come gradually into soft focus. I stretch my arm towards a long shape covered in more of the rough hessian sacks lying a few feet to my left. Perhaps it is the meat, which must have been left out in the sun too long. Suddenly, the shape next to me is illuminated by strong, bright sunlight as a cloth cover lifts from above me and I am temporarily blinded, but not before I realise that I am lying next to a corpse.

"This one's dead, sir."

The tall black man speaks in English, his accent clipped. He is one of four uniformed men who peer down at me, but unlike the others, he does not wear a jacket. His muscled forearms glisten. Another man, who wears the peaked cap of a British officer, responds, his voice soft, gentle and controlled.

"Thank you, Trooper Mojela. Lieutenant Drake, perhaps you will come with me to my office so that we can record the particulars and allocate a status to the woman."

Then I hear a different man who must be Lieutenant Drake. He sounds Scottish, maybe from Edinburgh.

"Certainly, Major Rogerson. My scouts here found her in this state before I arrived with the patrol, and it was Trooper Clarke here who brought the man down."

Trooper Clarke, a fair-haired young Londoner, grins and says, "Shot him straight through the back of the head as he was escaping, sir."

Klaus. Klaus is dead.

Lieutenant Drake nods and continues, "When the rest of my patrol reached the farm, it had all been sorted out. Trooper Mojela here saved the woman." He indicates towards the tall black soldier.

Major Rogerson turns to Trooper Mojela and looks at me, "What happened to her?"

Mojela's staccato reply is immediate, "The dead man must have beaten her, sir. You know what these Boers are like with their women folk. And their whores. Found one of those big horse whips next to her. She's been delirious and ranting on in Afrikaans for hours. Didn't think she would make it. She must have banged her head too."

Lieutenant Drake nods thoughtfully, "And the bandages?"

Young Trooper Clark looks quickly and with some admiration at his older, jacket-less comrade. "Trooper Mojela did it, sir. Right good job he made of her an' all. Cut up a woman's dress he found lying around to make them bandages. And he lent 'er his jacket, sir."

There is something familiar about Trooper Clarke's jovial tone and his accent is making me smile. I run my fingers over the jacket I am wearing and a flash of memory comes to me. I think that I recall the handsome black trooper taking off his jacket for me.

"Place was burnt out, sir. Living like pigs, they were, sir. Stank, it did, sir. All that was there was a bit of whiskey and this old cart."

Pain ricochets through my body when he rattles the cart, and thankfully, Trooper Clarke's reminisces are halted by the arrival of two men bearing a stretcher. They set about the grim task of removing the reeking body that lies beside me. As they load this burden onto a stretcher, the sacks slip away to reveal the man. He is about forty. His red hair and beard the same shade as his weathered face are now matted with blood. I feel a pang of something like sadness, because Klaus has been my travelling companion after all.

I find my voice, "Meneer?"

Everyone stops to look at me and Major Rogerson swaps from gentle English to soft Afrikaans. "We thought you were sleeping. How are you feeling, my dear?"

My lips are so dry it feels like minutes go by before my reply leaks out. "Thirsty, sir," I reply in English.

"Good. You can speak English. That will be helpful for the medical staff. I am Major Rogerson, I am the temporary superintendent of this camp. What is your name?"

I think. More seconds go by. Nothing comes to me. I open my mouth but the answer remains lost.

"I asked her name when we found her, sir," offers Trooper Mojela. "She said something that sounded like Anna to me. That was all." He and Trooper Clarke regard one another with concerned, tacit agreement.

"Perhaps the bang on the head has affected her memory?" volunteers Lieutenant Drake and Major Rogerson nods in agreement.

"Ah good. Here you are, Sister Fairfax."

A tall thin nurse with sunburnt cheeks and kind eyes joins the group. Her uniform is very neat and clean and I feel ashamed at how I must look.

"Let me introduce Anna. Anna will be with us for some time, I think. Lieutenant Drake, perhaps your men here will help move her to the nursing station while you and I sort out the paperwork. Between us, I think we have all the information I need."

At a nod from Lieutenant Drake, his subordinates place me face down onto a stretcher, watched over by Sister Fairfax, who smiles and tells me that I will soon be feeling more comfortable. We snake our way across acres of parched earth, guided by lines of white stones that mark out pathways and from my one eye that is not pressed into the canvas, I see her bid another nurse to join us.

I hear Sister Fairfax ask for chloroform and the other nurse, who wears an ordinary day dress under her white apron, does as she is bid, taking long, purposeful strides in the wake of the camp superintendent. When our convoy reaches a small but airy tent, my stretcher is placed down and I am lifted onto a bed and my body sinks into a soft mattress. With joy and trepidation in equal measure, I make a mental note of the tin bath in the corner. Nurse Fairfax asks the two troopers to wait with me while she goes to find me some clean clothes.

When we are alone, each man assumes a position on either side of my bed. Judging from their swift assured movements they seem to know what they are doing. Although it really hurts, I try not to cry out when they turn me onto my back. Trooper Mojela sits on the edge of my bed and carefully begins to unfasten the jacket that I am wearing, button by button, starting at the neck. Slowly and deliberately, he helps me out of the rough garment, his hands cradle my back as he gently peels my arms out of the sleeves. I try to resist because I know that I am quite naked underneath, but he is powerfully built and strong. I wriggle myself away, but his firm hands press my shoulders into the cot and his gaze lingers.

"Rest there, ma'am." He impresses on me the need to stay still.

When I am freed from his jacket, he whispers something softly that I am not quite able to hear. I smell something familiar about him, mixed in with stale whiskey, old sweat and tobacco and I shiver suddenly. The tips of his fingers brush accidentally against my body and I feel my face turn scarlet.

"Simeon!" hisses the younger soldier who is now standing at the tent flap, closed to protect my dignity. Mojela stands quickly as Matron returns with a pile of pale grey linen in her arms. My modesty compromised, the man, I now know is called Simeon Mojela, gleams a white smile my way before he turns his back to me.

"Trooper Mojela! If you please!" with relief, I hear the authority in the woman's tone.

"Sorry, ma'am. But I need my jacket, or I'll get what-for from my lieutenant."

I begin to feel sorry for these men who have gone to such pains to save me. "Well, quite so, but you could have waited five more minutes."

My rescuer gives her a knowing look as he gives my nakedness a cursory glance.

"We have seen it before, ma'am. We did find her in this condition."

The nurse's expression softens. "Yes, of course you did. Well done for dressing her and bringing her to us." She turns her patient smile to me, "Lucky for you, dear, that they showed up when they did." She coos over me and covers me with a sheet then says, "Are we going to say thank you?"

My mouth is so dry and I think about the jug of water on the table by the tin bath.

"Thank you, Trooper Mojela…Trooper Clarke…" I whisper and almost manage to raise myself into a sitting position to shake hands with my rescuers, but the room swims around me and I lower my throbbing head to the pillow. My scalp feels oddly rough and makes an unfamiliar scratchy sound on the crisp bedclothes. I reach up to my long hair but it is gone, and I find just scrappy tufts in places and shorn patches in others.

"That's quite a bump," the nurse sounds concerned.

"Yes, ma'am. I shaved her hair to get a better look at the injury. Got some cold water from the river onto it."

A recollection prickles in my aching head, but it is gone as quickly as it appeared.

"As well as a knight in shining armour, it appears that you are a fine nurse too. She is a very lucky young woman."

He bows graciously, picks up a piece of cloth and hands it to me. It is my damaged linen cap. I quickly put it on to cover my shaved head, even though it smells of smoke and the action causes me immense pain.

"Well, Sister, we must be on our way back to the camp now. Glad to be of service." He pulls his khaki jacket firmly shut, buttons it rapidly then turns to look directly at me. "We will be sure to come by to see how your new patient…how Anna…is doing."

Sister Fairfax smiles apologetically, "I am so sorry, but we do not normally allow soldiers, apart from officers of course, into the camp. Today, Lieutenant Drake made a special arrangement with our superintendent because, well to be honest, we are a little short-staffed."

The Sister's remarks cause Trooper Mojela to raise his brows as he bids his farewell, "Well then, Anna, it seems like goodbye. Ma'am. Sir."

Trooper Clarke holds the tent flap open and both men salute a harassed-looking Major Rogerson as he enters carrying a pile of precariously balanced papers.

I watch my two British soldier-heroes stride through the lines of white stones to where Lieutenant Drake awaits them next to a group of the tethered horses, and I hope that one day, I might repay their good deeds.

As well as seeming harassed, the camp superintendent is frowning when he returns. Major Rogerson doesn't look at me when he directs what he has to say to Sister Fairfax. He also ignores the other nurse who has appeared clutching medicine bottles and bandages, wide-eyed and out of breath.

"Well, Sister, I have spoken at length to Lieutenant Drake who has enlightened me as to the background of our new guest."

Sister Fairfax glances nervously at me and asks the superintendent, "Do we have enough information to categorise the patient, sir?"

It is now that the Major looks at me, and his eyes are steely. "Well, from what Lieutenant Drake has gleaned from his men, it appears that this young woman is a category U. And given her command of the English language and the hideout where she was found, it could be more serious. But there appears to be no firm evidence yet that she is a spy even if she is a prostitute."

The sister shakes her head, purses her lips and this time, it is she who avoids my gaze. Category U. A spy. A prostitute. What is he talking about? Where in God's name have they brought me?

"Category U, sir. What does that mean sir?" I ask.

Now he turns and looks down at me, "The letter U stands for undesirable. Do you understand that English word? U.N.D.E.S.I.R.A.B.L.E." His tone has lost all its previous kindness and he speaks to me as if I were a child, slowly and deliberately enunciating every word and letter.

"Yes, sir. I know the word sir. Of course, I know the word. But I do not understand, sir. Why am I an undesirable? What does it mean?"

He ignores me and looks at Sister Fairfax, "See that she is washed immediately and get rid of those stinking clothes." He addresses the other nurse abruptly, "Nurse Le Roux, this patient's rations will be the reduced quantity as usual for undesirables. No potatoes and half sugar and milk. Brief treatment, but only if necessary in the hospital then I think tent twenty-eight will be suitable. Room for one more in there."

Nurse Le Roux reacts for the first time and like Trooper Mojela, she speaks English with a clipped accent, "Sir, there are already ten people in tent twenty-eight. We put the Van de Berg family in there last night."

His smile is not warm when he speaks, "As I said, nurse, tent twenty-eight." He looks directly at me and there is no possible way that I can misinterpret the look of disdain upon his face. "You are an undesirable, miss, because you and the dead man you were brought in with have been assisting Boer commandos by providing food, shelter and goodness knows what else. These Boers certainly have appetites."

"But sir, I…"

They wait for me to finish my sentence, but I have nothing to say. The doctor's words break the silence.

"Well, miss…what is your surname?"

As I try to raise myself to a sitting position, my unfastened cap slips from my head. Nurse Le Roux picks it up off the ground and I notice that there is no groundsheet covering the floor of compacted earth. I feel a jolt of recognition. I know this earth. But who am I?

"I…don't remember, sir."

Sister Fairfax interjects. A sympathetic note has returned to her voice. "Possibility of trauma to the head, sir. Some kind of amnesia. We believe that her first name is Anna."

I nod. It does sound familiar.

"Anna. Well, Anna, do you have something to say that might refute the information about you that we have on such good authority?"

"I'm sorry, sir. I do not remember, sir."

"I see. Right. I thought not. Well, perhaps you will let me know when you do."

Then he barks another command at Nurse Le Roux who is gripping my kappie so hard that her sun-browned hands have turned white. "Get her head properly shaved. And throw that filthy bonnet away."

He does not deign to pay me any more attention and strides out, dropping the pile of papers onto my bed whilst issuing a curt instruction to Sister Fairfax that they be returned to him as soon as they are appropriately completed.

Once the superintendent is out of earshot, Nurse Le Roux flings my offending bonnet to the ground and turns her frustration towards Sister Fairfax.

"How can we put her in tent twenty-eight, Sister? You know it's not big enough for six people never mind eleven."

The sister stoops to retrieve my kappie and I feel comforted by her calm tone. "By the time Miss…Miss Anna is out of hospital, things may have changed. You

107

saw the state of the Van de Berg children last night." Her face wears an impenetrable mask. I see Nurse Le Roux's anger change to something else, something more like compassion. She nods, then indicates towards my bound legs and holds up scissors and a glass bottle.

"Right, Miss Anna, we are going to have to take those off so that we can treat your injuries."

It occurs to me that none of us know what exactly we will find under the tightly wrapped, blood stained bandages, but the way that I smell tells me that the superintendent is right about my clothes and I raise my face to Nurse Le Roux.

"Is that chloroform?" I ask her. Her look of puzzlement turns to one of interest, maybe even respect. Sister Fairfax intervenes.

"Is chloroform familiar to you?" she asks gently. "Have you been involved in nursing or midwifery?"

New tears well up, blurring their kind faces. I simply don't know. But somehow, I do know that chloroform will help with the pain.

"Half the usual dose?" asks Nurse Le Roux and the sister nods. Once the medicine has been administered, Sister Fairfax indicates that I need to be moved again.

"Let's put you onto your stomach now, Anna, so we can clean you up."

While they turn me gently over using two of the new sheets, I hear the timid scuffle of several pairs of feet and from my prone position, I can just make out the three native African girls who enter. Each one carries a bucket so full that the steaming grey water sloshes over the rim and is immediately consumed by the parched, compacted earth. Two are wearing tight fitting floral caps that fasten with bows under the chin, but one girl has the more elaborate kappie like mine, with its face-framing frills. None of the girls wear shoes, and the rest of their attire is made up of simple patched rags of indeterminate colour. They need no instruction to tip the hot water into the tin bath, which the two nurses have pulled close to my bed.

"We did boiled it, missus," the tallest helper volunteers proudly with a smile that I think could mend my broken body. Then I realise that they are all trying not to stare at what is left of my hair.

"Thank you, Tombi, Bessie, Helena. That will be all for now, girls."

Sister Fairfax waits for them to close the flap of the tent before she holds out her hand for the scissors. The sharp sound of metal shearing through fabric breaks through the blur of semi-consciousness before the bindings fall away and blissful air caresses my bare legs. It is then that I hear Nurse Le Roux gasp, but I can understand only some of the expletives that she utters in Afrikaans.

Chapter 14
Tent Twenty-Eight

They tell me in the camp hospital how lucky I am that the whiplash wounds have not become too badly infected. I am grateful for the wooden framework that has been constructed to keep the air flowing around my lower body and legs, but after more than a week of lying on my stomach, time interspersed with brief turns around the ward aided by a stick, I am sore and stiff. Although I do not remember how I came to have rope burns around my wrists and ankles, I am impatient for it all to heal so that I can get out of bed permanently. I see the doctor rarely, in fact I am certain that he avoids me, but I don't mind because I like it here. I like the sparse functionality of the large brick building and the familiar sound of the rain on the tin roof comforts me.

I have discovered from Nurse Le Roux that I am in the hospital of a temporary refugee camp outside Bloemfontein, set up by the British to care for groups of local women and children who have become destitute because of the war. There are some men here, she tells me, but they are mostly old or what she referred to as 'hendsoppers'. She gave me one of her incredulous looks yesterday when I asked, "What are hendsoppers?"

I could not discover who these mysterious people, who raise their hands for goodness-knows-what, are because she had to rush off. An increasing number of young children are being admitted to the other ward. "It's measles," she notified me grimly as she departed.

Nurse Le Roux deals with most of my needs and we talk often in Afrikaans. For some reason though, I do not always understand what she says to me. She laughs when I forget perfectly simple words and puts it down to my head injury and the amnesia.

"Don't worry," she tells me reassuringly, "your memory will come back, Miss Anna. I will keep saying prayers for you."

In trying to find the correct Afrikaans words during our conversations, I almost always recall the elusive word first in English or occasionally German, then search for a translation. My dreams are filled with many languages that pursue me through the night so that I awake on most mornings feeling confused and troubled, searching empty chattering voids for words and memories.

In addition to the whiplash injuries and my sprained ankle, I have a lot of pain in my most private parts. Nurse Le Roux is gentle and reassuring in her attention to this area, always erecting a temporary screen around my bed when she makes her examinations. The hospital is usually crowded, and some days there are sick men as well as women lying very close to each other and to me, so I appreciate her discretion. On one of the occasions when she is attending to my intimate place, we try and converse again, but this leaves her very frustrated. I think she is trying to tell me something but I cannot understand the Afrikaans she uses. Because I am feeling so much improved, I hope that she is asking me if I feel well enough to leave hospital and so I am keen to understand her question.

Unusually, Sister Fairfax is also on the ward that morning and she enters my makeshift cubicle at Nurse Le Roux's request. After a brief exchange in Afrikaans that I only half follow, Sister Fairfax pulls up a chair next to my bed and sits down. Sensing her hesitation, I open the dialogue, "I think Nurse Le Roux would like to ask me something," I say in English.

Sister Fairfax too has questions in her eyes.

"Actually, she was trying to tell you something, Anna, not ask a question."

The two nurses exchange glances, and Sister Fairfax commences in the calm tone I have heard her use to a mother who must be told that the condition of her sick child has deteriorated during the night.

"Anna, we have found considerable damage. Internal damage. There were lesions, damage consistent with a hard, sharp object. We have managed to treat them but that is why the injuries, why those particular injuries, are taking so long to heal."

I nod as if she has just told me that it might rain this afternoon. And then it hits me like a falling branch. The sound of breaking glass, the smell of whiskey, the horror of my nakedness against a rough stone wall and of Klaus running out of the door. But why would he hurt me?

"Klaus?" I sound surprised. "But why?" I begin to whimper quietly at first, then I am crying and soon the sobs become screams. "Why, Klaus, why?" I screech the question at him. I scream at the shocked faces of Sister Fairfax and Nurse Le Roux. I am out of control. My whole body shakes as if I am about to erupt. I cannot breathe. As my flailing arms send a jug of precious water tumbling to the ground, Nurse Le Roux reacts to my terror. She steadies my shaking body, holds me firmly and Sister Fairfax swiftly leaves my cubicle, reappearing within minutes. The doctor is with her, holding a syringe. As someone holds my hand, the sharp sensation of a needle pierces my distress. The morphine takes over and the trembling mirages of burnt out farmhouses, Klaus, and galloping commandos drift into oblivion.

"Here, Anna, have this," urges Sister Fairfax, holding out a cup which I take from her. She watches me closely as I drink the sweet milk. Handing back the empty vessel, I feel warm creamy sunlight filtering through the cloth walls onto my arms. Realising that I am no longer in the hospital, I recognise the place that I was brought to on my arrival at the refugee camp. A slight breeze wafts under the loosely fastened tent flap and cools the still heat of the afternoon. We are alone.

"I think you have remembered things, Anna," she says. "Do you want to tell me about them?"

"It's September. September 1900," I say and her pretty laugh encourages me, but before I can speak again, she responds.

"Actually, it is October now. But it was September when you came to us." Her face suggests that I might continue, "You mentioned Klaus. Was he the red-haired man in the wagon with you?"

I nod and she takes a deep breath.

"Was he your husband, Anna? Your man?"

This time I shake my head. "No. No, he was not. We didn't share a bed. I slept in the barn. But we were on a mission together."

110

Did I see the look of hope vanish from her eyes? What is it that replaces her look of concern? Then she asks another question.

"What was the mission, Anna?"

I try and think what we had been doing at the burnt-out farm. "I was helping him protect his family. His friends." I can tell straight away by her shuttered eyes that I have given the wrong answer.

"I see. Do you remember anything more?"

Misery sits in my heart and makes me heavy with tiredness, as in vain, I try to summon my forgotten past.

"No, Sister." I'm not sure she even hears my whisper as sleep sweeps over me. Somewhere, a barn door slams shut and a bolt slides into place.

I wake to a new day's faintly rosy dawn, my disturbed dreams broken by tinny metallic sounds just outside the tent accompanied by a ghostly moving shadow. As the nightmares slip away, the ghost reveals itself to be a tall stranger who carries an enamel mug and bowl inside of which rest a tarnished knife, fork and spoon. Aware of the threadbare nightdress that I have been wearing since my first day here, I quickly sit up and pull the blanket tight.

"There is no need to hurry, Miss Anna," his deep throaty Afrikaans words reassure me, so I thank him when he hands me the eating implements.

"Ah, so you speak English, Miss Anna? Are you from The Cape?" He switches easily from Afrikaans to fluid, if slightly abrupt, English.

I nod noncommittally, adding, "I've been helping a friend on the veldt," before explaining a little about my head injury without giving away how little I know about myself. It is his turn to nod, which he does whilst respectfully averting his eyes. I remember my shorn head and feel a flush travel up my chest to my cheeks.

"My name is Eric Jeppe." He covers my embarrassment for me, flicking his eyes to mine for a second as he explains what he does. "I work at the camp. Help with the rations and suchlike." His next sentence is reluctant and I begin to realise the stigma that is attached to my 'undesirable' status when he hands me a paper chit. "Your rations, miss. Sorry, miss but you aren't entitled to the potatoes you would get if you were just a refugee."

I study the brief list on the paper he has given me and follow the words as he confirms my daily entitlement.

"Sugar; half an ounce, salt; half an ounce, condensed milk; one twelfth of a tin, flour; half a pound, coffee; one ounce and half a pound of fresh meat, including bones and fat. Collect the meat at the time allocated for your tent at the building by the main gate each day. The rest you get on a Tuesday."

I frown, not knowing where the entrance to the camp is.

"The others will show you, miss. Oh, and miss, one more thing." Smiling, he goes to retrieve a larger bowl from where he left it outside the tent and points out a small bar of blue soap. Because of his expectant look, I sense that I should show some appreciation. So, I smile to convey my gratitude, because now I will be able to wash myself, and my clothes.

"All prisoners…refugees, are allowed to go to the river to bathe." He looks to make certain that my pleasure is what it should be. "Accompanied of course. Until the construction of the bathhouse is complete. Should be soon." He casts an uncomfortable glance towards the pile of folded clothes that lie on the chair by my bed, walks slowly to the tent door and speaks with his back to me, "I will return when you have dressed to escort you to your billet, miss."

On inspection, the collection of garments left by Sister Fairfax yesterday contains no corset, at which I feel both relief and concern. I do need some kind of underwear, but it has long been my belief that corsets are an unnecessary encumbrance. Happy at this new realisation about myself, I rifle through the assortment of linens in the hope that more memories might be triggered. No further revelations are forthcoming.

I discover a full-length sleeveless article with ties at the front that will pass for an undergarment. I hold it up and although the sun shines directly through, the lightweight gauze making it rather less than decent, at least its voluminous size means that it will be a generous fit. A faded, patched brown two-piece costume in cotton cambric is not so promising, because although it looks big enough to fasten around my waist, I guess that the skirt will be too short. Then I notice, pinned to the skirt, a piece of red felt in the shape of a letter 'U'. 'Undesirable' is what Major Rogerson called me. U.N.D.E.S.I.R.A.B.L.E.

Dressed in this outfit and with my shorn head, it perfectly describes how I feel. I almost laugh. Climbing off my cot, I search about for a bonnet and shawl or pelisse but find only a pair of dusty leather boots with worn out soles placed neatly under the bed. Their familiarity fills me with pleasure and thus encouraged, I quickly slip off my nightdress and gingerly begin to dress myself.

My new trousseau is much as I predicted, except that as well as being not quite long enough, the brown cambric skirt, which barely reaches the top of my boots, is tight around my middle. The overly snug bodice of the hand-me-down dress is a little short-waisted and effects a gap between bodice and skirt that reveals my shift beneath. Ruefully, I imagine that its previous owner was more Joy's size. Deliberations on my wardrobe stop dead in their tracks as an image of a petite copper-haired woman with a delicate nose, handing me a threaded needle as we sit laughing, flits across my mind and is gone like a butterfly. No amount of concentrated thought recalls this fleeting memory or brings any further elucidation, so with some difficulty and not a little frustration, I bend down to fasten the buttons of my boots and await the return of my escort, praying for the miraculous appearance of a shawl to cover the problematic brown dress and for anything at all to cover my shaved head.

The difficult journey across the camp with Mr Jeppe to my allocated billet is the first opportunity I have had to properly survey my surroundings. Progress is hampered by my inexperience at walking with a stick. I somehow manage to collide it at every other step with the white stones that mark the route between the many tents and fewer tin shacks, one of which I realise must be the hospital. The canvas structures, tin huts and sparse brick buildings are dotted across an arid landscape interrupted by small bushes, hillocks and rocks. In the crook of my right arm nestle, my scant possessions wrapped in my nightdress; two bowls, one cup, three pieces of cutlery and the precious blue soap. The grubby children who are occupied in a game with a piece of wood, and a group of women who appear to be washing clothes in a puddle, are oblivious to me as I walk past.

We thread our way around the larger oblong tents to one of the more modest round ones. Our reception on entering is mixed. Seated before the open front of the tent is a group of perhaps eight or more people. I endeavour to engage them with what I hope is a friendly expression. My stiff smile is not returned. I face a wall of blank hostility, all except for one woman who stands and liberates my bundle before her stern features are finally transformed by a grin.

"Welcome. I am Elinor van de Berg. These are my children," she says in Afrikaans.

Elinor places my possessions on a makeshift table covered with an intricately embroidered cloth and indicates towards a group of girls, some seated, others standing around what looks like a large leather valise. Their young, pale faces are rigid with fearful expectation. The costume of each displays a badge in the shape of now familiar scarlet letter 'U' stitched firmly to either hem or sleeve.

"Our brothers are collecting wood," explains one of the older sisters and she introduces her siblings. "My name is Rykie. I am fourteen. This is Martha, this Lenie, and Hester. Deneys and Jurg will be back soon. And this is Tombi. She helps look after us." I recognise the timid face of one of the native African girls who brought water for my bath when I first arrived at the camp. Acute embarrassment at my lack of head covering returns to me as Tombi peers from beneath the frills of her neat kappie. Before I have chance to respond, Mr Jeppe announces his departure.

"Right then. Meat distribution at four o'clock," and he moves off, unhampered by his invalid charge. He bids me a personal farewell in English as he leaves, "Goodbye, miss. And don't forget to stitch that patch onto your dress. Where it can be seen."

I study the red letter 'U', and the name of 'Hester' comes to mind. Hester Prynne. But I have no idea who she is.

Mrs Van de Berg waits until Mr Jeppe is out of earshot, "Filthy hendsopper!"

I am shocked to see this well-dressed dignified woman spit after him. She senses my reaction and smiles apologetically. "He should be fighting with the commandos like the rest of our men, not hiding here like a coward. Even the Kaffirs are fighting, even though some of them have gone over to the British – pah."

A murmur of agreement breezes through the group outside my new home. "After all, his wife is not in the camp so there is no excuse for him to be here."

I listen in to the ensuing conversation. I participate only when I know I will not give my ignorance away. It seems that Eric Jeppe has signed an Oath of Allegiance to the British, and like all those who have thus become traitors to the Boer cause, he is called 'hendsopper' in Afrikaans or 'hands-upper' in English. Many former Boer fighters have been driven to such treachery, according to old Mrs Jacobs, another of my new roommates. She defends the decision of those men who have come to the camps to care for sick wives and children. A younger woman, whose name I don't manage to ascertain, and I assume because of their striking similarity, is Mrs Jacobs' daughter, sides with her mother. The conversation has become increasingly animated and the argumentative talk of traitors and betrayal is making the children fidget. The tiniest girl, Hester, flutters about like an autumn leaf and might easily be carried away by the faint breeze that blows through the tent, has started to cry.

"Are there many camps?" I ask, in an attempt to change the course of the discussion.

Mrs van de Berg switches her attention from Mrs Jacobs.

"My dear girl. How discourteous of us. We have not even been properly introduced. What must you think of us?"

When the inevitable question is posed, I consider inventing a family name, but decide that because we will be living in such close quarters, truthfulness might prove to be the more worthy and sensible option. I imagine that in the coming weeks and perhaps months, we refugees and undesirables will become very well acquainted and life will be challenging enough without having to explain away lies about my past life. So, I tell them:

"I only remember my name is Anna, and I was brought in from the veldt. The British brought me here with a man who they shot. Dead. A farmer. From near Senekal. His name is…was…Klaus. They think I was his wife."

I pause and decide not to mention that I might have been his whore because the children are listening and because I know that I was not. I am sure that I was not. I continue, "But I am sure we were helping other Boers, some were injured…"

That I know things but cannot remember how I came to know them is difficult for my new friends to make sense of. But they listen avidly to what I can tell them of myself. Since I have not yet been able to collect my provisions, Mrs Jacobs' daughter, Martha Kies, whose husband is with a commando nearby, makes us all a most welcome and delicious brew of coffee. As I watch the ceremonial lighting of a small fire to heat the water, I learn that Mrs Kies' husband had initially signed the oath to the British but was later persuaded to re-join the fighting with General de Wet's commando. Mrs Kies lowers her voice at the mention of this man's name. An attractive bearded face framed with a mass of dark hair flashes across my mind and I flinch. She looks at me, waiting.

I hear myself say, "Stabberts Nek Pass."

She judges my reaction with a smile and a nod. She has no idea where her husband is now or even if he is alive. I have no idea how I know about General de Wet but I have been through Stabberts Nek Pass with Klaus and am sure de Wet was there too. Fragments return to me now and again.

We appear to have a small stack of firewood to one side of the tent and this is increased, although not by much, when the two Van de Berg boys return from their fuel-gathering mission. Curious at my arrival, they are intrigued about what they refer to as my funny accent and of course my shaved head, lack of bonnet and clothes that don't fit. This causes their younger sisters, Lenie and Martha to giggle until Rykie, who they clearly obey in all matters, scowls at them and reminds them of their manners. Little Hester breaks the uncomfortable pause that follows with an outbreak of her own giggling that neither she nor anyone else knows the cause of.

I believe that she too is amused by my state of disarray, for she thrusts a beautiful, though scratched, porcelain doll into my hands. Chootie is her name, dressed in a fine muslin summer dress belted with a blue silk ribbon. Her bonnet and attire are far more suitable for a lady than is my own tatty costume. Neither, it seems, is she forced to wear the red badge of the undesirables.

I am only allowed to hold the doll for a few seconds. Hester takes firm repossession of clearly the one toy the little girl managed to rescue when, she says, they were 'captured'. I am puzzled by this particular word to describe how she and her family came to be at Bloemfontein refugee camp, but before I can quiz her, Jurg thrusts a wooden gun at me – so realistic that I almost shriek.

Of the two brothers, it is clearly Jurg who sees himself as the man of our billet.

"You are just like my brother! Always rushing around with guns!" I say to him as he brandishes the weapon, even down to the blonde hair, but the image of my sibling fades so quickly that I wonder for a minute if I saw it at all.

"Do not worry, Miss Anna, I have an annoying brother too. He does not like guns."

Deneys, is nine and quite different from his older sibling. He is thoughtful and reserved. Inside our tent, the children delight in competing to show me their few special possessions and Deneys hands me his much thumbed, treasured leather-bound copy of 'Great Expectations' by Charles Dickens. At sight of the book, I experience another jolt of recognition. I find that I can entertain my eager audience with descriptions of the Kentish towns of Rochester and Chatham. Fleeting images of bow-fronted shops, narrow streets and shingle beaches flutter through my head as I speak, but I cannot tell if these are memories or just conjured places of my imagination.

I explain to Deneys that although I particularly enjoyed the stories of *Oliver Twist* and *David Copperfield* when I was his age, my favourite English author would have to be either Charlotte or Emily Brontë, but I can never decide which of the sisters' books I like the most.

"But why do streets in England need to have these cobbles?" asks Jurg.

"Why are the houses built so close together?" Deneys wants to know when I tell them about the narrow streets of the Brontë sisters' home village of Haworth in the northern English county of Yorkshire. He is particularly interested to hear about the miniature books written by the Brontë children and how the future authors were schooled by their father for much of their education. I make a mental note to tell him about Cowan Bridge, where two of Charlotte Brontë's older sisters died and which was turned into Lowood School in *Jane Eyre*.

I look up from my thoughts of the school where the young Jane experienced such hardship to find Mrs Van de Berg staring at me as if I were the ghost of Christmas Past. Fully expecting to be challenged about my knowledge of English towns and authors and wondering how I will explain it all, she surprises me instead with a gift. From beneath one of the two beds that occupy most of the space in our billet, she retrieves a parcel, wrapped in thick paper and tied with string. The bed is piled with thick, down-filled quilts and I have a sudden desire to wrap my aching limbs in their luxurious softness.

"Your need is much greater than my own, Anna," she says as her family gathers round in anticipation. Six pairs of eager eyes are upon me, whilst Mrs Jacobs and her daughter look from a respectful distance in the doorway. Mrs Van de Berg pats the bed on which she sits and so I follow her lead, resting my walking cane between us. My hands are trembling and it takes an age before the first knot of the package is undone. Five-year old Lenie, who I took to be no more than three because she is so very small and thin, rushes forward to help.

"Here, Miss Anna, use my scissors!"

I feel honoured because I know that the sewing case she proffers is the special thing she chose to bring from their home and has a 'secret' hiding place under the mattress, guarded, along with her knitting needles, as though it was a stash of precious gems. Lenie takes the scissors from their place between a leather tape measure and a tiny delicately etched thimble, and places them gently into my hand and waits.

Unlike me, the two boys are singularly unimpressed when the contents of the parcel are revealed. As I admire the gift of exquisite and carefully folded clothes, they are allowed to go and play outside with strict instructions to stay clear of the hospital and the possibility of contracting an infectious disease. Waves of gratitude threaten to render me speechless as I admire the garments, but I manage to stammer a few words.

"Mrs Van de Berg…" I begin.

"Elinor. Please call me Elinor," she says.

"Thank you. Thank you, Elinor, however can I repay you?"

"Anna, it is but a small thing to give you these gift," she says in English.

"Gifts, mama. It is these gifts, with an 's'," Rykie corrects her mother. "I was learning English and French before… Before we came here," she looks at me then casts her eyes down.

Mrs Jacobs gives one of her tutting sounds, "Girls have no need to go to school." Her lined face distorted into an unpleasant grimace, she purses her mouth, "Girls should be learning to cook and keep house. And you, miss, are practically old enough to be married."

Rykie stares at her feet and twists the pencil that hovers over the page of a notebook already crammed with words and figures, but she does not defend herself.

"Do you miss school?" I ask, and Elinor smiles fondly before answering for her oldest daughter.

"Rykie loves to learn. She is a very clever girl. History, languages, mathematics. It will not be long before we can go back to the farm and you can go back to your studies, my girl. Just wait and see, this wretched war will be over soon. Our commandos will see to it."

"Perhaps you would allow me to teach Rykie? I know English and some German," I offer. "In exchange for these. These gifts." I grin at Rykie, who spins around for her mother's approval, eyes bright.

"On one condition."

All of us look to Elinor Van de Berg who looks at me sternly. "That Anna puts on her new clothes at once."

Mrs Kies and Mrs Jacobs have shut the flaps of the tent. I carefully unwrap the clothing and feel the quality as I touch each article. There are an eight-panelled corset, a white chemise, a pair of drawers of the softest linen with ribbon ties, and a day dress that looks like it could be brand new. A crisp cotton apron completes the package. In the sweltering heat of the enclosed canvas tent, I wonder how long I will be able to wear the corset, beautiful as it is. Then I cast my ungrateful thoughts to one side and emerge to show off the exquisitely tailored gown of blue and grey striped silk faille that fits almost perfectly. My audience murmurs in unison when Elinor tells me what a striking figure I make, but I sense a touch of disappointment from the girls. It is then that Tombi steps forward from behind everyone else. When she unfastens the ties of her kappie, presents me with it and slips silently back to her place, she barely raises her velvet eyes. I hear Mrs Jacobs give a sharp intake of breath, then the slightest tutting sound before she mutters something unintelligible in Afrikaans, which is lost in the litany of appreciation that greets Tombi's generosity and which rises to a crescendo when I put on the bonnet. Mrs Kies is the first to put the murmurs and cries into a sentence.

"Why, my dear, you are a very picture! What a beautiful dress and kappie of course!" I do not miss the sideways glare that she passes to her mother.

Eight-year-old Martha has said little until this moment. She is the only person who hasn't told me yet what special item she brought from home and she regards me as though I were indeed an agreeable sight.

"Mama had that dress made just before we were captured."

That word again. I make a mental note, decide that now is not the moment to investigate and twirl around as best as I can with the assistance of my walking cane.

"Really, Elinor, it is too generous a gift," I protest later that afternoon as we stand together in the queue for our daily meat ration.

She merely smiles and says, "Truly, Anna, giving those clothes to you gives me more pleasure than wearing them. Besides, I have these," and she gestures to her own deep russet silk twill two-piece outfit.

"But they are new. And I think unworn..." I watch the dimple appear that accompanies her stunning smile.

"Martha is right. I had collected the parcel from my dressmaker the very day before we were taken. I wasn't going to leave it behind to be thrown on the fire by those British and their khaki Boers."

Since none of the children are with us, I decide to ask Elinor about the circumstances that led to her family being at the refugee camp.

"Refugee camp! Who has filled your head with such nonsense?"

"Why, that is what they told me when I was brought here. What other sort of place could it be?" I am puzzled at the ardour of her tone and the ferocity in her eyes. Because a group of women in the line ahead of us have turned to look, Elinor speaks more quietly now, her soft words still imbued with anger.

"We are prisoners, not refugees. It is true that some, a very few, people are here because they had nowhere to go, Anna. Perhaps they are refugees. But only because of the war."

I sense that this conversation will be a long one and I am glad of the long wait that will lead to our meat ration.

"Many farming folk who did not own their own homes found themselves here because there was no room and no food for them in the towns."

"But you have your own home, Elinor. You and your husband."

A shadow crosses Elinor's face and I wonder if she knows where her husband is, and if he is alive.

"We had a home. A beautiful home. The last time I spoke to my husband, he warned me to prepare to leave. That British soldiers would come." There is love and anguish in Elinor's eyes. "We built that house together, Johannes and I. Grew crops. Our first child Pieter was born there. All my babies were born there."

I take Elinor's rigid hand.

"Now Peiter is dead, murdered. The farm is a charred ruin. Who knows if we will survive this place?"

As our doleful parade creeps forward towards the piles of ration meat laid out on grubby tarpaulins, Elinor explains how she heeded her husband's warnings and buried some of the family heirlooms in preparation for what might happen. Beds, chairs and essential furniture were moved to the hall. Each day, the children wore two layers of clothing ready for a swift departure and stayed close to the farmhouse. As the days passed with no sign of British soldiers, hope grew that they might have been spared. The children began to play on the veldt again and the boys rode out on horseback. Food was plentiful, thanks to their flock of sheep, the pigs, and cattle. The larder was stocked with flour, coffee, and all kinds of vegetables grown on their land, which was tended by Tombi's father. Tombi's mother helped in the house.

"It was when Jurg returned alone that I knew something was wrong," Elinor says. "His horse, Caspar was injured and Jurg was in shock." She looks to the distant hills. "Neither of my sons had stopped when the British officer shouted at them to halt. So, the British shot Pieter dead and another volley hit Jurg's horse, Caspar. Jurg loved that creature."

My heart pounds as memories crowd themselves into my head. How I long to share the thrill of remembering.

"Oh, Elinor. I am so sorry."

But further words that might console my new friend do not come to me and although I think I was with a man called Klaus and we cooked and worked together on the veldt, I cannot explain why we were there.

The spent tears have left moist tracks down Elinor's cheeks.

"It was not long before they came for us. The British 'gentlemen' soldiers, their khaki Boers and the native turncoats." She faces me with her pain. "First, they shot Jurg's horse dead. 'You are all coming with us', they said. Then told us to gather our possessions, which we did. Beds, chairs, food, all kinds of clothes. Money. These." From her skirt pocket, she retrieves a small black velvet pouch. "This," she corrects herself. "My jewellery, diamonds, some money. They have not found it yet."

"You managed to bring your beds. Those in the tent?" I ask. "And the table and drawers?"

Elinor's laugh is bitter, "All the furniture in our tent belongs to Mrs Jacobs and her daughter. They let me use one of the beds just now because Lenie is sick. You have seen the tarpaulins piled on the ground?" Indeed, I have, as well as the hunks of meat hanging up to dry for biltong.

"Yes. Below the meat. And with some dirty old blankets," I say and she nods. "Those dirty old blankets are our bedding. And yours, Anna." She sees my shock and laughs again, this time almost amused, "Do you *still* think we are in a refugee camp, Anna?" Her question is rhetorical. "When we dragged our furniture and other belongings from the hallway and piled it outside, ready to be loaded onto the transport, I saw there was no transport. Just soldiers on horseback leering at my Rykie."

"Elinor, you do not have to talk about this," I say and grip her hand with mine.

"They threw oil over my things, Anna, then set light to them. My beautiful things. My grandmother's piano. The doll's house my mother gave to the girls before she died."

It is a scene that I wished I were not familiar with because I know what is coming next.

"They threw anything that was not burning on the bonfire back into the house. Martha had forgotten her special thing, her flute and ran to fetch it but she was too late. They grabbed her and made her watch them torch our house."

"But how did you get here, Elinor? It is a long way from your farm to Bloemfontein."

"They burnt our cart, because they said we would have no use for it where we were going. That my son, Pieter was a commando, that he had shot at them, and

118

because we had been harbouring him, they had orders to take us away and to destroy our farm."

"Your son, Pieter, wasn't a commando," my words are a statement, not a question.

"He was fifteen, Anna, and he did want to fight, but his father was adamant that he stays and look after me, the children, the livestock."

"His gun?" I ask.

"Hunting. Protection," she replies, desolate. "A trooper came with Pieter's body slung over his horse. They wouldn't let me bury him. No time, they said. They pointed at Tombi's father and told us that he would do it because he would be going to a different place."

"How so? Tombi is here. What happened to Tombi's father? What about Tombi's mother?"

Elinor explains that Tombi had been allowed to stay with the Van de Berg family but that Tombi's parents had been sent to the separate camp for the native Africans. She thinks it is nearby but has no idea where.

"My children were all crying. My house was burning. My son was dead. But we carry on, Anna. It is the human nature." She has been slipping between Afrikaans and English and I answer her in English.

"How right you are, Elinor. The human spirit is strong."

"With God's help, we persevere."

This is the first I discover of her inclination towards religion and I want to contradict her, but I don't know why.

"We walked for eight hours. If we couldn't keep up with the horses, one of the khaki Boers would crack a whip behind us. It frightened Martha. But it was worse for Rykie."

I think of Rykie's flawless complexion, white blonde hair and graceful figure.

"She is a very beautiful girl," I say.

"They all looked at her in *that* way. One of the soldiers rode right beside her and kept telling her that soon, she would be his wife. I insisted she was next to me when we slept that night on the open ground. We had no food or water until the morning as they had kept the food that we put aside to give to their troops."

By now, the much-decreased piles of ration meat, still buzzing with flies, are in sight but when we reach the head of the queue and it is finally our turn, all that remains is bones.

"Say nothing," Elinor warns me – too late.

I hand back what Mr Jeppe has given me, "Please, could I have some meat, sir?" I ask as politely as I can, given we have been standing in the heat of the sun for so long. With not a glance and no reply he tosses the bones I have returned to one side, studies Elinor's chit, looks at her, studies the list again, gives her a pile of bones not much bigger than what was offered to me and orders us to move on. Elinor's eyes are cast to the ground throughout the encounter. My friend pulls me away from Mr Jeppe before I have time to make any more foolish mistakes, and at her sudden, jerky movement, the meat bones rattle around in the tin dish. I realise that my outspokenness has cost not only my ration but has meant Elinor's family will go short today.

"There is much to learn here, Anna," she says and I have several silent minutes to consider her words as we make our way back to the tent.

Chapter 15
The Birthday Party

In my delight at Elinor's gift, I had forgotten to stitch the scarlet letter 'U', given to me when I came out of hospital, to my new clothes. The punishment for not indicating my status is one week's latrine-cleaning duty in the hospital, a task that seems strangely familiar, so I do not mind the work. As I start to get to know more people, I soon discover the ways of the camp and learn when to be invisible, when to speak up and how to flatter Mr Jeppe in English so that our ration, albeit bones, will at least have enough meat to make a decent broth.

It transpires that because our tent houses 'Undesirables', we are always last in the queues for food. Somehow, Mrs Jacobs and her daughter have managed to bring meat with them and it hangs, mouth-wateringly tempting from ropes strung up high inside the tent. Drying meat in this manner is not at all approved of by the British who consider it to be unhygienic, but Mr Jeppe enjoys the bribes given to him and we believe that it is he who has convinced the camp superintendent to allow Mrs Jacobs and Mrs Kies to continue with this practice of making biltong. On special occasions, Mrs Kies lowers one of the hunks of meat and then holds it steady for her mother to cut off strips. We greedily and gratefully devour these.

The first such day is soon after my arrival, in mid-October. We usually know not to call attention to ourselves by flouting or breaking the rules, but the younger children are used to an active, noisy and joyful outdoor life and find the constraints and strict bell-driven camp timetable difficult to understand. Today, there is much distraction for the officials. A continuous stream of ox wagons pulls up at the perimeter fence to disgorge their cargoes of scrawny, coughing, wailing waifs and their distressed mothers. Nurse Fairfax, who was sent away after she became ill with typhoid, has been replaced with an erect, angular English woman in her forties who speaks no Afrikaans. As Jurg begins to scrawl huge black letters across a banner, I notice the new sister with hands on hips standing next to the camp superintendent who directs the mass of human traffic. Bare-chested, sun-burnt arms and faces in stark contrast to their white torsos, unfamiliar British soldiers shake out rolled-up packages and create waves of dusty canvas as they launch more tents.

We watch Jurg as he clambers on the valise outside our tent, facing the main thoroughfare and hangs the banner that he has borrowed Rykie's paints to inscribe: 'Happie Birthday to President Kruger!' He has been getting on so well with the English lessons he and his younger brother share with Rykie, that I don't have the heart to correct his spelling of happy and it takes observant Mrs Jacobs, who does not particularly like the spirited Jurg, to draw everyone's attention to what he has used to make the birthday greetings flag.

"Why, Anna, I do believe that is your old underwear!"

With horror, I recognise the thin voile of my old sleeveless shift and I reach up with my cane to try and dislodge the offending article, but Jurg has tied tight knots and his homage to the Orange Free State's president flies steadfastly.

Hair blowing in the wind, a young woman approaches the throng that we have become and she presents a wrapped parcel to Elinor.

"Hello. I am Emmie. Here is a small contribution to the festivities."

Our gasp at the sight of what looks like a fruit cake is louder than the wind and as I help cut it up into tiny pieces, Elinor whispers that Emmie Fraser is the sister of M. T. Steyn, President of the Orange Free State, so we feel doubly connected with the Boer cause. I want to tell Emmie that I know her brother, but I do not mention the fact because I cannot remember where I met him.

"Watch out for glass in the sugar!" Mrs Jacobs sifts through the new ration of sugar until she pronounces, "One batch they didn't manage to tamper with. Damned British!" Her glee is so infectious that soon, we are all laughing at Mrs Jacobs' hair-raising tales of foiled plots; sugar contaminated with glass, maggot-infested biscuits, bread made with sawdust. Acts of revenge, she claims with fierce conviction, carried out by the British and foiled by the Boer women of the camp. In cheerful mood, we are eating some celebratory biltong with our coffee and cake when the camp superintendent's voice interrupts the party, "Goodness me, it is an afternoon birthday tea party!" He nods genially in our general direction. "To whom does that belong?" his playful tone encourages more giggles from the girls and when Lenie cries, "It is Miss Anna's underwear!"

We all laugh some more.

"Cut it down," he orders, his face inscrutable.

Mr Jeppe quickly slices through the ties and is rewarded by a curse from Mrs Jacobs. The superintendent turns to me, "You will come to my office tomorrow morning at eight." With that, he nods peremptorily at the other women and he and Mr Jeppe make haste towards the ramshackle rows of new tents and the ox-pulled carts full of flapping humanity that gather at the camp's perimeter. I have no idea where all these new arrivals will go. There are so many.

Jurg is deeply apologetic that I am the one to be admonished for his misdemeanours, but I reassure him that the superintendent did not appear to be angry. We then discuss the spellings of 'angry', 'happy' rather than 'happie', and the other English words 'party', 'comedy' and 'fly', at which point, we decide to stop since there have been too many of those wretched creatures buzzing around of late and besides which it is starting to rain, which means we will have to borrow Mrs Jacobs' umbrella to queue for the meat.

I reach out in the black dark towards the quiet sobs that wake me during the night. Instead of the scratchy blanket, my hand finds a sodden mass that is Martha's bed. Mere drops at first, the rain has invaded our canvas home and when we try to light a candle, the wind grabs the flame and extinguishes the momentarily illuminated scene of chaos. I shine a lantern onto the water that courses down the tent walls onto the tarpaulin sheets and blankets that are our beds. After weeks of drought, the rock-hard earth is impermeable and we are soon trying to rescue ourselves plus anything that is not soaked from the small lake we now flail around in.

"Mama!" shrieks little Hester as she slips in the mud and drops her doll, Chootie, who becomes submerged.

"Here, Hester, I have you!" I grab the child, but her doll slips back into the mud.

"Want Mama! Want Chootie!" shrieks Hester again.

Mrs Jacobs and Mrs Kies are in one bed and Elinor cradles Lenie who is sick in the other. Rykie, Deneys and I hoist the little ones up, shouting instructions in the flickering dark above the howling wind, the crashing rain, and Martha's sobs.

"Hold the flaps down!" urges Jurg. "Don't let the wind get hold!"

Deneys and Rykie take one set of flaps as the canvas balloons out in the gale as though to set sail. I deposit the soaking, upset masses that are Hester and Martha onto their mother's bed, find Chootie, and help Jurg to hold down the second set of door flaps. As we battle the elements, sounds of screeching, creaking and shouting come and go with the rise and fall of the wind, then gradually subside into the slushing, slopping slurs of the broken dawn.

When we venture outside, we are met with a scene of devastation. All around are the flattened, mud-crushed tents of our neighbours. The reluctant sun drags itself up and through the shocked silence, periodical stifled sobs and groans can be heard. Ours is not the only structure still standing. Many of the tents occupied by the men, either soldiers or hands-uppers, were cast about at rakish angles by the gale, but appear to be unscathed. Bedraggled, our nearest neighbours, the Roos family, poke around their plot. Disconsolate, they lift and shake wet ropes, pull up wooden pegs, and look first to one another then up into the sky for divine guidance. The two sets of twin boys pay no heed to their elderly grandparents and splash gaily around the new baby who has been propped up in an old wooden crate. Desperation on her face, Mrs Roos, whose husband is fighting with his commando, sees Mr Jeppe and some of the other hands-uppers as they stand around a small fire nearby, coffee brewing and cigarettes lit, their tent intact. She makes her way over to the group, who each turn their backs to her.

"Stepan, please help us?" she says pointedly to one of the men who stands, hands on hips, facing her.

"Go call your husband back from his commando so he can look after you. Or mend it yourself."

I grab Jurg as he darts past me, a revengeful look on his face, and shake my head. "Let's go and *help* Mrs Roos. It's better that way." I turn back for the nods of approval that I know will come from Elinor, Mrs Kies and Mrs Jacobs, before I let go of Jurg's arm and follow his not so cautious steps across the mire.

Through her tears, Mrs Roos tells me that in earlier times, Stepan, the hands-upper who refused to help, was on commando with Mr Roos and that many a time, she would get up from her bed in the middle of the night to provide refreshment for him or tend his minor wounds.

"Where is that friendship now?" she wants to know. But we are unable to answer because this war has turned kith against kin, neighbour against neighbour and I am ever more uncertain as to who is the enemy.

Not even half way through our rescue mission and hungry now for breakfast, I remember my eight o'clock appointment with the camp superintendent. Bitterly, I realise that by attending the meeting, I will miss the weekly distribution of milk, flour, coffee and sugar. If I choose not to be at the superintendent's office and go instead to the ration queue, I may bring more trouble to Elinor and the others. Full of conflict and conscious that it's unlikely he will be given my rations, I ask Jurg to stand in line for me. Then I straighten my mud-splattered clothes and head across the camp.

"You are late," the superintendent raises his attention from the piles of paper and unopened mail that cover his desk. Folded neatly next to an elaborate inkwell is Jurg's offending birthday tribute to President Kruger. Major Rogerson scrutinises my face while he dismisses the man who brought me here.

"Thank you, Sergeant. You may leave us."

I wait for his next words but he casts his eyes down and continues to write. The hands of the old grandfather clock behind his desk move slowly and the minutes clunk by. The damp cold from my clothes, heavy with rain and mud, numbs my body through to its core. After the passage of a quarter hour has been marked three times by the clock, I speak.

"Sir, I am sorry that I was late, but the storm…"

His voice rises to drown out the nine chimes that tell me I have been standing here for fifty-five minutes, "You will speak when spoken to. When I am ready. Is that clear?"

There is a knock on the door and the rich aroma of coffee reaches me before the sergeant enters with a steaming coffee pot, jug of hot milk and a plate covered with a napkin. Some minutes later, having eaten thick slices of buttered bread, Major Rogerson sips his drink, decides that he has waited long enough to admonish me, picks up my folded undergarment and spreads it out on his desk.

"Happie birthday to President Kruger. Explain," he orders.

Cold, overwhelmed by tiredness and distracted by the heady scents of coffee and freshly baked bread, my response does not come quickly enough.

"I am teaching the Van de Berg children to speak English. Jurg didn't know the correct spelling of happy." My flat, lame tone is not what I planned for this confrontation.

"And pray tell me why, exactly, are you teaching English to these children?"

I am puzzled by this question but it is easy to answer.

"Why, sir, they are missing their schooling and I speak English, German and Afrikaans, and they want to learn, sir. And their mother gave me these clothes so I wanted to thank her." Holding out what was Elinor's beautiful silk gown and is now a ripped, wet mess, I offer a smile to go with my inarticulate words.

His face is like ice when he answers.

"I see. You would not, I suppose be teaching them English so that they too can become enemy spies? And you invited the sister-in-law of a prominent Boer general purely by chance, I suppose?"

"We didn't invite Emmie, sir, she just arrived with some cake. We had not planned the party. It just happened."

Then I think back to the British soldiers who delivered me to this place and who put the idea into the superintendent's head that I might be a spy.

"I am not a spy, sir. I am teaching the children because they desire to learn."

He takes the birthday banner and moves around from behind his desk to stand next to me. He is so close that I can smell his oily pomade and feel his hot buttery breath. He shakes out the garment and holds it up to me.

"Then your teaching is not very good, is it? Next time, perhaps he will spell his treacherous messages correctly."

I nod, praying that Jurg won't be next in line for interrogation.

"This may remind you of your other profession. Put it on." He thrusts the garment at me.

"Put it on, sir?"

He smiles for the first time. "It is no use pretending that you do not understand English." He waits. "Put it on. Take those wet things off. All of them. Now." I look around, not quite believing what he wants me to do. "I will be back in five minutes. Do not test me on this."

The door clicks shut and is followed by the heavier double click of a lock being turned. I try the external door. It is locked and there is no key. The two open windows that lead out onto the main thoroughfare through the camp are too small to offer an escape route and anyway, where would I go? I begin to unbutton my dress.

On his return, he is accompanied by one of the older native South African women who I have seen washing the officers' clothing. The defaced undergarment is, as I remember, quite translucent, so I hold all my filthy damp clothes in front of me, ready to retain at least a modicum of modesty as I walk back to my tent.

"Give those to her," he commands impatiently and when I do not obey him, he takes them, thrusts them to over to the woman, and instructs her to take them to tent twenty-eight. "You have wasted quite enough of my morning."

I understand his words to mean that he wishes me to leave and I move to follow the other woman but he tells me to wait.

"You will stand outside my office until I bid you to return to your quarter."

I move towards the internal door.

"Not that one."

He retrieves a key from his desk drawer and moves to the external door between the two windows.

"I cannot stand there, sir. This garment is not decent." My arms are crossed against his gaze, but he isn't looking at me.

"That is an order. If you choose not to do as I say, the families in tent twenty-eight will have their rations stopped for one week."

The passing traffic is relentless as people come and go. In their endeavours to sort out the storm damage and accommodate new inmates, there is a fevered urgency in the camp. My boots soon begin sink into the rain softened and much trampled ground outside the superintendent's office, but I fear that if I move, I will only draw more attention to myself.

"Give us a birthday kiss, missus!" is one of the more polite comments that come my way from the passing soldiers for whom a scantily dressed woman is an instant distraction.

I try and shrink closer to the wall, but soon the men begin to cross the thoroughfare to get a closer look and some risk a quick prod. It is at the height of my mortification that I see Mrs Jacobs and Mrs Kies' shocked faces as they silently observe my predicament from across the way. I stare back, willing them to give me one of their voluminous shawls so that I might hide my shame, but they whisper conspiratorially and move on. Who can blame them for not interfering and incurring the wrath of the superintendent?

I pray that none of Elinor's children or the twins next door will walk this way. I know exactly how long I have been standing here because I can just make out the chimes of the superintendent's grandfather clock, and it is at precisely eleven o'clock that the doctor emerges from one of the hospital buildings, laden with files and heading in my general direction. In the week since I last saw him, he is much altered. Hollow cheeks, grey skin, stooped shoulders and slow gait have replaced his previously purposeful demeanour and flushed countenance. I look down, hoping that he will be too distracted to notice my disgraceful state. But he is not.

"What on earth?" his exclamation draws more attention.

His pace picks up and he roughly opens the front door of Major Rogerson's office and takes me with him.

"What is the meaning of this, superintendent?"

The files that he throws down jettison their contents across the neatly organised surface of the superintendent's desk. The doctor thrusts his jacket around my shoulders, sits me on a chair and continues to berate my persecutor.

"This woman is not one of your troopers, Major. She has not long left hospital and with this kind of treatment, she will be back there imminently. As if we don't have enough sick people here." He gestures towards the scattered files of patient notes.

Full of self-righteous indignation, Major Rogerson explains my multi-lingual misdeeds and stands with arms folded, but it is Doctor Brown who decides on a course of action. "This woman. Anna. Will come and work for me in the hospital. Sister Fairfax's departure, typhoid and the outbreak of measles among the children have left us short-staffed. We are admitting more patients each day. The new sister speaks no Afrikaans and most of the children do not speak English. Anna will act as translator for Sister Pelly and will help generally on the wards."

My heart is beating at least five times faster than the clock and I wait for the superintendent to refuse such an outrageous proposal. At the chime that signals it is fifteen minutes past eleven, Major Rogerson straightens the files on his desk, says, "As you will, Doctor Brown," opens the door and we leave, as if we have shared a convivial cup of morning coffee having decided who will play the church organ for the Sunday service.

"Anna, thank the Lord!" Sister Pelly greets me when I arrive for work the next morning. "I could have kissed Doctor Brown when he told me!" She throws her arms around my neck, kisses me instead and then, decorum recovered, leads me onto the ward. Judging by this over-excited response and by the sour odour of her breath, I guess that she has probably been drinking.

I cannot explain to him or Sister Pelly how I know the best way to treat the mouth ulcers of those poor souls suffering from the typhoid fever whose lips are stiff and caked with sores. When I have finished seeing to twenty or thirty tremulous pairs of lips, the same number of quivering tongues and the lesions in the mouth that accompany them, exhaustion overtakes me. I stop to take stock of how many more such patients await my administrations, to discover Sister Pelly watching me, transfixed. Her eyes, her stance, everything about her exudes gratitude and surprise in my direction.

"It is the most trying work, Anna. There is coffee at the nurses' station. Please, help yourself."

And thus passes my day, nursing the afflicted, translating the trembling words of the sick children from Afrikaans to English for Sister Pelly until my presence is requested in Doctor Brown's office so that, as we had agreed, we might assess my suitability for the role he has so rashly advocated me for.

"I hear that you have quite a remarkable ability with the typhoid patients, Anna."

In Doctor Brown's quiet, unassuming tone, I hear relief and perhaps a question about my previous experience. Another question that I cannot answer. "And your talent does not stop with nursing, Anna. Several mothers have been to see me." I do not understand what he is telling me.

"Doctor?"

He laughs. "To ask me to thank you, Anna. To say thank you for helping calm their little ones when they couldn't understand Sister Pelly. It seems that I should thank Major Rogerson after all for making you stand outside his office in that ridiculous outfit like a naughty schoolgirl. Otherwise I would not have found out about your skills as a nurse and a translator."

It is my turn to smile now. Yesterday seems a long time ago. The doctor and Sister Pelly agree a schedule that I am happy with and, although my foot is practically recovered and my walking stick has been dispensed with, I limp back to tent twenty-eight. I am very much looking forward to seeing everyone and telling them about the day I have had and my new role at the hospital.

When I arrive, the children are jumping around outside, excited not to see me, but to tell me the news. It seems that Doctor Brown has arranged the delivery of three new mattresses plus clean blankets and that night's sleep is the best and longest I have had at the camp. Mrs Jacobs and her daughter remain thankfully discreet and say nothing either to me or to Elinor's family of yesterday's events.

Chapter 16
A Surprise

After several weeks, the routine settles down for the inhabitants of tent twenty-eight, but we cannot escape the sickness that pervades the camp. Lenie's condition has worsened, little Hester has also become very poorly with measles and after many heated exchanges on the subjects of 'bad British medicine' (Mrs Jacobs and Mrs Kies) and 'benefits of careful nursing in a controlled environment' (me), I have persuaded Elinor to allow both her daughters to be treated at the hospital. We have more volunteer helpers, which means that although the work is exhausting, at least we can take a few hours off to sleep each night.

It is just before Christmas, and although there has been no repeat of the October gales, the dust storms coat everyone and everything with a fine layer of grit and the temperatures soar during the day. The dreary task of washing our clothes has become more backbreaking, what with the children's clothes becoming even filthier much faster than usual and with the added complication of the lack of water due to the drought. Rykie and Martha accompany us as usual, laden with dirty laundry but once the troughs are half-filled with the water we have been saving all week from our tent's two bucket a day allowance, instead of staying with us, they are directed back to the tent by their mother.

"Look after the little ones. You know they are not so well today. A little hymn singing might help." She watches them skip off and gives a jaunty permissive wave when they turn back, not quite believing their luck.

"Rykie is learning fast."

I press down the first batch of clothes from the laundry mountain until it is submerged in the shallow water. The water turns cloudy as dried mud leeches from the boys' shirts.

"You are a good teacher, Anna. I wonder if this is what you did before."

I hesitate, because I have not been entirely truthful with my friend. Wash days and queuing for rations have given us many opportunities to get to know one another. Elinor has been happy to talk about her life, her husband, Johannes, and the children I have come to love. Mostly, I have just listened. Not because I have nothing to say about my own history, but because it seemed easier not to reveal what I do remember. Elinor's questions about my previous life have been guarded and sensitive because she thinks it is my inability to remember that causes me distress. But as the weeks have passed, much of my time with Klaus on the veldt has become clear in my mind and in truth, I am a little ashamed and frightened by what I recall.

"Tell me about Klaus," she says, and I wonder if she has been reading my thoughts. I think carefully before answering.

"What do you wish to know?"

She becomes almost girlish. "What was he like? Was he handsome?" The vision of Klaus's wild mane and chest length beard as red as Rowan berries makes me smile.

"Perhaps handsome is not quite the best way to describe Klaus. He was very tall. And big," I remember. "His hands were the size of dinner plates. But even though he pretended to hate the colour of his hair and said only girls should have red hair, secretly he liked it."

"What were you doing with him, Anna? Were you living as man and wife?"

I drop the last remaining precious sliver of soap into the water and swing around to face her.

"No, Elinor, no! Certainly not. We helped his wife and children escape after their farm was burnt by the British."

"Are you sure, Anna? Why were you with him? What brought you together? What were you doing together I mean?"

"We were helping the Boer commandos. Once his family were safe, we used burnt-out or deserted farms to provide shelter for the soldiers. We hunted and caught hare and small deer. I cooked. I nursed some of them. I met President Steyn and General de Wet."

"Did his wife visit?"

"No, it was too dangerous. Klaus thought it best that she stayed with the children – with all the other families in the Basin. We were all together at first and then they went…" I stop mid-sentence because in truth, I cannot remember why they left, so I invent a reason. "They went to stay where Klaus thought they would be safer…" I know my words sound limp.

"Did you fall in love with him?"

Did I? It is a question that has remained unanswered in my quest. A dim, foggy image of a long, passionate kiss hovers for a second or two before Elinor brings me back to reality with a thumping question.

"Anna, did you lie with Klaus?"

I smell the whiskey. Feel the pain of the whip. The thirst. Klaus running away. I reject the memory.

"Lie with him! How can you think that? When we were on the veldt or in the laager, I slept inside the wagon and he slept underneath it. If we were at a farm, I would sleep in an outbuilding." I push away the memory of the great barn door slammed shut and the clang of the bolt. Surely, he didn't lock me in there. Did he?

"Anna, I believe that you have lain with Klaus because I see that you are with child."

Elinor holds me by my arms.

"Anna, you are going to have a baby."

"With child! Have a baby!" I am repeating her words for the second time.

"My dear, Anna, I have had enough babies to recognise the signs. Just look at you! Like a rose in bloom."

My expanding waist. No monthly menstruation. New hair growing back more thick and shiny than ever… I have put the increase in my girth to the improved rations since I joined Doctor Brown's team. Many women do not menstruate at the camp and I thought I was no different.

"Well, my dear, Anna, it seems as though we might expect a flame-haired baby in our tent within a few months!"

I look at Elinor. I put a hand on my belly. I am with child. I am expecting Klaus's baby. I am speechless.

Chapter 17
Not a Glengarry Bonnet

Elinor sits face to face with the delicate porcelain doll Hester adored. Impassive, Chootie stares back, nonchalant. Insolent. I resist the urge to throw the wretched doll who has no right to outlive the little girl who loved her across the hospital ward. I want to smash that shiny white smugness into a thousand pieces. Elinor picks up Chootie, strokes the doll's smooth face and places it next to her little daughter. The two sets of pale effigies side by side, their souls already departed to a happier place. Not that I concur with Hester's mother on her idea of the happier place, because I do not believe in heaven. That Hester is no longer suffering on earth is a good enough reason for me, except that if only the hospital were not so crowded, she might not have died. If only there were more than the three of us who attend to the sick. If only we had more and better water. If only the Boer mothers did not insist on keeping their children out of hospital until it is too late. If only.

Elinor raises her Madonna-like face heavenwards, eyes glowing and says,

"She is with God now."

I plant my feet wide apart, stand mute behind my friend and rest my hands on her shoulders. *What God? How could any God allow such suffering as is here? Surely, careful nursing and medical attention are worth a thousand prayers. Why can't these men just stop fighting? What is the point of this wretched war? Please God, let there be no more anguish for Elinor. Please don't let Lenie die too.* I gently stroke my friend's hair and study her dead daughter's waxen features. The vague whisper of a smile sits upon the child's still lips because she is happy to be reunited with her brother, Pieter, in heaven and because Chootie can go there too.

"What do you mean we have run out of coffins?"

It is later that same day and I fix my disbelief on the man before me. Eric Jeppe shifts his weight from one foot to the other.

"I am sorry, Nurse Anna, but as well as the Van de Berg girl, there have been four other deaths already today and ten yesterday."

Ten. Sadly, he is right. The measles epidemic is spreading its tentacles and grasping any child who dares to get in its way.

"What are we going to do about it? Can we get more coffins from the town?"

"The superintendent says to use blankets."

"Blankets! But we need them for the patients. The live ones."

My heart pounds against my rib cage and the heat rushes up to my cheeks. Does my baby kick in protest inside me? I steady myself against the desk.

"Miss Anna. Nurse Anna, I think you need to sit down."

"There is no time to sit down, Mr Jeppe." I wipe the sweat from my forehead and push damp tendrils of hair behind my ear.

"At least have a drink. Some coffee. I will bring the blankets."

I watch him wade through the detritus of the ward as he circumnavigates beds, people, and sacks of unwashed bedding. Then I steel myself to face the mothers and plan how I will tell them that their children will be buried in a mass grave wrapped in old blankets.

We have a new superintendent, Captain Holmes, who I have observed from time to time when he has visited the hospital going about his business, either deep in conversation with the Doctor or joking with our new orderly, for whom we have the superintendent to thank. Captain Holmes calls Dr Brown, Nurse Le Roux, and me to his office at the end of the second week of January. It is the first occasion I have had to visit the place since Dr Brown rescued me from the punishment meted out by Captain Rogerson after the ill-fated celebration for President Kruger's birthday in October and the room seems different somehow. In the stillness, I realise that the room's new tranquillity is because the grandfather clock with its incessant time tolling is gone and I relax into one of the leather chairs. After the mayhem of the ward, the peace soothes our exhaustion and we bask in its luxury with only the sound of coffee being poured to disturb the calm. Captain Holmes passes the cups around before his announcement snaps us back to attention.

"It appears that Bloemfontein Camp will be the first port of call for that bloody woman."

"Sir?" Dr Brown is as baffled as the rest of us.

"Miss Emily Hobhouse. Seems like she wants to interfere with the running of the camps. Make a report to the government. She's got the Liberal Party and the Manchester Guardian behind her." Captain Holmes clatters his empty cup onto its saucer. "What's more Sir Alfred Milner and Lord Kitchener have given their permission!"

I have no idea who any of these people are and my sideways look at Dr Brown is rewarded by an answer.

"Milner and Kitchener – the British army chiefs," he says and then turns back to the superintendent. "How can we help, Captain Holmes?"

"I believe Nurse Anna can help us with Miss Hobhouse's visit, Doctor."

"Anna has done a remarkable job at the hospital, considering the circumstances. I am sure she will be only too delighted to assist, but as you must realise, we are very short staffed."

"Quite so, quite so. Nurse Anna, will you act as escort for Miss Hobhouse during her visit with us? Apparently, she has no knowledge of the language of these wretched people. As you indeed do. I understand that you are an able translator." He regards me directly for once. There is a pause as he deliberates his next words. "I should be most obliged. And grateful."

A sudden knock at the exterior door heralds the late arrival of Sister Pelly and provides a moment where I am not the source of everyone's attention, so have time to think. Sister Pelly has been tending to the younger set of Roos twins, who have been in the hospital since before Christmas and whose condition had begun to improve until the heatwave of the last week seemed to trigger a relapse. Her bloodshot eyes dart around the room, alight on me, and she shakes her head in a small but vigorous movement. She flings herself onto the empty chair and uninvited, pours a cup of lukewarm coffee. She adds a surreptitious dash of something from the silver flask she thinks we do not know she keeps in her apron pocket.

"Well, nurse?" Captain Holmes curbs his irritation at Sister Pelly's entrance and head slightly tilted, stares me into submission.

"Yes, sir. Yes, Captain. I am happy to be of assistance."

"Thank you, nurse. I am indeed in your debt."

At which point, we are dismissed and the situation has to be explained to an unhappy Sister Pelly as we make our way across the bustling thoroughfares back to the hospital.

Unlike me, both my colleagues have read some recent English newspapers and seem to know something about Miss Emily Hobhouse.

"She seems very pro-Boer to me. What does she think she can achieve, I wonder?"

I can see that Sister Pelly is determined to side with Captain Holmes who seems to have scant regard for the British woman's humanitarian quest to improve things for the camp's residents. Given the conditions that we all inhabit and which have deteriorated so badly since I first came here in September last year, I'm surprised at her vociferous tone and raise my eyebrows at her.

"I'm sorry, Anna, I know you are one of them but really we have enough difficulties to overcome without having to justify ourselves to some pacifist zealot."

As usual, Doctor Brown assumes the role of peace-maker and before I make a comment that I will surely regret, he adds the voice of reason to our conversation. "There is much that might be improved here. We all know this, including Captain Holmes."

I nod, thinking how the Captain has recently secured a second orderly to help on the wards, and although being an 'undesirable' remains a status, the badge is now an invisible one thanks to our kindly superintendent.

"It is my belief, sister, that we might use Miss Hobhouse's visit as a lever." He stops and so do we. His frustration and anger, evident in his drawn, solemn face is cool, controlled, curt.

"You know and I know that the situation here is untenable. It was different when there were only three hundred people in the camp. The three of us, two orderlies and a handful of inexperienced volunteers are simply not enough to provide medical care for nigh on two thousand. And before we know it, winter will be upon us and who can tell what the rain and the cold will bring to all these people living in tents? They are not soldiers; they are not prepared for this kind of life."

I think hard before I make my point. "Not even soldiers should have to live like this, sir."

The Roos twins and Hester are buried later that same day. By some miracle, Eric Jeppe has found coffins for them all and although I do not have time to attend the burial, I say my farewell to Hester before the lid is closed on her too-short life and I watch the sombre column disappear towards the camp's graveyard, in the certain knowledge that very soon her hand-carved tombstone will stand sentinel with the many others in a sun-drenched brigade at permanent attention in the red dust.

My body is showing small outward signs of impending motherhood and I have no idea when my baby will come. Elinor carefully examines and feels my belly and is confident that I will give birth in late May or June. Doctor Brown has no experience of obstetrics so defers to Sister Pelly who, after an examination, agrees with Elinor. Aware of my state, Eric Jeppe not only gives our tent more meat these days but has located some of the herbs requested by Mrs Jacobs. A peppery green tea is made from them and I need to hold my nose to mask the bitter undertone whenever I gulp it down. Since I started to drink this murky infusion, the nausea that has plagued me for weeks has gone and I feel truly robust and healthy.

Elinor has made it clear to me and to everyone that I was married to Klaus and that he is the father of my child. As soon as the war is over, she says, she will help me find my family and the baby will be well cared for. Surely by then, my memory will have fully returned, she says encouragingly. Although I have reminded Elinor that Klaus had a wife and family, she never mentions them and I realise that it is in my future interest and that of my unborn child to follow her example. So, I gradually become used to the idea of being a widow which seems infinitely less problematic than being an unmarried mother and mistress of someone else's dead husband.

If Captain Holmes has been told of my condition and the situation, he does not refer to it but there is a definite thaw in our previously cool relationship. Whether his initial opinion of me was coloured by his predecessor's views I know not, but we have met twice since I accepted his request to help with Miss Hobhouse's visit. His willingness to listen to my views about how the camp should be run means that I am now much more kindly disposed toward him.

Miss Hobhouse is due to arrive at the camp tomorrow and we are to discuss the final arrangements for her visit. Captain Holmes pours tea for us both and passes a plate of biscuits. The familiarity of this puzzles me, and the fleeting image of sitting in a shady garden with an elderly woman flutters away as I try in vain to hold on to a delicious memory.

"Yes, nurse, we have British biscuits. McVitie's Digestive biscuits all the way from Edinburgh. Please take one."

I do not hesitate. "How on earth did they get here?"

"New arrivals from home. My request for more staff has finally been heeded and it seems that one of the officers picked up a parcel from my mother. Digestive biscuits, a cholera belt and these."

I smile at the mention of a cholera belt because so many of the British soldiers have them. They believe the chilling of the abdomen brings on foul disease and other ills. Long woollen belly-scarves lovingly knitted and then sent to them by wives, mothers, girlfriends, and grannies from home seem to give the men some comfort but provide the nurses with one more barrier and one more item to shrink in the wash. I stop myself. How do I know these things?

As if he senses my question, Captain Holmes pulls a pile of knitted artefacts from his desk drawer and shakes them out. He quickly shoves the long red cholera belt back and I absorb the colourful jungle of texture and pattern before me.

"One pair of fingerless mittens, one woollen scarf and one tam o' shanter."

I hold up the bright yellow and blue tartan hat with its red pom-pom at the crown next to the vividly striped scarf.

"You will cut quite a dash in these, sir."

"Given the temperature outside is almost ninety degrees Fahrenheit, nurse, you may have to wait some months to witness that display."

It is the first time that we properly laugh together and while we enjoy more digestive biscuits, I learn of Captain Holmes' Scottish heritage and his mother's love of, and dubious talent for, knitting.

"One of the little girls in my billet is a keen needlewoman."

I think of Lenie lying in the hospital, so keen to pick up the sampler she began before she became sick with measles. "She has knitting needles but no wool. But she does have some cotton threads and has begun a beautiful embroidery piece."

I think of the three lines that are the subject of her sampler so far and hope she might complete the passage from the Bible.

"Please. Give these to her." Captain Holmes passes me the scarf and the tam o'shanter. "Thanks to my mother, I am familiar enough on the subject of knitting to know that the little girl will be able to unravel them and knit something else."

"Those are certainly the wrong colours for your regiment, sir. I think green and blue are the Fusiliers colours, are they not, sir?" If I say that his look is one of astonishment, I doubt that he would disagree. I feel heat in my cheeks and dare not look at the Captain. Not only do I know the colours of the regimental tartan of the Royal Highland Fusiliers, but somehow, I know that that they wear a glengarry bonnet not a tam o'shanter.

Chapter 18
The Compassionate English Woman

"At least it is not covered in red dust today," Miss Emily Hobhouse laughs as she fixes her windswept soft brown hair with two tortoiseshell combs inlaid with mother of pearl.

"What a sight I must be!" Her soft brown eyes twinkle up to meet mine as she dusts herself down. "It is a pleasure to meet you, Anna. I am delighted that you are here to help me. I met many bilingual ladies in the Cape when I arrived in South Africa. I wanted to bring one of the Dutch ladies with me, but sadly it was not permitted." She smiles knowingly at Captain Holmes. "But now, I have you. That is more than enough. Please do call me Emily." She reaches towards me, and like her smile, the handshake of my new companion is warm and comforting and I know immediately that I am going to like this 'bloody woman'.

Initial introductions and pleasantries dispensed with, Captain Holmes takes his leave and I am left to escort our guest on a tour of the camp. We chatter on like old friends until we are inside the hospital when Emily becomes quiet.

"It did not used to be so busy," I feel somehow defensive. "When I arrived here in September, there were only three hundred people in the entire camp."

She replies abruptly with the question I do not want to answer, "How many now?" Her voice is terse.

"Near to two thousand. Probably a little less, but more wagons arrive each day. It's not so much those who have lost their own farms. Often, those people have families to go to. Or they go abroad if they have money and connections. It's the tenant farmers and the workers. They go to the towns but the towns are either full or burnt down. And, honestly, thank goodness there is somewhere for them to go."

Emily stops and surveys the lines of canvas bell tents from our vantage point at the top of the camp where we can also see queues standing or moving raggedly towards their goal. I provide a commentary for the scene before us.

"They are waiting for the latrines or to use the wash troughs. Those families by the ox wagons are waiting to be admitted. The women by that small building are waiting for visiting time to start. It's the hospital. We will go there first."

She looks at me, frowning slightly as she smiles.

"I hope you don't mind me saying so, my dear Anna, but your English is impeccable. Where did you learn?"

By now, I am so familiar with the story that Elinor tells that the words flow without hesitation. Emily listens attentively as I explain that I was raised in Cape Town but moved to the Orange Free State where I married a Boer farmer who is no longer alive, that I am expecting his child but that the medical staff believe that a trauma to my head has caused a form of amnesia which means I can only recollect certain events… "Like islands of memories floating in the sea of my past."

"I like that. Islands of memories. Quite poetic." The expectant look that she gives me reminds me that she is waiting for me to answer her question.

"I really don't remember where I learnt English. I speak German too, as well as Afrikaans. I used to speak German with Klaus. My husband. Klaus Meyer." I feel a fluttering in my stomach and my hands move quickly to feel what was a definite kick. Another follows in rapid succession. The life inside me is growing, moving, exploring. My body feels alive. Vibrant. Emily laughs and puts out her arm to support me. And I have remembered something new.

"When will your baby come?"

I take her arm gratefully, "I am not terribly sure. But Sister Pelly, who you will meet at the hospital, and my friend, Elinor both think that it will be in June or even as soon as May."

"Perhaps I will meet him. Or her. Your baby, I mean. I plan on returning to Bloemfontein later in the year once I have visited the camps in the north. If I can obtain permission, of course."

My thoughts race ahead and I think of Christo, Isabel and Klaus and Magrieta's other children and wonder if my baby will have red hair and blue eyes like them. How will I be able to cope? Will I have a boy or a girl? I must tell Elinor that I have remembered Klaus's surname! Then I pull myself back to the present.

"Whose permission do you need to visit the other camps?" I ask.

"I saw Sir Alfred Milner when I was in Cape Town and eventually after a deal of persuading by me, he gave me the go ahead, but with the caveat that the whole mission must be sanctioned by Lord Kitchener." She sees my puzzlement and adds, "Kitchener is Commander in Chief of the Imperial forces. The top man."

"And Sir Alfred is the High Commissioner for South Africa?"

"That's right. I spent two days in a complete blue funk before meeting him at Government House," Emily giggles and grins at me.

"Were you not afraid?"

"I wasn't afraid of meeting His Excellency despite what I had heard. But I was afraid that I wouldn't be able to plead my case at all adequately. I was quite sick with terror beforehand. Then there was an interminable luncheon – just me, alone – with eight gentlemen. Then he and I went off to the drawing room where we talked and talked – hammer and tongs – for a whole hour. He was actually very charming and surprisingly sympathetic. Everyone says he doesn't have a heart, but I think I found one, atrophied somewhere inside!"

I think of Elinor and how she and her family came to be at Bloemfontein camp.

"Did he have a view on the burning of the farms?"

"That is what surprised me the most. I think because he had seen truck-loads of women with his own eyes when he came down the line, he was uneasy about the situation and it had occurred to him that the burning and the blowing up of the farms was all rather terrible. Even though he went on to justify what happened and told me that 'war is war', and if the Boer commandos insist on blowing up our trains and railways, that this kind of retribution is appropriate. Even so, he listened to my views – and I did not mince matters – and he then said he would do all in his power to expedite my visit to the camps. And take a Dutch lady to help."

"But Lord Kitchener did not agree to a companion?"

We have been walking towards the hospital and as we approach, I notice that one of the native girls, who has been on watch, darts inside, no doubt to alert Doctor Brown and Sister Pelly to our arrival. Emily turns to me as we come to a halt. Her tone is rueful but accepting.

"I met a wonderful Afrikaner girl called Ellie Cronje who volunteered to accompany me. But her father had been a Boer general, so she was considered unsuitable. In fact, Kitchener forbade me any Dutch companion and only allowed me one – not two – trucks of provisions. Even Sir Alfred Milner had urged and recommended a second." Her eyes dim a little, "Kitchener made it quite clear that he did not approve of my visit. Interference is what he called it. I don't believe he liked me one little bit."

"And you were not granted permission to go any further north than Bloemfontein?"

"For now." Emily's eyes light up with the determination that has brought her thus far. "Shall we go in?"

If you have never witnessed one, I do not think that anything prepares you for the sights and the stench of a typhoid ward. We have been trying hard to train the few women volunteers who expressed willingness to help in the hospital but the scene roots Emily to the ground.

"Why is all this dirty linen piled here? Where are the nurses?" she asks Sister Pelly whose shadowed face bears the hallmarks of not enough sleep and poor diet. And something worse. My colleague's red-rimmed eyes blaze and when she speaks, I detect, not for the first time, the hint of liquor on her breath.

"I am the Sister here, Miss Hobhouse. Anna usually helps and we have four volunteers."

"For all these people? There is no matron?"

"We manage, Miss Hobhouse. We have to."

No one speaks because it is abundantly clear that we do not manage. We do not manage at all.

The first of several groups of camp residents that Emily and I visit together is Eric Jeppe and his family. I am thankful that neither Elinor nor Mrs Jacobs and her daughter are present since Mrs Jacobs' venom towards Mr Jeppe has not lessened over time. Rather, it has grown more vengeful and blatant since the news of the capture and banishment of her commando son in law to a prisoner of war camp in Ceylon. Elinor has no time at all for any of her compatriots who have refused to join the fighting, whatever their reasons.

I feel the usual stab of envy and a prickle of nostalgia when we enter the Jeppes' canvas home, for everywhere is adorned with hand-stitched quilts and exquisitely embroidered hangings. Rag rugs are everywhere underfoot and beneath them a groundsheet dulls the stench of dried dung that is used for flooring in most of the camp's tents. A jug of wild flowers adds cheerful colour and over this are three canaries in a bamboo birdcage. Their delicate chirruping adds to the homely atmosphere. There is even a washstand upon whose marble countertop sits a proud china jug and bowl. An enormous leather-bound Bible fleetingly reminds me of a church that I must have once attended. This takes pride of place on a polished set of mahogany drawers with brass handles so shiny that my gawping eyes are reflected back at me.

Although Mr Jeppe speaks some English, his wife, Elsa, does not, so I listen carefully and translate the answers she gives to Emily's questions. In my translation, I try to capture Emily's kindness and persuasive manner, but my Afrikaans vocabulary seems somehow inadequate. The words I choose sound abrupt and overly simple, making me wish that I was better able to convey the complexity and depth of Emily's questions and comments. I learn that Elsa and Eric Jeppe and their four children were some of the first people at Bloemfontein camp which they refer to as a 'refuge' camp rather than the refugee camp I understood it to be on my arrival. Mr and Mrs Jeppe are adamant that they never wanted there to be a war and when it came, found themselves in bitter conflict with friends and neighbours who thought that it was every Boer's duty to fight to the bitter end to maintain independence. So, in the face of much animosity, the Jeppe family had packed their belongings and led their livestock from their small farm to the nearest British garrison, only to be moved to the refugee camp soon after, when there became too many Boer families for the garrison to accommodate. Thus, has Mr Jeppe come to secure the trust of, and work for, the British administration.

When Emily comments on the cramped living accommodation and asks how six people can possibly live in a tent such as this, I begin to anticipate the horror she will feel when she visits other billets, such as mine, far less comfortably equipped, that house as many as twelve. As I worry about what will she make of the stench. I nearly choke when the oldest of the Jeppe children, a pink-cheeked girl, offers us egg sandwiches with some tea. Last week when Jurg managed to find eggs for sale on one of his forays to the town, he returned empty-handed since the price had reached one shilling and sixpence per egg. We have not had tea since before Christmas.

138

Chapter 19
Conspiracy

Emily's departure leaves me spiritless and without energy. The supply of herbs provided by Eric Jeppe that Mrs Jacobs used to make my special medicinal infusion has run out, and although many mothers who speak to me about my condition have assured me that the nausea and vomiting will disappear, or at least diminish after the first three months, I am already past that date and am still sick every day without fail. Dulled by inertia, I continue to drag the heavy burden that grows inside me through long days at the hospital, accompanying Elinor to the weekly laundry sessions and visiting families with sick children who refuse to come to the hospital. I have begun to lose count of who or how many are dying. The heavy air hangs listless, as I queue for hours in the sweltering heat to use the latrines or to collect rations.

Lenie has returned from the hospital and the sampler that I helped her to design hangs proudly from the roof of the tent, replacing the dried meat that we finished weeks ago. The words are a little unevenly embroidered in places, and framed by a delicate, exquisitely crafted border depicting flora and fauna in birds-eye and satin stitch:

The fear of the Lord tendeth to life:
and he that hath it shall abide
satisfied; he shall not be visited by evil. Prov 19 ver 23
Happy is the man that findeth wisdom,
And the man that getteth understanding.
For the merchandise of it is better than
the merchandise of silver, and the gain thereof than fine gold.
She is more precious than rubies and
all the things thou canst desire
are not to be compared unto her.
Prov 13_15 verses
Lenie Van de Berg, aged 6 years, 31 January 1901

Since the death of her little sister, Lenie talks often to God. Elinor has given up trying to discourage her daughter's endless sad pleas for the Almighty to send Hester and Chootie back to us. To the disapproving looks of Mrs Jacobs, Lenie goes each day to visit the Jeppes' tent where Mrs Jeppe allows her to read the beautiful leather-bound bible. Having taken our girl under her wing, Elsa Jeppe also feeds eggs and extra milk to the child so that a little flesh now covers the skeletal creature she became in hospital. Sometimes, an egg finds its way to me like a gift from the heaven

I cannot bring myself to believe in. From time to time, anonymous parcels of tinned corned-beef, salt or potatoes appear which also come from the Jeppes. They pretend to know nothing about it all when I try to thank them.

"It is nothing to do with us, Mrs Meyer," they always say.

They use the title by which Elinor thinks I should become known now that I have remembered Klaus's family name. She is convinced that being a married woman and a widow will add some hitherto-lacking respectability to my story. Deep inside, I know that this is not my name, but having any name at all is infinitely preferable to remaining in the shade of ambiguous obscurity.

Lenie sits now in the shade outside the tent, engrossed in a little pair of booties, the click clicking sound of her knitting needles; our metronome of the passing minutes, hours, and days. Elinor's face too is puckered with concentration as she repeatedly weaves a needle in and out of a piece of fabric.

"There! Finished at last." She shakes out her work and Lenie and I gasp in unison. Elinor holds up a tiny nightgown, exquisitely smocked front and back with silk thread so that the fine linen falls in soft folds.

"There is more."

She is like a child herself as she rummages in her sewing bag. She pulls a series of carefully folded garments out. She has sewn a whole trousseau of baby clothes for my unborn child. The urge to touch the miniature garments overwhelms me and as I do so, I feel acute, deep love and protection for the life inside me.

Elinor suddenly turns away from our admiring looks and scowls at her young native servant who approaches, head cowed. "Tombi! Where have you been all this time?"

"I sorry, Mrs Van de Berg, ma'am, but there are no thorn bushes left."

Tombi unclenches her fist to reveal a handful of twigs so thin that they might be straw. Elinor's face twitches with impatience and disappointment.

"So, nothing to heat the water again. No coffee."

With no meat left to cook, there is no need to worry about that, but I sigh inwardly at the thought of hard, salt-less biscuits again for supper.

"But what took you so long, girl? Did you go to that camp again?" Elinor's voice has risen and I fear that Tombi may be about to get another beating. It is usually Mrs Jacobs who finds fault with the girl and metes out punishment for one of many lapses in standards that she believes 'these damned kaffirs' are bound to succumb to. Tombi shifts from one leg to another and shaking, produces a wrinkled root from the patch that serves as a pocket on the front of her filthy dress.

"I thought there might be fire wood there. But it is all gone. Everywhere gone." Her black eyes are wide and she holds out the twigs and the root for me to see. "I see my mother who send these to Miss Anna, I mean for Mrs Meyer. Good for baby."

Elinor sits back down and drops the ruler that is the instrument she uses to deliver chastisement for less grave misdemeanours. Physical punishment is one of the few matters about which Elinor and I fervently disagree, but this time Tombi does not escape correction because Mrs Jacobs, who has been watching the scene unfold, clips Tombi around the ear and snatches the root from the child's hand. Not waiting for the thanks that sit on my too-slow lips, Tombi places the straw in my lap and disappears soundlessly as Mrs Jacobs brandishes her prize.

"I do not know how the child's mother came by such a thing but she is right. Tea made from ginger root will help calm your sickness, Anna."

140

If the lethargy, which accompanies my ever-present nausea, might also be banished is too much to hope for, but I nod anyway.

"What do you think this is?" I ask.

Mrs Jacobs and Elinor inspect the other gift from Tombi's mother, who I know has recently given birth herself. Closer scrutiny reveals the bunch of twigs to be oats and oat straw. These ingredients, so my friends tell me, will help with my restlessness and will cure the rash on my legs.

One morning in early March, I am forced to admit defeat. Despite the fresh morning air, I am hot with exertion and I fold open the tent flap next to me, trying not to wake everyone else. Lying next to me, Lenie grumbles sleepily and turns over. The moon waits in the sky as a leaden sun rises, a cool pink imitation of the white blinding self she will become later. I breathe in the beauty and try again, but no matter how hard I pull together the two edges of my thrice-altered skirt, they refuse to meet, bringing the realisation that I will finally have to go cap-in-hand to the sanctimonious Mrs Rousseau.

Something else for which we have Emily Hobhouse to thank is the arrival of much-promised donations of apparel from concerned and well-meaning local ladies, of which worthy band Mrs Rousseau is a stalwart. It had become apparent to Miss Hobhouse that prior to her visit, both the censorship and system of espionage were not merely military in character, but political and personal. The extent of this was such that even to feel, much more to show, sympathy to the people in the camps was to render oneself a suspect. Miss Hobhouse succeeded in banishing this disapprobation, which had hitherto prevented any kind of charitable scheme getting off the ground. Nevertheless, the proud women and men of the camps take no joy and feel much demeaned by the manner in which the second-hand clothing is distributed. I include myself in this number.

It is staggering to think that I have gained any weight at all because I have been so sick. The quality of the camp's food has certainly not improved in recent weeks, and although tea and coffee rations have been reinstated, there are no tasty morsels of anything new to tempt me. However, another beneficial consequence of Miss Hobhouse's visit, namely the weekly distribution of coal to each tent, means that we can boil water again to make tea and to cook stews and soups.

As I struggle one more time to squeeze my expanding belly into my clothes, the tent flap snaps roughly back and a breathless Jurg stands in the doorway and thrusts a bag onto my mattress. His wild eyes and white face frighten me and when I take hold of his arm, blood drips onto my useless skirt.

"Come with me," I whisper and push him out of the doorway, stopping to rip a piece from the hem of my skirt to make a tourniquet. He winces as I bind his arm tightly above the elbow to staunch the flow of blood. A few inches above the wrist is a small clean wound and parallel to it on the back of his arm is another similar but slightly larger gash. Then I remember. I have treated gunshot wounds like this before. I know that his arm will be broken. I know that in the worst scenario, both bones in his lower arm will be shattered. He needs urgent and immediate treatment.

Our ungainly trail breaks the soft silence of the sleeping camp and Jurg slumps against me just as we limp to the back entrance of the hospital where I steady him gently onto the ground.

"That is not a pistol wound. It is from a rifle. What happened, Jurg? Who shot at you?"

Through the shell-shock, his scared eyes search my face.

"I am not angry, Jurg, but please tell me what happened so I can treat you."

He nods and through laboured gasps, he tells how he left the camp under cover of darkness, as he often does now that we are not allowed to leave without the express permission of the superintendent, but that he was caught stealing food from the British army garrison's kitchen and although he managed to escape, was shot as he fled. I lean over him, creating a make-shift bed with blankets when a slight movement makes me turn around. Dr Brown stands behind me with a fixed expression that leaves me in no doubt he has heard everything.

"Thank you, Nurse Anna. An excellent tourniquet. Now, fetch me some boiled water, dressings and two short splints. Quickly, if you please."

Heart pounding, I hoist up my semi-fastened skirt and make haste to where the stores are.

On my return, Jurg lies sedated with eyes closed and the doctor kneels next to him, hands bloodied. I slip to the ground and between us we dress Jurg's wounds and splint the broken arm. Dr Brown pauses from time to time so I can mop his brow and I stop too when I see his pain-contorted face.

"Headache," he confesses. "This damnable heat. Your friend was lucky, Nurse Meyer. The bullet missed the radius altogether and the break of the ulna is a clean one." He rises, and when he holds out his hand to help me stand, I take it and we face one another. "No one need know exactly how this injury occurred, nurse. There are many ways for a young active man like Jurg to break an arm. Make sure you hide the food he stole. Go and do it now."

He is still gripping my hand and as a torrent of relief courses through me, I think I will never know how to express my indebtedness, so I speak the words that must suffice.

"Thank you, Doctor."

As Dr Brown makes his way back to the typhoid ward, I move across the deserted camp as hastily as my condition will allow. I wave at Mrs Jacobs on her usual morning routine to the latrines. When I arrive at our tent, my own rapid shallow breathing is the only sound. The bag, whose contents include several tins of meat, potatoes, an onion and some precious sugar, is where it was left less than an hour earlier. I expect a jar of jam or pickle when I feel the cold smoothness of glass. I am astonished to pull out an unopened bottle of brandy. We do not have anywhere private for personal possessions and so, apart from the cognac, which I will give to Dr Brown, I add the booty to our meagre pantry. I plan to explain it away as another anonymous gift from the Jeppes, which they will then deny as usual. I re-fasten the safety pins I took from the stores, which now hold my gaping skirt together and hurry back to the hospital. As I go, I deliberate how I will explain Jurg's broken arm to Elinor and the others.

Fortunately, Dr Brown takes on this act of deception and conspires with his new patient. They invent the very plausible story that the injury occurred when Jurg helped move the stack of bricks and large metal tanks for the new water boilers requested by Miss Hobhouse. No one questions this explanation probably because it is so typical of Jurg to help with the heavy and difficult jobs around the camp. I worry about others who may tend to him. Two of the new volunteers are sick themselves and when it is Sister Pelly's turn to change Jurg's dressings, she is so inebriated that I am forced to redo them myself. I doubt that she will have registered the true nature of his wounds. In fact, her drinking has become so heavy that I am worried enough to approach Dr Brown on the matter. He nods when I finish relating my concerns, then shifts from one leg to another, and leaves me wondering what he is afraid to say.

"Do you know how many we are in the camp, nurse?"

Realising how pre-occupied I have been with my own ailments for the past weeks, I acknowledge that I haven't given much thought to the exact number of those who inhabit our densely concentrated world.

"I am not sure, Doctor. According to Miss Hobhouse, there were nigh on eighteen hundred in January. Have we exceeded two thousand?" His bitter laugh is one of resigned scepticism.

"Three thousand and ninety-four." He takes in my surprise and adds, "Four hundred in hospital or sick, fifteen deaths this week so far. Who will replace you when...?" He looks down trying to avoid landing his gaze upon my huge belly. "When your time comes?" I'm not sure if I see accusation or sheer frustration in his tired eyes. "My dear Anna, is it any wonder that Sister Pelly has taken to the drink?"

Chapter 20
A Gift

As she stands and leans towards me, throwing a conspiratorial sideways look to no one in particular, a huge stabbing sensation in my abdomen causes me to double over with pain.

"Anna, please sit. Sit down!"

It is April, and Miss Hobhouse has returned to Bloemfontein after a tour of the camps in the Cape Colony and what was the Orange Free State but now, we must refer to as the Orange River Colony. My stomach has knotted itself into a tight ball and my whole body seems to be clenching. Sweat runs into my eyes, down my back, between my legs. Of the women seated around Miss Hobhouse, several, including Elinor stand quickly and press me into the vacant chair. Their skirts, faces and voices swim together into a vibrating, multi-coloured blur.

"Is it her time?"

"Is her husband in the camp?"

"Should we fetch Mrs Jacobs?"

"Her husband was killed by the Khakis. A hands-upper, found aiding the commandos."

"Fetch some water, she is very hot."

"No, it cannot be her time. It is too soon. Anna, Anna dear, can you hear me?" Elinor grips my hand and relief floods through my wracked body. The pain subsides and I breathe again. Someone thrusts a cup of water into my hand.

"Drink this, Mrs Meyer."

I look round in shock, expecting to see Magrieta but remember they are addressing me.

"She has been doing too much at the hospital for someone in her condition."

It is true, I know, but since Dr Brown has been struck down by the enteric fever and two of our four trainee volunteer nurses are dead, what choice did I have? The cool water soothes my parched lips.

"Please, there is no need to fuss," I say. "I'm fine now. Really." And I do feel nearly fine because I am so very happy to see Emily Hobhouse again and wait eagerly to hear news from her travels and what further improvements she may have achieved through her persistent lobbying. Casting my eyes around, I quietly sip my drink and note the many unfamiliar faces gathered here.

Some weeks later, in the pitch dark, the cramping pains wake me, and for a moment I think I must be dreaming because I can hear celestial singing very close by. I hoist myself into a sitting position, expecting to find that there is a heaven after all and that I have arrived there. But another excruciating stabbing sensation spasm through my lower body, a candle flickers into life and I realise that my mortal soul remains firmly connected to its earthly home.

"It's the Theunissen family again, and their midnight offering of psalms to the Almighty."

Elinor and Mrs Jacobs each hold a lighted candle taken from the small bundle keep hidden.

"Hoping to save a few souls," Mrs Jacobs adds drily as she holds the flame where she can examine my state. She nods curtly at Elinor who begins our rehearsed evacuation procedure. The children's quiet grumbles turn obediently to soundless movement when they realise what is happening, and like clockwork they rise themselves, gather their bundles and disappear into the cool night. I stand up, gripping the bed frame and watch them go.

Rykie returns minutes later and hands a parcel to her mother, "Sister Pelly is too…busy but she says to use this if…if Anna…"

Her mother gently touches Rykie's arm as she takes the packet, "I doubt very much that this will be necessary, but you go and thank Sister Pelly."

Rykie fiddles with her skirt and switches to English, "Good luck with the baby, Anna," she says and I manage a smile before the next wave of pain hits me and a rush of wetness that pools on the parched ground causes another knowing glance between my friends.

"This child is taking its time. Twelve hours already."

I hear Mrs Jacobs through the dream-like haze of the sounds and shadows of daily camp business. Limp, I gaze at the pale creamy canvas through half closed eyes, but although the pain has stopped again, I do not have the energy to focus and I long to sleep. I lie back, breathe in the thick, hot air and force myself to prepare for the next bout of agony, which have been regularly tearing through my insides all day. The old flannel petticoat that I was given to wear under my nightdress is long dispensed with and the heat pounds my body, no matter how many cold compresses Elinor presses upon my head and neck. I tense myself, but still the pain does not return. I relax a little. I will just sleep for a moment. Just a moment. One moment will not matter surely. My eyelids close and I am drifting, drifting, drifting…

"Anna!" Elinor presses another cool, damp cloth to my forehead, "Stay awake. Breathe. Breathe. Good. That is good." And then the pain comes. And keeps coming. I breathe. Cry out. Breathe. More pain. No pain. Breathe. Breathe. Grip my friend's hand.

Mrs Jacobs nods at Elinor and leans close, "Now your baby comes, Anna. Push now, help your baby."

Push, rest, push, breathe, pain, push, pain, pain, stop, push, breathe, pain. Elinor and Mrs Jacobs' voices encourage, cajole, praise and I push one more time before their excitement and anticipation turns to sudden and complete silence. The calm is broken by a faint mewling that escalates to a high-pitched wail.

"You have a daughter!" Elinor almost shouts above the cry of my little girl and gently places the swaddled child into my arms.

Mrs Jacobs fusses around the room clearing this and that, then finally peers down at us. Her expression puzzles me, "Congratulations, Anna," she says flatly and heads to the door. She looks back, face inscrutable, begins a sentence, thinks better of it and leaves. Elinor shrugs, we giggle, decide that we will never fathom Mrs Jacobs and turn our attention to my daughter. "Grace," I decide, "Grace Elinor."

145

Tears brim in my friend's warm, tired eyes.

"Welcome, Grace. Welcome, Grace Elinor Meyer," she says and pulls back the blanket that has slipped over my baby's forehead. "No Meyer red hair," she laughs and strokes Grace's little dark head with its tight curls. Elinor's hand recoils and she pushes back the blanket further. I hear fear, anger, an accusation when she speaks. "What have you done, Anna?"

I wake in the night. The memory of a man's distinct smell comes to me first. Then, his hungry, hateful eyes. The sound of the knife slitting through my clothes. The roughness of him against my skin. The searing pain, as the other one thrashed me again and again with the sjambok. I recoil at the shocking things he did to me. But the shameful wave of what happened to me at the hands of the British troopers is overpowered by stunning, joyful love for my child.

"Don't take her away! Give my baby to me!"

I force myself back to the present, summon the strength that comes from fierce, protective joy and reach out towards my friend in panic. But Elinor slowly finishes changing Grace's diaper before she wordlessly passes her into my arms. "Mrs Jacobs has been back. She knew before I did. She asked me if you know the laws about – she called it – miscegenation?"

I shake my head. "What is it?" I ask.

Elinor hesitates, then takes a breath "…Certain interracial relationships are against the law," she doesn't look at me.

I spill the truths of my part-remembered past to Elinor. She listens intently, but as the confessions mount and the incredulity on Elinor's face grows, the enormity of the lie that I have been enacting for the past nine months hits me.

Chapter 21
Undesirable

Two weeks later, I stand as requested and face the Llandrost, the magistrate, of the South African court. It seems that Mrs Jacobs has prevailed upon friends in high places to press charges, charges that I do not fully comprehend. Captain Holmes has been supportive to a point, but Dr Brown's illness and my absence from the hospital have only added to his burden. Even he could not argue against what is written in my camp record. I know that the 'undesirable' status ascribed upon my arrival will not stand me in good stead here in court, but I believe that Captain Holmes' testimony as camp superintendent will be enough to counter all negative perceptions of my character. He has told me to think myself lucky that neither Mrs Jacobs nor anyone else could produce credible evidence of my being a spy. This is one of the allegations that was laid against me and documented in Major Rogerson's initial report. Thankfully, it has been dropped, but I discovered that had the charge of spying been pursued, Captain Holmes' superior would have overseen the proceedings in a military court. The other charges concern local law so it is in the nearby civil magistrate's court that I must appear. I feel confident – it should not take very long to sort out this misunderstanding.

"Mrs Anna Meyer. This is your name?"

I shake my head.

"Speak up for the court please."

"No, sir, that is not my name." I answer him in Afrikaans. "I do not know my name, except that I believe my first name is Anna. At the camp, I was called Miss Anna, until I remembered, or thought I remembered that my name was Meyer. But I know now that this is not my name."

Following a discussion and much note-writing, the oldest of the three magistrates peers over his spectacles and speaks to me as though he has much better ways to spend his time.

"I will now read, for the court's benefit, the charge that is brought against you. It is alleged that you, a white woman, contra to the laws of this district, have performed sexual acts with a native black South African man and received money for your services. If you are found guilty of this crime, the sentence will be two years' hard labour. Do you understand?"

"I understand, sir. But that is not what happened. I was attacked by that man and…"

"The accused will not speak unless and until she is questioned under oath. Is that understood?"

I understand. I need to stay calm. I am innocent. I have written pages of explanation for the magistrate about the attack. I wrote about what I remember of my time helping wounded Boer soldiers and then serving as a nurse at the camp. There can be no possible evidence against me. I have also handed over the letter Dr Brown wrote before the enteric fever took him. This states my abilities as a nurse in glowing terms and how he is certain that I must have trained in a hospital, possibly in the Cape, which would explain my excellent command of the English language.

My trepidation and mounting fear subside somewhat when Elinor enters the court. She is guided to her place by an official but gives me a cool half-smile that only serves to set off my anxiety once more. I realise that one of the magistrates has begun to speak, and as he raises his voice in irritation at my apparent lack of regard, I switch my attention quickly to him.

"…and through the camp's administrative records, we have traced one of the British Troopers by whom you allege you were attacked. We have had permission from his commanding officer to invite him to give evidence to this court."

The shock that I might have to face my assailant causes an overwhelming desire to run, but I am hemmed in by the wooden railing. I grip it tightly. My rapid breathing calms after I take an oath to tell the truth, and then I sense the onlookers' interest in the male figure that enters. I look to the back of the room where he saunters into the court – a fair-haired British soldier all neatly dressed and spruce in khaki.

A translator is called who invites Trooper Clarke to relate what happened on the day that the British arrived at the farm. He looks directly at the magistrates and I immediately recognise the soldier by his London accent. I staunch the vomit that rises from the pit of my memory.

"Me and Trooper Mojela were ahead in the scout party. Found this whore in what was left of the farm kitchen, practically naked. Offered herself to me but I refused. Left Trooper Mojela to it, I did, sir. I 'ad to pursue me duty."

"And where is your Trooper Mojela now?"

"Dead, sir. Or gone at any rate."

"I see. And upon your return to the farm what happened?"

"Well, sir. Them two 'ad all but finished their business if you know what I mean."

Once this sentence is translated, the court erupts and Trooper Clarke enjoys his moment. Galvanised by his audience, he continues his story and pieces of memory begin to shudder into place. The reason he can relate such detail of that day is because he was there. He was there all the time. He held the whiskey bottle. I fight the humiliation and close my mind to what Trooper Clarke did to me.

"She didn't 'ave a stitch on 'er, sir. Seemed to 'ave banged 'er 'ead, sir. She 'ad fainted or some such. Trooper Mojela 'ad got some water an' was bathin' 'er 'ead. Think their game might 'ave got a bit out of 'and, if you know what I mean?" He waits for the translation and subsequent response from the court. Once the chuntering and laughter dies down, he continues, and for a second time, relishes his time in the limelight, "Then Simeon, Trooper Mojela that is, bandages 'er up, we drink some of their fine Scotch whiskey and then our lieutenant and the others turns up to 'elp. That's when we took 'er to the camp."

More questions follow about what happened when I was taken to the camp and Trooper Clarke regales how: "Lucky she was that she was took there. To be looked after an' all that."

All my attempts to intervene are ignored.

Once the court has finished with Trooper Clarke, we revert to Afrikaans and the translator stands down. It is only then that one of the magistrates addresses a question to me.

"What were you wearing at the time of the alleged attack?"

"Sir, I did not offer myself to him or the other man."

"Please answer the question. What were you wearing when the British troops happened upon the farm?"

"It is true. What Trooper Clarke says. It was so hot. We had been on the veldt for weeks in the heat. There was nowhere to wash clothes."

"The accused will answer the question. What were you wearing?"

"A chemise. And a petticoat."

"You were dressed only in your underwear?"

"Yes. It was so very hot, sir. But I covered myself with a shawl when the troopers arrived."

"And did you offer whiskey to the Troopers even though it was the middle of the day?"

"There was no tea or coffee left. There was only the whiskey. It was all we had."

"We?"

"Myself and Klaus. The man who I was with."

"The man who you thought that you were married to?"

"Sir, I do not know whether I was married to him or anyone."

"And how did you and Mr Meyer come by such fine whiskey?"

"As I have explained, sir, I cannot remember. He had money, a great deal of money and he spent it on whiskey."

"I see."

"In your written statement, you claim that you were kept against your will, but you state that Klaus Meyer was a kindly man. Who taught you to ride, to swim, and to shoot?"

"Yes. He was a good and kind man."

"And who your friends at the camp were led to believe was the father of your child? Your husband, in fact."

"Yes. I know how this all sounds, sir. But as I have explained in my letter and as Doctor Brown would affirm were he still alive, I was suffering from amnesia. After the attack. I must have banged my head. I did not remember hardly anything of my past until after the birth of my daughter. Before she was born, I did think for a time that Klaus must be the father of my child."

"And that you were married to him."

"I only said that I was married to him so that people would not think badly of me, sir. I knew he was married to someone else, but I had lost all memory of what really happened. Now, I am sure that we never lay together."

I do not have the Afrikaans to explain the true complexity of the situation and as the words come out, I know it all must sound very far-fetched and quite lame.

"So, now you say you are sure that you never lay together."

This is posed as a heavily ironic fact and not as a question, so I do not respond. "Tell the court when you became sure that you did not lie with Klaus Meyer. Was it when you discovered that your child was in fact the result of your union with Trooper Mojela?"

"I did not choose to lie with Mojela. He attacked me. He whipped me. I was defiled by that man. He violated me!" The dreadful scene plays in my mind as it has every day since my daughter's birth.

I grip the wooden rail and lean towards the Llandrost, willing him to believe me. How can he not?

"Mrs Meyer," at last, the magistrate has a decidedly friendly tone to his voice. I begin to remind him that this is not my name, but then I see that it is not me whom he addresses.

Magrieta Meyer appears, as serene and as beautiful as I remember her. Even dressed in sombre dark-grey bombazine she draws a gasp of admiration from the court. A brief exchange occurs and Magrieta's face softens as she listens to the condolences offered by the Llandrost for the loss of Klaus.

Over the next few minutes, the court hears something of the fighting in and around the Brandwater Basin. They listen to an account of the sequence of events from when the British scouts happened upon the farm where Klaus held me. The Llandrost pauses for effect, "But it is not for this court to judge the circumstances of Mr Meyer's death."

He goes on to philosophise about the war, but he uses many words that I do not know and I cannot understand much of what he says. After a short pause where Magrieta glances stonily in my direction, the magistrate continues,

"Mrs Meyer, please convey to the court what you know of the relationship that existed between your husband, Klaus Meyer, and the accused."

Magrieta fixes her eyes on the Llandrost and begins hesitantly, "My husband arrived with this young woman just after...just a few days after..."

The sight of slaughtered sheep and the smell of the Meyers' burnt farmhouse slots into place in my library of recollection. Other, sunnier, flashbacks play out: playing charades by firelight, the euphoria of learning to swim, Klaus berating the oxen Tafelburg and Englesman. The next question jolts me back to the present.

"Can you tell the court why your husband and this woman were travelling together?"

"I cannot tell you why a young, attractive, unmarried woman would venture alone with a strange man in a foreign land riven by war, sir. I do not know why she did not stay with her people. The English."

A buzz reverberates around the room and I remember! My name is Anna Lieberman! I live in London, England.

More scribbling. More discussion. I stand to gain their attention but am pressed back down by an official.

"You say that you believe the accused to be an English woman?"

"That is what my husband told me. He told me that her name is Anna Lieberman."

At last, the truth! I want to hug Magrieta.

"Lieberman. Not a very English name. I am sorry to press you, Mrs Meyer, but what do you believe was the relationship between your husband and the woman you say is Miss Lieberman?"

"I trusted my husband, sir. But there is no doubt in my mind that this woman had a hold over him. I saw..."

If she speaks the truth, she will dishonour the name of her husband. I pray for her to lie.

"What did you see, Mrs Meyer?"

"I recognised the way he looked at her. It was a look he once had for me only."

As the truth slips quietly through her sadness, I know that it is not just her dead husband who the magistrates will judge. I am complicit even though I did not mean to be.

There is a short break during which the magistrates disappear and I take the opportunity to survey the court. Rows of vaguely amused faces, scornful looks and quiet disgust, amount to a montage of animosity. I long for Magrieta's testimony to be over and for the court to hear from Elinor.

"Mrs Meyer, do you have any idea why your husband might have been travelling with this particular English woman, who we will now refer to as Miss Lieberman?"

She pauses and deliberates the answer she will give.

"He thought that she would be useful for the Boer cause, sir."

"Useful how, Mrs Meyer?"

"As a nurse, sir. But also, she speaks several languages and I did find her..." she looks across at me for the first time. "I found her studying maps of the Brandwater Basin when we were with General de Wet's laager."

"And why do you think she was studying maps, Mrs Meyer?"

"I know my husband thought she should get to know the terrain, in case something happened to him."

Thank you, Magrieta, I think, and hope that her comment will steer the court away from the ridiculous notion of my being a spy.

Magrieta continues, "But he was worried that she wanted to re-join the English and he thought she was trying to plan an escape route."

"And is that what you thought, Mrs Meyer?"

She shakes her head. "She had my husband under her spell. He only thought the best of her. My son and I did not quite trust her in the same way. We...I wondered if she might be a British spy."

The court is buzzing again.

"And do you have any evidence to support your view, Mrs Meyer?"

Magrieta looks at me and shakes her head as she speaks, "Not really, sir. Except..."

"Yes, Mrs Meyer?"

"Except that she did ask many questions. She even questioned one of the generals. I think she wanted to find out General de Wet's plans and somehow get the information back to the English who were camped not far away."

What start as gasps of outrage turn to noisier cries and cause a halt to the cross examination. When it resumes, Magrieta is not able to enlighten the court further and is dismissed with more kind words from the magistrates, who then pause the proceedings for a few minutes to write copious notes. The crowd begins to show their impatience. More papers are sifted and then I hear Elinor's name called, with not a little irritation. I relax a little when my friend stands to provide her testimony.

"Mrs Van de Burg, we understand that you helped the accused when she arrived at the camp and during her confinement. Is this correct?"

"Yes, this is true, sir. Anna has been a great help to me. And my children. She is a fine teacher and nurse." At last, my friend smiles at me.

"What did you understand of her position prior to her arrival at the camp, Mrs Van de Burg?"

"Anna was suffering from amnesia, sir. In truth, none of us knew anything much about her past – including Anna herself. Sometimes, small recollections would come to her. Including some of the time she spent with Klaus. With Mr Meyer, that is. It was easier for her to say she was married. But I did not imagine…when the child was born, I did not know what to think."

"And what do you think now, Mrs Van de Burg?"

Her head is bent over clasped hands and I wish that she would look up.

"I believe that what Anna says must be true."

I do not understand the lack of conviction in her voice and will her to say more, to say anything that might help persuade these people that I am neither a prostitute nor an adulteress. After a brief, hushed exchange between the magistrates, Elinor returns to her seat and when the next witness is called, the apprehension in her face reflects my own fear.

Mrs Jacobs swoops into position and after a few preliminary, straightforward introductions and factual clarification of events, including my arrival at tent twenty-eight and the birth of my child, she is asked about my relationships with others in the camp.

"Very close to Eric Jeppe, she is. That traitor. Same allegiances and morals, or lack of them, I should say. He is always bringing her gifts. Herbs, extra milk and suchlike for her condition. I saw her alone with the doctor too. She would creep away early, when she thought the rest of us weren't awake. But I was. I watched her. She would take him gifts. Brandy and suchlike. And whatever else a woman like her has to offer, I suppose. I wouldn't be surprised if it was, she who put glass in our sugar. And it…"

Interrupted in full flow, Mrs Jacobs finds it difficult to suppress her annoyance when the magistrate holds up a hand and bids her be silent. He looks directly at me.

"Did you ever give the doctor a gift of brandy, Miss Lieberman?"

"Only once. It only happened once."

And I cannot tell the court when they ask me where the brandy had come from, because then they would know that Jurg had stolen it along with food from the British army garrison, and Elinor who is still in the courtroom, would know that I had lied to her. Goodness only knows what would happen to her son if the truth were known.

"And did you receive gifts from Mr Jeppe?"

"Our tent received gifts from the Jeppe family. They were not just gifts to me alone."

"And why did your tent receive gifts from Mr Jeppe?"

I really do not know the answer to this except that Mr Jeppe and his wife are thoroughly decent folk who felt sorry for Elinor and her fatherless brood. And sorry for me too. Mrs Jacobs snorts at my silence before she is thanked by the Llandrost and dismissed. It is clear from her reluctance to leave that she has more to say, but the magistrates have listened to enough hearsay.

The three men adjourn to make their deliberations. They are gone longer than I expect. I am eager to get back to my baby and I begin to feel impatient when, after what must be at least an hour, they make their solemn return. I stand in anticipation.

"Miss Lieberman, although we feel a certain sympathy for your plight, we have heard no conclusive evidence to support your version of how you came to be in this situation. We have, however, heard a deal of evidence to support the case brought against you, and therefore, we find you guilty as charged."

I hear shrieking and realise that I am screeching at the judges and that the court is cheering. Cheering! This is impossible. I am a nurse. I am a British nurse. I do not belong here. I did nothing wrong. I lean over the wooden bar but am forced back by rough hands and rougher threats. The Llandrost raises his gavel and his voice. The noise subsides.

"Usually in such cases, the punishment of two years' hard labour would be served on one of the large farms in the area, but since many of them are out of action, this is no longer possible. We might have sentenced you to an alternative two-year term of hard labour at a laundry attached to one of the mines in Kimberley. But, as you may know, the mines have been closed since the beginning of the war. There is, however, a shortage of domestic staff because many of those originally employed in such positions, no longer regard it their place. You will be sent therefore to a reputable mine owner, who is happy to accept persons such as yourself and for whom you will assume whatever domestic tasks are allocated to you. Arrangements will be made for the adoption of your child within an appropriate family."

The heavy emphasis on the word appropriate strikes me out of my shock and disbelief.

"No! No! I am not guilty! You cannot take away my child! I am an English woman!"

Frantic now and sobbing, I search the room for a friendly face, someone, anyone who might help me.

"Elinor! Do something!" But she is being led away back to the camp and now two people are ushering me from the court too. When I resist, and plead after the retreating magistrates, who do not turn around, two pairs of muscular arms propel me roughly down the steps. I am dragged out of the court's back entrance and across the street to the railway station. There, a train, made up of several open and a few closed wooden cargo trucks, lies in wait.

As we approach the stationary train through the gathering smoke and commotion of its imminent departure, I see that some of the open trucks contain not animals or provisions, but people. There are women and children wearing typical Boer kappies or sheltering from the sun under parasols. Elderly couples and the occasional younger man are packed tightly together. All of them are surrounded by odd pieces of domestic paraphernalia and some excited dogs yap from time to time before being hushed momentarily by a child. Some of this shabby collection of people and possessions has the luxury of a patched canvas cover draped across the truck and flaps untidily over the side. One truck even has a metal frame over which a ripped tarpaulin is stretched, but I am escorted past these noisy, jovial transports towards the three closed, window-less wagons. The sliding doors are firmly secured with giant padlocks, and from within, there is only silence. Purposeful men in khaki stride past us, Lee-Metfords slung over their shoulders, pointing skywards.

I start to beg for assistance. I lunge towards one British soldier but I am pressed towards the now-open door of a truck and ignored by my countryman.

My escort yells an admonishment, "Here's an English whore to entertain you. And a mad woman to boot."

They tip me head first onto the train before the door screeches on its oil-less runner and clangs shut.

Disentangling my limbs and skirt takes a few seconds during which time the train shudders forward and I fall back. When the long screech of metal on metal fades into a more regular rattle, I sit up. I have to hold my hand across my face against the stench. My eyes adjust as I peer into the flickering semi-darkness.

Part Four
Mining for Diamonds

Chapter 22
Ripponden House, Kimberley

4 August 1902

That the war has been over for three months now seems incomprehensible. More astonishing is the realisation that I have been at Ripponden House for over a year. I had the latest present from Mr Chambers with me this morning when I called at Mr Barnato's office in Stockdale Street after my usual weekly tour through the workers' compound at the mine. The Kodak folding pocket-camera was much admired, but I managed enough time by myself to take what I think will serve as wonderful reminders of my time here in Kimberley for when I return to London.

Mr Chambers spoils me so. My embarrassment is such that each time I receive another gift, I protest that I will never be able to repay his generosity. He shrugs this off like the opera cloak he had made for a recent trip to New York.

A flurry of activity in the garden below diverts my thoughts and I put down my pen.

"Up here, Christabel!" I wave as the elegant woman dressed in white makes her way past the shaded bank of evergreen ferns that border the lily pond. Laden with cleverly balanced candy-striped, ribbon-tied boxes so that her right hand is free to hold the exquisite parasol bought by her husband in Paris, she navigates around the spray from the cherubic fountain, and laughs as a sparkling shower of droplets lands unbidden upon her elbow-length, ivory kid gloves. As intense a blue as the speedwell flowers dotted around the garden, Christabel's eyes twinkle up from beneath her extravagant coiffure and then disappear. Seconds later, she emerges from the exterior stairwell, just one of the inspired architectural jewels of this stunningly designed villa.

"Here they are, Anna. You will simply adore them!"

She deposits the parcels unceremoniously upon the wooden deck of the first storey veranda.

"But where are your things, Christabel?" I ask.

Before she has time to answer, a riotous kerfuffle ensues and a pile of humanity lands in a heap next to my writing table that almost topples over in the excitement. My fifteen-month-old daughter Grace.

"Please do open them, Anna!" Christabel removes an elaborate pearl and ruby hatpin, gently places her latest fine straw chapeau onto the wicker chair and smiles expectantly.

How can I resist this woman with hands clasped in anticipation and eyes that sparkle more than any diamond I have ever seen retrieved from the Big Hole?

But first, I pick up the smaller of the two just-landed bundles of humanity and kiss the top of her head. I am rewarded with the most precious word I know. Twice.

"Mamma. Mamma!"

"Baby girl, what have you got there? Christabel, tell me you have not?"

"It is not from me, Anna! It arrived from your uncle in Germany this morning. Along with a host of gifts for all the children. There is a letter addressed to you too – in the red room."

I scoop up my little girl who clutches the Stieff family's latest creation in her tiny hands. This toy giraffe will add to the growing menagerie that has made its way across the world from Salzburg to Kimberley.

"It is adorable. Tombi, please take Grace to the nursery. She will be hungry, I expect."

"Tom Tom!" cries my little daughter and reaches chubby arms towards her nursery-maid, adding almost a full sentence in what sounds like Afrikaans to me.

"Yes, Miss Anna. Come, baby Grace." There follows the identical command in Afrikaans and much giggling from them both.

No longer wearing the rags I became accustomed to seeing her wear in the camp and now sixteen years old, Tombi has blossomed into a full-figured, striking young woman who takes her duties in our household very seriously. It was only when she came to Ripponden House that Tombi shared with me the correct pronunciation of her name, which in fact has the letter 'N' before the 'T' of Tombi. Tombi told me that she had tried to explain this once before to Elinor but had received a sound beating for such disrespect. However, because little Grace cannot pronounce with an N, we have decided to stay with the name that we all love and are familiar with and so N'Tombi is now forever Tombi to us, and Tom Tom to Grace.

"Now, Miss Grace, I tell you story of little girl who made the stars. Remember she made them so that we can all find our way home in middle of the night…It had been a cold night and when the embers of the fire had died away, the little girl said to the wood ashes…"

Laughing together and with Grace perched on her right hip, the pair slip through the double door into the nursery at the far end of the veranda and I turn to Christabel.

"Grace loves that story. Especially the part about how the ashes from the little girl's fire turn into the Milky Way."

What I do not add is how much I have come to love the African folk tales that passed many hours at Bloemfontein camp. Magrieta's younger children enjoyed Tombi's storytelling there as much as Grace does now.

"Will you take Tombi back to England with you, Anna?"

Her face now serious, the mood is instantly transformed. I watch the rhythmic movement of her wicker rocking-chair as it creaks to-and-fro then halts.

"It all rather depends," I say. "Henry might be opposed to the idea but it is one of the matters that I will be able to put to him later."

"What time are they expected?"

"I have said that I will meet the five o'clock train."

"I see. And go to the hotel?"

"We have much to discuss, Christabel."

"But they would have been so very welcome to stay here."

"I may yet be able to persuade him. Although his letter does suggest that he is set on being at the Kimberley Club. He feels a loyalty somehow and a desire to return there. After what happened during the siege."

"I understand. And we are strangers to him, of course."

"But I am his sister."

"And Grace is his niece."

Christabel stands and contemplates the unopened packages.

Yes, I think to myself, *but will he want to be Grace's uncle? Will he accept her as his niece?*

"Let us save these until after luncheon," Christabel proposes and continues to chatter on as we gather up the parcels. What she says does not register because my mind has already begun to churn over how I will tell Henry that my daughter will not remain in South Africa after all, but will be travelling with me to London and that Tombi will be coming too.

I was initially reticent about the precise details of Grace's arrival into the world when I wrote to my brother, Henry. I had no idea how much Captain Holmes had revealed through the correspondence with him that ultimately led to my acquittal and freedom. Eventually, when we met three months ago, just after the peace treaty was signed at Vereeniging, Henry and I discussed how Grace might be adopted here in Kimberley or even in the Cape. Such a simple solution, he advised.

Of my family, it is only Henry who knows the truth. My parents in London and my aunt and uncle in Germany have been led to believe that I live with the Chambers family as a companion to Christabel after a bout of enteric left me too weak to continue nursing. My uncle sends generous presents to the Chambers' children – Ernest, Bede and Augusta – about whose antics I write. I have left unchallenged his assumption that they are Grace's siblings.

Do not worry, Anna. Henry has scribed. *No one need know. And once you are back in London, you will be able to re-apply for your place at Oxford. Or you can decide to pursue a career in medicine. Or maybe you will do something unexpected? Get married for example!*

The fear and doubt about what I have decided to do mean that I barely touch the salmon in aspic with fresh minted potatoes lovingly prepared by Tombi's mother, Mieta. It is cook's day off, which gives Mieta a chance to show off some of what she has been taught since she joined the below-stairs staff in January this year. I do not know why I refer to the servants as below-stairs staff, since most of them have rooms in an extensive wing of the house dedicated to staff accommodation. Force of habit perhaps. Of course, the coachman has his own cottage, the head gardener lives over the stables and there is a separate block for the native African servants, which is where Tombi's parents live, as is the custom here.

I have specifically requested that the new nursery-maid is close to my daughter, so Tombi has been permitted to move into the small chamber adjacent to the nursery. And as an obviously reluctant Mr Chambers points out, it will only be a short-term arrangement. No positions could be found for Tombi's brothers at Ripponden House, but they work at the mine and live at the compound there.

Unusually, Mr Chambers has returned from the mine office in the middle of the day. He greets us effusively as our paths cross in the hallway outside the dining room and he gathers Christabel in his arms. His words are as warm as always, "Darling girl!"

The footman swiftly gathers his coat and a stiff nod given before the master of the house turns his smiles back to us. "I am sorry, Christabel, but I will not be taking luncheon with you and Anna. I will be going to the club once I have changed."

I try to hide my relief at not having to make small-talk with my friend's husband. I believe his act of taking in a 'fallen woman' was not as charitable as he would have people think. After all, servants are becoming more and more difficult to find. He has never warmed to me nor me to him. I have always been much closer to Christabel than to John Chambers. It was Christabel who identified my plight in the first place when she found me crying over the dolly-tub. She took the bold step of contacting the Bloemfontein authorities and the even braver decision to write to my brother, Henry, before she brought everything to her husband's attention. I have a very great deal to thank her for. Since the Chambers children typically take their weekday meals upstairs with the governess and Grace eats with Tombi in the nursery, it is only myself and Christabel who dine today, for which I am grateful because I am not in the mood for chit-chat.

I push my food around the plate, and as always, she senses my pensive state but says nothing until she has finished eating.

"Let us take our coffee in the orangery," Christabel knows that I love that place above all the other beautiful spaces in this house. "I will join you and have Mrs Jackson bring in your parcels."

The orangery opens to the west through a part-glazed double door with finely etched glass panels, and by mid-afternoon, the refracted light pools brightly coloured art-nouveau swirls from the stained-glass windows upon the pale cream floor-tiles. Where the glowing shadows dance between floor and greenery, the effect is enchanting and I tread softly there so as not to disturb the magic. My favourite plants are the waxy orchids, of which there must be fifty varieties here. I make my way through the lush canopy of tall palms and jasmine-covered trellises to sit in their company where I can absorb their smooth, sculpted loveliness.

After a few minutes, Christabel joins me and pours the coffee left not by Mrs Jackson, the housekeeper, but by the new parlour-maid whose name I do not remember. She looks to be no more than fourteen years old and her hands shake when she puts down the china cups and saucers. Despite the apparent difficulties in finding experienced and trustworthy domestic staff, there are so many servants here that it is difficult to keep up with all their names.

"I realise why it is difficult for you, Anna, but he would so very much like you to call him John," Christabel smiles warmly at me.

I nod and grimace slightly because I still find it impossible to refer to her husband by his first name.

"What happened to you was not his fault," she adds.

I know that it frustrates them both, but I was his servant for six months and it feels inappropriate and wrong somehow to use his Christian name. Neither did he always treat me as well as he does now.

"We will both miss you, Anna. And so will the children."

"And I will miss you too, Christabel. But we will meet when you come to London. I cannot wait to introduce you to my family."

And to the man I hope to marry.

This silent dream brings a smile to my face. Christabel senses my mood and pushes the pile of presents within my grasp. She tells me again how much I am going to love the fruits of her shopping trip.

"Very well, I can see that I will not receive a moment's peace unless and until they are unwrapped. Now, which one shall I open first...?" As I begin to feign indecision, the deep, round box with a carrying handle is thrust into my lap.

"Now what can possibly be inside this hat-box, I wonder?"

We spend a deliciously decadent time opening the presents, but after more than an hour, I make my excuses. There are four letters addressed to me on the silver post platter when I make a detour into the red room on my way upstairs for a supposed rest. I recognise the thick cream parchment of Asprey's finest writing stationary and the weight of this letter causes a flood of anticipation. I will save this one until last. I turn over the envelope whose lightness and soft, orchid-pink hue means that it can only be from my mother and smile at her utter femininity in all things. The Austrian postmark indicates which correspondence is from my aunt and uncle in Salzburg and there is one more, addressed in a hand that I do not recognise and with an unfamiliar stamp.

The chime of the mantelpiece clock reminds me that I have less than an hour before I must leave for the station to meet my brother Henry. Resolving to save the letters until my return this evening and seizing the new gown that was in the largest of the parcels, I ring for Winnie, the lady's maid I share with Christabel. We meet in the hall and I practically race up the stairs, raising my skirts and taking two steps at a time in the satisfying knowledge that were this act to be witnessed either by another of the servants or especially Mr Chambers, certain admonishment would follow. Winnie quickly lays the dress on the thick eiderdown quilt and I stand back to fully appreciate its beauty.

"Quickly, Winnie, I shall wear this with my velvet coat and new hat. Can you find the purse with the gilt clasp and my kid evening-gloves? It will be cold later."

I survey the other fine garments. Even the corset is of the utmost quality and I knew as soon as I saw the dreaded item that this one would turn out to be comfortable. The standard of workmanship is just as good as the corsetiere used by my mother at Swan and Edgar in Regent Street, but the fine mesh chosen by Christabel means that it will be more bearable when the warm weather comes. But of course, by then I will no longer be here.

"Do you think the pearls are best, ma'am?" Winnie holds up a long string of pearls and a diamond choker for me to choose. I reach for the longer necklace.

"Yes, the pearls will be perfect."

Reflected in one of the hall's many mirrors, the peach-coloured ostrich feathers that adorn the crown of my new hat shimmy in the slight breeze from an open window. The soft up-turned brim tilts forward and is a perfect accompaniment to Winnie's arrangement of my hair. The sheen of my coiffure glints in the sun's late afternoon rays. Since there is no one in the hall, or upon the galleried landing above, I swivel around to glimpse the back detail of the navy-blue lace that falls in a slight train over the dove-grey satin, which two fabrics complement one another perfectly in this copy of a Jacques Doucet gown. I blink away the memory of my shaven head and the stinking rags I wore on my arrival at Bloemfontein camp, pull on the velvet coat and pirouette for one final appraisal, agreeing to myself with Christabel, who thinks that the outfit will also be suitable for London. Even Paris or New York come to that, I shouldn't wonder.

Chapter 23
Henry's News

It is impossible to stand on the platform at Kimberley station, feeling cool and clean in my finery, and not re-live the terror of my initial arrival here after a three-day ordeal in the semi-darkness of a barely ventilated, closed wooden truck. I was in the company of several women like me who had been sentenced to hard labour for sexual misconduct. There were others found guilty of a range of criminal offences, mostly involving men and many which do not bear repeating.

I did not think I had slept at all that first night, so terrified was I of my travelling companions, but I must have done. And when I got to know the girls, although I never trusted Sally entirely, it was compassion that I felt above all else. I was most sorry about Celia, who found the strength to string herself up to a hook and remain silent as she died. I can still hear the quick slit of fabric being cut away as I tried in desperation to untie the knotted garments that the poor girl had fashioned into her own noose. Sally, who was a prostitute from Port Elizabeth, came to my aid with the knife that she kept 'just in case her clients got any funny ideas' and I guessed from the alacrity with which the knife was wielded that it had been much used.

Celia's death brought our miserable crew together, and from the angry old scars and new painful marks on Celia's naked body, we came to understand why she had killed her husband.

"Couldn't stand the thought of never seeing her wee ones again," was Sally's conclusion of the night's events and what brought me to confessing my own history and 'crimes' to this most unlikely confidante.

The imminent arrival of Henry's train does not permit me to dwell upon the past any longer and when the locomotive thunders to a hissing, clanking halt, I see my brother's familiar blonde hair and grinning face framed by one of the open carriage windows. He leans out and waves his peaked officer's cap with a vigour that would lift even the most crushed of spirits.

In no time at all, we are embracing, his baggage flung to the ground. Then I am sobbing and he is trying very hard not to and so we are laughing and then I am crying again and he is laughing because my tears are interspersed with hiccups. He gives me one final breath-crushing hug, takes my wrists and holds me at arms' length. He is alone.

"If I were not so happy to see you, my dear sister, I would be speechless. I have never seen you looking so...well damn it, Anna...so very beautiful!"

And if only you had seen me when I first arrived at this very station, Henry. If only I could tell you about it, about what those soldiers did to me. Perhaps I will, one day.

"You are different somehow, Anna. Let me see you." He spins me around so that my skirt flares out like a dancer's and the layers of my fine petticoats froth out. I feel like I might fly.

"I do believe that you are taller!" he declares.

Of course, I am not. Stronger, tougher, maybe. Damaged, certainly. Mended, definitely. But the cracks remain. I grab Henry's wrists and come to a standstill.

"Silly boy! I stopped growing when I was fourteen. Ah, but maybe it is these boots?" I lift one of my ankles to the shock of a passing porter and display one of the kitten heels that do give me an extra half inch. "I cannot believe you are here, Henry. Look at you! And a captain too! I did not know. And what is this?"

I gently reach beneath his greatcoat to touch the ribbon over the left breast pocket of his khaki jacket.

"Oh, that bit of old metal." He brushes my hand away and his abashed look reminds me of the time he rescued a young boy, in trouble and out of his depth while swimming in the lake near our uncle's house. "It is nothing, honestly. In the cause of King and country and all that."

"I have nursed enough soldiers to know that you must have done something very brave and special to be given that particular bit of old metal."

He laughs again and confesses. "Well, I did wear the thing to impress my big sister. I can take it off now." He unpins the cross and pops it into his pocket. "Right then, shall we go? I think we better had!"

Our demonstrative discussion, repeated embraces and the sight of my ankles are causing raised eyebrows and disapproving backward glances from alighting passengers and busy railway staff. I am reminded that no one could possibly imagine that we are siblings, even less twins, given our entirely different physiognomy. I had thought that my days of needing a chaperone were finished, but it seems that we must revert to the old ways and moral behaviours now that the war is over.

"The carriage is waiting," I tell Henry and it is his turn for raised eyebrows. "It is nothing. Mr Chambers… John and Christabel insisted that I take it for the evening since they have no need of it tonight. You would be welcome to stay at Ripponden House, you know, Henry."

"I do know. But the Kimberley Club is up and running again. And the girls are staying there – they arrive tomorrow, by the way. They thought we might appreciate some time together. Just the two of us."

I nod. This is typically thoughtful of Marjorie and Florence.

"That is kind of them. So much has happened."

We stop again at the end of the platform and are the focus of more stares as Henry holds me tight to him when I bury my head into his chest. As my memory-laden tears soak through the layers of his uniform, I care not a jot what anyone might think.

Two hours and a calming carriage ride later, we are seated by the maître d'hôtel in a quiet corner of the Kimberley Club's restaurant. The menu of turtle soup, followed by mutton cutlets, aspic of foie gras, steamed pudding, and Stilton, appeals more to Henry than to me. I am so happy to be with my brother that I would not have minded if we had been served with mealie porridge.

"Did you meet Captain Holmes in person?" I ask Henry as our cut-glass champagne coupes are filled by one of the waiters.

"We met twice. Once, soon after his first letter reached me and again when your diaries and letters came to light."

"I have Magrieta Meyer and her family to thank for that."

"And Elinor."

"And her son, Jurg, of course."

"Astonishing, really, that the letters and your diary survived intact for all that time."

I think back to the loose stone in the barn where I slept and behind which were concealed the evidence to support my story.

"They were well hidden."

"And cleverly retrieved by Jurg."

"Who could never have found them had it not been for Magrieta's help in revealing the location of the hideaway farm."

"Can you bear to talk about it, Anna?"

I fend off the recurring nightmare that comes, unbidden and often, usually just after I fall asleep.

"About the attack, do you mean?"

He puts down his glass.

"I suppose I do mean that, yes. About all of it, really. Who have you spoken to?"

I begin to see where this conversation might lead.

"What I mean is," he continues, "who at home knows? In England, that is."

"If you are trying to discover how many people know the truth about my illegitimate daughter, Henry, there is one important fact not to be forgotten – I was interrogated in court, remember? Many people know of my shame. But the answer to your question is, you know. And Captain Holmes knows. That is all."

"I am sorry, Anna. I truly did not intend to upset you. But you will be able to put it all behind you very soon. Look, here is the soup."

My brother has always been a good listener, so I begin my tale with the arrival in Cape Town of the RMS Dunottar Castle from which elegant vessel, Marjorie, Joy and I witnessed the spectacle of Lord Roberts' disembarkation. We laugh at recollections of the calisthenics classes on board, my attempts to learn to sew, life at the various hospitals, the antics of Durban, the hospital dog with his red cross panniers, and at Marjorie's tireless dedication both as a nurse and to chatting up young men. Henry is thus adequately prepared and forewarned about the arrival tomorrow of my great friend, confidante and consummate flirt. By the time we have eaten our main course, Henry has heard all that is to be told of my time at Kroonstad. That is, apart from my decision to travel behind enemy lines to Lindley with a complete stranger who also happened to be a married man.

"And so," he takes his time over his next sip of champagne, "you have not been in touch with Major Oliver…"

"Edwin," I interrupt.

"…with Edwin…for almost two years?"

"Actually, we have been writing to one another for some time now."

I predict my brother's raised eyebrows just before they react for the umpteenth time this evening.

"How did you get in touch with him? Did he recover? Where is he now? Did he go back into action? A Royal Engineer? How old did you say he was?"

Our combined mirth at his protective interrogation and my defensiveness towards the man I love draws the attention of our waiter who glances at my ringless finger and wants to know, "Would sir and madam like another bottle of champagne?" which of course, we would, and another is delivered post-haste with not a further hint of disapprobation, once Henry has informed him of our familial relationship.

My brother listens carefully as I speak about the hopes and plans that Edwin and I have shared in our correspondence.

"Three children! That will be quite an undertaking, Anna. And John is little more than a baby."

"He is two and a half now, Henry. John's sister, Katie, is five and Charles, the oldest, is seven. I will show you their photographs when you come to Ripponden House. Katie is the image of her mother, Joy."

And then there is Grace, I think to myself, *about whom Edwin knows. Except I have held back the full truth.* Henry interrupts my worrisome thoughts of the future with a question about the here and now.

"Dinner on Friday evening, you say?"

Rising apprehension and anticipation in equal measures prompt me to pick up the champagne coupe, now refilled for the fourth time.

"Seven for seven-thirty. You will love the house, Henry; it has a sort of Queen Anne Revival style. And I cannot wait for you to meet…everyone."

"But tomorrow, it will be just Marjorie, Florence and us?"

I nod.

I decline the offer of steamed pudding from the waiter and reflect on how this extravagant food would have been fought over at Bloemfontein camp. During our conversation, my brother and I have barely touched on that experience or exactly how I came to be at the camp in the first place, although I am aware that Henry has been well briefed by Major Holmes.

Between mouthfuls of sponge and custard, Henry asks about the Chambers family, the mine, the house and the children. It is another conversation that demands more than the few minutes it takes him to polish off his pudding, but I begin nevertheless.

"At the outbreak of war, the shortage of servants was a problem for Mr Chambers but not so great as it became. That is how I came to work for him. He was happy to keep 'fallen women' such as myself in some of the more menial positions."

"Not at the mine, surely?"

I laugh at the very thought.

"Not there! I was put to work in the laundry at Ripponden House. In any case, the mine was shut because of the war and so there was no need for workers there. Consequently, the family spent a lot of time in England. In Yorkshire, where Mr Chambers Senior is also in the mining business."

"I see. Is Mrs Chambers from Yorkshire too?"

"She is, although she hales from the West Riding and he is from South Yorkshire. And her mother is French, from near Paris, which has something to do with Christabel's love of shopping and haute couture."

"She would get along splendidly with our mother then," Henry deduces this fact, of which I have often mused. Our grandpa on our mother's side was brought up in France, although to hear his flawless command of the English language, you would never believe it. Mother inherited Grandpa's love of all things French, especially fine wine.

"How are mother and father, Henry?"

A cold blanket of fear enfolds me when I see the expression on my brother's face.

"I will have to tell you sometime, Anna. There is no best time for what I have to say."

"No. Not papa? Not mother?" I cannot bear the thought of more sadness.

"No, no, Anna, not that. Papa is well and his firm has a great deal of work. There are so many court cases that he has even had to take on more attorneys and barristers. And secretarial help. And mother is just fine. Still painting. Did she tell you that one of her seascapes went into the Academy exhibition last year?"

He searches my face and waits for an answer that does not come. He steals himself and continues.

"No, not them. They are both well. It is Grandpa. Grandpa died. Two months ago; he passed away in June."

"But why, how? Why have I not heard?"

Our grandpa was a healthy, active man who played golf, bridge and tennis even though he had certainly exceeded his three score years and ten. Poor mother doted on her papa and must be devastated.

"His heart stopped. Just stopped working. I am sorry, Anna but we…we thought it best to tell you in person. Although I know mother has written. I thought her letter might have reached you before I did."

I remember the unopened envelopes waiting for me at Ripponden House.

Now we are crying again, and the waiter circumnavigates our table pondering, no doubt, whether this is the right moment to offer a third bottle of Veuve Clicquot.

Aided by Forbes the coachman, I climb gingerly into the carriage after my new grief has been tempered by sweet words from my brother and a large glass of brandy. A short drive later, overwrought, exhausted and not a little tipsy, I cannot bear to open the letters that await me at Ripponden House. Instead, I dismiss Winnie's attentions, fling clothes, shoes and hairpins across the ottoman at the foot of the bed, crawl between the linen sheets and pull the eiderdown around my shoulders. As sleep closes in, further comfort comes in a jigsaw of dreams where I am certain that the faces in that unfinished picture belong to Edwin and Grace.

My daughter's sweet face greets me when I awake late next morning. Although rather frowned upon by Nanny and by Christabel, I often allow Tombi to bring Grace into my bedroom. Someone, probably Winnie, has hung up my navy lace gown on the front of my wardrobe. It serves as a sombre reminder of last night's events and of the news of my grandfather's passing. Having bounced Grace a little on the bed – a game that brings on the usual fits of baby giggles – I hand her back to Tombi and tell them that we will meet for a trip around the garden in the dog-cart once Tombi has tamed Grace's hair. I have tried to do it myself with the special comb that Tombi uses, but whenever I go near Grace with it, she shrieks in dread horror.

Because I already know the sad tidings contained in the letter from my mother, I put it to one side to read later along with news from my aunt and uncle. Then I ring for Winnie, who helps me decide on a dove-pink, challis frock and paisley wrap. Once the trickle of morning servants has run its course, I find precious solitude in the gentle spring sunlight on the downstairs veranda with its far-reaching views across the terraced gardens.

My impatience to discover who has sent the mysterious envelope does not get the better of me. Instead, I slip my ivory handled paper-knife beneath the flap of the envelope addressed by Edwin's hand. From between the many sheets of correspondence, falls a small package wrapped in white tissue paper. Inside is a tiny silver filigree locket in the shape of a heart. I open it and a photograph of Edwin sits within. His dark eyes gaze out at me and the facing side is empty, awaiting my own image. I unfold the thick sheaf of paper and relax into the gentle swing of the rocking chair.

Dearest Anna,

I do hope you like the necklace. I think will suit your beautiful neck. It is quite old and belonged to my grandmother before my mother, who in answer to the question you asked in your last letter; yes, is looking forward to meeting you and soon, as is my father. Then afterwards, perhaps I can do the proper thing and speak to your father. There is so much I want to say to you, my darling Anna, so forgive my impatience. It is hard that we can only write and not speak to one another, although I look forward to the post each day, hoping for more sweet words from my darling girl.

I have not long been in possession of all the letters you wrote to me during your time on the veldt with Klaus Meyer. Thank you for sending them on. That they came to light at all is nothing short of a miracle. I do not really know where to begin or even how to express the relief, pride, sorrow, joy and admiration that overcame me on reading of your travels. Reading between your lines, my darling, I think there is much more to tell but it struck me that your journey unfolds rather like one of Isabella Bird's, except that Africa is one of the few continents she did not explore, I think.

Of course, you probably know by now that the man you set out to help, turned up back at Kroonstad about two weeks after you left. Maud had been the very soul of discretion, and neither Marjorie nor I knew the real purpose behind your vanishing act until the injured Colonel Roddeston returned. At first, everyone assumed that Henry had been wounded and that you went to be with him. How is that gallant brother of yours by the way?

Since I have already written reams on the subject, I do not need to spell out here again what a worry it was when we discovered that you had gone missing. Suffice to say that when the party sent out to the Meyer farm returned to tell of its abandoned, burnt out state, we did think the worse.

I am trying to understand why you cannot write to me about your time at the camp in Bloemfontein. From what I have read in Emily Hobhouse's reports and those subsequently from the Ladies Commission and everything published here in the British newspapers, I can imagine some of the horrors that you must have witnessed in the camp's hospital. But it is something you say that you would prefer to speak about rather than write and so I will just have to be patient for just a short while longer. The date is writ large in my mind and I will be at the Southampton quayside hours before the Avondale Castle is due in. I shall take the Red Funnel packet steamer from Cowes the day before you arrive and stay at the Southwestern Hotel so as to avoid any possibility of missing you!

168

Please worry not about me. I am now patient-turned-visitor at Frank James Hospital, where a sorry lot of the chaps still reside. I consider myself to be hugely fortunate when I see the impairments that some of them suffer. It is also good to be living at my parents' house and to be able to spend so much time with the children.

You asked after my parents' positions now we have a new King. There was a great deal of uncertainty about the future of Osborne House after the old Queen's death, but things are slowly falling into place. It seems that King Edward does not have the same love of the Isle of Wight that his mother did, God rest her soul. The King does not wish to keep the house on, and after much rumour and speculation, there does now appear to be a plan. My mother will, for the time being at least, continue with her work and my father is involved in the scheme to develop the household wing at Osborne into a convalescence home for the Navy and the Army.

But enough of the Isle of Wight and my family. You will discover its delights and meet them all when you come over here next month. You will particularly love Princess Beatrice, I know.

Next month! That sounds soon even though it is nearly eight weeks away. By the time you receive this letter, it will be only five weeks. Does it seem to you as though I am counting the days? Well, I am, my darling.

There is something I want to ask you…

Close by, I hear "Mamma! Mamma!" and I stand to look over the wrought iron balustrade and wave at neatly coiffured Grace who is already in the dog-cart. Tombi leads Kim, the family's black and white part-Pointer, part-Labrador Retriever, as he ambles gently around one of the lawns. Grace sits up in the miniature cart, supported by a mound of pillows and gives what passes for a little wave.

"Keep the cart away from the croquet lawn!" I warn and wave back as they move towards that sacrosanct and elegantly manicured part of the garden. An angry, male voice bellows from the shadows as I make my way to the steps.

"Get that kaffir and that half-breed child off my lawn!"

Holding on to my temper with every ounce of restraint that I can muster, I reach Tombi and Grace before the head-gardener does.

"They are doing no harm, Fred."

I try and pacify him, but to no avail. He has never understood my change in status and his dim view of me has not changed since I moved from the small room at the back of the laundry into the main house. Fred shouts more insults when I steer the unhappy procession of elderly dog, sobbing baby and terrified Tombi back to the stable block, but his curses are mostly lost in the wind-rustled trees and shrubs. I pick up my baby girl and hold her close until the sobs subside.

"Come, girls, let us unhitch the cart. I think Kim is a little tired now."

"Yes, Miss Anna. This is good idea," Tombi raises her eyes at last and I know that she will be smiling again soon enough.

It will be hours before I can finish reading Edwin's letter, or begin my reply due to another of the interminable rounds of 'visiting' or 'being visited' that happens almost every afternoon. Thus, I will have plenty of time to ponder his question. But it is not Edwin's desire to know whether I am set on living in London once we are married that causes me to make my excuses. The unexpected heat of the afternoon provides an opportunity for me to retreat upstairs to change my attire and to open the remaining letters, whose contents are enough of a shock for Christabel to forgive my absence.

"But it is such a vast amount!"

It is Friday evening after a wonderful dinner of fricassée of chicken à la chevalière followed by roast lamb, accompanied by a bottle of Chateau Latour. I have managed to drag my brother away from the others while Marjorie and Christabel exchange places at the piano.

Masked by the strains of Dvorjak's Song to the Moon from Rusalka, Henry's whisper is barely audible, "Our grandfather has made you a very rich woman. You should be happy with your inheritance, Anna! And you will be able to send money back here to support the child."

"Grace. My daughter," I hiss back. "And I will not have to send money back here," I return my brother's direct stare, "because she is coming to England with me."

At that moment, the room erupts with applause just as Christabel concludes the stylish rendition of her husband's current favourite opera piece. Henry neither applauds nor smiles, and although I know it will be perceived as the height of rudeness by our hosts, I follow him outside onto the terrace.

"Henry, please. She is my daughter."

"She is the illegitimate child of a black man. He violated you. How on earth do you think you can impose such an offspring on our family, Anna? Have you gone completely mad?"

"I am quite sane, brother dear. Do you imagine that this has been an easy decision for me?"

This time, he says nothing but begins to walk away from the orange glow and animated chatter of the drawing room and down the steps. I move quickly to keep up with his rapid pace. He slows as we turn into the shadows where light from the house does not reach. His anger has subsided but become something that I like much less.

"What man will want to have anything to do with you, Anna?"

"A good man, Henry. A good one."

"And would that happen to come in the person of Major Edwin Oliver?" He stops walking and holds me by the wrists, and continues, "Whose parents work for the new King? Whose only experience of coloured people is in their servants' hall? Or on the streets?"

I slap my brother so hard across the face that the sound reverberates momentarily before losing itself amidst the quivering rhododendrons.

"She is my blood. She is your blood. She is our blood!"

I stoop to pick up the handkerchief that I have dropped in my distress. Henry is there before me and retrieves the sodden cloth. He guides me onto the stone seat by the lily pond and wipes away my anger.

"I know," he says. "I know."

We sit there for a while, volleying 'what ifs?' and 'buts' until the faint sound of Christabel's voice calling my name reminds us of our neglected hosts and the evening's unfinished entertainment.

"Was my playing so deplorable?" quizzes Mrs Chambers as we step back into the house and there follows a little nervous laughter from the other guests. That they have noticed my red eyes and my brother's inflamed cheek is apparent from the way they do not look directly at either Henry or myself. But no one remarks upon these things, and it is not long after a short hand of cards that Henry, Marjorie and Florence depart.

"What a pleasure it was to meet another Yorkshire girl. And from the West Riding too. Quite a coincidence that she should know the Calder Valley and even Ripponden!" Christabel tries a jolly approach.

"It is. I had no idea that you named this house after a village near your parents' home."

"But Florence guessed straight away!"

"And you had no problems understanding her accent! When she and I first met, I had to have practically every sentence translated. '*Yu shud no betta, yuv read Wutherin' eyets'*, is how she used to scold me."

Christabel's laugh tinkles its merry tune and I realise that I feel better. Calmer. Happier.

"Dare I ask?" she ventures.

"I think he will come around. But it was a difficult conversation. And yesterday…no, it is not important…"

"Go on, Anna. Tell me."

I think of the author of the unopened mystery letter and smile.

"Yesterday I had a letter from Emily Hobhouse. She plans to return to Africa next year."

"But you will be gone."

"Yes, I will have been back in England for some while by the time of her visit. She has friends though, Lady Jane Frankton and Miss Elizabeth Molteno, in Cape Town, who she insists that I meet."

"Well, that was not such a difficult revelation, Anna! Miss Molteno may have a certain reputation here but she is from a well-regarded and respectable family. And by all accounts, Lady Frankton is a charming host who is terribly well-connected."

"That is not it. I had another letter. From my mother. You know already that my grandfather died in June."

Christabel nods.

"My mother wrote that…I learned that…that my grandfather has named me the sole beneficiary of his estate."

"The sole beneficiary?" I detect the raised note of surprise in her tone.

"So, Henry inherits nothing?"

"Henry says that his allowance from our father is more than enough for his needs."

"Does he mean that?"

"I think he does."

"Why, Anna? Why did your grandfather leave everything to you?"

"My mother wrote to me that Grandpa thought that life was easier for Henry, as a man that is. And that he wanted me to have the money so that my life would be easy too."

After airing admiration for my grandfather's enlightened views, we discuss how I might invest my inheritance and the challenges of building a house from scratch. It is something of which Christabel and John have much experience, and a project that I would dearly love to undertake if I decide to sell Grandpa's Kensington house. We touch on the difficult problem of how my parents will respond to Grace, but I do not

171

reveal my worries about how I will share the truth about my daughter with Edwin. When pressed, I tell Christabel how much money I will inherit. Her face becomes porcelain pale and she reaches for the bell.

"This calls for a toast, my dear. I am happy for your good fortune, Anna. Goodness only knows you deserve some."

Chapter 24
Decisions

Saturday's visit to the mine is not an event that I have been looking forward to. For Tombi, however, it is an important day and she wears a clean, newly pressed uniform when we congregate even though I do not insist upon it.

I have had a charming cotton print dress made especially for her but she has kept it, wrapped and neatly folded, in a drawer. Because the carriage will be somewhat cramped with five of us plus Grace, Christabel declines our offer of 'squeezing her in'.

John was keen for Henry to experience a trip in his brand-new Wolseley but we managed to persuade him of the impossibility of everyone being comfortably accommodated in that motor-vehicle, not to mention being appropriately attired against the dust or the danger of breaking down, which happens with alarming regularity.

Grace, Tombi and I enjoy the glorious August spring sunshine on the drive into town before Forbes draws to a stately halt outside the Kimberley Club, where my brother, Marjorie and Florence hover expectantly. They are bedecked in clothes that are far too smart for where we are going, especially Marjorie, who seems to think that we are headed for a garden party. I understand her choice of white organdie embossed with tiny flowers when she expresses her disappointment at not being able to sit up-top next to Forbes and Henry.

"How long did my brother have to wait before you decided to make him your next victim?" I ask when she takes her petulant place beside me inside the carriage.

"About ten minutes."

"You took your time then!" I tease her.

"I would say it were no more 'n five," chimes Florence, who at least wears a sensible coat over her frock. She gathers Grace into her arms and nuzzles her neck while Marjorie puts on her outraged face and turns to me.

"I had no idea that you had such an adorably handsome twin. You are a woman of deep secrets, Anna."

The last said, she gives my free hand a gentle squeeze, compliments Tombi on how smart she looks and takes Grace from Florence's lap to sit her firmly upon her own. But Florence is having none of it and, making a game out of this child-ping-pong, seizes her back with a look that might well have changed the result of the Wars off the Roses. Grace screams with laughter and demands, 'gen, gen!' so that soon my two friends are glowing with exertion.

Our arrival at the mine confirms my indecision about what bothers me the most. Forbes pulls up the horses at the gate, where the smiling security officer opens the carriage door. His expression changes from deference to disgust on seeing its occupants and he jabs a finger at Tombi then notices Grace, now nestled in Florence's victorious arms.

"Are these all going in with you, miss?" he asks, but before I can give him a piece of my mind, Henry is asking if there is a problem, and with a "No, sir," from the guard, we move ahead into the vast tract of open land that my guests would never know is enclosed by miles and miles of barbed wire.

"Where will we go first?" asks Marjorie. "Will there be tea? It is just that all this dust is making me terribly thirsty."

"No tea just yet, I am afraid. And first, we will see the great pit. In fact, here we are!"

We pile out and gather near the edge of the deep chasm in the earth.

Marjorie peers into the void and steps back hurriedly, "How far down does it go?" The pink in her cheeks that vanished momentarily is now resuming its rightful place.

"It has been excavated to about a hundred feet."

"Why are they all rushin' about so?" Florence wants to know.

I do not need to look down to visualise the barely clothed native men in their oddly braided straw hats scurrying into the numerous burrows situated around the floor of the great pit.

"They are getting ready for the next explosion. We need to move away."

Time seems to freeze while we count down to the detonation. Then it happens. The blast is short and sharp, but the reverberations that splinter the air and rock the ground so that it shakes, last for an age. Clouds of dust deposit a fine, pale film on our hands and faces and for a moment, we are in a soundless vacuum. I cannot get close to Tombi, whose terrified eyes search mine for answers.

The blast over, we watch the men heap the broken clay into buckets. These are then raised to the surface by pulleys and put into little trams. This is something I know that Grace will love because the trams are drawn by donkeys along narrow rails to the pulsator. Each of us, in turn, except Henry, dangles Grace so that she has a good view of the creatures. Then tiring one by one, the girls go back to the edge of the pit to rest their arms in anticipation of what will happen next. It is then that Henry comes to stand beside me.

"She is beautiful. Like her mother. I am so sorry, Anna." He takes his niece in his arms, kisses her hair and joins in as she chortles merrily when he lifts her high above the diamonds in the dark pit of the earth.

At the sound of a high-pitched siren, Marjorie, Florence and Tombi turn puzzled faces towards my brother and me.

"Meal time," I say, trying not to infect the jolly mood with my discomfort.

"But why they go down big tunnel in big hole?" Tombi knows that we are to see her brothers during their break and is clearly mystified as to how that will happen.

"It is a tunnel to the workers' compound. But we are not permitted to use it. It's for the miners only. Quickly, everyone, come this way and we will make our way to the kitchens."

The place where the workers live and eat is a large area enclosed by a high white-washed facade that is surrounded by a continuous ring of mud brick rooms, also painted white. The corridor opens out into a long room where there are ten steaming iron kettles, each the size of a barrel. The pale glutinous mush that is revealed when the metal lids are removed does nothing to heighten our appetites. Quite the reverse, in fact. A Caucasian man who is clearly in charge nods in Henry's direction, but it is I who step forward.

"We are here to see Esaia and Jeso Ntswana."

Although my remark is addressed to him, the man blatantly directs his response to my brother.

"Yes, sir, so I understand. Please wait here."

Glistening with sweat and dressed in not much more than their straw hats, the native men emerge robotic from the tunnel past an overseer who ticks off each name on his notepad in turn. Silently, we watch the men file into the kitchen and observe each one as he collects a metal pail.

Marjorie pulls at my sleeve.

"It is like a zoo."

"It is work. These men need to work," I hear the lack of conviction in my voice, but Marjorie is so transfixed that I do not think she notices. So fluid is the movement of men and pails, as ten by ten, each group hives off from the line to an allocated kettle, that it has the semblance of a well-rehearsed and oft-performed military tattoo. The activity does not have the same distracting fascination for my brother as it does for my friends, and he tugs my other arm.

"What are we doing in this place, Anna? We do not belong here."

"We are here, brother, so that Tombi might to say goodbye to her brothers," I reply and wait for the realisation to hit.

"Which means that you intend to bring Tombi back to England too, I suppose."

His voice is cold but quiet. He gives me one of his steadfast looks. That my brother's statement is not a question leaves me with a sense of his acceptance.

After a short conversation with Henry, a different white man, who has been speaking animatedly with the head of the overseers approaches and ushers our party through a door whose sign reads Inspection Room. Tombi has not yet been able to identify Esaia and Jeso, partly I suspect due to the identical hats they all wear and partly because there are just so many uniformly muscular, similarly unclothed bodies. She glances back repeatedly as we are led away.

"Do not worry, Tombi. They will be brought to us."

But it is tea that is brought to us first and once we have drunk our fill, Henry picks up Grace who has begun to wriggle and asks Marjorie and Florence to accompany him outside for some fresh air. Florence, who has said not a word since we arrived at the compound, rises to her feet and Marjorie gives me a knowing wink before hooking her arm around Henry's.

"Perhaps we can visit the rest of the mine once Tombi has spoken with her brothers?" she says.

I am thankful to Henry now that Tombi and I are alone, but then I wonder if she would rather I left too. It seems that she would like that and so I close the door on their farewells and wait for her in the corridor to the muted sound of gentle words and soft sobs.

"What d' they inspect in t' Inspection Room?" Florence wants to know when we meet up with them by the washing lake a short while later. Grace is asleep in my friend's arms despite the noise of the driverless trucks rattling along their rail-journey high overhead to deposit their precious mud-bound gems into the lake's jigging machine.

"Do you really want to know, Florence?" asks my brother, who is evidently enjoying the company of my blunt Yorkshire friend and the kittenish attention of Marjorie.

"S' long as I do not drop the little 'un."

"The value of diamonds is such that it is considered to be a great temptation for those men who work in the mine."

"Yes, I can see that might be the case."

"When a man's contracted time comes to an end, he is searched thoroughly to make sure that none of the goods are leaving the mine with him, if you get my meaning? And for good measure, an emetic is given prior to the inspection, just to make sure."

The look Florence gives my brother, who is only the messenger after all, speaks a lengthy tirade that has never been Florence's way. The brusque retort that is her usual trademark does not happen either and it is Marjorie who breaks the uneasy silence.

"It is as well that we are all nurses, Captain Lieberman. Thank you for the insight, but no further explanation is needed."

Marjorie's look of mock horror seems to amuse Henry, and for some reason, I bristle. I hope that Marjorie will not thumb through my brother, only to cast him aside like an old book that does not warrant a second read. Her library of second-hand literature is substantive. Then I remember Tombi. A sideways glance assures me that she did not fully comprehend or even hear Henry's comments. Whether in the past or future, I see that her thoughts are faraway.

Chapter 25
The Journey South

From the balcony outside the atrium of the ogee dome at Ripponden House, it is possible to see the baobab trees. I watch the flaming sun sink behind these African giants and vow to ask Tombi if there is a bushman story about how they came to be. As burning red cools finally to indigo, I watch for the rising stars and wonder if I will ever return to this land of rich earth and deep secrets.

I have been sitting here with my thoughts for a long while when I hear footsteps and the creak of the door.

"Are there stars in England, Miss Anna?"

Tombi knows that I come up here often just before supper and has brought Grace to say goodnight.

"The skies in England are not so big as in Africa. Not in London at least," I say.

"But there are stars?"

"The same stars. Perhaps not quite so bright. There are a great many buildings in London and gas lamps in the street make the stars appear to dim a little."

I do not mention the London smog, winter mists or grey, small-island clouds that often obscure the night skies. So, it is in silent companionship that we perch on the window ledge under the celestial cloak that covers both our worlds and soak up the beauty until the dinner gong sounds.

Next morning, the entire household is up before dawn to help, and by ten o'clock, we are ready. John Chambers has been conspicuously absent during the hours of packing, re-packing, loading, unloading and final counting and checking. With all the stealth of a big cat, his un-moving eyes blink as he emerges from the shadows of the curved front steps. His stance deliberately casual, he lifts the chain of his gold pocket-watch and studies the hour.

"You are sure that you have all your passes?" he asks. Because military rule is still in place and permits are notoriously difficult to come by, I am grateful for his intervention in procuring ours and pat the large pocket in my travelling cloak wherein they lie.

"It has been arranged that you should have hot dinners each evening at the station restaurants. And cook has packed hampers for the train. There may be delays of course, and there is still a great deal of troop movement, but you should reach Cape Town by Thursday at the latest."

At the station, I spot the harried-looking ticket inspector and herd my little party towards him. Upon his request, I hand over the travel permits and he summons another man who appears older and less harassed. He indicates towards Tombi and Grace with a dismissive flourish of his thin hand.

"Will these two be in third class, ma'am? I can show them to their carriage."

"Thank you, sir, but we are travelling together."

"These…are accompanying you ladies? I am sorry, madam, it is just that servants do not usually travel in first class."

I am about to make the foolish mistake of revealing Grace to be my daughter, not Tombi's, which he has clearly assumed, when Florence bustles up to confront him.

"You 'eard the lady. We are together."

Florence so rarely intervenes that our surprise makes us slow to follow when the ticket inspector reluctantly discharges us into the care of another young railway worker who guides us to a first-class corridor coach – one of two sandwiched between sections of a goods train.

None of our luggage or food is here and there follows an anxious few minutes, made more so by screaming officials and an impatient, repeated whistle that commands the train to leave at once, even though we are not due to depart for another hour. From under the shroud of steam that threatens to engulf us, emerges a familiar but sooty leather trunk, then another and another. Transported on the bent backs of native African and Chinese porters from the longer train that waits impatiently at the opposite platform, our worldly goods are deposited without ceremony in the corridor outside our carriage. At an elongated, shrill blast from the guard's whistle, we begin to move and the last of the porters practically topple from the train.

An agitated Marjorie, who has been scanning the platform, begins to wave frantically. "Henry!" she cries then laughs at my brother's confused face.

"You are on the wrong train!" he bellows above the noise, accosts a railway official, gesticulates towards our train and increases his stride to keep up. He is parallel to our carriage for only a second but it is enough time to allow him to thrust a tiny package into my hand.

"Wear it," he commands. Then there is a great nodding of heads and a final shrug and a grin from Henry as he waves us off before he is swallowed by the swirling smoke.

In the parcel is a gold band that fits my ring finger perfectly.

Hot, bothered and hearts pounding, we arrange ourselves with our food hamper in the carriage and pray that we are travelling South. This happy fact is soon verified when Florence announces that the sun is in her eyes and so we celebrate in style with a picnic and some tepid champagne drunk straight from the bottle as the glasses seem not to have made the transition from one locomotive to another.

The signs of war trundle past as we settle into our journey. Here and there are bleached carcasses mostly of horses begun to merge with the parched earth. Lines of sun-lit, immortally white-washed wooden crosses bear witness to those who will not be returning home. Glinting their now unnecessary sharp warnings, tangled networks of barbed wire run un-interrupted on either side of the track and at irregular intervals are military blockhouses of various sizes and construction. Some are of stone, some of mud-brick and some of tin; all well-fortified with stone walls and sandbags, some ravaged by gunfire but all uniformly desolate.

"Was Edwin involved in the construction of these fortifications, Anna?" asks Marjorie after we pass yet another turreted edifice at the side of the track.

"Yes, after he recovered and left Kroonstad hospital and before he was injured again. Lord Kitchener decided that the building of the blockhouses would make the railways safer and would also make life difficult for the Boer commandos."

"How so?"

"Well, so many blockhouses were built, all linked by signalling equipment and manned by small garrisons, it became increasingly difficult for the Boers to destroy the railway lines. And of course, our lines of communication and supply were therefore in much better shape."

I click my Kodak and think of Edwin's oft-read words so deeply imprinted in my memory that they speak to me now.

...If it were not for the use of corrugated iron on some of these buildings, which are mostly made of stone and shingle, you might be forgiven for thinking that you had somehow slipped back into the realm of Henry Tudor. But then, of course, the passing locomotives and all the barbed wire might rather give the game away.

This letter continues, as usual, to anticipate our future together.

Once these latest wounds are healed and you are back in England, I must take you to Carisbrooke castle, Anna. It is at Yarmouth, not so very far from my parents' home and the old Queen's youngest daughter, Princess Beatrice, takes a great interest. In fact, the island's museum was opened there in 1898, in memory of her husband, Henry, and she is having Percy Stone, the architect, undertake much renovation. I cannot wait to...

Edwin's words fade from my mind. Thoughts of visiting castles and meeting English princesses seem inconsequential unless I can find a way of explaining how and why I am bringing my dark-skinned child out of Africa, where most people would probably say she belongs.

Monday night brings us to de Aar Junction where we stop for dinner and to replenish the oil for our lamps. But after wading through ankle deep dust, no paraffin can be found at the station and so we spend an eerie evening by candlelight and that night, our restless sleep is haunted by mysterious shadows. Marjorie and Florence are in the overhead bunks and Tombi sings softly to Grace on the seats opposite me. My daughter is soon lulled to sleep by the unfamiliar and beautiful native song. One or other of us is wakeful by turn in this cramped sleeping accommodation as the noises of the African night each take their gleeful turn to remind us how far from home the rest of us are.

Next day, I stay on the train to write my journal when the others decide to leave the confines of the carriage and walk beside the engine while it crawls to the summit of a gradual incline. I have barely written today's date when Marjorie reappears.

"Do you mind if I stay here with you, Anna?" she asks.

I clip the top back on the fountain pen that was a parting gift from Mr Chambers and pat the seat next to me. "Sit. I was not particularly in the mood for writing anyway and this wretched joggling up and down does make it rather difficult."

"We have had little chance to be alone together."

She takes my left hand and touches the gold ring. When she looks up into my eyes, I see that she wears her serious face. It is the one that always makes me want to laugh and today is no exception. Soon, she has become infected and we giggle until I see that in twice beginning a sentence, my friend is troubled about something. I wonder if she is going to confess her feelings for my brother.

"Is there something you would like to say to me, Marjorie?" I imitate her previous serious countenance and she relaxes into her usual smiling self. She glances out of the carriage window at Tombi, who waves, out of breath as she climbs the hill with Grace strapped onto her back.

"We do not have long. So, I will say what I must."

She hesitates for only a second.

"Anna, are you sure that you are doing the best thing for Grace?" She does not wait for my reply but wades right in. "By taking her to England, I mean. You see, I know what it feels like to be an outcast. An illegitimate child. A bastard, Anna. That is what people will call your daughter. Whether or not you wear a wedding band. And I am not…"

She struggles not to mention the words coloured, black or half-caste, so I say them for her and she blushes as she continues,

"…and I am white. A white woman in a white man's country, Anna. You know very well that had not my father paid for my schooling at that vile convent, I would have been put in the workhouse. My mother was a servant. And a disgraced one at that. She could not have kept me. Thank goodness my father had some shred of decency about him, even if he could never, would never, marry my mother. How much worse would it have been for me had I been…"

"Like Grace?" I say.

"Like Grace," she affirms then pauses and continues when I do not speak.

"What have you told Edwin?"

I try to persuade myself that it is not any of Marjorie's business, but in her own blunt way, she is merely expressing what I have churned over and over in my own mind so what I say is, "I have told him a half truth."

"And which half have you neglected to tell the man you intend to marry, Anna?"

"He does not know that Grace is my child."

"But he does know that you are bringing a child back to England?"

"He knows that I have decided to adopt a child from the concentration camp. A child who would have no one, were I not to do so."

"A child from the camp. A camp populated almost entirely by Dutch people. White, Dutch people."

Marjorie is correct in this assumption and in the assumption that she knows Edwin will have made. I can only nod. I am barely able to look her in the eye.

"How could I have explained all that has happened in a letter?" I hear the defensive tone in my voice and do not like it one bit.

"So, let me think this through. Edwin is expecting a little blonde Dutch girl with pigtails and you will present him with coffee-coloured Grace and her unmistakably African hair? Will that be before or after you drop into the conversation that you were violated by a black British soldier who thought you were a Boer whore?"

Desperation floods over me, and gulped waves of fear confound my thoughts. Then Marjorie flings her arms around me and it is as we clutch one another in hopeless helplessness at our inability to predict the future or change the past, that Florence, Tombi and Grace climb back aboard the train.

Beaufort West is our next meal stop and where we find two armies. The first is a dust-raising British column on their homeward march. It is led by sunburnt scouts in shirt-sleeves on war-wasted horses with broken harnesses and followed in turn by donkey-drawn wagons, a mounted guard and finally foot soldiers whose battle-ravaged uniforms tell their own silent story. The second is an army of eager Chinese, who are keen to offer a myriad of comforts to weary travellers. Florence organises hot, sweet tea while Marjorie uses her charms to secure what we are told is the very last of the paraffin.

Progress along the single narrow-gauge rail track towards Cape Town is hampered by the surprising number of trains carrying troops bound for all the pink places of Empire. We return the men's joyful waves but not the colourful language, each time we are forced to wait in a siding. When we think that the great Karoo will go on forever, we finally reach Matjiesfontein. After the great expanse of wild land which stretches across the interior of Cape Colony, where our train has been dwarfed by the barren mountains and untamed, natural beauty of this country, a change of scene into the station's restaurant with its man-made accoutrements is a most welcome pleasure, even if the roast mutton is as stringy as old rope.

Chapter 26
Return to Cape Town

Although I smile at the intake of breath from Florence who has never been to Cape Town before, my own wonderment is just as great as the first time I came here. I am certain that today, the surrounding gardens are greener and more fecund than ever.

After I have taken some snaps, we return to the front of the building and approach the familiar, welcoming entrance to the Mount Nelson Hotel, where it has been arranged that our little party is to stay for our short sojourn in Cape Town. John and Christabel have also organised for us to meet several of their Cape acquaintances who they believe are best placed to introduce us to some of the finer sights. The first of these is to be an accompanied visit to Groote Schuur, but thankfully not until tomorrow morning, because despite the high-spirited delight at our arrival, the thought of hot baths and the renowned cuisine of the Mount Nelson are uppermost in our minds. Nonetheless, we are full of anticipation for our visit. We have heard a great deal about the beauty of Cecil Rhodes' estate and house, rebuilt after a catastrophic fire in 1896 by architect Sir Herbert Baker, who is not only a great friend of Christabel, but who played a significant part in the design and furnishing of Ripponden House. It is to be a friend of Emily Hobhouse, Lady Frankton, who will accompany us to Groote Schuur and then on to her own residence for afternoon tea afterwards. Had it not been for his early demise only five months ago, we would doubtless have been dining at Groote Schuur with Mr Rhodes himself, as he was a famously generous host and a close business colleague of John Chambers, who attended the great funeral here in April.

A commotion ahead brings my thoughts back to the present and I lengthen my stride to catch up with the others. Marjorie's raised voice and Florence's strident accent have already drawn a small audience at the hotel's main entrance, where our trunks and other baggage are stacked. Awoken by the noise, Grace has begun to bawl and Tombi is being forcibly held by a uniformed hotel porter. It is the more senior footman that I address, however, once I have calmed my friends. There is so much noise from arriving guests, carriages, and even an automobile, that I am forced to shout to make myself heard.

"What appears to be the problem?"

"As I explained to the other members of your party, the booking is for three rooms in the hotel and a place in the servants' accommodation. For the maid."

I lift a now screaming Grace from Tombi's rigid arms and Marjorie starts to argue with another of the hotel's guests who has joined the throng and is pointing out the folly of employing 'kaffirs'. His wife, a hippo of a woman wearing unflattering stripes, thrusts herself into the fray. The exchange of words becomes a jostling, angry argument so I raise my voice again.

"This is my daughter's nursery maid and I expect her room to be close to my own."

"I understand, madam, but that is not what has been arranged by Mr Chambers and our hotel policy clearly states…"

An elbow jabs into my side and the woman in the striped dress knocks me sideways in her eagerness to be heard. Tombi steps in front of me to stop me falling and misses her step. The automobile is trying to reverse and sounds its horn right next to the carriage horses, whose front pair rear up and when I steady myself, there is Tombi lying on the ground. Blood seeps from the back of her head. She is very still and her neck is twisted so that her face is angled towards the ground.

"Thank goodness you were holding Grace," Marjorie says once the ambulance has taken Tombi to the hospital and we have been ushered inside the hotel with some deference and an outpouring of apology from the manager. Florence insisted that she go with Tombi but that Marjorie must stay with me and so the two of us find ourselves alone in the hotel's best suite with Grace who is now asleep.

"Should I have a telegram sent to Christabel? So that Tombi's parents know what has happened?" I wonder aloud.

"Let us wait. She may be quite recovered by the time we embark. But we should contact her uncle."

A fleeting shadow eclipses the brightness in Marjorie's eyes, but despite the doubt that clouds my own judgement, I agree with her proposal and after we arrange for a message to be sent to the nearby farm where Tombi's uncle works, we plan how we might visit the hospital on our way to Groote Schuur tomorrow.

When tomorrow comes, our stay at the hospital is all too brief.

"I am sorry," the sister who greets us at the nurses' station has a soft reassuring Afrikaans burr, "Tombi is still unresponsive. We are not permitting visitors just at the moment. Might I suggest that you return tomorrow, Mrs Lieberman?"

I twist the false wedding ring around my finger.

"But, how is she?" I want to know. I need to hope.

"She is young, strong and in the best place, ma'am."

"Thank you, Sister."

With a brisk nod and firmly placed hands, Marjorie guides me back to the fresh air and to Florence who pushes Grace's newly acquired perambulator, a gift from the hotel. Marjorie thinks I do not see when she gives a cursory but definite shake of the head as an indication of Tombi's condition in response to Florence's puzzlement at the brevity of our visit.

"Please let me take Grace back to the hotel, Anna."

I know that practical Florence is not interested in visiting houses and gardens or in socialising with people who she regards as alien to her working-class roots. In any case, Grace will need to be fed and changed soon, so I agree. Also, Florence is the only one of us who has mastered the technique for styling Grace's hair, and so I make sure she knows where Tombi keeps the special comb.

Marjorie and I ride in our old favourite mode of transport to meet Lady Frankton as arranged and our mood lightens as the Cape cart rattles from the comparatively scanty vegetation of the town to the more verdant Rondebosch, four miles away. The fresh yellows, oranges, reds and violets of the African spring's awakening blossom in oddly idiosyncratic harmony alongside British oaks, palm trees, cacti and bamboos.

"You must be Anna. And Marjorie. I would have recognised you anywhere, so vividly were you described in Christabel's letters!"

This bespectacled elderly woman, whose personality would appear to be larger even than her ample, padded frame, hoists herself indelicately into the cart, which plunges alarmingly to the right.

"Please, allow me to introduce myself. I am Jane Frankton but call me Jane." She grips each of us by the hand in turn and more words tumble from her lips before we can even draw breath.

"But no Florence, I see. And no baby. I do trust that all is well? Groote Schuur, please driver!"

As the cart slowly gains momentum and we circle our way around the gravel sweep of the drive, we endeavour to return Jane's warm greeting, admire her beautiful home and explain about Tombi's accident. Lady Jane Frankton listens attentively and once our sorry tale is concluded, she takes my hand again. She looks down at the wedding ring on my glove-less hand.

"My dear, Miss Lieberman. Anna."

I see that there is no need to explain the circumstances that have brought me here and a silent understanding passes between us.

"Forgive my boldness, but you have seen my house, in which I rattle around like a pebble in a bucket. If you or your friends ever have need of a place to stay, you must please consider my home to be your home. What need does one person have for seventeen rooms? If I had had children of course, there would be grandchildren… Oh, but look! I am talking so much – my dear husband, God rest his soul, always said that I had more words than Webster's Dictionary but that I would insist on saying them all at once – and he was right. Oh dear. We are missing the splendid views! Oh, and what a good thing that we are here on a Friday because the grounds of Groote Schuur are open to the public tomorrow and again on Sunday and really some of them – the people who come here that is – are wilder than the wild animals that dear Cecil introduced into the grounds. We will see them later. The animals, that is. Oh, and look, my dears! Well, sadly, you cannot see how magnificent the hydrangeas are because they are not in season, but the trees, as you can see, are beautiful at any time of the year. Well, here we are!"

Even though it is hardly likely, the idea of an immediate encounter with a lion or other hungry beast makes my descent from the cart somewhat hesitant. Behind me, Jane's laugh rings out as she becomes wedged somehow until Marjorie secures the aid of the wide-eyed driver. Cork-like, and to the obvious amusement of the driver, Jane pops from the vehicle and we find ourselves in the shadow of a quite beautiful white house with curved, Dutch-style gables at either end of a slate-topped roof. The many chimneys remind me of liquorice twists except that they too are white. Steps lead up to the hall door, on one side of which is a narrow window with a little seat inside, which in Dutch houses, so Jane tells us, is where the lady sits to be courted by her admirers. I pull my coat tight around me and put my gloves back on because the day is not warm. I see that despite the temperature, Jane unfolds a large fan with which she cools herself in the shaded recess of the grand and very masculine, columned front stoep.

Around the back of the house, we find a stunning park-like garden whose tree-dotted slopes rise all around us towards the jagged ridges of Devil's Peak Mountain. Beneath these towering purple rocks, valleys unfold before us to reveal clumps of fir trees and swathes of spring-time flora about to burst into colour. Something moves across the distant hillside and I lower my camera to get a clearer view.

"Zebra. And ostriches. But do not concern yourselves, my dears. There is a fence." Panting a little with exertion, Jane has managed to catch up with us. Her chin quivers when she speaks.

"I do hate to interrupt your enjoyment of this splendid scenery, my dear girls, but we really should move on. I have arranged luncheon for one-thirty. We cannot stay here long, but it would be such a pity not to see inside the house. It is a very fine interior indeed and shows excellent taste. The old house was burnt down a few years ago, but it has been rebuilt – without the thatch of course – on exactly the same lines. All very Dutch and with old Dutch furniture of the very best kind. Except, of course, when necessary and when Dutch things are not so quaint and pretty, there is English furniture. Always in good taste and never incongruous. Come, girls, come!"

Inside, the house appears so solid that it might have been hewn from one single, enormous piece of wood. What it might lack in lightness of touch is compensated for by surprising treasures such as the lines of blue tiles that are let into the walls in unexpected places. A parade of blue and white vases stands erect above the entrance hall's stone fireplace and even the chubby columns of the wooden screen seem to stand to attention. I admire the distinctive bannisters and move closer to inspect the carved newels. I stroke the wood.

"Phoenician. The bird."

I swing round in embarrassed shock at the man's accent-less yet familiar voice. "Captain Dawlish!"

185

Chapter 27
Captain Dawlish

The uniformed man swings his wheelchair around so that he is next to me.

"Major, now, actually. How are you, Miss Lieberman? Not in uniform I see. Have you given up nursing?"

His confident manner and charming smile are exactly as I remember them from our first meeting on the Dunottar Castle in the new year of 1900. I am temporarily dumbstruck and find myself staring at where his legs should be.

"Only one left as you can see. But I am told that I am quite lucky to be still alive."

"Captain Dawlish!"

Marjorie's voice rings around the hall as she emerges from the library with Jane.

"It is Major these days, Marjorie." I find my voice at last then add, "Forgive my rudeness, Major Dawlish. It is just that a British officer, especially one who I know, was the last person I was expecting to see here!"

"Ah, I see that you three are already acquainted," Jane puffs into view.

The Major laughs and seems genuinely pleased to be in our company. Not one for beating around the bush, as Florence would say, Marjorie's question is the one of the many that fly all at once to shock the rest of us into embarrassed silence.

"What happened, Major? To your leg?" Before he can summon his answer, Jane bustles into action and commands Major Dawlish to join us for luncheon.

Lady Jane's seventeen roomed-mansion is but a five-minute carriage ride from Groote Schuur, and within the hour, Marjorie and I have had an escorted tour around most of the splendid interior while Major Dawlish, undaunted by the ad-hoc invitation, has changed into more formal attire and joins us in the drawing room. He walks a little unsteadily across the room with the aid of crutches until he reaches Jane, where he stops, manages to lift her hand, kisses it and turns to face Marjorie and me. His delight at our evident surprise at his mobility causes a less than ladylike guffaw from our hostess which turns to tears of mirth when a tap of the Major's fake leg with her own walking stick, leads the parlour maid to gasp aloud.

"As you can see, ladies, it takes more than the loss of a limb to keep an officer of the Yeomanry down!"

"A gunshot wound?"

Marjorie's unflinching directness was one of the reasons for her popularity amongst the patients. It is an approach that elicits an equally blunt response from Major Dawlish.

"We were in the thick of an attack. For once, heavily outnumbered by the Boers but luckily, we had the Pom-Pom. Unluckily, it was jammed."

He seems to forget that Marjorie and I have nursed hundreds of battle-wounded men when he pauses to check that we are familiar with the term for this large mobile gun. He does not notice that Marjorie rolls her eyes at his lack of insight because he has to concentrate hard to lower himself onto the window seat where I join him, taking a glass of champagne for us both from the tray offered.

"And in any case, we were holed up in one of the blockhouses with only forty men when we needed a hundred to defend the place. He grins at me. That is where I met Major Oliver."

"Edwin! You know Edwin!"

"A splendid fellow indeed, Miss Lieberman. I understand that you set out on a very brave venture, which had rather unexpected consequences?"

He laughs at my surprised reaction and I find myself worrying about how much he knows.

"Sadly, Miss Lieberman, the reason I came to know Major Oliver so well, was that we were both injured in the same damn battle."

"Defending the railway line at the Witkop blockhouse?"

"Exactly. Then we recuperated together at the field hospital before he was sent back to England and I went back into the fray. Tweebosch. March. That is where this happened."

He bangs his wooden leg heartily.

"I went down to the Pom-Pom to tell the men to clear back to the rear and tinker it up. I kept riding around, getting the men to shoot away and I was on my way back to the big gun when there was a huge bang on my leg and what felt like a load of red-hot skewers pass through my calf. My mount was hit and she fell dead on top of me. I must have passed out because the next thing I knew, I was drinking Bovril and Brandy in the field hospital and the leg was gone."

"How did you come to be at Mr Rhodes house?" Marjorie asks.

"I may well ask you the same question!" he retorts.

"Well, Mr Rhodes was a friend of the Chambers, where Anna has been staying since she left that terrible camp at Bloemfontein. I know she would like to use some of her grandfather's inheritance to build a house for her and Edwin once they are married. Groote Schuur has many inspiring design features and Lady Frankton wanted to show us."

By now, I am only half listening because all this talk of Edwin makes me imagine his face and I long to see him. I also remember that Tweebosch was where the British general, Lord Methuen had been captured and then released by Koos de la Rey. I am quite certain that this is not the moment to share the fact that I have met this Boer general who I know was subsequently court-martialled for freeing such a valuable prisoner.

"Miss Lieberman?"

I have been aware of chatter in the background and it seems that Major Dawlish has posed a question.

"I do apologise, Major. My thoughts had wandered. I am so sorry, what was it that you asked me?"

"It is still rather a mystery, is it not?"

I begin to feel uncomfortable under his penetrating gaze, and shift my position on the window seat, plumping up one of the cushions behind me.

"Major?"

"How you came to be in the refugee camp at Bloemfontein in the first place."

The others have stopped their conversation and try in vain to feign a merely casual interest.

"When did you say that you spent time in hospital with Edwin?" I ask.

"Early in 1902. At that point, you were still missing. Edwin was wracked with guilt for not intervening in your plan to go to the aid of Colonel Roddeston. Roddeston was injured behind enemy lines, after all. Even back then, Major Oliver's feelings for you were plain to see. He was transfixed. I believe you had bewitched him, Miss Lieberman."

Although Major Dawlish speaks with humour in his voice, there is an undertone in his tease that I do not like. His stare is fixed on my face when he continues.

"It was only when we corresponded once he was back in England and I decided to take up Cecil's, that is Mr Rhodes', offer to stay at Groot Schuur, that Edwin told me you had become…reconnected. But there are great…gaps…in what he knows of your experience."

Marjorie decides to come to my aid, jolly as ever.

"Yes, the poor girl lost her memory after a terrible head injury. She was mistaken for a Boer farmer's wife and taken to the camp. Can you imagine the horror? Still, it is all over now, thank goodness. And we set off for England on the Avondale Castle in just three more days!"

I frown at Marjorie, willing her not to divulge any more of my secret history.

"And I am helping these girls make the most of their short stay in Cape Town, Major," adds Jane, brightly. "Shall we go through?"

No more is said on the topic concerning any 'gaps in what Edwin knows of my experience', and eventually, I relax. The whole meal is convivial and entertaining until the cheese course is interrupted by sound of raised voices outside the dining room. Eyes-blazing and with full-blown Yorkshire expletives accompanying her entrance, Florence marches into the room with Grace attached firmly to her hip. A tall, agitated native man hovers behind the footman who stands protectively in the doorway. Florence glares at me. It is a look I recognise as the one that she uses when she is scared. Her tone belies that fear.

"I am sorry t' interrupt, but there's been word from the hospital. We need to go there. Now."

She takes in the assembled company and nods first at Jane and then at Major Dawlish.

"Florence. Florence Wheelwright. I am a friend of these two. And this is Anna's daughter, Grace."

Grace's smile reveals the two, new bright white teeth that have recently appeared and her huge black eyes make my heart melt, but when I catch his eye, I see that the Major's smile is not warm.

"My, Miss Lieberman. You are an even darker horse than I thought."

It is only now that I remember his abrupt manner on the RMS Dunottar on discovering my surname and how he subsequently quizzed me on my German heritage. He raises himself from the table and casts a deliberate and disdainful look between me and the native man who I assume to be Tombi's uncle and who he clearly thinks is Grace's father.

"You will forgive me, Lady Frankton, but I see that it is time for me to leave."

"Yes, yes. Quite so, Major Dawlish. Yes. I quite understand. Quite."

The colour rises in Jane Frankton's already flushed cheeks as she lowers the glass of port, which she was about to raise in a toast only moments before. She summons the footman who does not know whether to keep the unwelcome guest at bay or to show the invited guest out. Jane makes the decision for him.

"Frobisher, you will kindly escort Major Dawlish to the carriage. Goodbye, Major. I am sorry that our afternoon had to end so hastily."

When I discover that the reason for our sudden journey to the hospital is due not to Tombi's worsening condition but because her uncle insists that he takes her back to the family home on the outskirts of the city, I feel curiously aggrieved and vent my exasperation on Florence.

"Why did you have to bring him to Lady Frankton's house?" I hiss at her when we arrive at the ward. She is furious in return.

"How was I t' know you would be entertaining some bloody man that you have never once mentioned before?"

"Florence, that is not fair. I had no idea that we would meet Major Dawlish. Who, as bad luck would have it, and thanks to you, now knows my many secrets. Including a mixed-race daughter, an as-yet unspecified relationship with a native African, but who the Major believes to be the person you brought to the house today and huge gaps concerning my whereabouts during the war. Oh, and thanks to the vagaries of war, the Major already knew that I am engaged to be married to Edwin, who turns out to be his friend. Could it get much worse?"

Florence softens but her temper remains inflamed.

"Praps y' should have told Edwin the truth in the first place!"

We have fallen behind Marjorie who is trying to pacify Tombi's uncle. The poor man has told me his name, but I have already forgotten in my distress. Tears of acknowledgement at Florence's barbed but truthful observation run freely as my friend puts her free hand around my shoulder.

"It'll be alright, you'll see. Won't it, Grace?" And she jiggles my daughter until her giggles make me smile too.

However hard I try, it is impossible to persuade Tombi's uncle, Joshua, that his niece should come to England with me. He is adamant that she must remain in South Africa and promises that he and his wife will care for her until she is well enough to return to Kimberley. I send a telegram to Christabel, briefly outlining the change of plan and decline Marjorie's invitation to join her and Florence for an evening soiree with one of the South African nurses they worked with at Kroonstad hospital during the time I spent with Klaus on the veldt.

Back in my room and with Grace soundly asleep in her cradle next to me, I sink into an armchair with my journal and two unexpected letters that have reached me from England. Looking forward to what I know will be his warm and loving words, I slip Edwin's familiar cream envelope to one side. My mother's orchid-pink stationary has been superseded by another equally feminine shade that reminds me of sugar-coated almonds and it is her letter that I open first.

My dearest daughter,

I am rather hoping that this letter reaches you before your ship departs for England, so forgive me if what I write comes as somewhat of a surprise. Your father and I thought initially that we would prefer to share what I must impart in person.

But now that your grandfather's will is in the public domain and rumours spread so quickly, we did not want you to hear about it from strangers.

You know that as well as the large sum of money, Grandpa also had the house in Cheyne Walk.

I pause here, because of course I know about the house in Chelsea, close to the river Thames. My great dilemma has been whether to keep the house and its servants on, or whether to sell up and use the money to have an architect build a house so that Edwin and I can have a say in its design. I know that my mother is keen to retain the Chelsea villa and so I sigh before I read on, fully expecting another list of reasons not to sell.

What you are not aware of, my dear, are your grandpa's assets in the United States of America. California, to be precise.

I stop dead to consider this extraordinary news. How is it possible, I wonder, that the grandfather to whom I was so close has never told me about his 'assets' in America? And what are these assets exactly? And why have my parents not said anything about them until now? I know that his family originated in south west France and that they were great wine-makers, hence grandpa's love of fine French claret. But how does the United States fit into the puzzle?

Before your grandpa was married to your grandmamma, he had another wife. Julia was American and he met her when he was tempted to California by the possibility of finding gold. All this was a long time ago, Anna. Like many others, Grandpa did not strike gold, but his experience of growing vines and wine production in France stood him and Julia in good stead and they established what became a very successful vineyard in the foothills of the Sierra Nevada...

Tragically, Julia died giving birth to their first child, a boy. Grandpa was so grief-stricken that he could not bear to stay in San Francisco and it was on his return to Europe, soon after Julia's death, that he met your grandmamma. They eventually decided to settle in England, as you know. It appears that the estate in foothills of the Sierra Nevada and the house in San Francisco were never sold and because you are named as the sole beneficiary in his will, they are now yours.

There are complications, my dear, which are too perplexing for me to explain in a letter, but worry not because in just a matter of weeks, we will be together again and your father and I will explain.

Until then, my dearest daughter,

Fondest love,
Your mama

All I can do is shake my head since there is no one with whom to share this startling revelation. I cannot shake off the feeling of incredulity and consider the possibility of a walk in the tranquil hotel gardens. Then I remember my sleeping child and decide instead to read Edwin's letter.

I have barely unfolded the precious sheets of parchment when there is a loud rat-tat-tat on the door. Grace stirs and begins to whimper but I ignore her, anticipating

Florence or Marjorie's return because they have forgotten something. The idea that something bad has happened to Tombi also crosses my mind but these are only fleeting thoughts because when I open the door, I see one of the hotel's bellboys, who hands me a sealed envelope. The young man shifts from foot to foot, but does not look at me, probably because I am wearing the rather flimsy peignoir given to me by Christabel as part of my bedroom 'trousseau'. Overcoming my embarrassment and smiling to myself at the thought of his, I remember the bellboy's expectation of a tip.

"Wait a minute," I tell him and retrieve a ten-shilling note, plus a now-screaming Grace. The look of shock on the young man's face confirms that I have given him far too large a tip, but I have no coins and it is the smallest note in my possession. He hands it back.

"I cannot take this, miss. They will think I stole it."

"I am sorry. I will make it right before I leave. What is your name?"

He looks up at me for the first time and holds out his hand to Grace, who immediately grabs it and stops crying.

"Simon, miss."

"Thank you for bringing this, Simon. Goodnight."

I watch his tiny frame disappear down the corridor, and wonder if he has ever been to school, then turn over the envelope and study the slightly smudged letters that make up my name. Miss Anna Lieberman. That there is nothing else written there is puzzling. Not even the customary 'By Hand', indicating a personal caller. My curiosity that the letter is not addressed vanishes when I read its content.

My dear Miss Lieberman,

How enchanting it was to meet you again today after all this time and to hear of your good fortune. I was especially delighted, not to say a little surprised, to meet your daughter. So charmingly...exotic. What a dark-eyed, dusky beauty she will become I am sure. Although, and forgive me, Miss Lieberman, you must be delighted that her skin is not quite as black as her father's, who I take it was the rather inappropriately dressed man who appeared at Lady's Frankton's during luncheon. That you are full of surprises, Miss Lieberman, would be rather an understatement, would you not say?

I have a small proposition that I think you might be interested in, and therefore await your company in the hotel garden. I will be on the terrace until nine o'clock after which time, should you decide not to accept my invitation, I will assume that you are not interested in what I have to say.

Major Dawlish has signed his note off with an ostentatious signature and without the usual pleasantries. With panic rising, I glance at my watch and see that I have fifteen minutes to make my decision. I dare not leave Grace alone in the room because in her wakefulness, she seems to sense my tense mood and is already upset. Her alert eyes dart around after me as I cast off my dressing gown and try to banish the fear that threatens to overwhelm me. It is two minutes before nine by the time I have searched for my daughter's coat, donned my own and made my way downstairs.

It takes a moment for my eyes to readjust to the night-dark outside. I search the blackness for him, but there is nothing. No sound, no sight. I let go of the breath I have been holding. When I breathe in again, the air is thick in my mouth somehow. Then the acrid smell of smoke reaches me and in the far corner of the terrace, close against the wall, I notice the smouldering red tip of a lighted cigarette.

His back is towards me when I approach but he does not turn around when he speaks. I shiver at the low sound of the now-familiar, accent-less voice.

"Do sit, Miss Lieberman. I took the liberty of ordering us both a digestif. I hope you like cognac. Ah, I see you have brought your daughter."

"Grace. My daughter's name is Grace, Major Dawlish."

He offers one of the brandy glasses which I decline.

"Perhaps you would like something else?"

"No, Major Dawlish. What I would like is for you to explain yourself. You say that you have a proposition?"

"I see. Straight to the point."

He reaches across and runs the tip of his index finger slowly across my mouth, pausing once to press my lips open a little.

"I like a woman who knows what she wants."

More than anything, I want to walk away from this man. I hate his smug face. I want to tell him that his hands stink of stale tobacco and his fingernails need cutting. I want to tell him that he is a disgrace to his profession and as a man. But I dare not. I dare not say or do anything.

"And clearly, you know how to get what you want, Miss Lieberman."

It is only now, as he looks directly at my sleeping child that I stand up.

"If you thought to bring me here for your own pleasure, Major Dawlish, you are sadly deluded. As you are perfectly aware, I am engaged to be married to…"

"…to my esteemed friend, Major Oliver. Yes, Miss Lieberman. But it seems that you have not been so…choosy…during your stay in South Africa as you are being this evening."

"Edwin is quite aware that I will be arriving in England with a little girl. With Grace."

"Indeed, he is, my dear. But he does not know that the little girl in question is your little girl, does he?" He lights another cigarette and inhales deeply as he anticipates the answer he already knows.

"I thought not. I wonder what else you have not told him?"

"What has happened is none of your business, Major Dawlish. Neither is what I have or have not told my future husband."

"One thing I am sure will delight Major Oliver, is the good news about your grandfather's will. I have your friend Marjorie to thank for that little nugget of information, so guilelessly given at luncheon. Major Oliver's family is rather grand after all, and your inheritance makes you a much more suitable match. N'est-ce que pas?"

"My wealth matters not to Edwin!" I exclaim. "We love each other. It is enough."

"But would that change if Major Edwin Oliver knew of your affair with that farm-worker? He seemed so keen to see you earlier on today at Lady Frankton's."

"That man has nothing to do with me! He is not Grace's father!"

"So, it is another, *different* native African who is the father of your child. I see."

Grace awakens at the sound of the agitation in our voices.

"You see – nothing! What is it that you want from me, Major Dawlish?"

"I think that we find ourselves in a position to help one another, Miss Lieberman. I will not be able to continue in my own business. Not in this state. But I forget, you do not know anything about my family."

I take a breath at his arrogance, "And neither do I wish to know anything more about you or your family. Your previous actions have told me all I need to know."

My cheeks are ablaze as he continues regardless, "I am the youngest of three sons, and destined to run the farm on my return from this war. Wiltshire. Lovely county. But with a little help, in the form of a monthly allowance, it would be very easy for me to employ a farm manager. Or perhaps with one larger sum, I could invest the money... And in exchange, I will keep quiet about your...little...indiscretions."

My next words spill out even though I have not fully considered his threat.

"I have done nothing to be ashamed of, Major Dawlish. I have absolutely no intention of giving you any sum of money, large or small. Goodnight."

"As you wish, Miss Lieberman. But it is an adieu and not a farewell that I must bid you, because as good fortune would have it, I will be joining you on your voyage home. I have secured my own passage on the Avondale Castle for the day after tomorrow. Plenty of opportunity on board to discuss the matter should you wish to reconsider my offer. Adieu for now, Miss Lieberman."

Having finished his own drink, he lifts what was intended to be my glass of cognac and makes a silent toast to no one in particular before downing it in one swift move; hunched in the wheelchair, wrapped tight in his own misfortune.

193

Chapter 28
A Little Morning Rain

An ominous red-streaked dawn greets the day of our departure. Unsurprisingly, it is followed by a rain squall during which we make our journey to the docks. In my mind, I make light of the weather with a few lines of Charlotte Brontë's poetry, desperate to break the hopelessness that fills my thoughts.

"Life, believe, is not a dream
So dark as sages say;
Oft a little morning rain
Foretells a pleasant day.
Sometimes, there are clouds of gloom,
But these are transient all;
If the shower will make the roses bloom,
O why lament its fall?"

Marjorie and Florence had been outraged when I showed them Major Dawlish's note and told them what happened that night. Each expressed their own ideas for how I might respond to his blackmail, but we all realise how the situation must appear to anyone other than us, and a gloom rather larger than a passing cloud, has descended upon our little group. We travel in silence until I decide to share Miss Brontë's sentiments. They listen, puzzled.

"And?" Demand Florence.

"And what?" I ask.

"Well, is there an answer? Why lament its fall? The rain, that is."

"There is another verse. Two more actually, but I like the end best."

"Go on then. Tell us the end," instructs Florence.

"It is about hope."

"We could do wi' some of that."

"And just a tiny bit of luck. Maybe Major Dawlish will fall overboard?" adds Marjorie, grinning as she enacts pushing someone out of the carriage.

"Marjorie! How could you?"

I am laughing now, as I share the last part of the poem with my dear friends.

"Yet hope again elastic springs,
Unconquered though, she fell;
Still buoyant are her golden wings,
Still strong to bear us well.
Manfully, fearlessly,

The day of trial bear,
For gloriously, victoriously,
Can courage quell despair!"

Our revived optimism is short-lived because when we arrive at the ship, there has been a mistake with the cabin bookings. On discovering that we have not been allocated the first-class accommodation that had been arranged by John Chambers, we make our way through the throng to the purser's office.

"I am sorry, ladies, but your booking was cancelled two days ago. The ship is full."

"How is that possible?" I ask.

"There are still many troops to be reunited with their homelands, Miss…"

"Lieberman," Marjorie interrupts, "and I am Marjorie Makepeace. Sister Makepeace. There is one more of us. Nurse Florence Wheelwright. And a child. And what my friend here means, is how is it possible that our booking has been cancelled? We have not cancelled it."

"The notes here say that we received a telegram. Unavoidable circumstances. I do not have the actual message here…"

"There must be two first class cabins left surely!" Marjorie chips in again.

"I am sorry, madam. There are no cabins left. Except…"

He leafs through the ledger on his desk to a page where a line of script has been crossed through.

"…one second class, four-berth, inside. Take it or leave it."

There is another impatient knock at the purser's door. The queue is building.

"We will take it," I say.

Ten minutes later, the four of us crowd into the narrow space several decks down, that will be our home for the next two and a half weeks.

Florence points out a metal shaft that takes up more than its share of the precious sleeping space.

"Here is a piece of good luck! P'raps Miss Brontë has put in a good word f'r us."

"What is it?" Marjorie asks.

"An air shaft. From the upper deck. Means we will get cool air even in the rough seas when you cannot open the ports on the outside cabins."

She slams her cabin box into its place. "I will take this top bunk."

Marjorie smiles, "And I will have the other. You and Grace can take the bottom ones, Anna. We can fix up some sides so that she does not roll out."

Later that afternoon, Marjorie and I take a turn round the ship. I need some air and crave a last look at the land where I have spent the first three years of the new century.

"Did you write it?"

To the whooshing sound of the waves parting beneath us, I lean over the starboard rail of the Avondale Castle, recall the final words to Edwin that may be too late to make a difference and watch Cape Town fade into the distance.

…You once told me that everything is not quite what it seems. Do you remember, Edwin dear? When we discussed Hester Prynne and her scarlet letter? So, in the hope that you can forgive not what I have done but what I did not do, which was to

tell you the complete truth, I seal my love with these words and pray that the badge of shame some would have me wear, is invisible to the man I love…

The shadow of Africa's land has disappeared over the past's horizon before I answer Marjorie's question.

"It is done. Twelve pages. I had it posted this morning."

"It is the best thing to have done, Anna."

"It took me four attempts! There are so many ways to say how sorry I am. I am sorry that I did not write before. I just hope that it is not too late."

"Your letter could be travelling with us on this very ship, Anna. You will probably see Edwin before he has chance to read what you have written."

"At least it is written."

"And your courage has quelled your own despair a little?" My friend's wide blue eyes are hopeful as she quotes Miss Brontë's words back to me.

"Yes," I lie.

"Come. Let us take a walk around the deck before dinner."

I slip my arm through Marjorie's.

We are still arm in arm and on our way to rescue Florence, who has been left in charge of a sleeping Grace, when we see him. Black hair slicked back, glinting almost blue in the late afternoon light and seated in a wheelchair, he is smoking and laughing with another man at the top of the companionway that leads down to the second-class inside cabins. The soldier beside him, who I take to be Major Dawlish's batman, makes himself scarce at the click of his senior officer's fingers.

"Good afternoon, Miss Lieberman, Miss Makepeace. What a happy coincidence. And what a surprise. I did not expect to see you in the second-class accommodation."

"It is perfectly clear, Major, that you are here because this is exactly where you expected to find us. Or perhaps you thought we would only find accommodation in steerage when you telegrammed to cancel our reservation?"

"That would have been perfect, of course. I hear that the stench in the hold is unbearable. Also, I understand that the division between the sexes is not carefully looked after. So, it would have suited you well, Miss Lieberman. Given your predisposition to promiscuity that is."

I have let go of Marjorie's arm to pass by him because his chair is placed so as to block the gangway. I am beginning to make my way down the stairs but the sharp sound of an angry slap draws me back.

"How dare you!"

Marjorie towers over the invalided man and is aiming a second blow when he grabs her around the thighs, grips her tight and presses her close between his legs.

"You will live to regret that, my dear."

"I do not think so, Major Dawlish."

The shock is so profound when Marjorie kicks his good leg that he immediately releases her. She stumbles backwards before regaining her foothold.

"Shall we dress for dinner?" she asks and takes my arm again.

Dinner that night is the last meal for several days that we truly enjoy due to the storm that takes hold the next morning. The first sign of rough weather is when a small flower vase that Marjorie has arranged on the shelf in our cabin, along with other pretty objects, crashes to the floor in the early hours. Such is the pitch and roll of the ship by breakfast time that Florence is vomiting into a bedpan and we decide to call the steward.

"Most of the other ladies are sick too, Miss Lieberman. You and Miss Makepeace must have very strong constitutions."

"Do you have any Mothersill's Sea Sickness Remedy on board?" Marjorie asks and the steward shakes his head but looks optimistic at the same time. Within minutes, the kindly man has returned with a supply of Tarrant's Seltzer. We feed this to Florence by the spoonful. It is all the worse because Grace, completely unaffected by sea-sickness, has decided that this is the moment she wants to walk. In our cramped cabin, she cries when the swell knocks her down and screams with frustration at not being allowed on deck where there is more space. The see-saw tilt of the ship makes it impossible for her to move at all without rolling into one fixture or fitting or another. Her shrieking is enough to test even Florence's patience.

The storm lasts for days and although the rough seas have subsided by the time we reach the island of St. Helena, we are all suffering from cabin fever and are dying to spend a few hours ashore.

"Thank goodness we can get rid of these!" Marjorie peels off the rubber-soled shoes that have been our habitual footwear during the bad weather. I laugh as she flings them under Grace's bunk-turned-crib.

"Thank goodness for them though, Marjorie. I cannot for a moment imagine how we could have stayed upright on the deck when the boat was at a forty-five-degree angle without them!"

"Think yourselves lucky that you were able to leave the cabin at all!" chirps a pale-faced, sunken-eyed Florence, who is the first of us to be dressed and ready for our foray. Grace sits like a doll on her lap and allows my friend to attend to those wild locks.

"One good thing about the storm was that we did not see him."

Upon which point, we agree and decide that we should endeavour to go ashore on one of the earliest tenders, thus avoiding a potential confrontation with Major Dawlish.

We feel very small aboard the landing craft as she punches through the waves. At sea-level so low down in the water, we can appreciate the magnificence and great beauty of the ocean. I look ahead, mesmerised by the bold, bare, volcanic bluff of St. Helena that rises perpendicular before us. We approach Jamestown, nestled in a valley between two rocky headlands, and we agree that the place has quite an English look about it. I decide that it must be the familiarity of the church towers and the rows of terraced houses that remind us of home. A daunting flight of seven hundred steps leads to the citadel, so we decide to follow an alternative route to the top of the island and as we make our way along the long, winding path between clumps of cacti, I feel Grace relax. She nestles into my back, held by a kind of sling made by Florence and is protected from the sun by the cotton bonnet she wears. The ingenious harness, which is tied around my shoulders and waist and holds my daughter close to me, must be comfortable because Grace is asleep long before we reach our destination.

Our climb is rewarded by magnificent views of sea and sky merged together in glorious blue harmony. Like a model-village, Jamestown is dotted beneath us, and in the hills beyond, we can see what must be one of the prison camps. I am struck by a sudden guilty thought of my Boer friends in the camp at Bloemfontein and their husbands, sons, and brothers sent here. When Marjorie points out Napoleon's tomb, which we have no time to visit, we decide that there are very good reasons for this being an isle of imprisonment and make our way back down into the town.

Here, we buy pounds and pounds of fresh bananas, tangerines, and loquats before taking tea at one of pretty cafes. Marjorie, Grace and I wait there for Florence who has been tempted by something she has seen in an Aladdin's Cave of a souvenir shop that we passed earlier. We sip from delicate porcelain cups and Grace sits on my knee until the sight of Florence across the square, laden with parcels, causes her to slip down to the ground. She hurls herself in crazy, tottering triumph towards our startled friend. I am flooded with pride at my daughter's first steps on St. Helena. Something that looks like a birdcage clatters into a hundred fragments across the stone flags and Florence runs to catch Grace. They collide loudly in a rush of Yorkshire, Afrikaans and other exclamations of no discernible language whatsoever.

We arrive back at the Avondale Castle exhausted and delighted with our day's adventure. Florence has colour in her cheeks, Marjorie is laughing like she used to, and my exhausted daughter is fast asleep in the harness on my back. Rows of now-vacated steamer chairs line the decks, a sure sign that those who did not make the day trip to St Helena have been enjoying the sunshine and fine weather on board.

"Just like the Kaffir women carry their babies when they are working in the fields. How very appropriate."

We were so engrossed in our conversation that we did not notice one of the few remaining passengers still lounging on the deckchairs is in fact Major Dawlish.

"Indeed, Major. A very practical way of carrying a baby," Florence defends her own ingenuity and we do not stop.

It is days before I come across him again. I am alone when it happens.

Marjorie and Florence are with Grace on the upper deck where a riotous game of shuffleboard has just concluded and one of ring-toss is about to commence. Yearning for some solitude, I have made my excuses and am now in the well-stocked library where our reliable and helpful steward, George, has directed me in my search for books on art and architecture. I am engrossed in a wonderful collection of essays on Italian buildings, landscapes and daily life, which are illuminated by watercolour sketches and beautifully reproduced photographs. George recommended this particular book because, he informed me proud in this knowledge, it has been much praised for its brilliant style and historic research. Ruskin's three-volume treatise on Venetian Art and Architecture also lies enticingly unopened beside me.

"The Stones of Venice by John Ruskin. Have you ever ventured to that fine city, Miss Lieberman?"

The smooth, accentless voice startles me from thoughts of the palazzos that line the Grand Canal and of the beautiful Basilica St. Marco with its bronze horses and glittering gold mosaics. I may be wrong, but I think I detect a note of surprise in Major Dawlish's voice.

"It is not somewhere that I have been yet, Major. But Edwin and I plan to go there during our honeymoon tour of Europe."

"No doubt you are looking forward to seeing him when you arrive in Southampton. But the worry of how you will tell him of your news must be rather dampening your anticipation?"

The emphasis he puts on the word news, makes it sound like a dirty rag or some vile disease. I feel my temper ignite and stand so heatedly that I knock over the chair that I have been sitting on and Ruskin's three volumes topple with a thud to the floor. When no one comes over to see what the commotion is all about, I realise that Major Dawlish and I are alone in the library and a deep unease enfolds me.

"Have you considered my proposal any further, Miss Lieberman?"

He stands so close to me that the heat of his breath touches my cheek and I can smell the detergent of his freshly laundered shirt mingled with a scent that belongs only to him. It is a scent that is at once cool and hot, alluring and yet repulsive. When he manoeuvres himself to within an inch of where I stand, the rough fibres of his jacket rub against the hairs on my arm and I shiver involuntarily. He uses his crutches as a barricade and I fear that I might knock the man down if I push by him. But that is what I do, answering his question as I make haste to the door.

"There is nothing that you or anyone can say, Major Dawlish, that will make me change my mind. You will never see a single penny of my money."

He does not reply and I do not look back.

Chapter 29
Counting the Hours

Soon, I begin to dare count the hours that bring me closer to Edwin.

Florence, Marjorie and I revel in the glorious heat and sunshine that fill our days now that the voyage has brought us beyond the Equator and there is no sign of the bad weather that plagued our journey last week. Florence has created some make-shift reigns for Grace, whose first tentative totter soon turned into steady and increasingly confident steps. My daughter is adored by our steward, George, and he sometimes takes her off to meet other crew who shower her with little tokens of their affection. Her latest gift is a miniature sailor-suit made by another of the stewards, who had joined the Avondale Castle after ten years as an able seaman in the British Royal Navy. Sewing one's own clothes, so he tells us upon seeing our surprise at his skill, is quite usual for sailors. He is so taken with our appreciation that he promises to make a little hat to complete Grace's nautical outfit and when that is produced, Grace teeters about entertaining everyone with the funny little ditties she sings in a mix of her many tongues.

We marvel at the early sunsets and toast the magic of that equatorial twilight-less hour with a cocktail almost every evening. We see Major Dawlish quite frequently, but no further dialogue passes between us. It is only when I catch myself as the subject of an unusually prolonged and deliberate stare that I think of the letter of confession I wrote to Edwin and wonder whether it will reach him before I do. Or before Major Dawlish does.

Frustratingly, we are scheduled to make another stop, which only serves to prolong the waiting. In the end, and despite our lack of enthusiasm, our day on Tenerife proves to be both interesting and entertaining. Tenerife is one of the Spanish Canary Islands with a great peak at one end. The top of this volcanic mountain disappears beneath the only cloud in the sky today, but nothing obscures the beauty of the pretty little town of Santa Cruz whose dainty pink and white houses are as delicate as icing on a cake.

Our ship is quickly surrounded by smaller boats selling fruit, tobacco, lace and Spanish drawn work. I see George's steward friend examining these fabrics somewhat surreptitiously. Marjorie and I employ all our powers of persuasion to prevent Florence buying a very sweet but rather mangy bright green parakeet from an especially persistent local vendor. Thankfully, she settles in the end for just the birdcage – to replace the one that was irreparably damaged on the day Grace walked for the first time. Her new purchase is stunningly decorative, although goodness knows where we will put it in our overcrowded cabin.

Eventually, we are mobbed by one of the boatmen ferrying passengers ashore and we climb aboard his bobbing craft. The barrage of demands to buy this or that is followed by another, immediately after we land ashore. This time, it is a band of beggars impossible to ignore. I give money to one man with no legs but we make a circuitous detour to avoid the group with fingerless hands, one of the many cruel disfigurements of leprosy. All these poor unfortunates seem to want to touch Grace, who looks like a little doll in her sailor costume and I think of my mother's Bible stories and wish Jesus was here to put an end to this cruel suffering.

In the central market-square are donkeys which we ride and which Grace loves. Then we raid the bazaars and shops and are soon laden with knick-knacks and souvenirs for everyone at home, including a painting of the Madonna that my mother will probably hate, and a framed watercolour painting of Santa Cruz in the shadow of Mount Teide, which I am certain that Edwin will love.

That night, I dream of being in the arms of my beloved but he holds me so tight in his embrace that I awake, gasping for breath. A small lantern that flickers in the cabin's darkness serves to soothe my nightmare and I discover that in the stifling heat neither Marjorie nor Florence can sleep. Before long, all of us have dragged our bedding onto the deck where we are caressed by a soft breeze and spend the night under the stars.

To sleep outside one's cabins is not at all approved of. But such is the oppressive heat that for the next two days, there is a mutiny of sorts. Refusing to go downstairs at night, we ladies take possession of one side of the deck and the gentlemen the other. We have already met Mr and Mrs Howard who are on their way back from central Africa where they have spent three decades as missionaries. It is Mrs Howard who lays down her bedding next to mine and is immediately captivated when she sees Grace.

"Such a dear little thing you have rescued, Miss Lieberman. Just like Topsy in Uncle Tom's Cabin! But so very young! What will you and Major Oliver do with her back at home? Will you train her for your own service, my dear?"

I think very hard before I reply.

"Yes, she is very young, Mrs Howard. Just sixteen months old. I intend to bring her up as my daughter." And although this is not an untruth, I am ashamed at my smooth denial. She is my daughter and I am a coward for the insinuation that she is not.

"Such a God-fearing act. I will pray for you and the little one. And for your future husband. What good shepherds you are."

Like meek lambs, we return to our quarters on the third day when the Captain issues an ultimatum to do with decency, strict moral codes, and our behaviour being akin to that of barbarians. There is to be no more sleeping on the deck.

"Goodness, it is like being back at my convent school," hisses Marjorie.

"Do you think he might wrap our knuckles if we misbehave again?"

"Highly probable," I whisper back, incurring the Captain's wrath in the form of a piercing glare of disapproval as we pad past him.

The whole incident and the terrible heat are forgotten by the time we approach the Bay of Biscay. Fuelled by much chatter with the new friends we have made during the outdoor sleeping rebellion, we are dreading the gale-force winds and giant waves for which this bay is renowned. This famously unpredictable piece of water is so flat-calm when we reach it however, that we perform the calisthenics manoeuvre that involves hopping around on one leg, with no difficulty whatsoever.

Passing north along the French coast reminds us that dear old England is but a day away and frantic packing ensues even though our cabin boxes are only big enough to contain the four outfits that we have been alternating daily.

Our final day aboard the Avondale Castle brings with it that memorable first view of the chalky dots that magically transform themselves into the Needles off the west of the Isle of Wight. Then we play cat and mouse with the swarms of welcoming small craft that are skimming along the sun-sparkling Channel or bobbing playfully at anchor. With two shuddering blasts of its horn, our great ship makes its final turn to port and we head to the starboard deck where we will have the best view of the dockside. The south-westerly breeze blows our hair over our eyes when we join the growing band of home comers who line the starboard-side guardrail and peer anxiously across Southampton Water. It is far too soon to pick out even the dock, never mind those loved ones who wait there with equal nervous anticipation, but we strain to look anyway.

I study the furrowed brows and bitten lips of my fellow passengers. It is so long since I have seen Edwin that I wonder if I will recognise him. Will he know me? I pull tight around my shoulders the brightly coloured paisley shawl that should identify me and hope that I will be able to spot him by the red silk handkerchief that he wrote he would wave.

Wanting to make the most of what might be their last opportunity for a while, Marjorie and Florence have been playing with Grace in the dining room. This has become a habitual event since George and his fellow stewards first invited us there after breakfast one morning when it was too windy to take my little girl outside. My dear friends are so out of breath when they arrive that I am completely certain they have worn themselves out rather than Grace.

"What a charming little outfit!" Mrs Howard hurries by to pass comment on my daughter's navy-blue sailor suit, now complete with a collar made from the cut-work fabric from Tenerife to complement the exquisitely crafted cap and tiny handmade leather shoes.

"Can you see him yet?" Marjorie hands me some binoculars and laughs.

"We have slowed down now, so it will probably be another quarter of an hour." Mrs Howard pitches in her final comment before disappearing towards the stern. Florence rolls her eyes and we laugh.

The longest fifteen minutes of my life comes to an end as the mass of movement on the quayside gradually comes into focus. And there it is – a flash of red. I wave madly with my shawl. But he does not appear to see me, so I wave higher, faster, more furiously. When my arms ache and we are a little closer, I realise that it is not Edwin's handkerchief, but a gaudy feather-trimmed red hat that belongs to a stout young woman who has removed the article to wave at her own loved one. A khaki-clad man in his twenties returns her eager gesticulations and I swallow a rising sob of disappointment.

I scan the scene through an increasingly fearful haze of doubt. Peddlers wind in and out of the swaying, waving, joyful crowd. Endless lines of trucks run up and down. Ripples of laughter and calls of welcome from the shore echo back from the deck, but we four maintain our silent, hopeful vigil as our eyes search for the red flash.

Our watchful hope continues as we follow the last of the passengers down the gangplank. We wait until we are alone on the dockside except for a few workers.

They soon disappear aboard to begin the tasks of clearing up and cleaning. We say a tearful goodbye to Florence who has a train to catch so that she can make her connection to Leeds that will depart from London Kings Cross Station very soon. There is no red handkerchief and no Edwin.

"What shall you do, Anna?" Marjorie's voice is small but not bleak.

"I will take Grace to the South Western Hotel since that is where we were meant to spend the night. I only hope that the room Edwin booked for me has not been given away."

"I will come with you. No argument."

I have no wish to face this situation alone and hug my friend in gratitude.

Within half an hour, we are standing at the reception desk facing a dour clerk. He can find no record of a booking for a Miss Lieberman. I feel such desolation that I cannot even summon a plea for him to look one more time. Marjorie has a little more presence of mind and asks to see the hotel's manager. We must look a motley crew, with little Grace dressed as a sailor and we two rather the worse for our weeks at sea, wearing salt-marked outfits that are scruffy at best. A tall, well-dressed man appears once the clerk realises that we will not go away until our repeated request is granted.

"How can I help, ladies?" the manager asks. He is calm, polite and cold. I do not like the look he gives Grace, who is crying now because she is hungry, and decide to try a different tack.

"We are looking for Major Edwin Oliver."

The man's demeanour changes in an instant at the mention of Edwin's name.

"I am sorry ladies, but Sir Edwin has left the hotel."

I realise that Edwin must have started using the courtesy title that is his birth-right.

"Left! When? Why? When did he leave? Where did he go?"

"He has gone back to the Island. The Isle of Wight. After the telegram."

"Telegram! What telegram?"

"I do not know the content of the message but he cancelled both room bookings immediately. But by the look on his face, I would say that the telegram did not convey good news."

"You do not have the telegram still, I suppose?" asks Marjorie, but the man shakes his head and gives her a patronising look, which he turns upon me when I speak.

"But why has he not left me a message?" I want to cry.

"Why would Sir Edwin leave you a message, Miss…"

"Miss Lieberman. I am Anna Lieberman."

"And she is Major Oliver's fiancé!" Marjorie's eyes dance like blue flames.

"And this is my friend, Miss Marjorie Makepeace."

The colour drains from the hotel manager's face.

"I must apologise, Miss Lieberman. I had no idea. You did not say. And…well…your costume…"

"We have been travelling for weeks, sir. I apologise if our attire is not…"

"Please, please, there is no need to apologise, Miss Lieberman, Miss Makepeace. And I have not even introduced myself. My name is Sowerby. Thaddeus Sowerby. Jones! Arrange for some tea for the ladies and some milk for the little girl. Now!"

The astonished clerk scurries into action and I ask the repentant Mr Sowerby what day Edwin left.

"What day? Why, Miss Lieberman, he left just an hour before you arrived. The four o'clock ferry to the Island is the last one of the day. I believe it was his intention to…"

We do not allow him to finish his sentence and are already at the main entrance just as Jones reappears with a tray piled high with silver teapot, a jug of milk, and a cake-stand groaning under the weight of thickly filled sandwiches and a mouth-watering selection of cakes. His face resumes the look of confusion that had been briefly replaced with that feeling of satisfaction one experiences upon getting something right after a mistake. Marjorie does not help his mood when she dashes back to seize a handful of cucumber sandwiches and a slice of Victoria sponge cake without so much as a please or a thank you.

The hands of the station clock read three twenty-five when our carriage hurtles past and it is a quarter to four by the time we reach the embarkation point for the Red Funnel paddle steamer ferry service to Cowes. We stare hopefully at the dockside that is all but empty. I dash across to the nearby office and purchase two single tickets. Precious minutes are wasted in a conversation to determine that Grace travels for free. It is four o'clock. I am certain that it is only because of the most winning smile that Marjorie has ever conjured that we are allowed onto the boat. The ferry-worker who kept the gangplank down just long enough for us to scramble aboard cannot believe his luck when my effervescent friend takes him in her arms and hugs him until he coughs.

"Well! Here we are. The last boat of the day." I cannot tell if Marjorie is happy or desperate.

"I know it is madness, but I have to at least try and find him," I offer.

"But of course, Anna." She squeezes my arm and wrinkles her nose. "Let us freshen up a little."

Our bags were sent from the Avondale Castle to the South Western Hotel and so we have no clean clothes to change into. At least, we will be able to wash, straighten our dishevelled hair and make ourselves look more presentable than we do now. The helter-skelter dash through the hot and busy Southampton afternoon has left us looking like oversized ragamuffins and this is not the vision I had intended to present to my future husband after two years apart.

"Do you think he changed his mind after receiving my letter, Marjorie? Do you think that is why he left?"

She bites her bottom lip, "It is possible, Anna. But Mr Sowerby said he left immediately after receiving a telegram. He definitely said telegram, not letter."

I feel heartened by this observation, but once we have made a demi-toilette, shared the Victoria sponge cake and begin wandering around the decks, I allow the doubt that gnaws away at my confidence to consume it entirely.

We repeat many futile promenades around all permitted areas of the paddle-steamer and several that are forbidden. Grace is strapped, in turn, to mine and then Marjorie's back and it is her presence when we climb an exterior metal ladder that leads to our most severe reprimand. The south westerly wind has risen to read thirty-five knots on the Beaufort scale according to a sweet elderly gentleman who informs us that he has been a sea-faring man for more than half a century and that we should go down below because there is a storm brewing. It would appear that the other passengers have already heeded what is very sound advice because we are the last to reach the top of the companionway steps down to the dining room. One thing is abundantly clear. Edwin is not here. The tears that come do not fall, but perch in their distress upon my lashes and the scene before me blurs.

"Please give me a moment, Marjorie."

The rebuke she was going to give remains unspoken when she sees my face and she nods.

"Grace and I will have a pot of tea waiting for you." And they are almost thrown down the steps as the boat lurches to the right.

I wear nothing to protect me from the elements except for the bright, paisley shawl that should have been a beacon for Edwin. As if it were the fault of this inanimate object, I pull the shawl viciously tight and turn to the port-side of the boat which is sheltered a little from the horizontal rain which attacks me like a thousand tiny sharp pins released all at once from their cases. Through the sheets of driving drizzle, I can just make out the promontory of land where we will turn left into the Medina River and I let my tears fall into the flood tide.

I do not anticipate the wind's change of direction when the boat turns sharply to port and gasp when my shawl is whipped up into the air and carried off towards the stern. By now, I am soaking wet and give up any idea of retrieving the useless article. Hair plastered down and drenched dress clinging where it should not, I make my way through the windswept gloom to join Marjorie and Grace below.

"Anna!"

Marjorie has been watching for me and holds up a teapot in welcome. But she is not the only person who has called my name. A simultaneous shout causes me to turn around.

"This is yours, I believe."

Edwin hands me a sopping wet, brightly coloured paisley shawl.

"What are you doing here, Anna?"

Raindrops teeter on the tips of his long lashes and his dark eyes are accusing, angry. Very angry.

"Hoping to find you. When you did not meet the Avondale Castle, I went to the hotel," I say.

"But your telegram!"

"I did not send a telegram, Edwin. To you or anyone else."

"If you did not send it, who would have sent a telegram in your name? And from the Avondale Castle."

"I can think of someone who might have."

"So, you have not changed your mind?"

I realise that I have mistaken the fear in his eyes for anger. Right now, they are full of hopeful expectation.

"I supposed from your message that you had found another…"

"Not my message, Edwin!"

He smiles the smile that first made me want to kiss away his pain. So, I do. Right there in the middle of the dining room. In front of wide-eyed passengers, he kisses me back as the boat comes to a shuddering halt at Cowes' quayside.

When we can bear to draw apart, I remember the letter.

"Edwin. I have something that I must tell you. I wrote a long letter explaining everything…but…"

205

"Yes of course. Grace! Your adopted daughter! The letter arrived two days ago. Where is she?"

Marjorie raises her eyebrows at me so that Edwin doesn't see and then turns to face him, "Right here, Major Oliver," Marjorie's grin has caused the rain to stop. "Or should I call you Sir Edwin? Lord Bradleigh? Or Earl Lanchester perhaps?"

"Nurse Makepeace! I am found out."

He turns to stroke my furrowed brow but not until he has kissed Grace on the forehead.

"Sadly, my father died. Unexpectedly." His eyes meet mine, his gaze steady.

"As the eldest son, I inherit the title. I think you knew that it would happen one day, Anna. And there's land. And the house of course. It is not far from here and there are a great many rooms. You are all most welcome."

The sound of an embarrassed cough interrupts Edwin's generosity. It is clear from the way the crew are standing expectantly around that we are being encouraged to leave the ferry. I decide that this is not the moment to reveal the truth about Grace's conception, the news of my grandfather's Californian assets and the fact that he has left me a substantial sum of money, plus at least two houses and a vineyard in his will. Instead, I say, "I think we have rather a lot to talk about."

Edwin holds out his arms and Grace goes to him as if she has known him always.

Printed by BoD™in Norderstedt, Germany